Look for these m
Pocket

Judith McNaught

"One of the finest writers of popular fiction."
—Barnesandnoble.com

NIGHT WHISPERS

REMEMBER WHEN

ALMOST HEAVEN

Jude Deveraux

"One of the all-time greats."
—Midwest Book Review

THE SUMMERHOUSE

TEMPTATION

HIGH TIDE

JUDITH McNAUGHT

JUDE DEVERAUX

Simple Gifts

POCKET BOOKS
New York   London   Toronto   Sydney

The sale of this book without its cover is unauthorized. If you purchased this book without a cover, you should be aware that it was reported to the publisher as "unsold and destroyed." Neither the author nor the publisher has received payment for the sale of this "stripped book."

This book is a work of fiction. Names, characters, places and incidents are products of the author's imagination or are used fictitiously. Any resemblance to actual events or locales or persons living or dead is entirely coincidental.

"Just Curious" and "Double Exposure" were previously published in *A Gift of Love;* "Miracles" and "Change of Heart" were previously published in *A Holiday of Love.*

 POCKET BOOKS, a division of Simon & Schuster, Inc.
1230 Avenue of the Americas, New York, NY 10020

"Just Curious" copyright © 1995 by Deveraux, Inc.
"Miracles" copyright © 1994 by Eagle Syndication, Inc.
"Change of Heart" copyright © 1994 by Deveraux, Inc.
"Double Exposure" copyright © 1995 by Eagle Syndication, Inc.

Originally published in trade paperback in 1998 by Pocket Books

All rights reserved, including the right to reproduce this book or portions thereof in any form whatsoever. For information address Pocket Books, 1230 Avenue of the Americas, New York, NY 10020

ISBN-13: 978-0-7434-4223-7
ISBN-10:   0-7434-4223-7

This Pocket Books paperback edition December 2001

10   9   8

POCKET and colophon are registered trademarks of Simon & Schuster, Inc.

Manufactured in the United States of America

For information regarding special discounts for bulk purchases, please contact Simon & Schuster Special Sales at 1-800-456-6798 or business@simonandschuster.com.

Contents

Jude Deveraux

Just Curious

One

"I DON'T BELIEVE in miracles," Karen said, looking at her sister-in-law with her lips pressed tightly together. Sunlight shone on Karen's shiny-clean face, making her look like the "before" photo of a model without makeup. But lack of makeup only revealed perfect skin, high cheekbones, and eyes like dark emeralds.

"I never said a word about miracles," Ann replied, her voice showing her exasperation. She was as dark as Karen was fair, half a foot shorter, and voluptuous. "All I said was that you should go to the Christmas dance at the club. What's so miraculous about that?"

"You said that I might meet someone wonderful and get married again," Karen answered, refusing to remember the car wreck that had taken her beloved husband from her.

"Okay, so shoot me, I apologize." Squinting her eyes at her once-beautiful sister-in-law, Ann found it difficult to believe that she used to be eaten up with jealousy over Karen's looks. Now Karen's hair hung lank and lifeless about her shoulders, with split ends up to her ears. She hadn't a trace of makeup on and with her pale coloring, Karen looked like a teenager without it. Instead of the elegant clothes she used to wear, she now had on an old sweat suit that Ann knew had belonged to Karen's deceased husband, Ray.

"You used to be the most gorgeous girl at the country club," Ann said wistfully. "I remember seeing you and Ray dance at Christmas. Remember that red dress you had, slit so high your tonsils were visible? But how you and Ray looked when you danced together was worth it! Those legs of yours had every man in the room drooling. Every man in Denver was drooling! Except my Charlie, of course, *he* never looked."

Over her teacup, Karen gave a faint smile. "Key words in that are 'girl' and 'Ray.' Neither of which I am or have any longer."

"Give me a break!" Ann wailed. "You sound as though you're ninety-two years old and should be choosing your coffin. You turned thirty, that's all. I hit thirty-five this year and age hasn't stopped me." At that Ann got up, her hand at her back, and waddled over to the sink to get another cup of herbal tea. She was so hugely pregnant she could hardly reach the kettle.

"Point made," Karen said. "But no matter how young or old I am, that doesn't bring Ray back." When she said the name, there was reverence in her voice, as though she were speaking the name of a deity.

Ann gave a great sigh, for they'd had this conversation many times. "Ray was my brother and I loved him very much, but, Karen, Ray is dead. And he's been dead for two years. It's time you started living again."

"You don't understand about Ray and me. We were . . ."

Ann's face was full of sympathy, and reaching across the table, she clasped Karen's wrist and squeezed. "I know he was everything to you, but you have a lot to offer some man. A man who is alive."

"No!" Karen said sharply. "No man on earth could fill Ray's shoes, and I'd never allow anyone to try." Abruptly, she got up from the table and walked to the window. "No one understands. Ray and I were more than just married, we were partners. We were equals; we shared everything. Ray asked my opinion about everything, from the business to the color of his socks. He made me feel useful. Can you understand that? Every man I've met before or since Ray seems to want a woman to sit still and look pretty. The minute you start telling him your opinions, he asks the waiter to give him the check."

There was nothing that Ann could say to contradict Karen, for Ann had seen firsthand what a good marriage they'd had. But now Ann was sick with seeing her beloved sister-in-law hide herself away from the world, so she wasn't about to tell Karen that she'd never find anyone who was half the man Ray was.

"All right," Ann said, "I'll stop. If you are bound and determined to commit suttee for Ray, so be it." Hesitantly, she gave her sister-in-law's back a hard look. "Tell me about that job of yours." Her tone of voice told what she thought of Karen's job.

Turning away from the window, Karen laughed. "Ann, no one could ever doubt your opinions on anything. First you don't like that I love my husband and second you don't approve of my job."

"So sue me. I think you're worth more than eternal widowhood and death-by-typing."

Karen could never bear her sister-in-law any animosity because Ann truly did think Karen was the best there was, and it had nothing to do with their being related by marriage. "My job is fine," she said, sitting back down at the table. "Everyone is well and everything is going fine."

"That boring, huh?"

Karen laughed. "Not horribly boring, just a little bit boring."

"So why don't you quit?" Before Karen could answer, Ann held up her hand. "I apologize. It's none of my business if you, with all your brains, want to bury yourself in some typing pool." Ann's eyes lit up. "So anyway, tell me about your divine, gorgeous boss. How is that beautiful man?"

Karen smiled—and ignored the reference to her boss. "The other women in the pool gave me a birthday party last week." At that she lifted her eyebrows in challenge, for Ann was always saying snide things about the six women Karen worked with.

"Oh? And what did they give you? A hand-crocheted shawl, or maybe a rocking chair and a couple of cats?"

"Support hose," she said, then laughed. "No, no, I'm kidding. Just the usual things. Actually, they chipped in together and got me a very nice gift."

"And what was that?"

Karen took a drink of her tea. "Aneyeglassesholder."

"A what?"

Karen's eyes twinkled. "A holder for my eyeglasses. You know, one of those string things that goes around your neck. It's a very nice one, eighteen-karat gold. With little, ah, cats on the clasp."

Ann didn't smile. "Karen, you have to get out of there. The combined age of those women must be three hundred years. And didn't they notice that you don't wear glasses?"

"Three hundred and seventy-seven." When Ann looked at her in question, Karen said, "Their ages total three hundred and seventy-seven years. I added it up one day. And they said they knew I didn't wear glasses, but that as a woman who had just turned thirty I would soon need to."

"For an ancient like you, support hose are just around the corner."

"Actually, Miss Johnson gave me a pair last Christmas. She's seventy-one and swears by them."

At that Ann did laugh. "Oh, Karen, this is serious. You have to get out of there."

"Mmmmm," Karen said, looking down at her cup. "My job has its uses."

"What are you up to?" Ann snapped.

Karen gave her sister-in-law a look of innocence. "I have no idea what you mean."

For a moment Ann leaned back against the bench and studied her sister-in-law. "At last I am beginning to understand. You are much too clever to throw away everything. So help me, Karen Lawrence, if you don't tell me everything and tell me *now,* I'll think of some dreadfully way to punish you. Like maybe not allowing you to see my baby until she's three years old."

When Karen's face turned white, Ann knew she had her. "Tell!"

"It's a nice job and the people I work with are—"

Suddenly, Ann's face lit up. "Don't you play the martyr to *me.* I've known you since you were eight years old, remember? You take extra work from those old biddies so you'll know everything that's going on. I'll bet you know more about what's going on in that company that Taggert does." Ann smiled at her own cleverness. "And you let your looks go so you don't intimidate anyone. If that dragon Miss Gresham saw you as you looked a couple of years ago, she'd find some reason to fire you."

Karen's blush was enough to tell her that she was right.

"Pardon my stupidity," Ann said, "but why don't you get a job that pays a little more than being a secretary?"

"I tried!" Karen said vehemently. "I applied at dozens of companies, but they wouldn't consider me because I don't have a university degree. Eight years of managing a hardware store means nothing to a personnel director."

"You only quadrupled that store's profits."

"Whatever. That doesn't matter. Only that piece of paper saying I sat through years of boring classes means anything."

"So why don't you go back to school and get that piece of paper?"

"I *am* going to school!" Karen took a drink of her tea to calm herself.

"Look, Ann, I know you mean well, but I know what I'm doing. I know I'll never find another man like Ray who I can work *with,* so maybe I can learn enough to open a shop of my own. I have the money from the sale of Ray's half of the hardware store, and I'm managing to save most of what I earn from this job. Meanwhile, I am learning everything about running a company the size of Taggert's."

Karen smiled. "I'm not really an idiot about my little old ladies. They think they use me to do their work, but truthfully, I'm very selective about what I agree to do. Everything in that office, from every department, goes across my desk. And since I always make myself available for all weekends and holidays, I always see what's most urgent."

"And what do you plan to do with all this knowledge?"

"Open a business somewhere. Retail. It's what I know, although without Ray there to do the selling, I don't know how I'll cope."

"You should get married again!" Ann said forcefully.

"But I don't *want* to get married!" Karen nearly shouted. "I'm just going to get pregnant!" After she'd said it, Karen looked at her friend in horror. "Please forget that I said that," she whispered. "Look, I better go. I have things—"

"Move from that seat and you're dead," Ann said levelly.

With a great sigh, Karen collapsed back against the upholstered banquette in Ann's sunny kitchen. "Don't do this to me. Please, Ann."

"Do what?" she asked innocently.

"Pry and snoop and generally interfere in something that is none of your business."

"I can't imagine what you could be referring to. I've never done anything like that in my life. Now tell me everything."

Karen tried to change the subject. "Another gorgeous woman came out of Taggert's office in tears last week," she said, referring to her boss, a man who seemed to drive Ann mad with desire. But Karen was sure that was because she didn't know him.

"What do you mean, you're 'going' to get pregnant?" Ann persisted.

"An hour after she left, a jeweler showed up at Taggert's office with a briefcase and two armed guards. We all figure he was buying her off. Drying her tears with emeralds, so to speak."

"Have you done anything yet about getting pregnant?"

"And on Friday we heard that Taggert was engaged—again. But not to the woman who'd left his office. This time he's engaged to a redhead." She leaned across the table to Ann. "And Saturday I typed the prenuptial agreement."

That got Ann's attention. "What was in it?"

Karen leaned back again, her face showing her distaste. "He's a bastard, Ann. He really is. I know he's very good looking and he's rich beyond imagining, but as a human, he's not worth much. I know these . . . these social belles of his are probably just after his money—they certainly couldn't like *him*—but they are human beings and, as such, they are worthy of kindness."

"Will you get off your pulpit and tell me what the prenupt said?"

"The woman, his bride, had to agree to give up all rights to anything that was purchased with his money during the marriage. As far as I could tell, she wasn't allowed to own anything. In the event of a divorce, even the clothing he bought her would remain with him."

"Really? And what was he planning to do with women's clothing?" Ann wiggled her eyebrows.

"Nothing interesting, I'm sure. He'd just find

another gorgeous gold digger who fit them. Or maybe he'd sell them so he could buy a case of engagement rings, since he gives them out so often."

"What is it you dislike about the man so much?" Ann asked. "He gave you a job, didn't he?"

"Oh, yes, he has an office full of women. I swear he instructs personnel to hire them by the length of their legs. He surrounds himself with beautiful women executives."

"So what's your complaint?"

"He never allows them to *do* anything!" Karen said with passion. "Taggert makes every decision himself. As far as I know he doesn't even ask his team of beauties what they think should be done, much less allow them to actually do it." She gripped her cup handle until it nearly snapped. "McAllister Taggert could live on a desert island all by himself. He needs no other person in life."

"He seems to need women," Ann said softly. She'd met Karen's boss twice and she'd been thoroughly charmed by him.

"He's the proverbial American playboy," Karen said. "The longer the legs, and the longer the hair, the more he likes them. Beautiful and dumb, that's what he likes." She smiled maliciously. "However, so far none of them have been stupid enough to marry him when they discover that all they get out of the marriage is *him.*"

"Well . . ." Ann said, seeing the anger in Karen's face, "maybe we should change the subject. How are you planning to get a baby if you run from every man who looks at you? I mean, the way you dress now is calculated to keep men at a distance, isn't it?"

"My! but that was good tea," Karen said. "You are certainly a good cook, Ann, and I've enjoyed our visit immensely, but I need to go now." With that she rose and headed for the kitchen door.

"Ow!" Ann yelled. "I'm going into labor! Help me."

The blood seemed to drain from Karen's face as she ran to her friend. "Lean back, rest. I'll call the hospital."

But as Karen reached the phone, Ann said in a normal voice, "I think it's passed, but you better stay here until Charlie gets home. Just in case. You know."

After a moment of looking at Ann with anger, Karen admitted defeat and sat back down. "All right, what is it you want to know?"

"I don't know why, but I seem to be very interested in babies lately. Must be something I ate. But anyway, when you mentioned babies, it made me want to hear all of it."

"There is *nothing* to tell. Really nothing. I just . . ."

"Just what?" Ann urged.

"I just regret that Ray and I never had children. We both thought we had all the time in the world."

Ann didn't say anything, just gave Karen time to sort out her thoughts and talk. "Recently, I went to a fertility clinic and had a complete examination. I seem to be perfectly healthy."

When Karen said no more, Ann said softly, "So you've been to a clinic and now what?"

"I am to choose a donor from a catalog," Karen said simply.

Ann's sense of the absurd got the better of her. "Ah, then you get the turkey baster out and—"

Karen didn't laugh as her eyes flashed angrily. "You can afford to be smug since you have a loving husband who can do the job, but what am I supposed to do? Put an ad in the paper for a donor? 'One lonely widow wants child but no husband. Apply box three-five-six.'"

"If you got out more and met some men you might—" Ann stopped because she could see that Karen was getting angry. "I know, why don't you ask that gorgeous boss of yours to do the job? He beats a turkey baster any day."

For a moment Karen tried to stay annoyed but Ann's persistence thawed her. "Mr. Taggert, rather than a raise," Karen mimicked, "would you mind very much giving me a bit of semen? I brought a jar, and, no, I don't mind waiting."

Ann laughed, for this was the old Karen, the one she'd rarely seen in the last two years.

Karen continued to smile. "According to my charts, I'm at peak fertility on Christmas Day, so maybe I'll just wait up for Santa Claus."

"Beats milk and cookies," Ann said. "But won't you feel bad for all the children he neglects because he spent the whole night at *your* house?"

Ann laughed so hard at her own joke that she let out a scream.

"It wasn't *that* funny," Karen said. "Maybe Santa's helpers could— Ann? Are you all right?"

"Call Charlie," she whispered, clutching her big stomach; then as another contraction hit her, she said, "The hell with Charlie, call the hospital and tell them to rush a delivery of morphine. This *hurts!*"

Shaking, Karen went to the phone and called.

"Idiot!" Karen said, looking at herself in the mirror and seeing the tears seeping out of the corner of her eyes. Tearing off a paper towel from the dispenser on the restroom wall, she dabbed at the tears, then saw that her eyes were red. Which of course made sense since she'd now been crying for most of twenty-four hours.

"Everyone cries at the birth of a baby," she muttered to no one. "People cry at all truly happy occasions, such as weddings and engagement announcements and at the birth of every baby."

Pausing in her wiping, she looked in the mirror and knew that she was lying to herself. Last night she'd held Ann's new daughter in her arms and she'd wanted that child so much that she'd nearly walked out the door with her. Frowning, Ann had taken her baby from her sister-in-law. "You can't have mine," she said. "Get your own."

To cover her embarrassment, Karen had tried to make jokes about her feelings, but they had fallen flat, and in the end, she'd left Ann's hospital room feeling the worst she had since Ray's death.

So now Karen was at the office and she was nearly overpowered with a sense of longing for a home and family. Making another attempt to mop up her face, she heard voices at the door, and without thinking, she scurried into an open stall and locked the door behind her. She did *not* want anyone to see her. Today was the office Christmas party and everyone was in high good spirits. Between the promise of limitless free food an drink this afternoon and a generous bonus received from Montgomery-Taggert Enterprises this morning, the whole office was a cauldron of merriment.

If Karen hadn't already been in a bad mood, she would have been when she realized that one of the two women who entered was Loretta Simons, a woman who considered herself the resident authority on McAllister J. Taggert. Karen knew she was trapped inside the stall, for if she tried to leave the restroom, Loretta would catch her and badger her into hearing more about the wonders of the saintly M.J. Taggert.

"Have you seen him yet?" Loretta gushed in a way that some people reserved for the Sistine Chapel. "He's the most beautiful creature on earth— tall, handsome, kind, understanding."

"But what about that woman this morning?" the second woman asked. If she hadn't heard all about Taggert, then she had to be the new executive assistant, and Loretta was breaking her in: "She didn't seem to think he was so wonderful."

At that, Karen, hidden in her stall, smiled. Her sentiments exactly.

"But you, my dear, have no idea what that darling man has been through," Loretta said as though talking about a war veteran.

Standing against the wall, Karen put her head back and wanted to cry out in frustration. Did Loretta never talk about anything but the Great Jilt? the Great Tragedy of McAllister Taggert? Wasn't there anything else in her life?

"Three years ago Mr. Taggert was madly, insanely in love with a young woman named Elaine Wentlow." Loretta said the name as though it were something vile and disgusting. "More than anything in life he wanted to marry her and raise a family. He wanted his own home, his own place of security. He wanted—"

Karen rolled her eyes, for Loretta was adding more to the tale each time she told it: fewer facts, more melodrama. Now Loretta was on to the magnificence of the wedding that Taggert had alone planned and paid for. According to Loretta, his fiancée had spent all her time having her nails done.

"And she left him?" the new assistant asked, her voice properly awed.

"She left that dear man standing at the front of the church before seven hundred guests who had flown in from all over the world."

"How awful," the assistant said. "He must have been humiliated. What was her reason? And if she did have a good reason, couldn't she have done it in a more caring manner?"

Karen tightened her jaw. It was her belief that Taggert waited until the night before or the day of the wedding to present his bride with one of his loathsome prenuptial agreements, letting her know just what he thought of her. Of course Karen could never say that, as she was not supposed to be typing Taggert's private work. That was the job of his personal secretary. But beautiful Miss Gresham was much too important to actually feed data into a computer terminal, so she gave the work to the person who had been with the company the longest: Miss Johnson. But then Miss Johnson was past seventy and too rickety to do a lot of typing. Knowing she'd lose her job if she admitted this, and since she had a rather startling number of cats to feed, Miss Johnson secretly gave all of Taggert's private work to Karen.

"So that's why all the women since then have left him?" the assistant asked. "I mean, there was that woman this morning."

Karen didn't have to hear Loretta's recapping of the events of this morning, as it was all the office staff could talk of. What with the Christmas party and the bonus, yet another of Taggert's women dumping him with almost more excitement than they could bear. Karen was genuinely concerned for Miss Johnson's heart.

This morning, minutes after the bonuses had been handed out, a tall, gorgeous redhead had stormed into the offices with a ring box in her trembling hand. The outside receptionist hadn't needed to ask who she was or what her errand was, for angry women with ring boxes in their hands were a common sight in the offices of M.J. Taggert. One by one, all doors had been opened to her, until she was inside the inner sanctum: Taggert's office.

Fifteen minutes later, the redhead had emerged, crying, ring box gone, but clutching a jeweler's box that was about the right size to hold a bracelet.

"How could they do this to him?" the women in the office had whispered, all their anger descending onto the head of the woman. "He's such a lovely man, so kind, so considerate," they said.

"His only problem is that he falls in love with the wrong women. If he could just find a *good* woman, she'd love him forever" was the conclusion that was always drawn. "He just needs a woman who understands what pain he has been through."

After this pronouncement, every woman in the office under fifty-five would head for the restroom, where she'd spend her lunch hour trying to make herself as alluring as possible.

Except Karen. Karen would remain at her desk, forcing herself to keep her opinions to herself.

Now Loretta gave a sigh that made the stall door rattle against its lock. Since Loretta had told every female in the office all about the divine Mr. Taggert, she wasn't worried about anyone overhearing.

"So now he's free again," Loretta said, her voice heavy with the sadness— and hope—at such a state. "He's still looking for his true love, and someday some very lucky woman is going to become Mrs. McAllister Taggert."

At that the assistant murmured in agreement. "The way that woman treated him was tragic. Even if she hated him, she should have thought of the wedding guests."

At those words, Karen could have groaned, for she knew that Loretta had recruited yet another soldier for her little army that constantly played worship-the-boss.

"What are you doing?" Karen heard Loretta ask.

"Filling in the correct name," the assistant answered.

A moment later, Loretta gave a sigh that had to have come straight from her heart. "Oh, yes, I like that. Yes, I like that very much. Now we must go. We wouldn't want to miss even a second of the Christmas party." She paused, then said suggestively, "There's no telling what can happen under the mistletoe."

Karen waited for a minute after the women were gone, then, allowing her pent-up breath to escape, she left the stall. Looking in the mirror, she saw that the time she'd spent hiding had allowed her eyes to clear. After washing her hands, she went to the towel holder and there she saw what the women had just been talking about. Long ago some woman (probably Loretta) had stolen a photograph of Taggert and hung it on the wall of the women's restroom. Then she'd glued a nameplate (also probably stolen) under it. But now, on the wall above the plate was written "Miserably Jilted" before the *M.J. Taggert.*

Looking at it for a moment, Karen shook her head in disgust, then with a smirk, she withdrew a permanent black marker from her handbag, crossed out the hand-written words, and replaced them with, "Magnificently Jettisoned."

For the first time that day, she smiled, then she left the restroom feeling much better. So much better, in fact, that she allowed herself to be pulled into the elevator by fellow employees to go upstairs to the huge Taggert Christmas party.

One whole floor of the building owned by the Taggerts had been set aside for conferences and meetings. Instead of being divided into offices of more or less equal space, the floor had been arranged as though it were a sumptuously, if rather oddly, decorated house. There was a room with tatami mats, shoji screens, and jade objects that was used for Japanese clients. Colefax and Fowler had made an English room that looked like something from Chatsworth. For clients with a scholarly bent there was a library with several thousand books in handsome pecan-wood cases. There was a kitchen for the resident chef and a kitchen for clients who liked to rustle up their own grub. A Santa Fe room dripped beaded moccasins and leather shirts with horsehair tassels.

And there was a big, empty room that could be filled with whatever was needed for the moment, such as an enormous Christmas tree bearing what looked to be half a ton of white and silver ornaments. All the employees looked forward to seeing that tree, each year "done" by some up-and-coming young designer, each year different, each year perfect. This tree would be a source of discussion for weeks to come.

Personally, Karen liked the tree in the day-care center better. It was never more than four feet tall so the children could reach most of it, and it was covered with things the children of the employees had made, such as paper chains and popcorn strings.

Now, making her way toward the day-care center, she was stopped by three men from accounting who'd obviously had too much to drink and were wearing silly paper hats. For a moment they tried to get Karen to go with them, but when they realized who she was, they backed off. Long ago she'd taught the men of the office that she was off limits, whether it was during regular work hours or in a more informal situation like this one.

"Sorry," they murmured and moved past her.

The day-care center was overflowing with children, for the families of the Taggerts who owned the building were there.

"If you say nothing else about the Taggerts, they are fertile," Miss Johnson had once said, making everyone except Karen laugh.

And they were a nice group, Karen admitted to herself. Just because she didn't like McAllister was no reason to dislike the entire family. They were always polite to everyone, but they kept to themselves; but then with a family the size of theirs, they probably didn't have time for outsiders. Now, looking into the chaos of the children's playroom, Karen seemed to see doubles of everyone, for twins ran in the Taggert family to an extraordinary degree. There were adult twins and toddler twins and babies that looked so much alike they could have been clones.

And no one, including Karen, could tell them apart. Mac had twin brothers who had offices in the same building, and whenever either of them arrived, the question "Which are you?" was always asked.

Someone shoved a drink into Karen's hand saying, "Loosen up, baby," but she didn't so much as take a sip. What with spending most of the night in the hospital to be near Ann, she'd not eaten since yesterday evening and she knew that whatever she drank would go straight to her head.

As she stood in the corridor looking in at the playroom, it seemed to her that she'd never seen so many children in her life: nursing babies, crawling, taking first steps, two with books in their hands, one eating a crayon, an adorable little girl with pigtails down her back, two beautiful identical twin boys playing with identical fire trucks.

"Karen, you are a masochist," she whispered to herself, then turned on her heel and walked briskly down the corridor to the elevator. The lift going down was empty, and once she was inside, loneliness swept over her. She had been planning to spend Christmas with Ann and Charlie, but now that they had the new baby, they wouldn't want to be bothered with a former sister-in-law.

Stopping in the office she shared with the other secretaries, Karen started to gather her things so she could go home, but on second thought she decided to finish two letters and get them out. There was nothing urgent, but why wait?

Two hours later Karen had finished all that she'd left on her desk and all that three of the other secretaries had left on their desks.

Stretching, gathering up the personal letters she'd typed for Taggert, one about some land he was buying in Tokyo and the other a letter to his cousin, she walked down the corridor to Taggert's private suite. Knocking first as she always did, then realizing that she as alone on the floor, she opened the door. It was odd to see this inner sanctum without the formidable Miss Gresham in it. Like a lion guarding a temple, the woman hovered over Taggert possessively, never allowing anyone who didn't have necessary business to see him.

So now Karen couldn't help herself as she walked softly about the room, which she'd been told had been decorated to Miss Gresham's exquisite taste. The room was all white and silver, just like the tree—and just as cold, Karen thought.

Carefully, she put the letters on Miss Gresham's desk and started to leave, then, on second thought, she looked toward the double doors that led into *his* office. As far as she knew none of the women in the secretarial pool had seen inside that office, and Karen, as much as anyone else, was very curious to see inside those doors.

Karen well knew that the security guard would be by soon, but she'd just heard him walking in the hall, keys jangling, and if she was caught, she could tell him that she had been told to put the papers in Taggert's office.

Silently, as though she were a thief, she opened the door to the office and looked inside. "Hello? Anyone here?" Of course, she knew that she'd probably drop dead of a heart attack if anyone answered, but still she was cautious.

While looking around, she put the letters on his desk. She had to admit that he had the ability to hire a good decorator; certainly no mere businessman could have chosen the furnishings of his office, because there wasn't one piece of black leather or chrome in sight. Instead, the office looked as though it had been taken intact from a French chateau, complete with carved paneling, worn flagstones on the floor, and a big fireplace dominating one wall. The tapestry-upholstered furniture looked well worn and fabulously comfortable.

Against a wall was a bookshelf filled with books, one shelf covered with framed photographs, and Karen was drawn to them. Inspecting them, she figured that it would take a calculator to add up all the children in the photos. At the end was a silver-framed photo of a young man holding up a string of fish. He was obviously a Taggert, but not one Karen had seen before. Curious, she picked up the picture and looked at the man.

"Seen all you want?" came a rich baritone that made Karen jump so high she dropped the photo onto the flagstones—where the glass promptly shattered.

"I . . . I'm sorry," she stuttered. "I didn't know anyone was here." Bending to pick up the picture, she looked up into the dark eyes of McAllister Taggert as all six feet of him loomed over her. "I will pay for the damage," she said nervously, trying to gather the pieces of broken glass.

He didn't say a word, just glared down at her, frowning.

With as much in her hand as she could pick up, she stood and started to hand the pieces to him, but when he didn't take them, she set them down on the end of the shelf. "I don't think the photo is damaged," she said. "I, uh, is that one of your brothers? I don't believe I've seen him before."

At that Taggert's eyes widened and Karen was quite suddenly afraid of him. They were alone on the floor and all she really knew about him personally was that a lot of women had refused to marry him. Was it because of his loathsome prenuptial agreements or was it because of something else? His violent temper maybe?

"I must go," she whispered, then turned on her heel and ran from his office.

Karen didn't stop running until she'd reached the elevator and punched the down button. Right now all she wanted on earth was to go home to familiar surroundings and try her best to get over her embarrassment. Caught like a teenage girl snooping in her boss's office! How could she have been so stupid?

When the elevator door opened, it was packed with merrymakers going up to the party three floors above, and even though Karen protested loudly that he wanted to go down, they pulled her in with them and took her back to the party.

The first thing she saw was a waiter with a tray of glasses full of champagne, and Karen downed two of them immediately. Feeling much better, she was able to calm her frazzled nerves. So she was caught snooping in the boss's office. So what? Worse things have happened to a person. By her third glass of wine, she'd managed to convince herself that nothing at all had happened.

Standing before her now was a woman with her arms full of a hefty little boy and juggling an enormous diaper bag while she frantically tried to open a stroller.

"Could I help?" Karen asked.

"Oh, would you please?" the woman answered, stepping back from the stroller as she obviously thought Karen meant to help her with that.

But instead, Karen took the child out of her arms and for a moment clasped him tightly to her.

"He doesn't usually like strangers, but he likes you." The woman smiled. "You wouldn't mind watching him for a few moments, would you? I'd love to get something to eat."

Holding the boy close to her, while he snuggled his sweet-smelling head into he shoulder, Karen whispered, "I'll keep him forever."

At that a look of fright crossed the woman's face. Snatching her child away from Karen, she hurried down the hall.

Moments ago Karen had thought she'd never before been so embarrassed, but this was worse than being caught snooping. "What is *wrong* with you?" she hissed to herself, then strode toward the elevators. She would go home now and never leave her house again in her life.

As soon as she got into the elevator, she realized that she'd left her handbag and coat in her office on the ninth floor. If it weren't zero degrees outside and her car keys weren't in her purse, she'd have left things where they were, but she had to return. Leaning her head back against the wall, she knew she'd had too much wine, but she also knew without a doubt that after Christmas she'd no longer have a job. As soon as Taggert told his formidable secretary that he'd caught an unknown woman—for Karen was sure the great and very busy McAllister Taggert had never so much as looked at someone as lowly as her— in his office, Karen would be dismissed.

On the wall of the elevator was a bronze plaque that listed all the Taggerts in the building, and toward the bottom it looked as though Loretta's new recruit had been busy again, for a piece of paper had been glued over McAllister Taggert's name that read, "Marvelous Jaguar." Smiling, Karen took a pen out of her pocket and changed it to, "Macho Jackass."

When the elevator stopped, she didn't know whether it was the wine or her defiance, but she felt better. However, she did not want another encounter with Taggert. While holding the door open, she carefully looked up and down both corridors to see if anyone was about. Clear. Tiptoeing, she went down the carpeted hall to the secretaries' office and, as silently as possible, removed her coat from the back of the chair and her purse from the drawer. As she was on her way out, she stopped by Miss Johnson's desk to get notes from her drawer. This way she'd have work to fill her time over Christmas.

"Snooping again?"

Karen paused with her hand on the drawer handle; she didn't have to look up to know who it was. McAllister J. Taggert. Had she not had so much to drink, she would have politely excused herself, but since she was sure she was going to be fired anyway, what did it matter? "Sorry about your office. I was sure you'd be out proposing marriage to someone."

With all the haughtiness she could muster, she tried to march past him.

"You don't like me much, do you?"

Turning, she looked him in the eyes, those dark, heavily fringed eyes that made all the women in the office melt with desire. But they didn't do much for Karen since she kept seeing the tears of the women who'd been jilted by him. "I've typed your last three prenuptial agreements. I know the truth about what you're like."

He looked confused. "But I thought Miss Gresham—"

"And risk breaking those nails on a keyboard? Not likely." With that, Karen swept past him on her way to the elevator.

But Taggert caught her arm.

For a moment fear ran through her. What did she really know about this man? And they were alone on this floor. If she screamed, no one would hear her.

At her look, his face stiffened and he released her arm. "Mrs. Lawrence, I can assure you that I have no intention of harming you in any way."

"How do you know my name?"

Smiling, he looked at her. "While you were gone, I made a few calls about you."

"You were spying on me?" she asked, aghast.

"Just curious. As you were about my office."

Karen took another step toward the elevator, but again he caught her arm.

"Wait, Mrs. Lawrence, I want to offer you a job over Christmas."

Karen punched the elevator button with a vengeance while he stood too close, looking down at her. "And what would that job be? Marriage to you?"

"In a manner of speaking, yes," he answered as he looked from her eyes to her toes and back up again.

Karen hit the elevator button so hard it was a wonder the button didn't go through the wall.

"Mrs. Lawrence, I am not making a pass at you. I am offering you a job. A legitimate job for which you will be paid, and paid well."

Karen kept hitting the button and looking up at the floors shown over both doors. Both elevators were stuck on the floor where the party was.

"In the calls I made I discovered that you've worked the last two Christmases when no one else would. I also found out that you are the Ice Maiden of the office. You once stapled a man's tie to your desk when he was leaning over you asking for a date."

Karen turned red, but she didn't look at him.

"Mrs. Lawrence," he said stiffly, as though what he said were very difficult for him. "Whatever may be your opinion of me, you could not have heard that I've ever made an improper advance toward a woman who works for me. My offer is for a job, an unusual job, but nothing else. I apologize for whatever I've done to give you the impression that I was offering more." With that he turned and walked away.

As Karen watched, one elevator went straight from the twelfth floor down to the first, skipping her on nine. Reluctantly, she turned to look at his retreating back. Suddenly, the image of her empty house appeared before her eyes, the tiny tree with not much under it. Whatever she thought of how he treated women in his personal life, Taggert was always respectful to his employees. And no matter how hard a woman worked to compromise him, he didn't fall for it. Two years ago when a secretary said he'd made a pass at her, everyone laughed at her so hard, she found another job three weeks later.

Taking a deep breath, Karen followed him. "All

right," she said when she was just behind him, "I'll listen."

Ten minutes later she was ensconced in Taggert's beautiful office; a fire burned in the fireplace, making a delightful rosy glow on the table that was loaded with delicious food and what seemed to be a limitless supply of cold champagne. At first Karen had thought of resisting such temptation, but then she thought of telling Ann that she'd eaten lobster and champagne with the boss and she began to nibble.

While Karen ate and drank, Taggert started to talk. "I guess you've heard by now about Lisa."

"The redhead?"

"*Mmmm,* yes, the redhead." He refilled her glass. "On the twenty-fourth of December, two days from now, Lisa and I were to be in the wedding of a good friend of mine who lives in Virginia. It's to be a huge wedding, with over six hundred guests flying in from all over the world."

For a moment he just looked at her, saying nothing. "And?" she asked after a while. "What do you need me for? To type your friend's prenupt?"

McAllister spread a cracker with a pâté de foie gras and held it out to her. "I no longer have a fiancée."

Karen took a drink of the wine, then reached for the cracker. "Excuse my ignorance, but I don't see what that has to do with me."

"You will fit the dress."

Maybe it was because her mind was a bit fuzzy with drink, but it took her a moment to comprehend, and when she did, she laughed. "You want me to pose as your fiancée and be a bridesmaid of some woman I've never met? And who has never met me?"

"Exactly."

"How many bottles of this have *you* drunk?"

McAllister smiled. "I'm not drunk and I'm absolutely serious. Want to hear more?"

Part of Karen's brain said that she should go home, get away from this crazy man, but what was waiting for her at home? She didn't even have a cat that needed her. "I'm listening."

"I don't know if you've heard, but three years ago I was . . ." He hesitated and she saw his eyelashes flutter quite attractively. "Three years ago I was left at the altar of my own wedding by the woman I planned to spend the rest of my life with."

Karen drained her glass. "Did she find out that you were refusing to say the lines 'with thee my worldly goods I share'?"

For a moment McAllister sat there and stared, then he smiled in a way that could only be called dazzling. And Karen had to blink; he really was gorgeous, with his dark hair and eyes and a hint of a dimple in one cheek. No wonder so many women fell for him. "I think, Mrs. Lawrence, that you and I are going to get along fine."

That brought Karen up short. She was going to have to establish boundaries *now*. "No, I don't think we will, since I do not believe your tragic little-boy-lost story. I have no idea what really happened at your wedding or all those other times women refused to marry you, but I can assure you I am not one of these lovesick secretaries who think you were 'Miserably Jilted.' I think you were—" She halted before she said too much.

Enlightenment lit his face. "You think I was 'Magnificently Jettisoned.' Or do you think I am a

'Macho Jackass'? Well, well, so now at last I know who the office wordsmith is."

Karen couldn't speak because she was too embarrassed—and *how* had he found this out so quickly?

For a moment longer he looked at her in speculation, then his face changed from feel-sorry-for-me to that of one friend talking to another. "What happened back then is between Elaine and me and will remain between us, but the truth is, the groom is her relative and she is going to be at the wedding. If I show up alone, with yet another fiancée having left me, it will be, to put it kindly, embarrassing. And then there is the matter of the wedding. If there are seven male attendants and only six female, women get a bit out-of-sorts about things like that."

"So hire someone from an escort service. Hire an actress."

"I thought of that, but who knows what you get? She could audition lady Macbeth at the reception. Or she could turn out to know half the men there in a way that could be awkward."

"Surely, Mr. Taggert, you must have a little black book full of names of women who would love to go anywhere with you and do anything."

"That's just the problem. They are all women who . . . well, they like me and after this . . . Well . . ."

"I see. How do you get rid of them? You could always ask them to marry you. That seems to cure every woman of you forever."

"See? You're perfect for this. All anyone has to do is see the way you look at me and they'll know we're about to separate. Next week when I announce our split, no one will be surprised."

"What's in it for me?"

"I'll pay you whatever you like."

"One of the engagement rings you give out by the gross?" She knew she was being rude, but the champagne was giving her courage and with every discourteous thing she said to him, his eyes twinkled more.

"Ouch! Is that what people say about me?"

"Don't try your sad-little-boy act on me. I typed those prenuptial agreements, remember? I know what you are *really* like."

"And that is?"

"Incapable of trust, maybe incapable of love. You like the idea of marriage, but actually sharing yourself, and above all sharing your money, with another human, terrifies you. In fact, as far as I can tell, you don't share anything with anyone."

For a moment, he gaped at her, then he smiled. "You certainly have me in a nutshell, but coldhearted as I am, it still embarrassed me that Elaine left me so publicly. That wedding cost me thirty-two thousand dollars, none of which was refundable, and I had to send the gifts back."

Refusing to give in to his play for sympathy, she repeated, "What's in it for me? And I don't want money. I have money of my own."

"Yes. Fifty-two thousand and thirty-eight cents, to be exact."

Karen nearly choked on her champagne. "How—?"

"My family owns the bank in this building. I took a guess that it might be the bank you use, so I tapped into the files after you left my office."

"*More* spying!"

"More curiosity. I was checking to see who you were. I am offering you legitimate employment, and since this is a very personal job, I wanted to know more about you. Besides, I like to know more about a woman than just the package." Taking a sip from his champagne glass, he looked at her the way a dark, romantic hero look at a helpless damsel.

But Karen wasn't affected. She'd had other men look at her like that, and she'd had one man look at her in love. The difference between the two was everything. "I can see why women say yes to you," she said coolly, lifting her glass to him.

At her detachment, he gave a genuine smile. "All right, I can see that you're not impressed by me, so, now shall we talk business, Mrs. Lawrence? I want to hire you as my escort for three days. Since I am at your mercy, you can name your price."

Karen drained her glass. What was this, her sixth? Whatever the number, all she could feel was courage running through her veins. "If I were to do this, I wouldn't want money."

"Ah, I see. What do you want then? A promotion? To be made head secretary? Maybe you'd like a vice presidency?"

"And sit in a windowed office doing nothing all day? No, thank you."

McAllister blinked at her words, then waited for her to say more. When she was silent, he said, "You want stock in the company? No?" When she still said nothing, he leaned back in his chair and looked at her in speculation. "You want something money can't buy, don't you?"

"Yes," she said softly.

He looked at her for a long moment. "Am I to figure out what money can't buy? Happiness?"

Karen shook her head.

"Love? Surely you don't want love from someone like me?" His face showed his bafflement. "I'm afraid you have me stumped."

"A baby."

At that McAllister spilled champagne down the front of his shirt. As he mopped himself up, he looked at her with eyes full of interest. "Oh, Mrs. Lawrence, I like this much better than parting with my money." As he reached for her hand, she grabbed a sharp little fish knife.

"Don't touch me."

Leaning back, McAllister refilled both their glasses. "Would you be so kind as to inform me how I'm to give you a baby without touching you?"

"In a jar."

"Ah, I see, you want a test-tube baby." His voice lowered and his eyes grew sympathetic. "Are your eggs—?"

"My eggs are perfectly all right, thank you," she snapped. "I don't want to put my eggs in a jar, but I want you to put your . . . your . . . in a jar."

"Yes, now I understand." Looking at her, he sipped his drink. "What I don't understand is, why me? I mean, since you don't like me or exactly think I'm of good moral character, why would you want me to be the father of your child?"

"Two reasons. The alternative is going to a clinic, where I can choose a man off a computer data bank. Maybe he's healthy but what about his relatives? Whatever I may think of you, your family is very nice and, according to the local papers, has been nice for generations. And I know what you and your relatives look like."

"I'm not the only one who has been snooping. And the second reason?"

"If I have your child—in a manner of speaking— later you won't come to me asking me for money."

It was as though this statement were too outlandish for McAllister to comprehend, because for a moment he sat there blinking in consternation. Then he laughed, a deep rumbling sound that came from inside his chest. "Mrs. Lawrence, I do believe we are going to get along splendidly." He extended his right hand. "All right, we have a bargain."

For just a moment Karen allowed her hand to be enveloped in his large warm one, and she allowed her eyes to meet his and to see the way they crinkled into a smile.

Abruptly, she pulled way from his touch. "Where and when?" she asked.

"My car will pick you up at six A.M. tomorrow, and we'll leave on the first flight to New York."

"I thought your friend lived in Virginia," she said suspiciously.

"He does, but I thought we'd go to New York first and outfit you," he said bluntly, sounding as though she were a naked native he, the great white hunter, had found.

For a moment Karen hid her face behind the champagne glass so he wouldn't see her expression. "Ah, yes, I see. Based on what I've seen, you like your fiancées to be well coiffed and well dressed."

"Doesn't every man?"

"Only men who can't see beneath the surface."

"Ouch!"

Karen blushed. "I apologize. If I am to pretend to be your fiancée, I will try to curb my tongue." She gave him a hard look. "I won't have to play the doting, adorable female, will I?"

"Since no other woman to whom I have been engaged has, I see no reason you should. Have some more champagne, Mrs. Lawrence."

"No, thank you," Karen said, standing, then working hard not to wobble on her feet. Champagne, firelight, and a dark-haired, hot-eyed man were not conducive to making a woman remember her vows of chastity. "I will see you at the airport tomorrow, but, please, there'll be no need to stop in New York." When he started to say something, she smiled. "Trust me."

"All right," he said, raising his glass. "To tomorrow."

Karen left the room, gathered her things, and took the elevator downstairs. Since she didn't feel steady enough to drive, she had the security man call a cab to take her to a small shopping mall south of Denver.

"Bunny?" Karen asked tentatively as a woman locked the door of the beauty salon. Looking at Bunny's hair, Karen couldn't decide if it had been dyed apricot or peach. Whatever, it was an extraordinary shade.

"Yes?" the woman asked, turning, looking at Karen with no recognition in her eyes.

"You don't remember me?"

For a moment Bunny looked puzzled, then her fine pale skin crinkled in pleasure. "Karen? Could that be you under that . . . that . . . ?"

"Hair," Karen supplied.

"Maybe you call it hair but not from where I'm standing. And look at your face! Did you take vows? Is that why it's so shiny and clean?"

Karen laughed. One of her few luxuries while married to Ray had been having Bunny do her hair and give her advice on makeup and nails, and pretty much anything else in life. For all that Bunny was an excellent hairdresser, she was also like a therapist to her clients—and as discreet as though she'd taken an oath. A woman knew she could tell Bunny anything and it would go no further.

"Could you do my hair?" Karen asked shyly.

"Sure. Call in the morning and—"

"No, now. I have to leave on a plane early in the morning."

Bunny didn't put up with such nonsense. "I have a hungry husband waiting at home, and I've been on my feet for nine hours. You should have come earlier."

"Could I bribe you with a story? A very, very good story?"

Bunny looked skeptical. "How good a story?"

"You know my gorgeous boss? McAllister Taggert? I'm probably going to have his baby and he's never touched me—nor is he going to."

Bunny didn't miss a beat as she shoved the key back into the lock. "I predict that hair of yours is going to take half the night."

"What about your husband?"

"Let him open his own cans."

Two

KAREN SETTLED BACK in the wide seat of the airplane, business class, and sipped her glass of orange juice. Beside her, McAllister Taggert already had his nose in the papers in his briefcase. Early this morning when she'd arrived at the airport, she was escorted to a lounge that she'd had no idea existed at the Denver airport.

Unobtrusively, she'd taken a chair across from him, and he hadn't bothered to greet her or even look at her. Ten minutes later, idly, he'd glanced up, lost in thought, then back down at his papers. Karen then had the great satisfaction of seeing him pause and look back at her— a long, slow look that went from her head to her toes then back up again.

"You *are* Karen Lawrence, aren't you?" he asked, making her smile, and making her sure that the three hours at Bunny's, with her head covered in foil, her face slathered in mud, then another three hours at home trying on everything in her closet, had been worth it.

He told her he had to work on the trip to Virginia, then looked back down at his papers, but several times he glanced at Karen. All in all, she found those looks quite gratifying.

Now, on the plane, she sat beside him, sipping orange juice and growing more bored by the minute. "Anything I can do to help?" she asked, nodding toward his papers.

He smiled at her in that way men do when they think a woman is pretty but had somehow managed to be born without a brain. "If I'd brought a computer, you could type for me, but actually, no, I have nothing for you to do. I just have some decisions to make."

Ah, yes, she thought, Men's Work. "Such as?" she urged.

A slight frown crossed his handsome brow. Obviously he liked his women to remain silent. "Just buying and selling," he answered quickly, in a tone that was meant to make her stop asking childish questions.

"And exactly what are you considering buying or selling this morning?"

The small frown changed to one that made his brows meet in the middle over the bridge of his nose. Love is such a funny thing, she thought. Had Ray looked at her like that, she would have backed off immediately, but this man did not frighten her a bit.

When he saw that she wasn't going to stop questioning him, he snapped, "I'm thinking of purchasing a small publishing company," then looked back at his papers.

"Ah," she said. "Coleman and Brown Press. Bad covers, mostly reprints. A few good books on regional history, but the covers were so bad no one bought the books."

McAllister looked at her as though she should mind her own business. "If I decide to buy it, I'll hire a new art director who can design good covers."

"Can't. The publisher is sleeping with her."

McAllister had just put his glass of orange juice to his lips and at Karen's words he nearly choked. "What?"

"I was curious, so when the publisher's secretary came to deliver the financial sheets to you I asked her to have lunch with me. She told me that the publisher—who is married and has three children—has been having a long-term affair with the art director. If he fires her, she'll blab to his wife—whose family owns the publishing house. It's a very sticky situation."

Mac blinked at her. "So what do you recommend?" he asked with great sarcasm.

"Buy the house and put some competent people in there, then consolidate several of the small history books into one fat one and sell it as a textbook on Colorado history to the schools. There's a great deal of money to be made in textbooks."

For a long moment Mac just looked at her. "And you found out all this because you were curious, right?"

Turning away, Karen looked out the window and knew she'd never missed Ray more than she did in that moment. Ray used to listen to her; he liked her ideas and her input. Unfortunately, she'd found that most men's minds were as closed as this man's.

It wasn't until the plane had taken off and they were cruising that he spoke to her again. "What other things have you looked into?" he asked softly. "Jet engines? Sewage plants? Road building equipment?"

She knew he was being ironic, but at the same time, she could hear that he actually wanted to know. "I'm only interested in the small things, especially the local Denver places."

"Such as?" he asked, one eyebrow raised.

"Lawson's Department Store," she answered quickly.

At that he smiled indulgently. "That place is an eyesore to downtown Denver. I already have an excellent offer from Glitter and Sass."

"Those stores that sell leather and chains?" she asked with a curled lip.

"More like leather and rhinestones." Leaning back in the seat, he looked at her in speculation. "And who would *you* sell it to?" When she didn't answer, he gave her a little smile. "Come on, don't chicken out on me now. If you're going to tell me how to run my business, don't stop after one suggestion."

"All right," she said defiantly. "I'd open a store that sells baby paraphernalia." At that she expected him to turn away in disgust, but he didn't. He just sat there, patiently waiting for her to continue.

She took a deep breath. "In England they have stores called Mothercare that sell everything for babies: maternity wear, strollers, nursery furniture, diapers, the works. In America you have to go to different stores for different items, and when you're eight months pregnant and your feet are swollen and you have two other kids, it's not easy schlepping to five different stores trying to get what you need for the baby. I don't know from experience, but it seems that it would be a wonderful convenience to be able to buy everything from one store."

"And what would you call this store?" he asked quietly.

"Sanctuary?" she answered innocently, making him laugh.

McAllister took a piece of paper and a pen from his briefcase and handed it to her. "Here. Write down all you know or think about Coleman and Brown Press. All of it, gossip, everything. I want to know how I can make that place a going concern."

Karen used all her strength to keep from smiling, but it was no use. She had a feeling he'd never before asked a woman her opinion of what he should buy or sell. His branch of Montgomery-Taggert was very small, and he had a few women executives, but everyone knew that McAllister Taggert was a law unto himself. He infuriated people in his employ by his stubborn insistence on doing things his own way. It further infuriated them that he was pretty much always right.

But now he was asking *her* opinion! "Aye, aye, sir," Karen said mockingly as she started to write, but out of the corner of her eye, she could see just a bit of a smile playing about his lips.

If Karen thought she was going to get any warmth out of Taggert, the notion was short-lived, for what time during the flight he didn't have his nose buried in papers, he was on the telephone. He ate with one hand, papers in the other. When they landed at Dulles Airport, outside D.C., he handed her three one-hundred-dollar bills, said, "Green hanging," then nodded toward the baggage carousel. Karen was tempted to give the porter one bill as a tip, but instead, she paid the five dollars out of her own pocket, then tried to find Taggert. He found her, rental car keys in his hand, and quickly, they went outside into the crisp, cold air to the car.

Once inside the warmth of the car, it felt almost intimate to be alone with him and she looked about for something to say. "If I'm to pretend to be your fiancée, shouldn't I know something about you?"

"What do you want to know?" he asked in a way that made Karen give him a look of disgust.

"Nothing really. I'm sure that knowing you are rich is enough for any woman."

Karen had expected the jab to make him laugh or respond sarcastically, but it didn't. Instead, he just looked straight ahead, his brow creased in concentration. For the rest of the drive, Karen didn't bother to talk. She decided if anyone asked why she was planning to marry M.J. Taggert, she'd say, "Alimony."

He drove them through the highways of Virginia to Alexandria, then through wooded countryside, past beautiful houses until he reached a graveled road and made a sharp right. Minutes later a house came into view and it was the place where all little girls dreamed of spending Christmas: three stories, tall pillars in front, perfectly spaced windows. She half expected George and Martha Washington to greet them.

The front lawn and what she could see of the rolling gardens in the back were alive with people playing touch football, gathering armloads of wood, or just strolling. And there seemed to be children everywhere.

The moment the car was spotted, what seemed to be a herd of people descended on them, opening the door and pulling Karen out. They introduced themselves as Laura and Deborah and Larry and Dave and—

One very good looking man grabbed her and kissed her soundly on the mouth. "Oh!" was all Karen could say as she stared at him.

"I'm Steve," he offered in explanation. "The bridegroom? Didn't Mac tell you about me?"

Karen didn't think about what she was saying. "Taggert never speaks to me unless he wants something," she blurted, then stared wide-eyed. These people were his friends, what would they think of her!?

To Karen's consternation, they burst into laughter.

"Mac, at last you found a woman who knows the true you," Steve yelled across the roof of the car as he put one arm around Karen's shoulders, then a pretty woman put another arm around her, and they led her into the house, all of them laughing.

They led her past heavenly rooms with huge fireplaces that blazed cheerfully, then up a grand staircase, down two halls to a wide white door. Steve opened it. "He's all yours," he said, laughing, then pushed her inside and closed the door behind her.

Taggert was in the room, their suitcases were already placed on luggage racks, and there was only one bed. "There's been a mistake," Karen said.

Mac frowned down at the bed. "I've already tried to rectify this, but it's impossible. The house is full. Every bed, cot, and couch is already assigned. Look," he said, frowning, "if you're afraid I'm going to attack you in the night, I can see if a hotel room can be found for you."

There was something about his attitude that always seemed to rub her the wrong way. "At least with a full house if I scream, I'll be heard."

He gave her a little half-smile then started unbuttoning his shirt. "I need to take a shower. The wedding rehearsal is in an hour." He was looking at her as though he expected her to be a heroine from a Regency romance and flee the room in fear at the very thought of a man undressing. But she wasn't going to let him intimidate her. "Please don't steam up the mirror," she said, chin in the air, then turned away as though sharing a room with a strange man was of no consequence to her.

With a bit of a chuckle, he went into the bathroom, leaving the door ajar for the steam to escape.

When he was out of sight, Karen let her breath escape and her shoulders relax. The room was lovely, all green silk and Federal furniture, and as she heard the shower running, she happily unpacked suitcases. It wasn't until she was finished that she realized that, out of habit, she'd unpacked Taggert's case too. As she put his shoes in the closet next to hers, Karen almost burst into tears. It had been so long since a man's shoes had been next to her own.

When she turned, Taggert was standing there, his hair wet, his big body encased in a terry-cloth robe, and he was watching her.

"I, ah, I didn't mean to unpack your case, but, uh . . . Habit," she finally managed to say before escaping into the bathroom and firmly closing the door behind her.

She took as long as she dared in the bathroom and was very pleased to see that he was gone when she reentered the room. After dressing as quickly as she could, she left the bedroom and ran down the stairs to join the rest of the wedding party, who were piling into cars headed to the church for the rehearsal.

All the way to the church, her annoyance toward Taggert built. If she was supposed to be his fiancée, shouldn't he be showing her some consideration? Instead, he dropped her at the front door and expected her to find her own way among strangers. No wonder so many women refused to marry him, she thought. They were all obviously women of sense and intelligence.

At the church the rehearsal went off smoothly until

at the end, when Taggert was to be the first to start down the aisle. He was to walk to the center, offer his arm to Karen, then walk with her out of the church. Maybe he hadn't heard what was said, but whatever his excuse, he walked to the center of the aisle, then started down alone, without Karen.

It was too much for her. "You know how Taggert is," she said, "he thinks he can partner himself."

Everyone in the church burst into laughter, and Taggert, turning, saw his mistake. With a great show of gallantry, he returned, bowed, and offered his arm to Karen.

"Getting me back for all those weekends of typing?" he said under his breath.

"Getting you back for all those women who were too timid to stand up to you," she said, smiling wickedly.

"I am not the monster you think I am."

"I shall ask Elaine's opinion on that. By the way, when is she coming?"

From the look on his face as they reached the back of the church, Karen regretted her remark.

"Christmas Day," he said softly, then turned away from her.

The rehearsal dinner was loud, with everyone talking at once about summers they had spent together and places they had visited. At first Karen looked at her food and listened but didn't participate in the conversation among these people who knew each other so well. Taggert sat on the other side of the big table, at the opposite end from her, and he, too, was quiet. Every once in a while, Karen glanced toward him and thought she saw him looking at her, but he turned away so quickly that she wasn't sure.

"Karen," one of the women said and the whole table quietened. "Where is your engagement ring?"

She didn't hesitate before she spoke. "Taggert had bought all the store had, so they're awaiting a new shipment of diamonds. He buys them by the dozen, you know."

The windows of the restaurant nearly exploded with the laughter of the diners, and even Mac laughed as Steve, next to him, slapped him on the back.

There were calls of, "I think you ought to keep this one, Mac," and, "It looks as though your taste in women is improving."

For the rest of the meal, Karen wasn't allowed to sit in silence. The two women across from her asked many questions about what she did and where she'd grown up and all the normal questions that people ask. When she told them that Mac was her boss, they were fascinated and wanted to know what it was like working for him.

"Lonely," she answered. "He doesn't need any of us, except to type a letter now and then."

Through all of this, Taggert ate his dinner without saying a word, but Karen could feel his eyes on her and even when Steve leaned forward to say something to him, Mac's eyes never left Karen's face.

It wasn't until they were alone in "their" room that Karen thought maybe she'd gone a little too far. "About tonight . . ." she began as he walked past her out of the bathroom. "Maybe I shouldn't have—"

"Going to chicken out on me now?" he asked, his face very close to hers.

Inconsequentially, Karen thought, he has a beautiful

mouth. But she recovered herself and stood up straight. "No, of course not."

"Good. Now, what did you do with my sweatpants?"

"Isn't it a little late for sports?" she said without thinking, not that it was any of her business what he did when.

Mac gave her a one-sided smile. "Unless you want me sleeping raw, they're the only alternative."

"Third drawer left," she said as she scurried into the bathroom. When she emerged, swathed in a puritanical white cotton nightgown, he was already in bed, and there was a long, thick bolster pillow down the center of the bed. Slipping into the vacant side of the bed, she said, "Where did you get this?"

"Stole it."

"So I guess some poor unfortunate is sleeping on a couch without a back cushion."

"Want me to take it back? You could sleep snuggled up with me or, better yet, we could have a serious discussion about this jar that you want me to—"

"Good night," she said firmly, then turned on her side away from him, but she was smiling as she fell asleep.

Three

KAREN AWOKE TO the sight of a gorgeous man wearing only a thick white towel about his waist, standing before the bathroom mirror shaving. In those few minutes before she awoke fully and remembered where she was, she had a vision of him coming toward her, kissing her, then tossing the towel aside and climbing into bed with her. For just those few seconds she could remember clearly how it felt to have a man in her arms, the size of him, the warmth of his skin, the weight of him, the—

"Want to share that thought?" he asked, not turning his head but looking at her in the mirror.

Turning away so he couldn't see her red face, she rolled out of bed, grabbed her robe, and moved toward the closet, out of his line of vision.

"What do you have planned for today?" he asked, coming out of the bathroom, still wearing only that tiny towel and wiping excess lather from his face.

Karen flung open a closet door so she couldn't see him. Did he work out every day? He must to keep his body looking like that. And was that warm honey his natural skin color? "Shopping," she mumbled.

"Shopping?" he asked, moving around the door to the other side of her. "As in Christmas shopping?"

"I, ah," she said, studiously looking at the clothes hanging inside, yet seeing nothing. "Yes, Christmas shopping. And a wedding gift." She took a deep breath. She *had* to get hold of herself! Turning, she looked into his eyes—and not one inch lower. "Tomorrow is Christmas and if I'm to spend it with these people, I can't very well turn up empty-handed. Do you know a good shopping mall around here?"

"Tyson's Corner,' he said quickly. "One of the best in the country. And I need to buy gifts, too, so I'll go with you."

"No!" Karen blurted, then tried to recover herself. "I mean, I concentrate better when I'm by myself." Even as she said it, she knew it was a lie. Christmas shopping alone became a chore.

"And how will you know who to buy for? Even how many kids are here? I assume you want to buy for the kids."

"Write down all the names for me and I'll get everything." She did not want to spend the day with this man—and it was getting very difficult to keep her eyes off the muscles of his chest.

"I don't have a pencil," he said, smiling. "Everything is in my head."

Karen almost smiled back at him. "You can dictate them to me. Besides, wouldn't you rather stay here and play football with the other guys?"

"I am a fat, out-of-shape desk jockey and they'd cream me."

At that Karen did laugh, for there was no one who was less out of shape than he was.

Without waiting for her to say yes, he grabbed a terry-cloth robe from the closet, put it on, then kissed her cheek. "Pick me out some clothes, would you? I have to make some calls. I'll be back for you in thirty minutes."

Before Karen could protest, he was out of the room, the door closed behind him. Of course, she thought, feminists everywhere would shudder at the notion of her choosing the clothing of an autocratic, arrogant, presumptuous man like Mac Taggert. But by the time she'd completed this thought, she had draped a pair of dark wool trousers, an Italian shirt, and a heavenly English sweater across the bed. Shaking her head in disgust at herself, she went into the bathroom.

An hour later, after a quick breakfast, she and Mac were walking to the rental car, and on the lawn were the bridegroom and other men playing ball. Steve shouted to Mac, asking him to come play with them.

"She's forcing me to go shopping with her," he yelled back.

"Ha!" Karen called to them over the roof of the car. "Like I need a man to go shopping with me, right? Truth is, he's afraid to stay here because you might hurt him."

Ignoring the laughter of the men, Mac shouted, "What do you want us to get you for a wedding gift?"

"From you, Taggert?" Steve called. "A Lamborghini. But from her, I'll take anything she offers."

"I'll second that," one of the other men called, then they all laughed in a very complimentary way.

Feeling quite flattered, Karen smiled brilliantly at all the young men playing touch football and she smiled even more brightly when she saw that Mac was frowning. "What a very nice group of people," she said as she got into the car.

Mac, his body twisted as he looked out the back window while he drove the car out in reverse, maneuvering it around the many other vehicles in the drive, didn't answer her.

Maybe it was because of the men's flirting with her and Mac's resultant silence, but by the time they arrived at the beautiful Tysons Corner mall, Karen was in very good spirits.

"Where do we begin?" she asked as soon as they'd entered the center of the mall near Hecht's. Looking up at him, she saw that male shrug that meant that she was in charge. "Elephant time," she muttered.

"I beg your pardon," he said stiffly.

"It's what I used to say when I was with my husband and we went shopping together. He'd refuse to participate in deciding what to buy anyone, but he'd carry anything I handed him. I called him my elephant."

For a moment Mac seemed to consider this, then he solemnly lifted his right arm, clenched his fist, and made his biceps bulge through his sweater. "I can carry anything you can pack onto me."

Karen laughed. "We shall see about that. By the way, if, as you said, 'we' are giving gifts, who's paying for these things?"

"Me?" he said with a mock sigh, as though he'd always paid for everything she'd ever bought.

"Perfect," she said over her shoulder as she took a right headed for Nordstrom's. "Your money, my taste."

"Just give me a peanut now and then and I'll be fine," he said from behind her.

Three hours later, Karen was exhausted but exhilarated. She'd completely forgotten what it was like to shop with a man. He never wanted to take the time to consider which of any two purchases was better. "This one," he'd say, or, "What does it matter?" And when it came to gift suggestions, he could rarely think past the music store. Twice she had him sit on benches, surrounded by shopping bags, while she went into stores and purchased sets of soaps and lotions, and some fruit and cheese baskets. She almost couldn't get him out of the Rand McNally shop, where he purchased a huge 3-D puzzle of the Empire State Building. And they visited all nine toy stores and made purchases from each one, so many purchases in fact that Karen suspected that they'd bought more toys than there were children.

"Does lunch come with this trip?" he asked after they'd visited the very last toy store the mall had to offer.

"Are you *sure* you want to eat? I think there was a toy car still left in that last store. Maybe you should go back and get it."

"Food, woman!" he growled, leading the way to the Nordstrom's cafe, where they placed their orders, then took their drinks and found a seat where Mac could put all the bags, for he wouldn't allow Karen to carry anything.

"You're a good elephant," she said as soon as they were seated, smiling at him.

After they were situated, he looked at her. "What plans have you made for Lawson's Department Store?"

Karen was in too good a mood to lie. "You don't have to patronize me. And you don't have to listen to my childish ideas. For all that this has been great fun today, you and I both know that as soon as we get back to Denver, it will end. You're the boss, and I'm just a typist."

"Just a typist, are you?" he said, one eyebrow raised as he reached down the neck of his sweater to his shirt pocket and pulled out several folded fax sheets. "You, your husband, and Stanley Thompson owned Thompson's Hardware Store for six years. You and your husband were everything to the store. Stanley Thompson was deadweight."

As Karen looked at him in astonishment, he continued.

"After you two were married, Ray worked two jobs, while you typed manuscripts at home. You two saved every penny you had and bought a half share in

Thompson's Hardware and you turned the place around. Ray knew about machines; you knew everything else. You wrote ads that made people come to the store and you handled the money, telling Ray how much you could and could not afford. It was your idea to add the little garden center and bring in women customers, and that was the most profitable part of the store. After Ray died you found out that the only way Thompson had originally been willing to sell to him was on the condition that on Ray's death he could buy you out for fifty grand."

"It was fair at the time the deal was made," Karen said defensively, as though he were saying that Ray had made a bad contract.

"Yes, at the time of purchase, half a share was only worth thirty thousand, but by the time he'd died, you and Ray had built up the business so a half share was worth a great deal more than fifty grand."

"I could have stayed as a full partner." Karen said softly.

"If you shared Stanley Thompson's bed."

"You do snoop, don't you?"

"Just curious," he said, eyes twinkling at her as their food was set before them. After the waitress left, he said, "You want to tell me about your ideas for this store for mothers?"

"I haven't really thought about it, just some vague ideas," she said, playing with the straw in her glass of iced tea.

At that Mac gave a little snort of laughter and pushed a pen and a napkin toward her."If you had unlimited money and owned Lawson's Department Store, what would you do with it?"

Karen hesitated but not for long. Truth was, she *had* thought about this for quite some time. "I'd put a children's play area in the center so mothers could watch their children at all times. If a mother is to be there a while, I'd tag the kids. You know, like clothing in department stores, so if the children wander outside the play area or someone tries to take them, bells go off as they exit the store."

Mac said nothing but his eyebrows were raised in question.

"They put tags on clothing so people can't steal them and children are a great deal more important than shirts, aren't they? And how can a woman try on clothes in comfort with a four-year-old screaming at her?"

After taking a bite of her food, she continued. "Surrounding the play area I'd have different departments: maternity wear, furniture, layettes, books on the various aspects of raising children, all the visual things. And I'd have clerks who were extremely experienced. And fat."

Mac smiled patronizingly at that.

"No, really. My sister-in-law just had a baby, and she was constantly complaining about anorexic sales girls who looked at her with pity every time she asked if they had something in extra large. And I'd have trained bra fitters and I'd have free brochures of local organizations the women could contact if they needed help or information, such as La Leche League. And of course we'd have contact with a local obstetrician in case of mishaps in the store. And—"

She broke off as she glanced at his face. He was laughing at her!

"Haven't thought about it much, have you?"

She smiled. "Well, maybe just a bit."

"Where are your financials? And don't you dare tell me you haven't worked out to the penny how much opening a store like this would cost."

Karen took a few bites. "I have done a bit of number crunching."

"When we get back to Denver, you can put them on my desk and I'll—" He broke off because Karen had removed a computer disk from her handbag. Taking it, he looked down at it and frowned. "When were you going to present me with this?"

She knew what he meant. He thought *this* was the real reason she'd agreed to this weekend. She was just one of the hundreds of people who tried to see him about or mail him their schemes for getting rich. Karen snatched the disk out of his hands. "I was *never* planning to show it to you or anyone else," she said through her teeth. "Millions of people have dreams in their heads and that's just where they stay: in their heads."

Angrily, she grabbed her purse and coat from beside her. "Excuse me, but I think this has all been a mistake. I think I'd better leave now."

Mac caught her arm and pulled her back down into the booth. "I'm sorry. I apologize. Really, I do."

"Would you please release me?"

"No, because you'll run."

"Then I'll scream."

"No you won't. You allowed Stanley Thompson to rob you blind and you didn't scream then because you didn't want to make a scene for his family. You, Karen, are not the screaming type."

She looked at his big, tanned hand clasping her

wrist. He was right, she was not a screamer—or much of a fighter. Maybe she needed Ray standing behind her telling her she could do anything before she believed in herself.

Mac's hand moved so his fingers were entwined with hers, and Karen made no attempt to pull away as he held her hand in his.

"Look, Karen, I know what you think of me, but it's not true. Have you ever told anyone else about your ideas for the baby store?"

"No," she said softly.

"But you must have been working on this idea since before Ray died. Did you tell him?"

"No." She and Ray'd had as much as they could handle with the hardware store. And she'd never wanted to give him the idea that she wanted something different—or even something more.

"Then I am honored by your confiding in me," Mac said, and when Karen gave him a look of suspicion, he said, "Really, I am." Pausing a moment, he looked down at their two hands entwined. "All those prenuptial agreements were only to see if she *would* sign."

Karen looked at him in disbelief.

"Honest. If any of those women had signed, I'd have torn it up immediately. But all I ever heard was, 'Daddy doesn't think I should sign,' or, 'My lawyer advises me not to sign.' All I wanted was to be *sure* that the woman wanted me and not my family's wealth."

"Rather a hateful little trick, wasn't it?"

"Not as hateful as marrying me and four years later going through a divorce. And what if we had kids?"

In spite of herself, Karen felt herself curling her fingers around his. "And what about Elaine?"

"Elaine was different," he said softly, then pulled his hand from hers.

As Karen opened her mouth to ask another question, he said, "Ready?" and the way he said it was a command.

Minutes later they were again in the mainstream of the mall, Mac moving ahead, loaded down with shopping bags. Behind him, thoughtful, Karen followed— until she was pulled up short at the sight of a shop full of the most beautiful clothes for children she had ever seen. In the window was hanging a christening gown of fine cotton, hand-tucked, dripping soft cotton lace.

"Want to go in?" Mac said softly from over her head.

"No, of course not," Karen said sharply, turning away.

But Mac, already large, was made even larger by all the bags he was holding and he blocked her exit as he moved forward.

"Really, I don't want . . ." she began, but she stopped speaking as soon as she was inside the store. Never had she allowed herself to look at baby clothes as something for a child *she* might have. For others, yes, but never for herself.

As though in a trance, she went toward the pretty dresses hanging on racks at eye level.

Mac, who had been relieved of his bags by a kind saleswoman, came up behind her. "Not those. The first Taggert baby is always a boy."

"Nothing is ever 'always,'" Karen told him, taking down a white cotton dress hand-embroidered with pale pink and blue flowers.

"Here, this is much better," he said as he held up a

red and blue striped shirt. "Good for playing football."

"I am *not* going to allow my son to play football," she told him, replacing the dress and looking at some white suits made for what could only be a little prince. "Football is much too dangerous."

"He's my son too and I say—"

It suddenly occurred to Karen what they were talking about, that they might have a baby together but it wouldn't be *theirs*. Not in any real sense. It wouldn't be . . . Before she could put together another thought, she ran from the store and was staring in the window of Brentano's when Mac found her.

"You mind if we sit awhile?" he asked, and all Karen could do was nod her head. Her embarrassment over what had happened in the baby store was still too fresh to allow her to speak.

She sat, he piled shopping bags around her, then he went to get the two of them ice cream cones, and for a while they sat in silence with their ice cream.

"Why didn't you and your husband have children?" he asked softly.

"We thought we had all the time in the world, so we put it off," she answered simply.

For a moment Mac was silent. "Did you love him very much?"

"Yes, very, very much."

"He was a very lucky man," Mac said and reached out to take her hand. "I envy him."

For a moment Karen looked into his eyes, and for the first time since Ray's death she saw another man. Not Ray superimposed over another man's features, but she saw Mac Taggert for himself. I could love again, she thought, and in that moment it was as though all the ice she had protectively put around her heart melted.

"Karen, I—" Mac began as he moved toward her as though he meant to kiss her right there in the midst of Tyson's Corner mall.

"My goodness!" Karen said. "Just look at the time. I have an appointment at the hairdresser for the wedding tonight, and I'm barely going to make it. It's here in the mall but on the next level, so I'd better run."

"When did you make an appointment?" he asked, sounding for all the world like a husband who couldn't believe she'd done anything without his knowledge.

"In between toy stores." She stood. "I have to go," she said, then started walking. "I'll meet you back here in two hours," she called over her shoulder, then disappeared around the corner before he could say another word.

The truth was, she had half an hour before her appointment, but she wanted to get a Christmas gift for Mac. And she wanted to get away from him. She could not possibly fall in love with a man like Mac Taggert. "He's out of your league, Karen," she told herself. A man like him needed a woman whose father was the ambassador to some glamorous country, a woman who could identify one caviar from another, who could . . . could . . .

"Idiot!" she told herself. You are as bad as all the others, thinking you're in love with him. Or worse! Thinking he is in love with *you*.

By the time she met him two hours later, she had managed to calm herself and regain her equilibrium. She saw him sitting on the bench, looking very pleased with himself. "What have you done?" she asked suspiciously.

"Merely had everything wrapped and labeled, and now they are all in the car."

"I am impressed," she said, wide-eyed.

"Stop laughing at me and let's go," he said, taking her arm. "Is that shellac they used on your hair? Or did they give you a wig made out of wood?"

"It's lacquer and I think it looks great."

"*Hmmm,*" was all he'd say as they hurried to the car.

Back at the house, everything was chaos as people scurried to get ready for the wedding. It seemed that nearly everyone had lost a vital piece of clothing and now was frantically trying to find it. When Mac closed the door to "their" bedroom, it was like a haven of calm, and when Karen came out of the bathroom, the bed was covered with boxes and a couple of hanging bags full of clothes.

"It all came while you were in there," he said, and when Karen started to comment that she'd heard no one enter, Mac scurried into the bathroom.

One box contained silk underwear, all of it white: lacy bra, teddy, and white stockings that ended mid-thigh in lacy elastic. Never before had she heard of a wedding providing underwear along with the dress.

"You don't have time to examine everything," Mac said as he entered the room.

"But—"

"Get dressed!"

As she picked up the underwear, then the dress that must have been made of three hundred yards of chiffon, she looked at the narrow space in the bathroom and back at the voluminous skirt.

"I won't attack you if I see you in your underwear—

but only if you make the same promise to me," Mac said, deadpan.

Karen started to protest but then smiled devilishly. "All right, you're on," she said as she took the white silk underwear and went into the bathroom. Moments later she emerged wearing makeup and her underwear and nothing else—and she knew that she looked great. She wasn't very large above the waist, but, as many people had told her, she had the legs of a showgirl.

"Do you know where—" Mac said as he turned toward her, then Karen had the great, oh, the enormous, satisfaction of seeing all the color drain from his face as he stared at her.

"Do I know where what is?" she asked innocently.

But Mac couldn't say a word as he stood there, his hands frozen, one held outstretched, the other trying to fasten the cuff link on his shirt.

"Could I help you with that?" she asked, striding toward him as he stared at her speechlessly. As sweetly as she could, she fastened first one then the other of his cuff links, then smiled up at him. "Anything else you need?"

When he didn't answer, she smiled again and started to walk away from him, knowing that the back view of her was as good as the front. Thank you, NordicTrack, she thought.

But she had no more time for thought because Mac grabbed her shoulder and pulled her into his arms, then brought his lips down on hers. How could she have forgotten? she wondered. She'd nearly forgotten the deliciousness of a kiss.

He kissed her long and thoroughly, and his big hands caressed her body, pulling her close to him.

Had it not been for the loud knock on the door and the call, "Ready to leave for the church?" Karen wasn't sure what would have happened. Even so, she had to push her way out of his arms, and it was with great reluctance that she did so. Her heart was pounding and her breath was fast.

"We must get dressed," she managed to say while he silently stared at her. With shaking hands, she picked up her dress and tried to get it on over her head without mussing her hair. She wasn't surprised when Mac helped her pull the dress down over her body, then zipped it up the back. And it seemed natural to help him into the coat of his tuxedo.

It wasn't until they started to leave the room that he spoke. "I almost forgot to give you your bridesmaid gift." Out of his pocket he pulled a two-strand pearl necklace and an earring with a long drop pearl.

"They're beautiful," Karen said. "The pearls almost look real."

"They do, don't they?" he said as he fished out the second earring, then he fastened the necklace on while she put on the earrings.

"Do I look okay?" she asked in earnest.

"No one will look at the bride."

It was a cliché, but the way he said it made her feel beautiful.

The wedding was enchanting. For all the chaos beforehand, everything went smoothly, and the reception was filled with laughter and champagne. Mac disappeared with a group of men he hadn't seen in years, and for a few moments Karen was alone at a table.

"Do you know how to dance?"

Karen looked up at Mac. "Wasn't that in your report

about me? Or did your spies forget such important things as dancing?"

With a laugh, he pulled her out of her chair and led her onto the dance floor. To say they danced splendidly together was an understatement.

Steve sailed by, his lovely bride, Catherine, in his arms, and told Mac he should keep "this one."

Mac smiled. "You know that no woman wants me for long."

After Steve had laughed and moved away, Karen frowned up at Mac. "Why don't you tell them the truth? Everyone blames you for all the breakups."

Mac pulled her closer into his arms. "Be careful, Mrs. Lawrence, it almost sounds as though you're beginning to like me."

"Ha! All I want from you is—"

"A child," he said softly. "You want to have my child."

"Only because you're—"

"What am I? Intelligent? A prince among men?"

"You're a reverse prince. When a woman kisses you, you turn into a frog."

"I didn't with the first kiss. Want to try again?"

For a minute he looked down at her and she thought he was going to kiss her again. But he didn't and she knew that her disappointment showed on her face.

Hours later she once again found herself alone in a room with Mac. When she returned from the bathroom wearing her chaste white nightgown, he was standing by the window, his back to her, looking out into the night.

"The bathroom is yours," she said.

"I'm going out," he said firmly.

To her horror, Karen said, "Why?" then put her hand

to her mouth. What he did was none of her business. Stiffening her body, she forced a smile. "Of course." She gave a great yawn. "See you in the morning."

Mac grabbed her shoulders. "Karen, it's not what you think."

"I have no right to think anything at all. You're free to do what you like."

Quickly, he pulled her to him, and held her tightly. "If I stay in this room tonight, I'll make love to you. I know I will. I won't be able to stop myself." Without giving her a chance to reply, he left her alone in the room.

"Right," Karen said to the closed door. "And next week it would be business as usual, the little fling with your typist forgotten. Better not to do anything that could get you sued."

She went to bed and only went to sleep after she had vented her frustration on the thick pillow separating the two halves of the bed.

Hours later she was sleeping so soundly she didn't hear him return, slip into bed beside her or feel him press a soft kiss on her forehead before he himself tried to sleep.

Four

KAREN AWOKE CHRISTMAS morning to screams. Thinking the house was on fire, she flung back the covers and started to leave the bed—but Mac's strong hand stopped her.

"Kids," he muttered, head buried in the pillow.

As the screaming increased, Karen pulled away from him, but his hand crept up her arm and pulled her down into the bed beside him. During the night the bolster pillow that separated them had slipped down (or been pushed) until it was nearer their knees.

Mac's hand crept upward into Karen's hair. He still had his face buried, still wasn't looking at her, but she could see his black glossy hair, could feel his warmth. The room was dim and the noise outside their room seemed very far away.

As he pulled her down to his level, as his face came next to hers and as his lips touched hers, he whispered, "Kids. Christmas. You know how they are."

"I was an only child. I had breakfast before opening my presents."

"*Mmmmm,*" was all he said as he kissed her, kissed her warmly, softly.

With the touch of his lips it was as though time fell away: to be in bed with a warm, sleepy man as he pulled her into his arms felt so very familiar. And so very right. It was easy to slide down so her body was stretched alongside his, to slip her arms about his neck and return his kiss with all the enthusiasm she felt.

Suddenly, the door flew open and in rushed two kids holding toys aloft, brandishing them over the heads of the couple in bed. Bewildered, Karen pulled her face away from Mac's and looked up at the toys the children were waving in the air. The girl had a Barbie doll in an outrageous dress with a handful of accessories worthy of any call girl, while the boy held a box full of trains.

In spite of this confusion, Mac was still kissing her

neck while Karen was half on top of him and trying to look at the children's new toys.

Before she could make a suitable comment, because Mac was kissing her throat, a third child came tearing in through the open door with an airplane in his hand, whereupon he crashed into the other two children and sent them flying. Everything—dolls, trains, children— landed on Mac's head.

Instantly the little girl started screaming that her doll was hurt, while the two boys tumbled to the floor in a fistfight over who had pushed whom. Getting out of bed, Karen scrambled to find the missing pieces belonging to the toys, but it was several minutes before she could find everything and get the children settled.

"Wait," she said to Mac as she picked toys out of the covers, "there seems to be a red high heel in your ear."

"It's not the first time," he muttered, annoyed that the children had interrupted them.

Giving him a quelling look, Karen rounded up the children and pushed them out the door.

Once they were alone again, Mac put his hands behind his head and watched her move about the room as she gathered her clothes. "Our kids will have better manners."

Karen was looking for her belt. "I hope our kids are just as happy and excited as they are and that they—" With a red face, she broke off, glanced at him lying there, grinning at her, then she scurried into the bathroom to get dressed.

But Mac bounced out of the bed and caught her before she could close the door. "Come on, Only Child, you're going to miss all the fun."

"I can't go downstairs in my nightgown and robe!"

"Everyone else will be," he said, pulling her, grabbing a T-shirt as he passed a chair.

Mac was right. Downstairs under the Christmas tree was chaos, with an ocean of torn wrapping paper and children everywhere. Adults were sitting in the midst of everything, exchanging gifts and laughing—and ignoring the children as best they could.

"Ah, the lovebirds," someone called. "You'd better get over here and see what Santa brought you."

"By the looks of them, I think Santa's already delivered," someone else called, making Karen drop Mac's hand, which she had been holding rather tightly.

It didn't take her long before she plunged into the middle of the paper and the people, and sat on the carpet beside a red wagon with a ribbon tied about on its handle. She was pleased that no one had yet opened the gifts she and Mac had purchased and she could have the pleasure of seeing their faces. However, she was surprised when people began heaping gifts into her lap. Each one had a tag telling who had given her the gift, but when she thanked them she saw a look of surprise on their faces, then they'd glance at Mac.

It didn't take her long to figure things out. He was sitting beside her, opening gifts, his face as innocent as a sleeping child's. "You were busy while I was at the hairdresser's, weren't you?" she asked softly, so just he heard. It was obvious that he had purchased all her gifts, had them wrapped, then labeled them as coming from his friends.

He didn't bother to deny it, but just smiled, his thick, black lashes half lowered. "Like your gifts?"

Her lap and some of the floor around her were covered with beautiful objects: a cashmere sweater, a music box, pair of gold earrings, three pairs of slouchy socks, a silver picture frame.

"What did *I* give you?" Steve called. He and Catherine had postponed their honeymoon until the day after Christmas.

Karen laughed. "Let's see," she said, picking up tags. "I think you gave me the string bikini."

"The *what?*" Mac blurted then turned red when everyone burst out laughing. "Okay, okay," he said, smiling, but he put his arm possessively around Karen's shoulders.

A woman who was Steve's cousin looked at Karen thoughtfully. "You know, Karen, I have met all of Mac's fiancées, and I can tell him now that I've never liked any of them, but you, Karen, I like. You are the first one who has ever looked at Mac with love in her eyes."

"Actually, I forgot my contact lenses," Karen said, "and—" She was halted by boos that made her blush and look down at her lap. Mac's arm tightened about her shoulders.

"So when's the wedding?" someone asked.

Mac didn't hesitate. "As soon as I can persuade her. Look, she won't even wear my ring."

"Maybe it's worn out from being slipped on and off the fingers of so many other women," Steve called, and everyone laughed.

It was at that moment that Steve's mother, Rita, stepped in from the kitchen. "Stop it, all of you! You're embarrassing Karen. And I need help in the kitchen!"

To Karen's consternation, the room cleared instantly. Within thirty seconds, there wasn't a single male, young or old, in the huge room, only women, girls, and a mountain of gifts and torn paper. "Works every time," Steve's mom said with a grin. "Now, come on, ladies, let's go gossip."

Laughing, the women went upstairs to dress before settling into their various tasks. Alone in the bedroom she shared with Mac, Karen dumped her gifts onto the bed and looked at them. It hadn't taken much sleuthing to find out that everything she'd received as a gift since she'd arrived had been from Mac. She'd been curious to find out what the other women had received as bridesmaid's gifts and was told the gifts had been given out last week. Hadn't she received hers?

More questioning had revealed that pearl necklaces and earrings had *not* been the gifts given. "If you're referring to the pearls you had on last night," one of the women said, "and if they were a gift from Mac, then you can bet your bank account that they are real."

Karen blinked. "So I guess the bride didn't give out complete sets of white silk underwear."

She'd said it more to herself than to the other women around her, but they heard and set up a howl of laughter that made Karen blush.

So now, alone in their room, she looked at what he'd heaped on her and knew she'd trade everything for an extra hour with Mac. Tomorrow they'd return to Denver and by the day after they'd be separated forever. Or at least as good as, she thought, remembering the office, with her desk about a million miles from his.

Turning, she noticed an envelope on the pillow, and when she moved the scarf she'd tossed onto the bed, she saw that it had "Merry Christmas, Karen" written on it.

Opening it, she saw that it was a short contract

signed by Mac and witnessed by Steve. Quickly, she scanned it and saw that it gave her control of a business to be housed in Lawson's Department Store. Mac would put up the capital and she'd supply the expertise. She was to have complete control to run the business in whatever way she saw fit and she was to repay him at five percent interest starting two years after the store opened.

"It's too much," she said aloud. "I didn't want—"

She stopped when she saw that there was a letter with the contract.

My dearest Karen,

I know that your first instinct will be to throw this in my face, but I beg you to reconsider. I am a businessman and you have the knowledge and experience to run a business that I believe will show a profit. I am not giving you this contract because I think you are beautiful and funny and excellent company, and because I enjoy being with you. I did this because I was forced to—by my constantly pregnant sisters-in-law. I have been told that I may not return home if I sell leather instead of diapers in that old department store.

Please don't turn me down.

Your future partner,
McAllister J. Taggert

For a moment Karen's head reeled with the meaning of what he'd written. But it wasn't the business offer that made her dizzy, it was the "beautiful and funny and excellent company, and because I enjoy being with you" that was about to do her in.

"Stop it!" she commanded herself. "He's not for you. He has women by the truckload and . . . and . . ." She went into the bathroom, where she stared at herself in the mirror. "And, you, you complete and total idiot, are in love with him."

Turning away, she turned on the shower. "Business," she told herself. "Keep it to business and nothing else."

But it wasn't easy to do that. When she went downstairs, she was wearing jeans and a red cashmere sweater set that Mac had given her (under the label of "Rita," Steve's mother) and the pearls that she couldn't help touching often. She would, of course, have to return them to him. They were much too expensive a gift.

People were slowly beginning to move about, some trying to clear the living room, some going outside to play games with the men, and some, like Karen, going to the kitchen to help prepare the Christmas feast.

Somewhere during the last days she had heard it mentioned that Steve's mother was Mac's mother's best friend. Not that it was any of Karen's business, but didn't best friends tell each other everything? And hadn't about thirty-five people mentioned that Elaine was supposed to show up this afternoon?

Karen was curious to know if Rita knew anything about the truth behind the breakup of Elaine and Mac.

She spent hours in the kitchen, chopping and peeling, while hearing some outrageous stories about Steve's family and a few about Mac's. Outside the kitchen window she could see Mac, wearing tight cotton-knit pants and an armless sweatshirt, playing touch football. Several times, whenever he made a goal or lost a goal, he looked at her in the window and waved. Happily, Karen waved back. She hadn't had a family in so long, and never had she known all the noise and confusion of this one, with children running around the kitchen, people laughing and, in the living room, singing carols. It was all the noise that small families missed.

She nearly jumped when Rita spoke behind her. "You like all this, don't you? You're happy in the midst of wrapping paper and kids screaming and stuffing onions inside some poor murdered creature, aren't you?"

"Yes, very," Karen answered honestly.

"Mac is a very good man."

Karen didn't say anything. Maybe he was and maybe he wasn't. The only thing she knew for sure was that he wasn't hers. "Do you know the truth about Elaine?"

She and Rita were alone in the kitchen, as most of the work was done, and for a moment Rita looked at Karen as though considering whether or not to tell her. "I have been sworn to secrecy," Rita said, looking down at her knife.

Karen drew in her breath. A woman admitting that she knew a secret meant that half the battle was won. All Rita needed was a bit of urging. But Karen hesitated. Part of her wanted to know and part of her didn't want to hear. What had made the woman walk out of her wedding like that? What had Mac done to her? "I would truly like to know," she said with feeling.

Rita stared into Karen's eyes for a moment, then smiled and looked back down at her knife. "You really do love him, don't you?"

"Yes," was all Karen could say; she didn't dare allow herself to say another word.

"Elaine was madly in love with some poor artist who all of us could see was more interested in her trust fund than he was in her. But love is blind and Elaine fought for him with all she had. Her father sent the artist—not that he ever painted anything—a letter saying that if he married Elaine, her trust fund would be cut off. He enclosed a check for twenty thousand dollars that would only be honored if the man left Elaine. When Elaine got home that night, her artist was gone. She blamed her father for everything, and said that if he wanted her to marry a rich man then she would."

Pausing, Rita looked at Karen with her lips tight. "Elaine systematically went after Mac, the oldest of the Taggerts who wasn't yet married. She's beautiful, talented, and confident. Mac didn't have a chance. The night before the wedding her artist came back, and when Mac returned to their apartment, he found them in bed together."

Rita gave Karen time to assimilate this information before continuing. "Mac refused to marry her, but, being the gentleman he is, he allowed everyone to think that Elaine was the one who walked out on him. Since then he's been scared to death of marriage. He wants to get married, to have his own home, but I think he purposely chooses women who only want his money, then he tests them with some ridiculous prenuptial agreement and when they won't sign, it reinforces his belief that that's all women want from him. I'm glad to see that at last he's going to allow that wound to heal. I'm glad he's going to marry you, someone who actually loves him."

Karen didn't look up from the celery she was dicing for the salad.

"I'm telling you this because Mac has some sort of

misguided sense of honor toward Elaine, so I didn't think he would ever tell you. And there're only two people outside of them who know the truth—his mother and I."

"But you told me this because I love him?"

"And because he loves you," Rita answered simply.

Karen smiled indulgently. "No he doesn't. We're not really engaged. He hired me to be his escort for the wedding and to—" She broke off because Rita was smiling at her in a *very* smug way.

"Karen, get real. Mac doesn't need to hire a woman for anything. He has women making fools of themselves wherever he goes. His mother is constantly complaining about the way the women who work for him make believe he comes with the job. She says he has two women executives so crazy about him they think that any work he gives them is proof of his love for them. His mother tells him to fire them, but Mac is so softhearted he won't. So he pays them outrageous salaries then does all the work himself."

"And the women complain to everyone because he doesn't share the load," Karen said softly.

"Probably. But Mac always takes the blame rather than allow a woman to look bad. His mother wanted to tell the world about Elaine, but Mac wouldn't allow it. Mac is from another era in time."

"Yes," Karen said in agreement. "I believe he is."

"Speak of the devil," Rita said, "a car just pulled up and it's Elaine. Karen! Don't look like that. Go out there and—"

Karen was looking out the kitchen window. The arrival of Elaine had stopped the ball game because *all* the men had run toward the car to help the elegant, beautiful, exquisite Elaine out of the backseat of the long, black limo. And at the head of the crowd was McAllister Taggert.

"If you'll excuse me, I have to . . . to . . ." Karen could think of nothing she needed to do, so she turned and ran out of the kitchen, then ran up the stairs to her bedroom.

five

THIRTY MINUTES LATER, Karen felt that she had lectured herself enough, and maybe she now had enough control to meet Elaine and not thrust a knife into her cold heart. Unfortunately, just outside the bedroom door, she found Elaine flanked by Steve and Mac.

Up close, Elaine was even more beautiful than she was from a distance. She was tall, blonde, cool-looking, and sophisticated enough to make Karen feel completely gauche. Elaine was exactly what Karen had envisioned as a woman Mac should marry. No doubt her father *was* the ambassador to some elegant foreign country, and no doubt she had a master's degree in something sophisticated and useless, like Chinese philosophy.

Just looking at Elaine made Karen feel as if she were wearing overalls and had straw sticking out of her hair. No wonder Mac had fallen head over heels in love with her, she thought.

Pausing at the head of the stairs, Elaine gave Mac a

look that could warm a steel I-beam, while Mac just started at her like a lost puppy, his heart in his eyes. He still loves her, Karen thought, and, against her best self-control, a flash of rage ran through her.

Steve paused only long enough to introduce Karen as Mac's fiancée, then he ran down the hall, football in hand, leaving the three of them alone.

"Still trying to get a woman to marry you, Mac?" Elaine asked softly, her eyes on Mac, as though Karen didn't exist.

"Still paying men to marry *you*, Elaine?" Karen shot back, then had the satisfaction of seeing Elaine's perfectly composed face crumble just before she turned and ran down the stairs. Obviously she'd thought her secret was safe forever and she could taunt Mac at will.

What Karen was not prepared for was Mac's reaction. His strong hand clamped around her upper arm and he half pulled her into their bedroom. When the door was shut, he faced her. "I didn't like that!" he said angrily, his face near hers. "What happened between Elaine and me is our business and no one else's, and I won't have you or anyone else sneering at her."

Karen straightened her body, ordering her muscles to remain rigid. If she hadn't, she would have collapsed on the bed in tears. What did it matter to her that McAllister Taggert was in love with a woman who had publicly made him a laughingstock? "Certainly, Mr. Taggert," she said stiffly, then turned toward the door.

But Mac caught her, shoved her against the wall, and kissed her hungrily. For a moment Karen's pride made her fight him off, but it wasn't long before she was pulling him closer to her, her hands in his hair, her fingers gouging into his back.

"I hate you," she managed to say as he kissed her neck, his hands moving all over her body.

"Yes, I know. You hate me as much as I hate you."

Later, she didn't know how it happened, but one minute they were against the wall, fully clothed, and the next they were naked and writhing on the bed. Karen had been celibate for over two years and the only way she had remained that way was by repressing all sexual desire. The combination of her anger at Mac and now his soft caresses made her erupt into flames, all her desires exploding at once.

Mac was a worthy opponent and his passion matched hers as he entered her with force, then more gently as he put his mouth over Karen's to keep her from crying out.

It didn't take long, but in those few minutes, a lamp fell crashing to the floor, Karen fell off the bed, and Mac lifted her so her feet were on the floor, her back on the bed.

When Mac came inside her, Karen wrapped her legs about his waist and pulled his body down onto hers, holding him tightly. Her heart was pounding, her breath ragged.

It was several minutes before she could think again, and when she did, she was embarrassed and ashamed. What must he think of her? The poor, uneducated little secretary making a fool of herself over the boss?

"Please," she whispered. "Let me up."

Slowly, Mac raised his head and looked down at her, and when she turned her head away, he put his hand on her chin and made her meet his eyes. "What's this?" he asked teasingly. "My little lioness can't be shy, can she?"

Karen looked away from him. "I would like to get up."

But Mac didn't allow her to move away from him. Instead, he pulled her onto the bed, wrapped his big naked body about hers, drew the bedspread over them, then said, "Tell me what's wrong."

Karen was having trouble thinking, for somehow, this cozy cuddling, their bodies naked, was more intimate than what they had just done. "You—I—" she said, but not coherent words came out of her mouth.

"We made love," he said softly as he planted a kiss onto the top of her head. "It's something I've wanted to do for what seems like years."

"You never knew I existed until a few days ago."

"True, but I've made up in intensity for what I've lacked in time."

She tried to push away from him, but he held her tight.

"I'm not releasing you until you tell me what's wrong."

"What's *wrong?!*" she said with feeling, pushing away enough to look at him. "I am one of your secretaries, one step up from the custodian, and you're the boss and . . . and . . ."

"And what?"

"And you're in love with Elaine!" she spat at him. After all, how could she make more of a fool of herself than she already had?

To her great annoyance, Mac cuddled her closer and she could feel him chuckling against her.

"*Ow!* What was that for?" he asked when she pinched him.

This time she almost got away before he pulled her back. "I am *not* one of your bimbos. I am *not* after your money. In fact I want nothing whatever from you, not a business, not anything. Including ever seeing you—" She broke off as he kissed her. "Again," she whispered, finishing her sentence.

"Gladly," he said, pretending to misunderstand.

It was when his hand moved to her breast and Karen could feel herself wanting him again, and feel that he was again ready, that she pushed away from him. She didn't try to get off the bed, but she looked him in the eyes and said, "No."

"All right," he said, removing his hands from her body. "Tell me what's bothering you. Just don't leave. Please?"

Karen turned on her back, the spread covering her, none of her body touching his. "I didn't mean for this to happen. I just wanted—" At that she turned to look at him. By her calculations, she was at peak fertility today and after what they had just done, maybe she was pregnant.

As though reading her mind, he lifted her hand and kissed it, first the palm, then the back of her hand. When he started kissing her fingertips, she pulled away from him.

But Mac drew her back into his arms, holding her tightly. "I don't love Elaine."

"That's not what I saw, and you defended her!"

"Whatever bad I wish to befall Elaine, it isn't worse than what has happened to her. A man married her for her money. I know how that feels, so I have only pity for her. If it helps her to make snide remarks to me, let her. At least *I'm* not married to her." His voice lowered. "And she's not the mother of my children."

"Do you have many?" she asked as though making conversation. More than anything, she wanted to remain cool and detached. Wasn't it all right in this day and age to have affairs with men? She was positively primitive to believe that people who went to bed together should get married.

"Maybe we made my first one today," he said softly, then held her as she tried to get away from him.

"It is *not* a laughing matter. I wanted you to be a donor, not a . . . a . . ."

"Lover? Karen, please listen to me. Today wasn't a mistake. I've never before been to bed with a woman without using protection." He lifted her chin to look into her eyes. "I love you, Karen. If you'll have me, I'll try to make you a good husband."

"Me and all the rest of the free world," she said before she thought, then was horrified when she saw the hurt in his eyes. Instantly, he turned away and started to get out of bed.

"I'm sorry," she said, flinging herself onto his back as he sat on the edge of the bed. "Please, I didn't mean that. You don't have to marry me or even ask me to marry you. I know your streak of nobility, how you're a chivalrous knight and—"

Turning, he smiled at her. "Is that what you think of me? You think I ask every woman I go to bed with to marry me?"

Her face gave a positive answer to that.

Mac's face softened with his merriment. "Sweetheart," he said, smoothing a strand of hair behind her ears. "I don't know what's made you decide I'm a saint, but I'm not. Your first opinion of me was the most accurate any woman's ever had. You want to know the truth?"

Karen nodded, her eyes wide, then he pulled her into his arms and lay down beside her on the bed, her head on his shoulder.

"I was never in love with Elaine. Not really. I know that now, but it was flattering to have someone like her allow me to chase her."

"Didn't *she* chase *you?*" Karen said, then bit her tongue for giving away too much information.

Mac just smiled. "You have to remember that I've been around Elaine most of my life, and she was the one all of us boys went after. But she was unattainable. She was gorgeous, and by the time she was fourteen, she was built. We used to take bets on who could get Elaine to go out with him, but none of us ever succeeded. She studied for her final exams the night of our high school prom; she must have turned down every guy in the school."

"So you wanted what you couldn't have?" she said with sarcasm.

"Of course. Doesn't everyone?"

Karen was too interested in the story to think about philosophy. "But *you* got her."

"In a way. About four years ago she came to my office telling me she wanted me to help her with some investments and I—"

"Made a fool of yourself over her and asked her to marry you so you could show the other guys that *you* won."

"In a word, yes."

At that, Karen had to laugh. "So the artist saved you, didn't he?"

Mac hesitated before he answered. "Someday I want to know how you wheedled this information out of my mother. Or whomever she told who told *you.*"

"Mmmm," was all Karen would answer. "So what about all the other women you asked to marry you?"

He paused, staring off into space. "You know, it was really quite odd, but every woman on earth seemed to think that after what happened with Elaine, I was dying to get married. Maybe they thought I wanted to show Elaine that I could get another woman if I wanted one."

"So they flung themselves on you," Karen said sarcastically. "You had nothing to do with all those engagement rings and prenuptial agreements."

He didn't laugh in return, but instead, turned so his face was above hers. "I'm serious. Two weeks ago I would have told you that I'd been in love with Elaine and maybe that I loved each of those beautiful girls I was engaged to. But now I know that I didn't love any of them, because when I'm with you, Karen, I don't have to be who I'm not. You're the first woman who has looked at me as just a man, not one of the rich Taggerts, not as a way to jump-start her own career. You saw *me* and nothing else."

He kissed her cheek. "I know it's sudden and I know you'll want to take time to think about this, and I'd love to court you, but I want to warn you what I'm after. I mean to marry you."

Karen's impulse was to throw her arms about his neck and say, "Yes, yes, yes," but instead she looked away for a moment, as though contemplating whether to marry him or not. When she looked back at him, her eyes were serious. "By courting do you mean candle-light dinners and roses?"

"How about trips to Paris, a cruise down the Nile, and skiing in the Rockies?"

"Perhaps," she said.

Pulling back, he looked at her speculatively. "How about I buy you two more buildings in cities of your choice for those baby stores of yours and set you up with a state-of-the-art accounting system?"

"Oh!" she said, startled. "With an instant inventory system?"

"Karen, honey, if you marry me, I'll give you the private code to my own accounting system and you can snoop to your heart's content."

"You do know how to court a girl, don't you?"

"Mmmm," was all he said as he moved his leg on top of hers. "Did you know that twins run in my family?"

"I have seen a bit of evidence of that fact."

He was kissing her neck as his hand moved down-ward. "I don't know if you know this, but the way twins are made is to make love twice in the same day."

"Is that so? And here the medical people think it has to do with the way an egg divides."

"No. The more love, the more kids."

Turning her hips toward his, she put her arms about his neck. "Let's try for quintuplets."

"I *knew* there was a reason I loved you," he mur-mured before his mouth closed over hers.

Epilogue

"KAREN!" SAID A WOMAN behind her, making Karen turn so quickly she dropped her packages. She was in a mall, people bustling about, and it took Karen a moment to recognize Rita, the woman she'd met on that remarkable weekend she'd spent with Mac.

To the consternation of both of them, Karen burst into tears.

With a motherly arm about the younger woman's shoulders, Rita led Karen to a tiled seat surrounding a quietly splashing fountain, then handed her a clean tissue and waited while Karen calmed herself.

"I am so sorry. I have no idea what is wrong with me. I seem to be bursting into tears constantly. I really am glad to see you. How is everyone? Steve?"

"Fine," Rita said, smiling. "Everyone is fine. So, when is your baby due?"

For several minutes Karen worked to control her tears. "Is it that obvious?"

"Only to another mother. Now, why don't you tell me what is bothering you. Something wrong between you and Mac? He *is* marrying you, isn't he?"

Karen blew her nose. "Yes, we're to be married in two months in a perfect little ceremony. You're on the guest list." She looked down at her sodden tissue. "Nothing is wrong. Nothing at all. It's just—"

"Come on, you can tell me."

"I'm not sure Mac wants to marry me," she burst

out. "I tricked him. I . . . I seduced him. I wanted a baby so much, and he—" She broke off because Rita was laughing.

"I beg your pardon," Karen said stiffly, and started to get up. "I did not mean to amuse you with my problems."

Rita grabbed Karen's arm and pulled her to sit back down. "I'm sorry, I didn't mean to laugh; it's just that I've never seen a man pursue a woman as hard as Mac pursued you. Whatever could have made you think he doesn't want to marry you?"

"You really have no idea what you're talking about. If you knew the truth about what went on between us, you'd know that this will be more of a business arrangement than a real marriage. Everything was my idea and—"

"Karen, forgive me, but you're the one who doesn't know what you're talking about. Did you know that there were only to be six bridesmaids in the wedding? Mac called Steve in a panic, said he'd met the love of his life and he had to have an excuse to spend the weekend with her. The addition of another bridesmaid to the wedding was *his* idea. He paid triple price for a custom-made dress in your size, then paid for a tux for a friend of his so there'd be a seventh groomsman."

Karen stared at Rita. "Love of his life? But he told me just after he met me about his problem with finding someone to fit the dress."

"Steve and Catherine have plenty of friends, they didn't need one of Mac's girlfriends. Certainly not when his girlfriends changed as often as Mac's did."

Karen shook her head. "But I don't understand. I don't think he'd even seen me before the night of the

Christmas party. What made him make up such a story? Why would he want to? I don't understand."

Rita smiled. "There's a saying in the Taggert family, 'Marry the one who can tell the twins apart.'"

Karen's face showed no understanding.

"In Mac's office, there is a photo of a man holding a string of fish, isn't there?"

Karen searched her memory, then remembered that night when she'd been snooping in Mac's office and picked up the photo from the shelf, then dropped it when Mac's voice startled her. "Yes, I remember the picture. It's one of his brothers, isn't it? I remember saying that I'd never seen the man before."

Rita smiled knowingly. "That was a photo of Mac's twin, a man who looks exactly like Mac."

"He doesn't look anything like him! Mac is *much* better looking than that man. He—" She stopped, then looked away from Rita's laughter, taking a moment to compose herself, then looked back. "He made up the whole bridesmaid story?" she asked softly.

"Completely. He offered to pay for the entire wedding if Steve would allow you to be in the ceremony. And he gave Steve free use of his precious speedboat for six months in return for putting both of you in the same bedroom. Those earrings Mac gave you came from the family vault, an heirloom, something given only to wives. Not girlfriends, wives. And I happen to know that twice that weekend he called home and told his family in detail about you, telling them how intelligent and beautiful you were and that he was doing everything he could to make you love him."

Rita gave Karen's hand a squeeze. "You must have noticed how tongue-tied Mac was around you. We were all laughing because he was so afraid of saying the wrong thing that often he wouldn't say anything. He told Steve that he kept pretending to ignore you because he'd been told by a man in the office that you ran from any man who showed the least interest in you."

"He told his sisters-in-law about the store I wanted to open," she said softly.

"Dear, if he wasn't with you, he was talking about you."

"But I thought he asked me to marry him because . . ." She broke off, looking into Rita's eyes. "Because I asked for something from him."

"I have never seen a man fall as hard in love with a woman at first sight as he fell for you. He said you picked up a photo in his office, he looked into your eyes, and he fell in love with you in that single moment."

"Why didn't he tell *me?*" Karen said.

"You mean Mac hasn't told you that he loves you?" Rita asked in horror.

"Yes, he has, many times, but I . . ." Karen stood. She wasn't going to say out loud that she hadn't believed him, that she couldn't believe that a man like McAllister Taggert could . . .

"I have to go," Karen said abruptly. "I have to—Oh, Rita, thank you," she said, then as Rita stood, she hugged her enthusiastically. "Thank you more than you could possibly know. You have made me the happiest woman on earth. I have to go and tell Mac that . . . that . . ."

Rita laughed. "Go! What are you waiting for? Go!"

But Karen was already gone.

Judith McNaught

~

Miracles

One

THE ROAR OF MUSIC and voices began to recede as Julianna Skeffington fled down the terraced steps of a brightly lit country house in which 600 members of Polite Society were attending a masquerade ball. Ahead of her, the formal gardens were aglow with flaring torches and swarming with costumed guests and liveried servants. Beyond the gardens, a large hedge maze loomed in the shadows, offering far better places to hide, and it was there that Julianna headed.

Pressing the hooped skirts of her Marie Antoinette costume closer to her sides, she plunged into the crowd, wending her way as swiftly as possible past knights in armor, court jesters, highwaymen, and an assortment of kings, queens, and Shakespearean characters, as well as a profusion of domestic and jungle creatures.

She saw a path open through the crowd and headed for it, then had to step aside to avoid colliding with a large leafy "tree" with red silk apples dangling from its branches. The tree bowed politely to Julianna as it paraded past her, one of its branches curved around the waist of a lady decked out as a milkmaid complete with bucket.

She did not have to show her pace again until she neared the center of the garden, where a group of musicians was stationed between a pair of Roman fountains, providing music for dancing couples. Excusing herself, she stepped around a tall man disguised as a black tomcat who was whispering in the pink ear of a petite gray mouse. He stopped long enough to cast an appreciative eye over the low bodice of Julianna's white ruffled gown, then he smiled boldly into her eyes and winked before returning his attention to the adorable little mouse with the absurdly long whiskers.

Staggered by the abandoned behavior she was witnessing tonight, particularly out here in the gardens, Julianna stole a quick glance over her shoulder and saw that her mother had emerged from the ballroom. She stood on the terraced steps, holding an unknown male by the arm, and slowly scanned the gardens. She was looking for Julianna. With the instincts of a bloodhound, her mother turned and looked straight in Julianna's direction.

That familiar sight was enough to make Julianna break into a near run, until she came to the last obstacle in her route to the maze: a large group of particularly boisterous men who were standing beneath a canopy of trees, laughing uproariously at a mock jester who was trying unsuccessfully to juggle apples. Rather than walk in front of their line of vision, thus putting herself in plain view of her mother, she decided it was wiser to go around behind them.

"If you please, sirs," she said, trying to sidle between the trees and a row of masculine backs. "I must pass." Instead of moving quickly out of her way, which common courtesy dictated they should, two of them glanced over their shoulders at her, then they turned fully around without giving her any extra space.

"Well, well, well, what have we here?" said one of them in a very young and very inebriated voice as he braced his hand on the tree near her shoulder. He shifted his gaze to a servant, who was handing him a glass brimming with some sort of liquor, then he took it and thrust it toward her. "Some 'freshment for you, ma'am?"

At the moment Julianna was more worried about escaping her mother's notice than being accosted by a drunken young lord who could barely stand up and whose companions would surely prevent him from behaving more abominably than he was now. She accepted the glass rather than make a scene, then she ducked under his arm, walked quickly past the others, and hurried toward her destination, the drink forgotten in her hand.

"Forget about her, Dickie," she heard his companion say. "Half the opera dancers and the demimonde are here tonight. You can have most any female who takes your eye. That one didn't want to play."

Julianna remembered hearing that some of the Ton's high sticklers disapproved of masquerades—particularly for gently bred young ladies—and after what she'd seen and heard tonight she certainly understood why. With their identities safely concealed behind costumes and masks, members of Polite Society behaved like . . . like common rabble!

Two

INSIDE THE MAZE, Julianna took the path to the right, darted around the first corner, which happened to turn right, then she pressed her back into the shrubbery's prickly branches. With her free hand, she tried to flatten

the layers of white lace flounces that adorned the hem
of her skirts and the low bodice of her gown, but they
stood out like quivering beacons in the breezy night.

Her heart racing from emotion, not exertion, she
stood perfectly still and listened, separated from the
garden by a single tall hedge but out of sight of the
entrance. She stared blindly at the glass in her hand
and felt angry futility at her inability to prevent her
mother from disgracing herself or ruining Julianna's
life.

Trying to divert herself, Juliana lifted the glass to
her nose and sniffed, then she shuddered a little at the
strong aroma. It smelled like the stuff her papa drank.
Not the Madeira he enjoyed from morning until supper,
but the golden liquid he drank after supper—for medic-
inal purposes, to calm his nerves, he said.

Julianna's nerves were raw. A moment later she
heard her mother's voice come from the opposite side
of the leafy barrier, making her heart hammer with
foreboding.

"Juliana, are you out here, dear?" her mother called.

"Lord Makepeace is with me, and he is most eager
for an introduction . . ."

Julianna had the mortifying vision of a reluctant
Lord Makepeace—whoever he was—being dragged
mercilessly by the arm through every twist and turn,
every corner and cranny, of the twisting maze and
torchlit gardens by her determined mother. Unable to
endure the awkwardness and embarrassment of one
more introduction to some unfortunate, and undoubtedly *unwilling,* potential suitor whom her mother had
commandeered, Julianna backed so far into the
scratchy branches that they poked into the pale blond

curls of the elaborate coiffure that had taken a maid hours to create.

Overhead, the moon obligingly glided behind a thick bank of clouds, plunging the maze into inky darkness, while her mother continued her shamelessly dishonest monologue—a few feet away on the other side of the hedge.

"Julianna is such a delightfully adventurous girl," Lady Skeffington exclaimed, sounding frustrated, not proud. "It is just like her to wander into the gardens to do a bit of exploring."

Julianna mentally translated her mother's falsehoods into reality: *Julianna is an annoying recluse who has to be dragged from her books and her scribbling. It is just like her to hide in the bushes at a time like this.*

"She was so very popular this Season, I cannot think how you haven't encountered her at some tonnish function or another. In fact, I actually had to insist she restrict her social engagements to no more than ten each week so that she could have enough rest!"

Julianna hasn't received ten invitations to social events in the past year, let alone in a single week, but I need an excuse for why you haven't met her before. With a little luck, you'll believe that rapper.

Lord Makepeace wasn't that gullible. "Really?" he murmured, in the noncommittal voice of one who is struggling between courtesy, annoyance, and disbelief. "She sounds an odd—er . . . unusual female if she doesn't enjoy social engagements."

"I never meant to imply such a thing!" Lady Skeffington hastened to say. "Julianna enjoys balls and soirees above all things!"

Julianna would rather have a tooth extracted.

"I truly believe the two of you would deal famously together."

I intend to get her off our hands and well wed, my good man, and you have the prerequisites for a husband: You are male, of respectable birth, and adequate fortune.

"She is not at all the sort of pushing female one encounters too often these days."

She won't do a thing to show herself off to advantage.

"On the other hand, she has definite attributes that no male could miss."

To make certain of it tonight, I insisted she wear a costume so revealing that it is better suited to a married flirt than to a girl of eighteen.

"But she is not at all fast."

Despite the low décolletage on her gown, you must not even try to touch her without asking for her hand first.

Lord Makepeace's desire for freedom finally overcame the dictates of civility. "I really must return to the ballroom, Lady Skeffington. I—I believe I have the next dance with Miss Topham."

The realization that her prey was about to escape—and into the clutches of the Season's most popular debutante—drove Julianna's mama to retaliate by telling the greatest lie of her matchmaking life. Shamelessly inventing a nonexistent relationship between Julianna and the most eligible bachelor in England, she announced, "It's just as well we return to the ball! I believe Nicholas DuVille himself has claimed Julianna's next waltz!"

Lady Skeffington must have hurried after the

retreating lord because their voices became more distant. "Mr. DuVille has repeatedly singled our dear Julianna out for particular attention. In fact, I have reason to believe his sole reason for coming here this evening was so that he could spend a few moments with her! No, really, sir, it is the truth, though I shouldn't like for anyone but you to know it. . . ."

Further down the maze, the Baron of Penwarren's ravishing young widow stood with her arms wrapped around Nicholas DuVille's neck, her eyes laughing into his as she whispered, "Please don't tell me Lady Skeffington actually coerced *you* into dancing with her daughter, Nicki. Not *you,* of all people. If she has, and you do it, you wont' be able to walk into a drawing room in England without sending everyone into whoops. If you hadn't been in Italy all summer, you'd know it's become a game of wits among the bachelors to thwart that odious creature. I'm perfectly serious," Valerie warned as his only reaction was one of mild amusement, "that woman would resort to anything to get a rich husband for her daughter and secure her own position in Society! Absolutely anything!"

"Thank you for the warning, chérie," Nicki said dryly. "As it happens, I had a brief introduction to Lady Skeffington's husband shortly before I left for Italy. I have not, however, set eyes on the mother *or* the daughter, let alone promised to dance with either of them."

She sighed with relief. "I couldn't imagine how you could have been that foolish. Juliana is a remarkably pretty thing, actually, but she's not at all in your usual style. She's very young, very virginal, and I understand she has an odd habit of hiding behind draperies—or some such."

"She sounds delightful," Nicki lied with a chuckle.

"She is nothing like her mama, in any case." She paused for an eloquent little shudder to illustrate what she was about to say next. "Lady Skeffington is so eager to be a part of Society that she positively grovels. If she weren't so encroaching and ambitious, she'd be completely pathetic."

"At the risk of appearing hopelessly obtuse," Nicki said, losing patience with the entire discussion, "why in hell did you invite them to your masquerade?"

"Because, darling," Valerie said with a sigh, smoothing her fingers over his jaw with the familiarity of shared intimacies, "this past summer, little Julianna somehow became acquainted with the new Countess of Langford, as well as her sister-in-law, the Duchess of Claymore. At the beginning of the Season, the countess and the duchess made it known they desire little Juliana to be welcome amongst the Ton, then they both left for Devon with their husbands. Since no one wants to offend the Westmorelands, and since Lady Skeffington offends all of us, we all waited until the very last week of the Season to do our duty and invite them to something. Unluckily, of the dozens of invitations Lady Skeffington received for tonight, mine was the one she accepted—probably because she heard *you* were going to be here."

She stopped suddenly, as if struck by a delightful possibility. "Everyone has been longing to discover how Julianna and her obnoxious mama happened to become acquainted with the countess and the duchess, and I would wager *you* know the answer, don't you! Gossip has it that you were *extremely* well acquainted with both ladies before they were married."

To Valerie's astonishment, his entire expression became distant, shuttered, and his words conveyed a chilly warning. "Define what you mean by 'extremely well acquainted,' Valerie."

Belatedly realizing that she had somehow blundered into dangerous territory, Valerie made a hasty strategic retreat to safer ground. "I meant only that you are known to be a close friend of both ladies."

Nicki accepted her peace offering with a slight nod and allowed her to retreat in dignity, but he did not let the matter drop completely. "Their husbands are *also* close friends of mine," he said pointedly, though that was rather an exaggeration. He was on friendly terms with Stephen and Clayton Westmoreland, but neither man was particularly ecstatic about their wife's friendship with Nicki—a situation that both ladies had laughingly confided would undoubtedly continue "until you are safely wed, Nicki, and as besotted with your own wife as Clayton and Stephen are with us."

"Since you aren't yet betrothed to Miss Skeffington," Valerie teased softly, pulling his attention back to her as she slid her fingers around his nape, "there is nothing to prevent us from leaving by the side of this maze and going to your bedchamber."

From the moment she'd greeted him in the house, Nicki had known that suggestion was going to come, and he considered it now in noncommittal silence. There was nothing stopping him from doing that. Nothing whatsoever, except an inexplicable lack of interest in what he knew from past trysts with Valerie

would be almost exactly one hour and thirty minutes of
uninhibited sexual intercourse with a highly skilled and
eager partner. That exercise would be preceded by a
glass and a half of excellent champagne, and followed
by half a glass of even better brandy. Afterward, he
would pretend to be disappointed when she felt obliged
to return to her own bed "to keep the servants from
gossiping." Very civilized, very considerate, very *pre-
dictable*.

Lately, the sheer predictability of his life—and
everyone in it, including himself—was beginning to
grate on him. Whether he was in bed with a woman or
gambling with friends, he automatically did and said all
the proper—and improper—things at the appropriate
time. He associated with men and women of his own
class who were all as bland and socially adept as he
was.

He was beginning to feel as if he were a damned
marionette, performing on a stage with other mari-
onettes, all of whom danced to the same tune, written
by the same composer.

Even when it came to illicit liaisons such as the one
Valerie was suggesting, there was a prescribed ritual to
be followed that varied only according to whether the
lady was wed or not, and whether he was playing the
role of seducer or seduced. Since Valerie was widowed
and had assumed the role of seducer tonight, he knew
exactly how she would react if he declined her suggestion. First she would pout—but very prettily; then she
would cajole; and then she would offer enticements.
He, being the "seduced," would hesitate, then evade,
and then postpone until she gave up, but he would
never actually refuse. To do so would be unforgivably

rude—a clumsy misstep in the intricate social dance they all performed to perfection.

Despite all that, Nicki waited before answering, half expecting his body to respond favorably to her suggestion, even though his mind was not. When that didn't happen, he shook his head and took the first step in the dance: hesitation. "I should probably sleep first, chérie. I had a trying week, and I've been up for the last two days."

"Surely you aren't refusing me, are you, darling?" she asked. Pouting prettily.

Nicki switched smoothly to evasion. "What about your party?"

"I'd rather be with you. I haven't seen you in months, and besides, the party will go on without me. My servants are trained to perfection."

"Your guests are not," Nicki pointed out, still evading since she was still cajoling.

"They'll never know we've left."

"The bedchamber you gave me is next to your mother's."

"She won't hear us even if you break the bed as you did the last time we used that chamber. She's deaf as a stone." Nicki was about to proceed to the postponement stage, but Valerie surprised him by accelerating the procedure and going straight to enticements before he could utter his lines in this trite little play that had become his real life. Standing on tiptoe, she kissed him thoroughly, her hands sliding up and down his chest, her parted lips inviting his tongue.

Nicki automatically put his arm around her waist and complied, but it was an empty gesture born of courtesy, not reciprocity. When her hands slid lower, toward the waistband of his trousers, he dropped his arm and stepped back, suddenly revolted as well as bored with the entire damned charade. "Not tonight," he said firmly.

Her eyes silently accused him of an unforgivable breach of the rules. Softening his voice, he took her by the shoulders, turned her around, and gave her an affectionate pat on the backside to send her on her way. "Go back to your guests, chérie." Already reaching into his pocket for a thin cheroot, he added with a polite finality, "I'll follow you after a discreet time."

Three

UNAWARE THAT SHE was not alone in the cavernous maze, Julianna waited in tense silence to be absolutely certain her mother wasn't going to return. After a moment she gave a ragged sigh and dislodged herself from her hiding place.

Since the maze seemed like the best place to hide for the next few hours, she turned left and wandered down a path that opened into a square grassy area with an ornate stone bench in the center.

Morosely, she contemplated her situation, looking for a way out of the humiliating and untenable trap she was in, but she knew there was no escape from her mother's blind obsession with seeing Julianna wed to someone of "real consequence"—now, while the opportunity existed. Thus far all that had prevented her mother from accomplishing this goal was the fact that no "eligible" suitor "of real consequence" had declared himself during the few weeks Julianna had been in London.

Unfortunately, just before they'd left London to come here, her mother had succeeded in wringing an offer of marriage from Sir Francis Bellhaven, a repulsive, elderly, pompous knight with pallid skin, protruding hazel eyes that seemed to delve down Julianna's bodice, and thick pale lips that never failed to remind her of a dead goldfish. The thought of being bound for an entire evening, let alone the rest of her life, to Sir Francis was unendurable. Obscene. Terrifying.

Not that she was going to have any choice in the matter. If she wanted a real choice, then hiding in here from other potential suitors her mother commandeered was the last thing she ought to be doing. She knew it, but she couldn't make herself go back to that ball. She didn't even *want* a husband. She was already eighteen years old, and she had other plans, other dreams, for her life, but they didn't coincide with her mother's and so they weren't going to matter. Ever. What made it all so much more frustrating was that her mother actually *believed* she was acting in Julianna's best interests and that she knew what was ultimately best for her.

The moon slid out from behind the clouds, and Julianna stared at the pale liquid in her glass. Her father said a bit of brandy never hurt anyone, that it eased all manner of ailments, improved digestion, and cured low spirits. Juliana hesitated, and then in a burst of rebellion and desperation, she decided to test the latter theory. Lifting the glass, she pinched her nostrils closed, tipped her head back, and took three large swallows. She lowered the glass, shuddering and gasping. And waited. For an explosion of bliss. Seconds passed, then one minute. Nothing. All she felt was a slight weakness in her knees and a weakening of her defenses against the tears of futility brimming in her eyes.

In deference to her shaky limbs, Julianna stepped over to the stone bench and sat down. The bench had obviously been occupied earlier that evening, because there was a half-empty glass of spirits on the end of it and several empty glasses beneath it. After a moment she took another sip of brandy and gazed into the glass, swirling the golden liquid so that it gleamed in the moonlight as she considered her plight.

How she wished her grandmother were still alive! Grandmama would have put a stop to Julianna's mother's mad obsession with arranging a "splendid marriage." She'd have understood Julianna's aversion to being forced into marriage with anyone. In all the world, her father's dignified mother was the only person who had ever seemed to understand Julianna. Her grandmother had been her friend, her teacher, her mentor.

At her knee Julianna had learned about the world, about people; there and there alone she was encouraged to think for herself and to say whatever she thought, no matter how absurd or outrageous it might seem. In return, her grandmother had always treated her as an equal, sharing her own unique philosophies about anything and everything, from God's purpose for creating the earth to myths about men and women.

Grandmother Skeffington did not believe marriage was the answer to a woman's dreams, or even that males were more noble or more intelligent than females! "Consider for a moment my own husband as an example," she said with a gruff smile one wintry afternoon just before the Christmas when Julianna was fifteen. "You did not know your grandfather, God rest his soul, but if he had a brain with which to think, I never saw the evidence of it. Like all his forebears, he couldn't tally two figures in his head or write an intelligent sentence, and he had less sense than a suckling babe."

"Really?" Julianna said, amazed and a little appalled by this disrespectful assessment of a deceased man who had been her grandmother's husband and Julianna's grandsire.

Her grandmother nodded emphatically. "The Skeffington men have all been like that—unimaginative, slothful clods, the entire lot of them."

"But surely you aren't saying Papa is like that," Julianna argued out of loyalty. "He's your only living child."

"I would never describe your papa as a clod," she said without hesitation. "I would describe him as a muttonhead!"

Julianna bit back a horrified giggle at such heresy, but before she could summon an appropriate defense, her grandmother continued: "The Skeffington women, on the other hand, have often displayed streaks of rare intelligence and resourcefulness. Look closely and you will discover that it is generally females who survive on their wits and determination, not males. Men are not superior to women except in brute strength."

When Julianna looked uncertain, her grandmother added smugly, "If you will read that book I gave you last week, you will soon discover that women were not always subservient to men. Why, in ancient times, we had the power and the reverence. We were goddesses and soothsayers and healers, with the secrets of the universe in our minds and the gift of life in our bodies. We chose our mates, not the other way around. Men sought our counsel and worshiped at our feet and envied our powers. Why, we were superior to them in every way. We knew it, and so did they."

"If we were truly the more clever and the more gifted," Julianna said when her grandmother lifted her brows, looking for a reaction to that staggering information, "then how did we lose all that power and respect and let ourselves become subservient to men?"

"They *convinced* us we needed *their* brute strength for *our* protection," she said with a mixture of resentment and disdain. "Then they 'protected' us right out of all our privileges and rights. They *tricked* us."

Julianna found an error in that logic, and her brow furrowed in thought. "If that is so," she said after a moment, "then they couldn't have been quite so dull-witted as you think. They had to be very clever, did they not?"

For a spilt second her grandmother glowered at her, then she cackled with approving laughter. "A good point, my dear, and one that bears considering. I suggest you write that thought down so that you may examine it further. Perhaps you will write a book of your own on how males have perpetrated that fiendish deception upon females over the centuries. I only hope you will not decide to waste your mind and your talents on some ignorant fellow who wants you for that face of yours and tries to convince you that your only value is in breeding his children and looking after his wants.

You could make a difference, Julianna. I know you could."

She hesitated, as if deciding something, then said, "That brings us to another matter I have been wishing to discuss with you. This seems like as good a time as will come along."

Grandmother Skeffington got up and walked over to the fireplace on the opposite wall of the cozy little room, her movements slowed by advancing age, her silver hair twisted into a severe coil at her neck. Bracing one hand on the evergreen boughs she'd arranged on the mantel, she bent to stir the coals. "As you know, I have already outlived a husband and one son. I have lived long, and I am fully prepared to end my days on this earth whenever my time arrives. Although I shall not always be here for you, I hope to compensate for that by leaving something behind for you . . . an inheritance that is for you to spend. It isn't much."

The subject of her grandmother's death had never come up before, and the mere thought of losing her made Julianna's chest tighten with dread.

"As I said, it isn't much, but if you are extremely thrifty, it could allow you to live very modestly in London for quite a few years while you experience more of life and hone your writing skills."

In her heart Julianna argued frantically that life without her grandmother was unthinkable, that she had no wish to live in London, and that their shared dream that she might actually become a noteworthy writer was only an impossible fantasy. Afraid that such an emotional outburst would offend the woman, Julianna remained seated upon the footstool in front of her grandmother's favorite overstuffed chair, inwardly a mass of raw emotions, outwardly controlled, calmly perusing a book. "Have you nothing to say to my plans for you, child? I rather expected to see you leap with joy. Some small display of enthusiasm would be appropriate here in return for the economies I've practiced in order to leave you this tiny legacy."

She was prodding, Julianna knew, trying to provoke her into either a witty rejoinder or an unemotional discussion. Julianna was very good at both after years of practice, but she was as incapable of discussing her grandmother's death with humor as she was with impersonal calm. Moreover, she was vaguely wounded that her grandmother could talk of leaving her forever without any indication of regret.

"I must say you don't seem very grateful."

Julianna's head snapped up, her violet eyes sparkling with angry tears. "I am not at all grateful, Grandmama, nor do I wish to discuss this now. It is nearly Christmas, a time for joyous—"

"Death is a fact of life," her grandmother stated flatly. "It is pointless to cower from it."

"But you are *my* whole life," Julianna burst out because she couldn't stop herself. "And—and I don't like it in the least that you—you can speak to me of money as if it's a recompense for your death."

"You think me cold and callous?"

"Yes, I do!"

It was their first harsh argument, and Julianna hated it.

Her grandmother regarded her in serene silence before asking, "Do you know what I shall miss when I leave this earth?"

"Nothing, evidently."

"I shall miss one thing and one thing alone." When Julianna didn't ask for an explanation, her grandmother provided it: "I shall miss you."

The answer was in such opposition to her unemotional voice and bland features that Julianna stared dubiously at her.

"I shall miss your humor and your confidences and your amazing gift for seeing the logic behind both sides of any issue. I shall particularly miss reading what you've written each day. You have been the only bright spot in my existence."

As she finished, she walked forward and laid her cool hand on Julianna's cheek, brushing away the tears trickling from the corner of her eye. "We are kindred spirits, you and I. If you had been born much sooner, we would have been bosom friends."

"We *are* friends," Julianna whispered fiercely as she placed her own hand over her grandmother's and rubbed her cheek against it. "We will be friends forever and always! When you are . . . gone, I shall still confide in you and write for you—shall write letters to you as if you had merely moved away!"

"What a diverting idea," her grandmother teased. "And will you also post them to me?"

"Of course not, but you'll know what I have written nonetheless."

"What makes you think that?" she asked, genuinely puzzled.

"Because I heard you tell the vicar very bluntly that it is illogical to assume that the Almighty intends to let us lie around dozing until Judgment Day. You said that, having repeatedly warned us that we shall reap what we sow, God is *more* likely to insist we observe what we have sown from a much *wider* viewpoint."

"I do not think it wise, my dear, for you to put more credence in my theological notions than in those of the good vicar. I shouldn't like for you to waste your talent writing to me after I'm gone, instead of writing something for the living to read."

"I shan't be wasting my time," Julianna said with a confident smile, one of their familiar debates over nonsense lifting her spirits. "If I write you letters, I have every faith you will contrive a way to read them wherever you may be."

"Because you credit me with mystical powers?"

"No," Julianna teased, "because you cannot resist correcting my *spelling!*"

"Impertinent baggage," her grandmother huffed, but she smiled widely and her fingers spread, linking with Julianna's for a tight, affectionate squeeze.

The following year, on the eve of Christmas, her grandmother died, holding Julianna's hand one last time. "I'll write to you, Grandmama." Julianna wept as her grandmother's eyes closed forever. "Don't forget to watch for my letters. Don't *forget.*"

Four

IN THE DAYS that followed, Julianna wrote her dozens of letters, but as one lonely month drifted into another, the empty monotony of her life provided little worth writing about. The sleepy little village of

Blintonfield remained the boundary of her world, and so she filled her time with reading and secret dreams of going off to London when she received her inheritance at eighteen. There she would meet interesting people and visit museums while she worked diligently on her writing. When she sold some of her work, she would bring her two little brothers to London often, so they could broaden their knowledge and share the wonders of the world beyond their little village.

After a few attempts to share this dream with her mama, Julianna realized it was wiser to say nothing because her mother was horrified and annoyed by the whole idea. "It's beyond considering, dear. Respectable, unmarried young ladies do *not* live alone, particularly in London. Your reputation would be ruined, completely ruined!" She was no more enthusiastic about any mention of books or writing. Lady Skeffington's interest in reading material was limited exclusively to the Society pages of the daily papers, where she religiously followed the doings of the Ton. She considered Julianna's fascination with history and philosophy and her desire to become an author almost as appalling as Julianna's wish to live on her own in London. "Gentlemen do not like a female who is too clever, dear," she warned repeatedly. "You're entirely too bookish. If you don't learn to keep all this fustian about philosophy to yourself, your chances of receiving a marriage offer from any truly eligible gentlemen will be ruined!"

Until a few months before the masquerade ball, the subject of a London Season for Julianna had never been discussed as a possibility.

Although Julianna's father was a baronet, his ancestors had long before squandered whatever modest fortune and lands that went with the title. His only legacy from his forebears was a thoroughly amiable and placid disposition that enabled him to ignore all of life's difficulties and a great fondness for wine and spirits. He had no desire to leave his favorite chair, let alone the secluded little village that was his birthplace. He was, however, not proof against his wife's determination, nor her ambitions for their little family.

In the end, neither was Juliana.

Three weeks after Julianna received her inheritance, as she was writing more letters of inquiry to the London papers about lodgings, her mother excitedly summoned the entire family to the salon for an unprecedented family council. "Julianna," she exclaimed, "your father and I have something thrilling to tell you!" She paused to beam at Julianna's father, who was still reading the newspaper. "Don't we, John?"

"Yes, my dove," he murmured without looking up.

After an admonishing look at Julianna's two young brothers, who were arguing over the last biscuit, she clasped her hands in delight and transferred her gaze to Julianna. "It is all arranged!" she exclaimed. "I have just received a letter from the owner of a little house in London in respectable neighborhood. He has agreed to let us have it for the rest of the Season for the paltry amount I was able to offer! Everything else has been arranged and deposits paid in advance. I have hired a Miss Sheridan Bromleigh, who will be your lady's maid and occasional chaperone, and who will help look after the boys. She is an American, but then one must make do when one cannot afford to pay decent wages.

"Dear heaven, your gowns were expensive, but the vicar's wife assures me the modiste I hired is quite competent, though not capable of the sort of intricate designs you will see worn by the young ladies of the Ton. On the other hand, I daresay few of them have your beauty, so it all works out quite evenly. Someday soon you will have gowns to go with your looks, and you will be the envy of all! You'll have jewels and furs, coaches, servants at your beck and call. . . ."

Julianna had felt a momentary burst of elation at the mention of inexpensive lodgings in London, but new gowns and a lady's maid had never been in the family budget, nor were they in her budget. "I don't understand, Mama. What has happened?" she asked, wondering if some unknown relative had died and left them a fortune.

"What has happened is that I have managed to put your small inheritance to grand use—and in a manner that will pay excellent returns, I am sure."

Julianna's mouth opened in a silent cry of furious protest, but she was incapable of speech for the moment—which Lady Skeffington evidently mistook for shared ecstasy.

"Yes, it is all true! You are going to London for the Season, where we will contrive a way for you to mingle with all the right people! While we are there, I have every confidence you will captivate some eligible gentleman who will make you a splendid offer. Perhaps even the Earl of Langford, whose estates are said to be beyond compare. Or Nicholas DuVille, who is one of the richest men in England *and* France and is about to inherit a Scottish title from a relative of his mama. I have it from several unimpeachable sources that the Earl of Langford and the Earl of Glenmore—which is what DuVille will be called—are considered to be the two most desirable bachelors in Europe! Just imagine how envious the Ton will be when little Julianna Skeffington captures one of those men for a husband."

Julianna could almost hear the sound of her dreams splintering and crashing at her feet. "I don't *want* a husband!" she cried. "I want to travel, and learn, and write, Mama. I do. I think I could write a novel someday—Grandmama said I am truly talented with a pen. No, don't laugh, please. You must get the money back, you must!"

"My dear, foolish girl, I wouldn't even if I could, which I cannot. Marriage is the only future for a female. Once you see how Fashionable Society lives, you'll forget all that silliness your grandmother Skeffington stuffed into your head. Now," she continued blithely, "when we are in London, I will contrive to put you in the way of eligible gentlemen, you may depend on it. We are not common merchants, you know—your papa is a baronet, after all. Once the Ton realizes we have come to London for the Season, we will be included in all their splendid affairs. Gentlemen will see you and admire you, and we will soon have eligible suitors lined up at our door, you'll see."

There was little point in refusing to go there, and no way to avoid it, so Juliana went.

In London, her mother insisted they browse daily in

the same exclusive shops in which the Ton shopped, and each afternoon they strolled through the same London parks where the Ton was always to be seen.

But nothing went as Lady Skeffington had planned. Contrary to all her hopes and expectations, the aristocracy did not welcome her with open arms upon discovering her husband was a baronet, not did they respond at all well to her eager efforts to engage them in conversations in Bond Street or accost them in Hyde Park. Instead of being given an invitation or invited to pay a morning call, the elegant matrons with whom she tried to converse gave her the cut-direct.

Though her mama seemed not to notice that she was being treated with icy disdain, Julianna felt every insult and rebuff enough for both of them, and every one of them savaged her pride and cut her to the heart. Even though she realized her mother brought much of the contempt on herself, the entire situation made her so miserable and self-conscious that she could scarcely look anyone in the eye from the moment they left their little house until they returned.

Despite all that, Julianna did not regard her trip to London as a total loss. Sheridan Bromleigh, the paid companion whom her mother had employed for the Season, proved to be a lovely and lively young American with whom Julianna could talk and laugh and exchange confidences. For the first time in her eighteen years, Julianna had a friend close to her own age, one who shared her sense of humor and many of her interests as well.

The Earl of Langford, whom Lady Skeffington had coveted for her daughter, threw a final rub into her plans by getting married at the end of the Season. In a quick wedding that shocked London and antagonized Lady Skeffington, the handsome earl married Miss Bromleigh.

When Julianna's mother heard the news, she went to bed with her hartshorn and stayed there for a full day. By the evening, however, she had come to see the tremendous social advantage of being very personally acquainted with a countess who had married into one of the most influential families in England.

With renewed confidence and vigor, she focused all her hopes on Nicholas DuVille.

Normally Julianna could not think about her disastrous encounter with him that spring without shuddering, but as she sat in the maze, staring at the glass in her hand, the whole thing suddenly seemed more amusing than humiliating.

Obviously, she decided, the horrid-tasting stuff she'd drank actually did make things seem a little brighter. And if three swallows could accomplish that, then it seemed logical that a bit more of the magical elixir could only be of more benefit. It was in the spirit of scientific experimentation, therefore, that she lifted the glass and took three more swallows. After what seemed like only a few moments, she felt even better!

"Much better," she informed the moon aloud, stifling a giggle as she thought about her brief but hilarious encounter with the legendary Nicholas DuVille. Her mama had spied him in Hyde Park just as his curricle was about to slowly pass within arm's reach of the path they were on. In her eager desperation to point him out and effect a meeting, Julianna's mama gave her a light shove that put her directly into the path of his horse and curricle. Off-balance, Julianna grabbed at the horse's reins for balance, yanking the irate horse and its irate owner to a stop.

Shaken and frightened by the animal's nervous side-stepping, Julianna clung to its reins, trying to quiet it. Intending to either apologize or chastise the driver of the curricle for not trying to quiet his own horse, Julianna looked up and beheld Nicholas DuVille. Despite the frigid look in his narrowed, assessing eyes, Julianna felt as if her bones were melting and her legs were turning to water.

Dark-haired, broad-shouldered, with piercing metallic-blue eyes and finely chiseled lips, he had the sardonic look of a man who had sampled all the delights the world had to offer. With that fallen angel's face and knowing blue eyes, Nicholas DuVille was as wickedly attractive and forbidden as sin. Julianna felt an instantaneous, insane compulsion to do something that would impress him.

"If you wish a mount, mademoiselle," he said, in a voice that rang with curt impatience, "may I suggest you try a more conventional means of obtaining one."

Julianna was spared the immediate need to react or reply by her mother, who was so desperate to accomplish an introduction that she violated every known rule of etiquette and common sense. "This is such an unexpected pleasure and privilege, my lord," exclaimed Lady Skeffington, oblivious to the ominous narrowing of his eyes and the avidly curious glances being cast their way by the occupants of the other carriages who had drawn to a stop, their way blocked. "I have been longing to introduce you to my daughter—"

"Am I to assume," he interrupted, "that this has something to do with your daughter stepping in front of me and waylaying my horse?"

Julianna decided that the man was rude and arrogant.

"That had nothing to do with it," she burst out, mortified by the undeniable accuracy of his assessment and by the belated realization that she was still holding on to the rein. She dropped it like it was a snake, stepped back, and resorted to flippancy because she had no other way to salvage her pride. "I was practicing," she informed him primly.

Her answer startled him enough to stay his hand as he started to flick the reins. "Practicing?" he repeated, studying her expression with a glimmer of amused interest. "Practicing for what?"

Julianna lifted her chin, raised her brows, and said in an offhand voice what she hoped would pass for droll wit rather than stupidity, "I'm practicing to become a highwayman, obviously. By way of an apprenticeship, I jump in front of innocent travelers in the park and waylay their horses."

Turning her back on him, she took her mother firmly by the arm and steered her away. Over her shoulder, Julianna added a dismissive and deliberately incorrect, "Good afternoon, Mr. . . . er . . . Deveraux."

Her mother's exclamation of indignant horror at these outrageous remarks muffled a sound from the man in the carriage that sounded almost like laughter.

Lady Skeffington was still furious with Julianna later that night.

"How could you be so impertinent!" she cried, wringing her hands. "Nicholas DuVille has so much influence with Society that if he utters one derogatory word about you, no one of any consequence will associate with you. You'll be ruined! Ruined, do you hear me?" Despite Julianna's repeated apologies, albeit insincere, her mother was beyond consolation. She paced back and forth, her hartshorn in one hand and a handkerchief in the other. "Had Nicholas DuVille paid you just a few minutes of attention in the park today, where others could see it, you'd have been an instant success! By tonight we would have had invitations to every important social function of the Season, and by the day after, eligible suitors would have been at our door. Instead, you had to be insolent to the one man in all London who could put an end to my hopes and dreams with a single word." She dabbed at the tears trembling on her lashes. "This is all your grandmother's fault! She taught you to be just like her. Oh, I should be *horsewhipped* for allowing you to spend so much time with that dreadful old harpy, but no one could oppose her will, least of all your father."

She stopped pacing and rounded on Julianna. "Well, I know more of the *real* world than your grandmother ever did, and I am about to tell you something she never did—a simple truth that is worth more than all her fantastical notions, and that truth is this—" And clenching her hands into fists at her sides, she said in a voice shaking with purpose, *"A man does not wish to associate with any female who knows more than he does!* If the Ton's gossip mill finds out how bookish you are, you'll be ruined! No gentleman of consequence will want you! You . . . will . . . be . . . ruined!"

Five

A TRILL OF FEMININE laughter pulled Julianna's thoughts back to the masquerade, and she listened to the sounds of adults behaving like naughty children, wondering how many feminine reputations were being "totally ruined" out there tonight. Based on what Julianna had gathered from her mother's frequent lectures, it seemed there were countless ways to be ruined, but there were two different and distinct kinds of ruination. Mistakes made by the female alone, such as appearing too intelligent, too clever, too bookish, or too glib, could "ruin" her chances of making a splendid match. But any mistake she made that involved the honor of a gentleman resulted in *"total* ruin," because it eliminated her chances of making any kind of match at all.

It was very silly, Julianna decided gaily as she reflected upon the myriad ways of blundering into *"total* ruin."

A female could be *"totally* ruined" by allowing any gentleman to be alone with her in a room, or allowing him to show a partiality for her, or even allowing him a third dance with her.

As Julianna contemplated all this, she realized she would have been far, far better off if she had done only one of the countless things that could "totally ruin" a female's chances of making any match. If she *had* been totally ruined, she realized with a sudden flash of new insight, she would not now be facing a repulsive marriage to Sir Francis Bellhaven!

The thought of him banished her momentary mirth and made the moon waver as her eyes filled with tears. She reached for her handkerchief, realized she didn't have one, and sniffled. Then she had another sip of her drink, trying unsuccessfully to buoy her plummeting spirits.

For several minutes after he had finished his cigar, Nicki remained where Valerie had left him, deliberating about turning to his right and returning to the garden of turning left and walking deeper into the maze until he came to a path that, he knew, led around to the side of the house and ultimately to his bedchamber.

He was tired, and his bedchamber had an enormous and very comfortable bed. If his mother hadn't specifically asked him to stop here on his way from London and to give her regards to Valerie's mother, he wouldn't have come. According to his father's note, his mother's health had taken a sudden and precarious turn for the worse, and Nicki did not want to do anything, no matter how minor, to disappoint or distress her. Turning, Nicki walked along the convoluted path that led out of the maze and into the garden, ready to fulfill his social obligation this night and his filial obligation on the morrow.

Six

JULIANNA WAS QUITE convinced that total ruination would cause Sir Francis to withdraw his offer, though she had no idea how she would survive if her parents disowned her for ruining herself. Sniffling again, she bent her head, closed her eyes tightly, and decided to resort to prayer. She asked her grandmother to help her find a way to ruin herself. Deciding that it might be wise to appeal to an even higher authority, Julianna took her problem directly to God. It occurred to her, however, that God might not approve of such a request, let alone consider granting it, unless He was fully apprised of her dire plight. She sniffled again, closed her eyes even tighter, and began explaining to God the reasons she wished to be ruined. She was just to the part about having to marry Sir Francis Bellhaven, and crying in heartbroken little gulps, when A Voice spoke to her out of the darkness—a deep, rich, male voice filled with quiet authority and tinged with sympathy: "May I be of assistance?"

Shock sent Julianna surging to her feet, her heart thundering, then leaping into her throat as her widened eyes riveted on a shadowy cloaked figure that materialized from the inky darkness and began moving forward.

The apparition stopped just beyond reach of a pale moonbeam, his face in shadow, his features indistinguishable. He raised his arm slowly, and something white seemed to float and flutter from his fingertips even thought there was no breeze.

Her senses reeling from shock and brandy, Julianna realized he was holding the white billowing thing out toward her. She stepped forward hesitantly and reached for his extended arm. The object that came away in her hand turned out to be an earthly, though still very soft and fine, handkerchief. "Thank you," she whispered reverently, giving him a teary smile as she dabbed at her eyes and nose.

Not certain what she was now expected to do with it, she held it out to him.

"You may keep it."

Julianna snatched it back, clutching it safely to her heart. "Thank you."

"Is there anything I can do before I leave you?"

"Don't have! Please! Yes, there is something I need, but I should like to explain." Julianna opened her mouth to finish explaining to God why she was praying to be ruined when two things struck her as a little odd. First, this celestial being who had evidently appeared in answer to her prayers seemed to have a slight accent— a French one. Second, now that her eyes had adjusted to the pool of darkness that concealed him, she noticed a small detail that struck her as more sinister than heavenly. Since she had been praying to be ruined, it seemed not only prudent but imperative to make certain the *wrong* sort of mystical being hadn't decided to pay her a visit in answer to that prayer.

Fighting against the dulling effects of the brandy, Julianna fixed him with a cautious stare. "Please do not think I am questioning your . . . your authenticity . . . or your taste in fashions," she began, carefully injecting as much respect into her voice as she possibly could, "but shouldn't you be wearing *white* rather than *black?*"

His eyes, visible through the slits of his half mask, narrowed at such an impertinent suggestion, and Julianna braced herself to be struck down by a bolt of lightning, but his tone was mild. "Black is customary for a man. Were I to appear here in white, I would draw too much attention to myself. People would begin trying to guess my identity. They would note my height first, then my other features, and begin trying to guess my identity. If they did, I would forfeit my anonymity and then my freedom to do the sort of things one expects to do on nights like tonight."

"Yes, I see," Julianna said politely, but she wasn't completely convinced. "I *suppose* that's not as extraordinary as I thought."

Nicki thought their entire meeting thus far had been a little "extraordinary." When he first saw her, she had been weeping. In a matter of moments, that expressive face of hers had already exhibited shock, embarrassment, awe, fear, suspicions, and now uncertainty . . . even apprehension. As he waited for her to screw up the courage to explain whatever it was she wanted of him, Nicki realized there was nothing ordinary about her. Her pale blond hair seemed to glisten with silver in the moonlight when she moved her head, and her large eyes actually appeared to be a lavender blue. They dominated a delicately molded face with smooth milky skin, winged brows, and a lovely mouth. Hers was a subtle beauty, easily overlooked at first glance. It came from a purity of features and a candor in those large eyes, rather than from vibrant coloring or exotic looks.

He couldn't assess her age, but she looked quite young, and there were certain things about her that did not quite fit.

She drew in a deep breath, pulling his thoughts back to the matter at hand, and he quirked a brow at her in silent inquiry.

"Would you mind," she said, very, very politely, "taking off your mask and letting me see your face?"

"Was that the favor you wanted to ask of me?" he asked, wondering if she were addled.

"No, but I cannot ask it until I see your face." When he showed no inclination to move, Julianna implored in a shaky, desperate voice, "It's *terribly* important!"

Nicki hesitated, and then sheer curiosity made him decide to comply. He pulled off the mask and even walked out of the shadows to give her a good look at his face, then he waited for a reaction.

He got one.

She clamped her hand over her mouth, her eyes as round as saucers. Nicki stepped forward, thinking she was going to swoon, but her sudden shriek of laughter checked him in midstride. That was followed by great gales of mirth as she sank onto the stone bench and covered her face with her hands, her entire body shaking with hilarity. Twice she peeked out at him from between her fingers, as if to ascertain that she had seen correctly, and both times the sight of his face made her laugh even harder.

With a supreme effort, Julianna finally managed to compose herself. She lifted her face to his, her eyes still sparkling with mirth as she stared in disbelief at the one face in all England that had made her heart pound. And now, as her shock subsided, that face was beginning to have the same effect on her that it had had on her last spring. Only this time there was a difference. This time there was a slight smile touching that chiseled mouth, and his eyes weren't cold and hard, they were merely . . . speculative. All in all, his expression was noncommittal but definitely interested.

That was flattering and encouraging enough to raise her spirits, bolster her confidence, and make her certain that she had made the right decision a few minutes before. She had prayed to be totally ruined, and it was going to happen at the hands of the most sought-after bachelor in Europe, Nicholas DuVille himself! That made it so much better—it gave it a certain flair, a style. In return for sacrificing herself to total ruin to avoid Sir Francis, she was going to have sweet memories to treasure. "I'm not demented, though it must look it," she began, "and I do have a favor to ask of you."

Nicki knew he ought to walk away, but he was as strangely captivated by her infectious laughter, her entrancing face, and her astonishing reactions as he was completely bored with the prospect of returning to the ball. "Exactly what is this favor you're hoping I'll grant you?"

"It's a little difficult to discuss," she said. He watched her reach for whatever it was she'd been drinking. She took a sip of it as if she needed it for courage, and then she raised those large candid eyes to his. "Actually it's *quite* difficult," she amended, wrinkling her pert nose.

"As you can see," Nicki responded, suppressing a smile and giving her a gallant little bow, "I am completely at your service."

"I hope you still feel that way, after you hear what I would ask of you," she murmured uneasily.

"What may I do?"

"I would like you to ruin me."

Seven

UNTIL THAT MOMENT, Nicki would have wagered a fortune that nothing a woman said could truly surprise him anymore, let alone reduce him to his current state of speechlessness. "I beg your pardon?" he finally managed.

Julianna saw him struggle to hide his shock, and she suppressed another siege of unacceptable giggles. She wasn't certain whether her urge to laugh came from nervousness or the wondrous, evil-tasting potion that men imbibed to make them feel so much more optimistic. "I asked if you would be willing to ruin me."

Stalling for time, Nicki studied her from the corner of his eye while he reached into his pocket and took out the last of the two cheroots he'd brought with him. "What . . . specifically . . ." he queried cautiously as he bent his head and lit the cheroot, "do you mean by that?"

"I mean, I wish to be ruined," Julianna repeated, watching him cup his hands around the flame, trying to get a better look at his features. "I mean, I wish to be made undesirable to any and all men," she clarified. "Rendered unmarriageable. Left on the shelf."

Instead of reacting, he propped a booted foot on the

stone bench beside her hip and eyed her in thoughtful silence, the thin cigar clamped between even white teeth.

"I—I really don't think I could possibly make it any clearer than that," she said anxiously.

"No, I don't think you could."

She leaned a little closer to his leg and tipped her head back, peering up at his unreadable face as he gazed off into the distance. "You do understand what I meant?"

"It would be difficult not to."

He did not sound very enthusiastic, so she blurted the first inducement that came to mind: "I would be willing to pay you!"

This time Nicki was able to suppress his shock through not his smile at her ability to cause the reaction. "That makes twice," he murmured aloud. "And in one night." Realizing that she was waiting for a reply, he lowered his gaze to her upturned face, bit back a wayward grin, and said gravely, "That's a very tempting offer."

"I would cooperate completely," she promised, leaning forward and looking at him with earnest, hopeful eyes.

"The incentives are becoming more irresistible by the moment."

Nicki let her wait for his decision while he gazed into the distance, analyzing the situation and the intriguing young woman seated on the bench beside his leg. He still wasn't certain how old she was, but he had known she was no gently bred debutante long before she'd asked him for a "favor." The clues had all been there from the first, beginning with the fact that she was alone in a dark, secluded area with a man to whom she'd never been properly introduced, and she'd made no effort to correct either situation.

Furthermore, the gown she was wearing was enticing in the extreme, seductively low cut to show off her swelling breasts and tightly fitted to emphasize her narrow waist. No respectable Society matron alive would have permitted her innocent daughter to appear in such a gown. It was a gown for a daring married woman—or a courtesan. She was not wearing a marriage ring, which left only the latter possibility. That conclusion was reinforced by the fact that it had become quite the thing, especially among the wealthy young bucks, to escort their lightskirts to masquerades as sort of a joke. Some of London's most beautiful and sought-after courtesans were in evidence at this masquerade, and Nicki assumed the angelic-looking one beside him had quarreled with whomever had brought her here. After crying her heart out, she was now looking for a replacement. He knew damned well she'd been "ruined" long before and often since, just as he knew she had absolutely no intention of paying him, but the latter approach was so marvelously creative that he was impressed. She was not only entrancingly lovely, she was unique. And extremely entertaining. With her looks and imagination, her soft, cultured voice, she was not going to have to look very far or very long for a new protector. In fact, if she proved to be half as entertaining in his bed tonight as she'd been thus far, he'd be sorely tempted to volunteer for the role.

In an agony of suspense, Julianna stared at his firm jaw and unreadable expression as he gazed off into the distance, his hands thrust into his pockets, his cloak thrown back over his shoulders. His eyes were creased at the corners, and it seemed almost as if he was smiling a little bit, but that may have been caused only by the way he was holding the cheroot clamped between his white teeth.

Unable to endure the wait any longer, Julianna said shakily, "Have you decided yet?"

He shifted his gaze to her face, and Julianna felt the full impact of the lazy, devastating smile that swept across his face. "I would not come cheaply," Nicki joked.

"I haven't a great deal of money," she warned, and Nicki bit back a chuckle that erupted into a shout of laughter when she actually started digging into her little reticule, searching for money.

Extending his arm to her, he said, "Shall we find a place more conducive to . . . ah . . ."

"My ruin?" she provided helpfully, and he sensed a slight hesitation that was gone before it materialized. Standing up, she squared her shoulders, put up her chin, and, looking like a queen going bravely and determinedly, announced, "Let's be at it, then."

He led her deeper into the maze, guided by a long-ago memory of the time when Valerie and he had been lost inside it for hours because they'd missed the secret path. It occurred to him as they walked along at a leisurely pace that introductions were in order, but when he mentioned this, she told him that she already knew who he was. "And you are?" Nicki prompted when she showed no inclination to volunteer him the information.

Somewhere in Julianna's hazy mind, tangled up in the dreamy unreality of the night and the moon and the handsome, desirable man at her side, caution finally asserted itself. Trying to think of a false name to give him, she glanced down at her gown. " 'Marie,'" she provided after a momentary pause. "You may call me 'Marie.' "

"As in 'Antoinette'?" Nicki mocked, wondering why she was lying.

In answer, she threw up her left arm in exuberation and called cheerfully, "Let them eat cake!" A split second later she stopped dead. "Where are we going?"

"To my bedchamber."

Julianna mentally recounted the possibilities for ruination. Three dances with the same man. Allowing a man to show partiality. And being alone in a room with a man. Room. Bedchamber. She nodded agreeably. "Very well, I suppose you know more about it than I."

I doubt it, Nicki thought dryly.

They strolled along in companionable silence, and Nicki liked that about her too. She did not feel a need to talk incessantly. When she finally broke the silence, even her timing was right, although her topic was another stunning first in his vast experience with females. She'd been looking down at the ground when she lifted her head and said very solemnly, "I often find myself wondering about worms. Do you?"

"Not as much," Nicki lied drolly, swallowing back a laugh, "as I used to do." He couldn't remember laughing this much in an entire week.

"Then consider this and see if you can think of an answer," she suggested in the grave tones of a puzzled scientist. "If God meant for them to crawl about on the ground as they do, why don't they have knees?"

Nicki stopped dead, his shoulders shaking with helpless mirth as he turned fully toward her. "What did you just say?"

A heavenly face lifted to his, eyes shining, breasts swelling invitingly above her bodice, generous lips forming words: "I asked why worms don't have knees."

"That's what I *thought* you said." Grabbing her shoulders, he hauled her abruptly into his arms and surrendered to the uncontrollable impulse to smother his laughter against the soft lips that had caused it. He let her go as quickly as he'd grabbed her, uncertain whether her expression was one of shock or reproof. Deciding it was unnecessary and undesirable to discuss either one with someone who was going to share his bed in return for payment, he stepped back and turned away.

Despite that, he couldn't stop himself from glancing at her several times in the dark to assess her reaction, and he relaxed when he saw the bemused smile touching her lips.

He was not completely certain he'd made all the right turns until they rounded the last corner and he found the secret exit that led around to the side of the house. Knowing in advance that they were going to be in plain view of the revelers for a few paces—albeit at a reasonably safe distance—Nicki carefully stationed himself on her left, between the house and her. "Why are we walking faster?" she asked.

"Because we happen to be in view of the gardens from here," he cautioned.

She peered around him to see for herself. "Let them eat cake too!" she announced cheerfully with another wave of her arm. Raising her voice, she called out, "All of you have my permission to eat cake!"

Nicki felt his shoulders shake with silent, horrified,

helpless laughter, but he said nothing to encourage another outburst.

Eight

IN HIS BEDCHAMBER, Julianna sat upon a small sofa upholstered in rich gold brocade, feeling as if she were in a dream, as she watched him slowly strip off his coat and loosen his snowy-white neckcloth. A thousand warning bells were clanging madly in her head, making her feel extremely dizzy. Or perhaps it was the memory of his mouth crushed to hers that made her head swim.

She lowered her gaze, because that seemed like the right thing to do, and then became preoccupied with what she saw.

Divested of his coat and neckcloth, Nicki loosened the top of his shirt and walked over to the polished table where a tray of glasses and decanters had been left. Pulling the stopper out of the brandy decanter, he glanced over his shoulder to ask if she wanted anything, but what he saw made him frown with concern and turn fully around. She was seated on the sofa, but bending as far forward at the waist as she could, looking at something on the floor. "What are you doing?" he asked.

She answered without looking up. "I don't have any toes."

"What do you mean?" Nicki demanded irritably as it began to occur to him that nearly everything she'd done and said in the maze that had seemed shocking or hilarious at the time, including her request to be ruined, could very likely be the result of intoxication or an unbalanced mind. His voice was intentionally sharp. "Can you stand up?" he snapped.

Julianna stiffened at his tone and slowly straightened. Transfixed by the change in him, she stood up as commanded, scarcely able to believe the forbidding man standing there was the same one who had joked with her and . . . and kissed her.

She looked completely dazed, Nicki realized. Dazed and disoriented. With an anger that was heightened by disappointment and self-disgust for his own naïveté, he said scathingly, "Are you capable of uttering anything at all that could convince me you are capable of intelligent thought at this moment?"

Julianna flinched from that all-too-familiar voice. It had the same clipped, authoritative tones, the same contemptuous superiority that had humiliated and antagonized her in the park. Tonight her reaction was slowed by brandy and shock, but when she did react it was just as instinctive and just as effective, although more restrained. She wanted this to be a night to remember, to cherish. "I think I am," she said softly, lifting her chin, her voice trembling only slightly.

"Shall we begin with Greek philosophy?" Clasping her hands behind her back, she turned sideways, pretending to study the painting above the fireplace, as she continued: "Socrates had some interesting observations about knowledge and ethics. Plato was more profound. . . ."

Julianna paused, trying desperately to clear her head and remember what else she knew of philosophers, ancient or otherwise. "In modern times . . ." she tried again, "Voltaire is a particular favorite of mine. I enjoy his wit. But of all the modern . . ." Her voice trailed off as Julianna heard him coming up behind her, then she made herself go on: "Of all the modern philosophers, the one I am best acquainted with was a woman. Her name was Sarah."

He stopped so near to her that she could actually feel him standing at her back. Shaking with uncertainty, Julianna said, "Shall I share Sarah's favorite theory with you?"

"By all means," he whispered contritely, his warm breath stirring the hair at her temple.

"Sarah's theory was that females were once considered superior to males, but that males, in their deceitful arrogance, found a way to—"

Julianna's entire body tensed as his hands curved around her shoulders, drawing her back against his full length. "Males found a way to convince us, and themselves, that women are actually birdwits and—"

His warm lips touched a sensitive place behind her ear, sending shivers racing down her entire body. "Go on," he urged, his voice like velvet, his mouth against her ear. Julianna tried, but her breath came out in a shuddering sigh. She was losing control again, letting the brandy soothe her and convince her this was right. It was either this or Sir Francis Bellhaven: sweet, forbidding torture with memories to cherish . . . or life with a man who sickened her. Surely she was entitled to a few more moments, she decided.

Nicki felt her heart racing beneath his hand as he slid it over her midriff, taking his time before he let himself touch the full, tantalizing breasts that were within his reach. He slid a kiss over her smooth temple and trailed another down the silken skin of her cheek.

She smelled like fresh air and flowers, and in his arms she felt like . . .

Wood.

She was breathing as if she were running, her heart was thundering from . . .

Fright.

Nicki lifted his head and wordlessly turned her around. In disbelief, he stared down at the hectic color on her cheeks and eyes, eyes that had darkened to violet pools, eyes that watched him in uncertainty. The color in her cheeks deepened with embarrassment as he inspected every feature of that elegant face, looking for something, anything, to indicate that this wasn't new and terrifying for her. He wanted to discover one thing that indicated experience.

And all he could find was innocence.

This was her first time.

She had *not* done any of this before.

He wanted her despite that. No, he realized with disbelief, he wanted her three times more *because* of that. She was there for the taking, she had asked him to do this, had even volunteered to pay him to do this. And still he hesitated. Taking her chin between his thumb and forefinger, he forced her to meet his gaze. In a voice that was devoid of anything except reassuring neutrality, Nicki asked, "Are you absolutely certain you want to be here . . . to do this?"

Julianna swallowed audibly and nodded slightly. "It's something I have to do—to get it over and done with."

"You're completely certain?"

She nodded, and Nicki did what he'd been longing to do all along. Except that as he bent his head, he had the disquieting thought that he wasn't merely despoiling a virgin, he was destroying an angel. He seized her mouth with violent tenderness, forcing her to respond and then pushing her harder until she was moaning in his arms and his hands were clamping her to him, then moving forward, sliding up to cup her trembling breasts.

"No!" She broke free with such suddenness that she caught Nicki off guard. "I can't! I can't! Not that!"

She shook her head wildly, and Nicki stared at her in frowning disbelief. One moment she'd been kissing him back, her arms twined sweetly behind his neck, her body molding instinctively to his. The next, she was running across the room, leaving him there, jerking the door open and leaving. . . .

Straight into Valerie, and another woman who was raving about her daughter being abducted and demanding a search of the house for her. As if in a dream, a nightmare, he saw the woman who had accosted him in the park wrap her arms protectively around the girl who had been his a moment before.

Only the older woman was different now. She wasn't groveling about what a pleasure it was to meet him, she was looking at him with triumphant hostility all over her face, saying, "After I have put my daughter to bed and summoned my husband, we will discuss this privately!"

Nine

"JULIANNA?" Her mother's normal speaking voice sounded like a screech. Julianna's head hurt so terribly that even her teeth seemed to ache in their sockets.

In all the world, the only thing that wasn't awful this morning was her mother. Her mother, who should have been livid, who Julianna had thought would disown her for less than what she'd done last night, was the soul of gentle understanding.

No questions, no recriminations.

Curled up in a tight ball of misery against the door of the coach, Julianna watched the house where it had all happened sway and pitch and lunge from view. "I'm going to be sick," she whispered.

"No dear, that wouldn't be at all pleasant."

Julianna swallowed and swallowed again. "Are we almost home?"

"We aren't going home."

"Where are we going?"

"We're going right . . . here," her mother said, leaning to the side and searching for something with narrowed eyes that widened suddenly with delight.

Julianna made an effort to see where "here" was and saw only a pleasant little cottage with her papa's carriage in front of it, and another carriage with a crest painted on its side. And then she saw the chapel. And in the yard of that chapel, ignoring her father and watching their coach draw up, was Nicholas DuVille.

And the expression on his dark, saturnine face was a thousand times more glacial, more contemptuous, than any she had seen in the park.

"Why are we here?" Julianna cried, feeling faint from shock and nausea and headache.

"To attend your wedding to Nicholas DuVille."

"My what?! But why?"

"Why is he marrying you?" her mama said dryly as she opened the door. "Because he has no choice. He is a gentleman, after all. He knew the rules, and he broke them. Our hostess and two servants saw you running out of his bedchamber. He ruined the reputation of an innocent, well-bred young lady. If he didn't marry you now, you would be ruined, but he could never again call himself a gentleman. He would lose face among his peers. His own code of honor requires this."

"I don't want this!" Julianna cried. "I'll make him understand!"

"I didn't want this!" Julianna was babbling a quarter of an hour later as she was shoved roughly into her new husband's coach. He had not spoken a word except in answer to his vows. He spoke now: "Shut up and get in!"

"Where are we going?" she cried.

"To your new home," he said with scathing sarcasm. *"Your* new home," he clarified.

Ten

HUMMING A YULETIDE melody as she sat before the dressing table in her bedchamber, Julianna tucked tiny sprigs of red holly berries into the dark green ribbon that bound her heavy blond hair into curls at the crown.

Satisfied, she stood up and shook the wrinkles from her soft green wool gown, straightened the wide cuffs at her wrists, then she headed for the salon where she intended to work on her new manuscript in front of a cheery fire.

In the three months since her husband had unceremoniously deposited her in front of this picturesque little country house a few hours after her wedding, and then driven off, she had not seen or heard from Nicholas DuVille. Even so, every detail of that hideous day was burned into her mind with such vivid clarity that it could still make her stomach knot with shame.

It had been an obscene parody of a real wedding, an eminently suitable ending for something that had begun at a masquerade. Far from condemning Julianna's breach of conduct the night before, her mother actually regarded it as a practical and ingenious method of snaring the Ton's most desirable bachelor. Instead of offering maternal advice about marriage and children before her daughter walked down a short aisle to become a wife, Julianna's mother was advising her on the sorts of *furs* Julianna ought to insist upon having.

Julianna's father, on the other hand, obviously had a clearer grasp of the real situation, which was that his daughter had disgraced herself, and her groom had participated in it. He had dealt with that by anesthetizing himself with at least a full bottle of Madeira before he walked her unsteadily, but cheerfully, down the aisle. To complete the gruesome picture, the bride was clearly suffering from the aftereffects of extreme inebriation, and the groom . . .

Julianna shuddered with the recollection of the loathing in his eyes when he was forced to turn to her and pledge his life to her. Even the image of the vicar who had performed the ceremony was branded into her brain. She could still see him standing there, his kindly face a mirror of shocked horror when, at the end of the ceremony, the groom responded to his suggestion that he kiss the bride by raking Julianna with a look of undiluted contempt, then turning on his heel and walking out.

In the coach, on the way here, Julianna had tried to talk to him, to explain, to apologize. After listening to her pleading in glacial silence, he had finally spoken to her. "If I hear just one more word from you, you will find yourself standing on the side of the road before your sentence is finished!"

In the months since she had been dumped here like a piece of unwanted baggage, Julianna had learned more about the agony of loneliness—not the kind that comes after losing someone to death, but the kind that comes from being rejected and despised and defiled. She had learned all that and more as the gossip about Nicki's flagrant affair with a beautiful opera dancer raged through London before the firestorm of gossip about his abrupt wedding had even gathered real force.

He was punishing her, Julianna knew. Publicly humiliating her in retaliation for what he believed—and would always believe—had been a trap set by Julianna and her mother. And the worst part of it was that when Julianna put herself in his place, and looked at things from his point his place, and looked at things from his point of view, she could understand exactly how he felt and why.

Until last week, his revenge had been completely devastating. She had wept an ocean of tears into her pillow, tormented herself with the recollection of the hatred in his eyes on their wedding day, and written him a dozen letters trying to explain. His only response had been a short, scathing message delivered to her by his secretary, which warned that if she made one more attempt to contact him, she would be evicted from the home she now occupied, and cut off without a shilling.

Julianna DuVille was expected to live out the rest of her days, in solitude, doing penance for a sin that had been almost as much his as hers. Nicholas DuVille had five other residences, all very grand and far more accessible to company. According to the gossip she read in the papers and what she gathered from the bits of information she pried out of Sheridan Westmoreland, he gave lavish parties at those houses for his friends, and intimate ones for two, Julianna was certain, in his bedchamber.

Until last week, her days had dragged by in an agony of emptiness and self-loathing, with nothing to give her relief except what little she found by pouring out her heart in letters to her grandmother. But all that had changed now, and it was going to improve more every day.

Last week, she had received a letter from a London publisher who wished to buy her new novel. In his letter, Mr. Framingham had compared Julianna in glowing terms to Jane Austen, he had commented on her humor and remarkable subtlety in dealing with the arrogance of Society and the futility of trying to belong where one can never truly belong.

He had also enclosed a bank draft with the prediction of many more to come, once her first novel was published. A bank draft was independence, it was validation, it was release from the bondage her wedding to Nicholas DuVille had placed her in. It was . . . Everything!

She was already daydreaming of a place to live in

London, something cheerful and tiny, in a respectable area . . . just the way she and her grandmother had always planned she would live when she received her inheritance. By the end of the coming year, she would have enough money to leave this silken prison to which she had been banished.

Her dreams at night were not so comforting. In the defenselessness of sleep, Nicki was there, exactly as he had been in the maze. With a booted foot propped on the bench beside her, he gazed into the distance, a thin cheroot clamped between his teeth, smiling a little as he listened to her outrageous request that he ruin her. He teased her in those dreams about expecting to be paid. And then he kissed her, and she would wake up with her heart racing and the touch of his mouth lingering on hers.

But in the morning, with sunlight streaming in the windows, the future was hers again and the past . . . She left the past in her bedchamber on the pillows. Now more than ever, her refuge was her writing.

Downstairs in the salon, Larkin, the butler, was already placing a breakfast tray containing a pot of chocolate and buttered toast on a table beside her desk. "Thank you, Larkin," she said with a smile as she slid into her chair.

It was late afternoon, and Julianna was completely engrossed in her manuscript when Larkin interrupted her, his voice taut. "My lady?"

Julianna held up her pen in a gesture that asked him to wait until she finished what she needed to write down. "But—"

Julianna shook her head very firmly, telling him to wait. Nothing of urgency ever occurred here, and she knew it. No unexpected callers arrived for cozy chats in this remote countryside, no household matter arose that couldn't wait. The small estate ran like a well-oiled machine, according to its owner's demands, and the staff only consulted her out of courtesy. She was merely a houseguest, though she sometimes had the feeling the servants sympathized with her plight, particularly the butler. Satisfied, Julianna put her pen aside and turned around. "I'm sorry, Larkin," she said, noting that he looked ready to burst from the strain of waiting for her attention, "but if I don't write down the thought while have it, I often forget it. What did you wish to say?"

"His lordship has just arrived, my lady! He wishes to see you at once in his study." Shock and impossible hope had already sent Julianna to her feet before Larkin added, "And he has brought his valet." Unfamiliar with the travelling habits of the wealthy, Julianna looked at him in confusion. "That means," Larkin confided happily, "he will be staying overnight."

Standing at the window of the study, Nicki stared impatiently at he same view of the winter landscape that used to seem so pleasing from here, while he waited for the scheming little slut he had been forced to wed to answer his summons. The night of the masquerade was no longer fresh in his mind, but his wedding day was. It had begun with a breakfast tray delivered personally by Valerie, along with several pointed and sarcastic references to his having been the only "fish" in London who'd been stupid enough to take the bait provided by Julianna and land in her mother's net. Before he ejected her from his bedchamber, she had done a good job of adding to his doubts about Julianna's innocence in the whole thing, and *still* he had refused to believe that Julianna had intended to entrap him

He had clung to the comforting delusion that it had been an accident of timing and circumstances.

With a streak of naïveté and self-delusion he didn't know he possessed, he had actually managed to concentrate only on how adorable she'd been, and how perfectly she'd fit in his arms. He had even gone so far as to convince himself that she would suit him perfectly as a wife, and he had clung to that conviction while he waited for her at the chapel. If he hadn't been so infuriated with his nauseating future mother-in-law, he'd have chuckled at the way Julianna looked when she alighted from the coach.

His little bride had been positively gray from the effects of the night before, but not so ill she couldn't chat about furs with her mother, not so ill that they couldn't stand in the back of the chapel and gloat about snaring themselves a rich husband. He had heard it all while he waited outside.

She would try some sort of play while he was here, Nicki knew. She was not only clever, she was intelligent—intelligent enough to know she could never convince him of her innocence. Based on that, he rather expected a confession, a claim that she had been coerced by her mother.

He turned away at the sound of the door opening, fully expecting to see her looking only slightly better than the last time he had seen her, and every bit as forlorn, perhaps more contrite. In that, he instantly realized, he was wrong.

"I understand you want to talk with me?" she said with remarkable poise.

He nodded curtly toward the chair in front of his desk, a silent command to sit down.

The brief flare of hope that had ignited in Julianna a minute ago when she learned he was here had already died the instant he turned and looked at her in that insolent, appraising fashion. He hadn't softened, she realized with a sinking heart.

"I'll come directly to the point," he said without preamble as he sat down behind his desk. "The physicians tell us my mother's heart is weakening and that she is dying." His face and voice were carefully blank, Julianna noted, completely devoid of all emotion, so much so that she instantly concluded the feelings he did have were extremely painful. "She will not see another Christmas."

"I'm very sorry to hear that," Julianna said softly.

Instead of replying he stared at her as if he thought she were the most repugnant form of human life he'd ever beheld. Unable to resist the need to try to convince him she was at least capable of compassion, Julianna said, "I was closer to my grandmother than anyone in the world, and when she died, I was desolate. I still confide things to her and think of her. I—I even write her letters, though I know it's odd . . ."

He interrupted her as if she hadn't spoken, "My father also informed me that she is deeply troubled by the state of our so-called marriage. Because of all that, it is my father's wish and my decision that her last

Christmas is going to be a happy one. And you are going to help insure that it is, Julianna."

Julianna swallowed and nodded. Driven by the same desperate eagerness she'd felt the day she encountered him in the park to say or do something to please him, she added softly, "I'll do whatever I can."

Instead of being pleased or even satisfied with her, he looked completely revolted. "You won't need to exert yourself in the least. It will be very easy for you. All you need do is pretend you're at another masquerade. When my parents arrive tomorrow, you are going to 'masquerade' as my tender and devoted wife. I," he finished icily, "have the more difficult task. I have to pretend I can stomach being in the same house with you!"

He stood up. "My valet and I will remain here until my parents leave in a sennight. Unless we are in their presence, I expect you to stay out of my sight."

He got up and walked out, his strides long and swift, as if he couldn't stand to stay in the same room with her another moment.

Eleven

WITH THE EASE of long practice, Nicki stood at the mirror, tying a series of intricate knots in his neckcloth, bracing himself to go downstairs. He had expected to dislike the time he spent here with Julianna, he had not expected it to be a week straight out of hell.

Thankfully, the ordeal was almost over; all he had to endure was the opening of Christmas presents tonight. Tomorrow his parents were leaving and he intended to be no more than a quarter of an hour behind them.

At least he had the satisfaction of knowing he had made his mother happy. There was no mistaking the fact that her eyes lit up whenever she saw evidence of affection between himself and Julianna, which had left him no choice except to make certain they gave her plenty of evidence.

To give Julianna credit, she cooperated. She looked at him with soft eyes, smiled back at him, laughed at his jokes, and flirted openly with him. She took his arm when they went in to supper, and walked close to his side; she sat at the foot of the table, glowing with candlelight and wit. She dressed as if pleasing her husband were her first concern, and she could fill out a gown as well as any woman he'd ever known.

She graced his table as well as any properly trained socialite could have done, but more naturally, and with more wit. Christ, she was witty! The dining room rang with laughter when she was present. She was also a wonderful conversationalist, attentive and willing to contribute. She talked of her writing when asked, and even of her grandmother, who'd evidently been closer to her than her mother.

If he didn't know what a fraud she was, if he didn't despise her, Nicki would have been incredibly proud of her. There were times—too many times—that he forgot what she really was. Times when all he could remember was the enchantment of her smile, the kindness she showed his parents, and the way she made him laugh. Twice, he had actually walked past her and started to bend down and press a kiss on her temple because it seemed so natural and so right.

All that, of course, owed itself to the unnatural situation he was in right now, with his mother bringing up names for grandchildren that were never going to exist. The Ton's efficient gossip mill had provided her with most of the information that led up to his marriage to Julianna, but despite that, his mother had insisted on drawing her own conclusions. She liked Julianna tremendously, and she made it abundantly clear. She'd actually brought little paintings of Nicki when he was young to show her. She knew she had little time left to spend with her new daughter-in-law and she was evidently determined to make the most of every moment, because she wanted Julianna there—and, of course, Nicki—with her whenever she was downstairs, which seemed to be nearly all the time.

Last night, Julianna had been sitting with her hip on the arm of his chair, her trim derrierre practically on his arm. His mother was describing some childhood antic of Nicki's and the whole family was laughing. Julianna laughed so hard she slid sideways into his lap, which made her blush gorgeously. She got up quickly enough, but Nicki's traitorous body had been reacting to the temptation of her before that, and there was little chance she hadn't noticed his erection when she squirmed off his lap.

He hated himself for his body's reaction to her. If he'd been able to keep his hands off her in the first place, he wouldn't be in this untenable situation. Finished with the neckcloth, Nicki turned as his valet held up his wine-colored velvet evening jacket. He shrugged into the sleeves, bracing himself for the last—and hopefully easiest—of the nightly ordeals as a "family."

It hit him then, that there would never be another family Christmas, not for him, and he stiffened his shoulders against the hurt of that knowledge.

At least by putting on this act with Julianna, he had made his mother feel reassured. She completely believed that he was happily married, sleeping with his wife, and diligently attempting to get heirs.

By this time tomorrow, he would be on his way to his house in Devon.

"Nicki will be on his way somewhere else as soon as our coach is clear of the drive," Nicki's mother told his father, as they dressed to go downstairs for supper.

In answer he pressed a kiss atop her head as he fastened a diamond necklace around her throat. "You cannot do more than you have, my dear. Don't vex yourself, it isn't good for your heart."

"It isn't good for my heart to know that, after years of associations with an endless string of unsuitable females, Nicki has managed to marry a female who is perfect for him, and for me, I might add—and he won't share a bed with her!"

"Please," he teased, sounding scandalized, "do not tell me you've stooped to asking the servants."

"I don't have to ask," she said sadly. "I have eyes. If he were sleeping with Julianna, she would not be watching him with that look of helpless longing in her eyes. That young woman is in love with him."

"You cannot make Nicholas feel something for her."

"Oh, he feels something alright. When he forgets he hates her, he is thoroughly delighted with her, you can see that. She's beautiful and enchanting," she added as she slowly stood up, "and I would make you a wager that he found her to be all those things, and more, the night of that dreadful masquerade."

"Perhaps," he said noncommittally.

"You know he had to have done! Nicholas may have a long history of defying propriety in his personal life, but there has never been a breath of scandal that involves anyone else. He would never have taken Julianna to his bedchamber when he was a guest in someone's house unless he were thoroughly besotted with her."

Since he couldn't argue that logic, her husband smiled reassuringly. "Perhaps everything will work out, then."

His wife's shoulders sagged. "I've thought of saying something to Julianna to encourage her efforts, but if she knew I was aware of her situation, she'd be mortified." She placed a hand upon his arm. "It would take a miracle to bring them together."

Twelve

ALONE IN HER BEDCHAMBER, Julianna stood at her dressing table, the box of letters she'd written to her grandmother in her shaking hands, the Christmas presents she'd received that night on the bed. Nicki intended to leave tomorrow, he'd told her that the day he arrived, and the butler had inadvertently confirmed it yesterday.

Nicki and his parents had been very generous to her, though Nicki's gifts were completely impersonal and only for appearances. He had given his parents their presents as if they came from Julianna as well, but it wasn't the same. And when the moment came for Nicki to open his gifts, there had been nothing there from Julianna—a fact which he'd explained away by saying she wanted to give it to him later. He'd even managed to imply with a smile that she wanted to be private with him when she gave it to him.

But the truth was, Julianna had given no gifts to any of them, because she had nothing to give . . . nothing except the contents of the box she was holding. She had that to give to Nicki. In the last week, she'd heard him called "Nicki" so much that she'd even started to think of him in that way. She'd also done everything she could think of to make him notice her, to make him see her in a different light. She'd flirted outrageously, spent ages on her hair and deliberated for an hour over what she ought to wear. And there had been a few times, when she thought she caught him watching her . . . times when he looked at her in the same way he'd done when he took her to his bedchamber that long ago night . . . as if he wanted to kiss her.

She was in love with him, she'd learned that during this wonderful, agonizing week with him. She'd learned other things, too, that made it seem essential to make one more attempt to heal the breach between them. First and foremost, according to Nicki's mother, Nicki loved children and doted on his nieces. He wanted children, she said, while Nicki's mother was hoping specifically for a grandson to carry on the family name. As things stood now, all that was impossible. Because of Julianna. She had caused this nightmare, and if there was any way to repair the damage she would do it. The scandal of a divorce would taint the whole family, not merely Julianna. Besides, there had only been a handful granted in the last fifty years anyway, so they were married for life.

An *empty childless* life, unless she did something, and there was only one thing left that she hadn't already done. She had not shown him the letters. They were the only "evidence" she could offer Nicki that she hadn't planned their meeting at the masquerade, nor schemed to trap him into marriage.

The problem was that she could not let him see the evidence without simultaneously letting him see all of herself . . . Everything she had been and wasn't and wanted to be. It was all in there, and once he read it, she would be more nakedly vulnerable than she had ever been in her life. It was still fairly early, and she could hear Nicki moving about. Uttering a fervent prayer that this would work, Juliana walked over to the adjoining door that connected both suites and knocked.

Nicki got up and opened the door, took one look at what she was wearing and nearly slammed it shut in self-defense. Clad in a cherry velvet dressing robe with a deep oval neck and her hair tumbling about her shoulders like molten gold, Julianna Skeffington DuVille was almost irresistible. "What is it?" he snapped, backing up.

"I—I have something to give you," she said, moving toward him in a halo of shimmering hair, alluring skin, and rich velvet. "Here, take it."

Nicki glanced at her and then at it. "What is it?"

"Take it, please. Just take it."

"Why in hell should I?"

"Because it's—it's a present—a Christmas present from me to you."

"I don't want anything from you, Julianna."

"But you do want children!" she said, looking almost as stunned by that announcement as he felt.

"I don't need you in order to sire children," he said contemptuously.

She paled at that, but persevered. "Any others wouldn't be legitimate."

"I can legitimize them later. Now get out of here!"

"Damn you," Julianna choked out, tossing the box that contained her heart and soul onto the table in front of the sofa. "I did not set out to trap you at the masquerade. When I asked you to ruin me, I thought you were someone else!"

A slow, sarcastic smiled crossed his saturnine face. "Really," he drawled in a scathing voice, "who did you think I was."

"God!" Julianna burst out tearily, so miserable and so insane about him that she almost stamped her foot. "I thought you were God! The proof is in that box, in the letters I wrote to my grandmother. My mother had them sent to me here."

She whirled on her heel and fled. Ignoring the box, Nicki fixed himself a drink, carried it over to the sofa, and picked up the book he'd left lying there when he answered her knock. He opened it to the first page, then glanced at the box of letters. Out of sheer curiosity to see what ploy his clever and imaginative young wife had concocted this time, he decided to read one of the letters instead.

The one on top was dated last spring, and he presumed he was supposed to start there, though he'd never set eyes on Julianna Skeffington as long ago as that.

Dear Grandmother,

I met someone in the park today and made such a cake of myself, I can hardly bear to think of it. There's always so much gossip about gentlemen in London—about how handsome one of them is supposed to be, and it's always such a disappointment when you see them. And then I saw Nicholas DuVille . . . He was beautiful, Grandmama . . . so beautiful. Hard, too, and cold, at least on the surface, but I think he laughed at what I said when I walked away. If he did, then he can't be hard at all, merely cautious.

Two hours later a log fell from the grate and crashed in an explosion of orange sparks as Nicki laid the last letter aside, then he picked up the one that he had already read twice, and he read the same lines that had filled him with self-loathing.

I know how ashamed you are of me, Grandmother. I only meant to dance those three dances with him, so that Sir Francis would withdraw his offer . . . I knew I shouldn't let him kiss me, I knew it, but if you'd ever been kissed by Nicholas DuVille, you'd understand. If you'd ever seen his smile or heard him laugh, you'd understand. How I yearn to see his smile and hear his laughter again. I long to make things right somehow. I yearn and I yearn and I yearn. And then I cry . . .

With her hip perched on the window seat, Julianna stared into the frosty night, her arms wrapped around her midriff as if she could keep out the chill that spread deeper and deeper as each moment passed and he didn't appear. Lifting her finger to the cold pane, she drew a circle, and another inside that one. As she began the third one, an image moved slowly into the center of it—a man in shirtsleeves, his hands shoved into his trousers pockets, coming toward her, and Julianna's heart began to pound in deep, painful beats.

He stopped close behind her and Julianna waited, searching his face in the window because she was afraid of what she'd see—or not see—if she turned and saw it clearly.

"Julianna." His deep voice was rough with emotion.

Julianna drew a shaking breath and slowly turned her head, watching a somber smile twist his lips as his gaze met hers and held it.

"When you were thinking I was God, and then the devil, would you like to know what I was thinking about you?"

Julianna swallowed over a knot of unbearable tension and nodded.

"I thought you were an angel."

Unable to move or breathe, she waited for him to indicate how he felt about her *now*.

Nicki told her. Holding her gaze, he said solemnly, "I yearn, too, Julianna."

Julianna stood up, took one step forward, and found herself crushed against him, his arms like iron bands around her. His mouth seized hers with gentle violence, his hands shifting over her back and sides in a possessive caress, pressing her ever tighter to his chest and hips and legs. Slowly, tantalizingly, he coaxed her lips to part, and when they did, he deepened the kiss. He kissed her until Julianna was breathless and leaning into him, fitting her body to his rigid length, her arms wrapped around his neck to hold him closer. When he finally broke the contact, he kissed her cheek and the corner of her eye and her temple, then he laid his jaw against her hair. "I yearn," he whispered tenderly. "I yearn."

Against her cheek, his chest felt warm and hard. Julianna waited for him to kiss her again. Shy and uncertain, she set about to make it happen again by sliding her own hands along his spine, and when that only made him hold her closer, she took a more direct means.

Tipping her head back, she gazed into his heavy-lidded, smoldering eyes and slowly slid her hands up his chest in an open invitation, watching the banked fires in his eyes begin to burn.

Nicki accepted the invitation by sliding his fingers into the hair at her nape, holding her mouth within his reach as he lowered his head and whispered gruffly, "God, how I yearn . . ."

Epilogue

THE SILK-UPHOLSTERED walls of the grand salon at
Nicholas DuVille's stately country house near London
were lined with priceless paintings by the great masters
and furnished with treasures that had graced palaces. It
was occupied at the moment by its owner and his four
closest friends—Whitney and Clayton Westmoreland
and Stephen and Sheridan Westmoreland. Also present
on this momentous occasion were the owner's parents—Eugenia and Henri DuVille. The seventh guest
was the Dowager Duchess of Claymore who, in addition to being a particular friend of the senior DuVilles,
had the honor of being the mother of both Clayton and
Stephen.

On this particular day, the guests themselves were
seated in two distinct groups in the vast room. One
group was comprised of the older parents, namely
Eugenia, Henri, and the Dowager Duchess. The other
group was comprised of Nicholas DuVille's four
friends, who were also parents, but, of course, younger
ones.

The seventh occupant of the room, Nicholas
DuVille, was not seated with a group, because he was
not a parent.

He was waiting to become one, momentarily.

His two male friends, who had endured and survived
this nerve-wracking wait were rather enjoying watching
him suffer. They were enjoying it, because Nicholas

DuVille was famous among the members of the elite aristocracy for his incomparable ability to remain supremely unruffled, and even amused, in situations that made equally sophisticated gentlemen sweat and swear.

Today, however, that legendary self-control was not in evidence. He was standing at the window, his right hand absently rubbing the tense muscles at the back of his neck. He was standing there because he had already paced across the carpet often enough to make his own mother laughingly tell him that she was becoming exhausted just watching him do that.

Since her heart had been so weak a year ago that she could not walk up a few stairs, and since no one understood how that same heart was now strong enough to allow her to do that and much more, her restless son ceased his pacing at once. But not his worrying.

His two friends eyed his taut back with amusement and sympathy—more of the first and less of the latter, actually—because Nicholas DuVille had once been vastly admired by their own wives for his supreme nonchalance. "As I recall," Stephen Westmoreland lied with a wink, "Clay had a meeting with some business associates while Whitney was in childbed. Afterward, I think we went over to White's for a few hands of highstakes whist."

Clayton Westmoreland looked over his shoulder at the silent-father-to-be. "Nick, would you like to run over to White's? We could be back by late tonight or early tomorrow."

"Don't be absurd," came the short reply.

"If I were you, I'd go," Stephen Westmoreland advised with a grin. "Once I spread the word that you paced like a caged lion and behaved like an ordinary lunatic, you won't be able to show your face in White's. The management will pull your membership. A pity, too, because you used to add a certain style to the place. Shall I use my influence and see if they'll let you sit in the window now and then, just for old times sake?"

"Stephen?"

"Yes, Nick?"

"Go to hell."

Clayton interceded, his tone deceptively solemn. "How about a chess game? It will help pass the time."

No reply.

"We could play for stakes that would keep your mind on the game. That Rembrandt over there against my son's most recent drawing of Whitney wearing a bucket on her head?"

Whitney and Sheridan, having failed to silence their husbands, got up in unison and walked toward the father-to-be. "Nicki," Whitney said, "it takes time."

"Not this long, it doesn't!" he said shortly. "Whitticomb said it would be over two hours ago."

"I know," Sheridan put in. "And if it's any consolation, Stephen was so upset when our son was born three months ago, that he called poor Dr. Whitticomb an 'incompetent antique' for not being able to do something to help me get it over with sooner."

That information caused Clayton to give his brother a look of amused censure. "Poor Whitticomb," he said. "I'm surprised at you, Stephen. He's an excellent physician, but you can't predict childbirth to the moment. He was with Whitney for nearly twelve hours."

"Really?" Stephen mocked. "And I suppose *you* thanked him very much for not rushing things along, and letting you wait downstairs hoping to God you still had a wife."

"I said something like that to him, yes," Clayton said, looking at the glass in his hand to hide his smile.

"You certainly did," Dr. Whitticomb agreed, startling everyone as he walked into the room, smiling and drying his hands on a white cloth. "But several hours before you said that, you threatened to throw me out on my—er—nether region and do the midwifing yourself."

He sent a reassuring smile at Nicki who was searching his face with narrowed eyes. "There are some very tired people upstairs who had a bit of a difficult time of it, but they would very much like to see you—" He stopped talking and grinned as the new father strode past him without a word and bounded up the stairs, then he turned toward the new grandparents who were waiting to discover whether the new arrival was boy or girl.

Somewhere far above and beyond the world where all this had taken place, Sarah Skeffington smiled down upon the proceedings, pleased with the way she had used the three small miracles each new arrival in her world was granted. There were limits and parameters on the use of these miracles, which were set by the true Maker of Miracles, but He had approved each one, including the restoration of Madame DuVille's health so that she could see her grandson.

Unaware of all that, Julianna sat propped upon her pillows, writing a letter to her grandmother.

My dearest Grandmother,
Five days ago, our son was born and we have named him John. Nicki is so proud of him, and he is utterly besotted with John's twin sister.
We have named her Sarah, after you.
You are always in my thoughts and in my heart . . .

Jude Deveraux

Change of Heart

One

THE MAN BEHIND the desk looked at the boy across from him with a mixture of envy and admiration. Only twelve years old, yet the kid had a brain that people would kill to have. I mustn't appear too eager, he thought. Must keep calm. We want him at Princeton—preferably chained to a computer and not allowed out for meals.

Ostensibly, he had been sent to Denver to interview several scholarship candidates, but the truth was, this boy was the only one who the admissions office was truly interested in, and the meeting had been set to the boy's convenience. The department dean had arranged with an old friend to borrow office space that was in a part of town close to the boy's very middle-class house so he could get there by bike.

"Ah hem," he said, clearing his throat and frowning at the papers. He deepened his voice. Better not let the kid know that he was only twenty-five and that if he messed up this assignment he could be in serious trouble with his advisers.

"You are quite young," the man said, trying to sound as old as possible, "and there will be difficulties, but I think we can handle your special circumstances. Princeton likes to help the young people of America. And—"

"What kind of equipment do you have? What will I have to work with? There are other schools making me offers."

As the man looked at the boy, he thought someone should have strangled him in his crib. Ungrateful little—"I'm sure that you'll find what we have adequate, and if we do not have everything you need we can make it available."

The boy was tall for his age but thin, as though he were growing too fast for his weight to catch up with him. For all that he had one of the great brains of the century, he looked like something out of Tom Sawyer: sandy hair that no comb could tame, freckles across skin that would never tan, dark blue eyes behind glasses big enough to be used as a windshield on a Mack truck.

Elijah J. Harcourt, the file said. IQ over 200. Had made much progress on coming up with a computer that could *think*. Artificial intelligence. You could tell the computer what you wanted to do and the machine could figure out how to do it. As far as anyone could tell, the boy was putting *his* prodigious brain inside a computer. The future uses of such an instrument were beyond comprehension.

Yet here the smug little brat sat, not grateful for what was being offered to him but demanding more. The man knew he was risking his own career, but he couldn't stand the hesitancy of the boy. Standing, he shoved the papers back into his briefcase. "Maybe you should think over our offer," he said with barely controlled anger. "We don't make offers like this very often. Shall we say that you're to make your decision by Christmas?"

As far as the man could tell, the boy showed no emotion. Cold little bugger, the man thought. Heart as cold as a computer chip. Maybe he wasn't real at all but one of his own creations. Somehow, putting the boy down made him feel better about his own IQ, which was a "mere" 122.

Quickly, he shook, the boy's hand, and as he did so he realized that in another year the boy would be taller than he was. "I'll be in touch," he said and left the room.

Eli worked hard to control his inner shaking. Although he seemed so cool on the exterior, inside he was doing cartwheels. Princeton! he thought. Contact with *real* scientists! Talk with people who wanted to know more about life than the latest football scores!

Slowly, he walked out the door, giving the man time to get away. Eli knew that the man hadn't liked him, but he was used to that. A long time ago Eli had learned to be very, very cautious with people. Since he was three he had known he was "different" from other kids. At five his mother had taken him to school to be tested, to see whether he fit into the redbirds or the bluebirds reading group. Busy with other students and parents, the teacher had told Eli to get a book from the shelf and read it to her. She had meant one of the many pretty picture books. Her intention had been to find out which children had been read to by their parents and which had grown up glued to a TV.

Like all children, Eli had wanted to impress his teacher, so he'd climbed on a chair and pulled down a college textbook titled *Learning Disabilities* that the teacher kept on a top shelf, then quietly went to stand beside her and began softly to read from page one. Since Eli was a naturally solitary child and his mother did not push him to do what he didn't want to do, he had spent most of his life in near seclusion. He'd had no idea that reading from a college textbook when he was a mere five years old was unusual. All he'd wanted to do was to pass the reading test and get into the top reading group.

"That's fine, Eli," his mother had said after he'd read half a page. "I think Miss Wilson is going to put you with the redbirds. Aren't you, Miss Wilson?"

Even though he was only five, Eli had recognized the wide-eyed look of horror on the teacher's face. Her expression had said, *What* do I do with this freak?

Since his entry into school, Eli had learned about being "different." He'd learned about jealousy and being excluded and not fitting in with the other children. Only with his mother was he "normal." His mother didn't think he was unusual or strange; he was just *hers*.

Now, years later, when Eli left his meeting with the man from Princeton, he was still shaking, and when he saw Chelsea he gave her one of his rare smiles. When Eli was six he'd met Chelsea Hamilton, who was not as smart as he was, of course, but near enough that he could talk to her. In her way Chelsea was as much a freak as Eli was, for Chelsea was rich—very, very rich—and even by six she'd found that people wanted to know her for what they could get from her rather than her personality. At six the children had taken one look at each other, the two oddities in the boring little classroom, and they'd become eternal friends.

"Well!" Chelsea demanded, bending her head to look into Eli's face. She was six months older than he, and until this year she'd always been taller. But now Eli was rapidly overtaking her.

"What are you doing in this building?" Eli asked. "You aren't supposed to be here." Smugly, he was making her wait for his news.

"You're slipping, brain-o. My father owns this place." She tossed her long, dark, glossy hair. "And he's friends with the dean at Princeton. I've known about the meeting for two weeks." At twelve, Chelsea was already on the way to being a beauty. Her problems in life were going to be the stuff of dreams: too tall, too thin, too smart, too rich. Their houses were only ten minutes apart, but in value, they were miles apart. Eli's house would fit into Chelsea's marble foyer.

When Eli didn't respond, she looked straight ahead. "Dad called last night and I cried so much at missing him that he's buying us a new CD-ROM. Maybe I'll let you see it."

Eli smiled again. Chelsea hadn't realized that she'd said "us," meaning the two of them. She was great at the emotional blackmail of her parents, who spent most of their lives traveling around the world, leaving the family business to Chelsea's older siblings. A few tears of anguish and her parents gave her anything money could buy.

"Princeton wants me," Eli said as they emerged into the almost constant sunshine of Denver, its clean streets stretching before them. The autumn air was crisp and clear.

"I *knew* it!" she said, throwing her head back in exultation. "When? For what?"

"I'm to go in the spring semester, just to get my feet wet, then a summer session. If my work is good enough I can enter full time next fall." For a moment he turned to look at her, and for just that second he let his guard down and Chelsea saw how very much he wanted this. Eli hated passionately the idea of high school, of having to sit through days of classes with a bunch of semiliterate louts who took great pride in their continuing ignorance. This program would give Eli the opportunity to skip all those grades and get on with something useful.

"That gives us the whole rest of the year to work," she said. "I'll get Dad to buy us—"

"I can't go," Eli said.

It took a moment for those words to register with Chelsea. "You can't go to Princeton?" she whispered. "Why not?" Chelsea had never considered, if she wanted something—whether to buy it or do it—that she wouldn't be able to.

When Eli looked at her, his face was full of anguish. "Who's going to take care of Mom?" he asked softly.

Chelsea opened her mouth to say that Eli had to think of himself first, but she closed it again. Eli's mom, Randy, *did* need taking care of. She had the softest heart in the world, and if anyone had a problem Randy always had room to listen and love. Chelsea never liked to think that she needed anything as soppy as a mother, but there had been many times over the years when she'd flung herself against the soft bosom of Eli's ever-welcoming mother.

However, it was because of Randy's sweetness that she needed looking after. His mother was like a lamb living in a world of hungry wolves. If it weren't for Eli's constant vigilance . . . Well, Chelsea didn't like to think what would have happened to his mother. Just look at the man she'd married, the horrid man who was Eli's father: a gambler, a con artist, a promiscuous liar.

"When do you have to give them your answer?" Chelsea asked softly.

"My birthday," Eli answered. It was one of his little vanities that he always referred to Christmas as his birthday. Eli's mom said that Eli was her Christmas gift from God, so she was never going to cheat Eli because she'd been lucky enough to have him on Christmas Day. So every Christmas, Eli had a pile of gifts under a tree and another pile on a table with a big, gaudy birthday cake, a cake that had no hint of anything to do with Christmas.

In silence, the two of them walked down Denver's downtown streets, forgoing the trolley that ran though the middle of town. Chelsea knew that Eli needed to think, and he did that best by walking or riding his bike. She knew without asking that Eli would never abandon his mother. If it came to a choice between Princeton and taking care of his mother, Eli would take care of the person he loved best. For all that Eli managed to appear cool and calculating, Chelsea knew that when it came to the two people he loved the most—her and his mother—inside, Eli was marshmallow cream.

"You know," Chelsea said brightly, "maybe you're overreacting. Maybe your mother can get along without you." "Without us," she almost said. "Who took care of her before you were born?"

Eli gave her a sideways look. "No one, and look what happened to her."

"Your father," Chelsea said heavily. She hesitated as

she thought about the matter. "They've been divorced for two years now. Maybe your mother will remarry and her new husband will take care of her."

"Who will she marry? The last man she went out with ended up 'forgetting' his wallet, so Mom paid for dinner and a tank full of gas. A week later *I* found out he was married."

Unfortunately, Randy's generosity didn't just extend to children but to every living creature. Eli said that if it were left up to his mother, there wouldn't need to be a city animal shelter because all the unwanted animals in Denver would live with them. For a moment, Chelsea had an image of sweet Randy surrounded by wounded animals and uneducated men asking her for money. For Chelsea, "uneducated men" was the worst image she could conjure.

"Maybe if you tell her about the offer, she'll come up with a solution," Chelsea said helpfully.

Eli's face became fierce. "My mother would sacrifice her *life* for me. If she knew about his offer, she'd personally escort me to Princeton. My mother cares only about me and never about herself. My mother—"

Chelsea rolled her eyes skyward. In every other aspect of life Eli had the most purely scientific brain she'd ever encountered, but when it came to his mother there was no reasoning with him. Chelsea also thought Randy was a lovely woman, but she wasn't exactly ready for sainthood. For one thing, she was thoroughly undisciplined. She ate too much, read too many books that did not improve one's mind, and wasted too much time on frivolous things, like making Eli and Chelsea Halloween costumes. Of course, neither of them ever told her that they thought Halloween was a juvenile holiday. Instead of tramping the streets, asking for candy, they would go to Chelsea's house, work on their computers while dripping artificial blood, and send the butler out to purchase candy that they'd later show to Eli's mom so she'd think they were "normal" kids.

Only once had Chelsea dared tell Eli that she thought it was a bit absurd for them to sit at their computes wearing uncomfortable and grotesque costumes while calculating logarithms. Eli had said, "My mother made these for us to wear," and that had been the *final* decree; the matter was never mentioned again.

Two

As ELI RODE his bike onto the cracked, weedy, concrete drive of his mother's house, he caught a glimpse of the taillights of his father's car as it scurried out of sight.

"Deadbeat!" Eli said under his breath, knowing that his father must have been watching for him so he could run away as soon as he saw his son.

Every time Eli thought of the word "father" his stomach clenched. Leslie Harcourt had never been a father to him, nor a husband to his wife. Miranda. The man had spent his life trying to make his family believe he was "important." Too important to talk to his family; too important to go anywhere with his wife and child; too important to give them any time or attention.

According to Leslie Harcourt, other people were the

ones who really counted in life. "My friends *need* me," Eli used to hear his father say over and over. His mother would say "But Leslie, *I* need you too. Eli needs school clothes and there are no groceries in the house and my car has been broken for three weeks. We *need* food and we *need* clothes."

Eli would watch as his father got that look on his face, as though he were being enormously patient with someone who couldn't understand the simplest concepts. "My friend has broken up with his girlfriend and he has to have someone to talk to and I'm the only one. Randy, he's in pain. Don't you understand? Pain! I *must* go to him."

Eli had heard his father say this same sort of thing a thousand times. Sometimes his mother would show a little spunk and say "Maybe if your friends cried on the shoulders of their girlfriends, they wouldn't *be* breaking up."

But Leslie Harcourt never listened to anyone except himself—and he was a master at figuring out how to manipulate other people so he could get as much out of them as possible. Leslie knew that his wife, Randy, was softhearted; it was the reason he'd married her. Randy forgave anyone anything, and all Leslie had to do was say "I love you" every month or so and Randy forgave him whatever.

And in return for those few words, Randy gave Leslie security. She gave him a home that he contributed little or no money to and next to no time; he had no responsibilities either to her or to his son. Most important, she provided him with an excuse to give to all his women as to why he couldn't marry them. He invariably "forgot" to mention that all these "friends" who "needed" him were women—and mostly young, with lots of hair and long legs.

But Eli and Chelsea had put an end to Leslie and all his Helpless Hannahs two years ago. When he was very young, Eli had not known what a "father" was, except that it was a word he heard other children use, as in "My father and I worked on the car this weekend." Eli rarely saw his father, and he never did anything with him.

It was Chelsea who first saw Eli's father with the tall, thin, blonde bimbo as they were slipping into an afternoon matinee at the local mall. And Chelsea, using the invisibility of being a child, sat in front of them, twirling chewing gum (which she hated) and trying to look as young as possible, as she listened avidly to every word Eli's father said.

"I would like to marry you, Heather, you know that. I love you more than life itself, but I'm a married man with a child. If it weren't for that, I'd be running with you to the altar. You're a woman any man would be proud to call his wife. But you don't know what Randy is like. She's utterly helpless without me. She can hardly turn off the faucets without me there to do it for her. And then there's my son. Eli needs me so much. He cries himself to sleep if I'm not there to kiss him goodnight, so you can see why we have to meet during the day."

"Then he started kissing her neck," Chelsea reported.

When Eli heard this account he had to blink a few times to clear his mind. The sheer enormity of this lie of his father's was stunning. As long as he could remember, his father had *never* kissed him goodnight. In fact, Eli wasn't sure his father even knew where his bedroom was located in the little house that needed so much repair.

When Eli recovered himself, he looked at Chelsea. "What are we going to do?"

The smile Chelsea gave him was conspiratorial. "Robin and Marian," she whispered, and he nodded. Years earlier, they called themselves Robin Hoods. Robin Hood righted wrongs and did good deeds and helped the underdog (or at least that's what the legend said).

It was Randy who'd first called them Robin and Marian, after some soppy movie she loved to watch repeatedly on video. Laughingly, she'd called them Robin and Marian Les Jeunes, French for "youths," and they'd kept the name in secret.

Only the two of them knew what they did: They collected letterhead stationery from corporations, law firms, doctors' offices, wherever, then used a very expensive publishing computer system to duplicate the type fonts, then sent people letters as though from the offices. They sent letters on law-office stationery to the fathers of children at school who didn't pay child support. They sent letters of thanks to unappreciated employees from the heads of big corporations. They once got back an old woman's $400 from a telephone scammer.

Only once did they nearly get into trouble. A boy at school had teeth that were rotting, but his father was too cheap to take him to the dentist. Chelsea and Eli found out that the father was a gambler, so they wrote to him, offering free tickets to a "secret" (because it was illegal) national dental lottery. He would receive a ticket with every fifty dollars he spent on his children's teeth. So all three of his children had several hundred dollars' worth of work done, and Chelsea and Eli dutifully sent him beautiful red-and-gold, hand-painted lottery tickets. The problem came when they had to write the man a letter saying his tickets did not have the winning numbers. The man went to the dentist, waving the letters and the tickets, and demanded his money back. The poor dentist had had to endure months of the man's winking at him in conspiracy while he'd worked on the children's teeth, and now he was being told he was going to be sued because of some lottery he'd never heard of.

In order to calm the man down, Chelsea and Eli had to reveal themselves to the son who they'd helped in secret and get him to steal the letters from his father's night table. Chelsea then sent the man one of her father's gold watches (he had twelve of them) in order to get him to shut up.

Later, when they weighed the good they had done—of fixing the children's teeth—against the near exposure, they decided to continue being Robin and Marian Les Jeunes.

"So what are we going to do with your father?" Chelsea asked, and she could see that Eli had no idea.

"I'd like to get rid of him," Eli said. "He makes my mother cry. But—"

"But what?"

"But she says she still loves him."

At that, Chelsea and Eli looked at each other without comprehension. They knew they loved each other, but then they also *liked* each other. How could anyone love a man like Leslie Harcourt? There wasn't anything at all likable about him.

"I would like to give my mother what she wants," Eli said.

"Mel Gibson?" Chelsea asked, without any intent at humor. Randy had once said that what she truly wanted in life was Mel Gibson—because he was a family man, she'd added, and no other reason.

"No," Eli said. "I'd like to give her my father as a real father, the kind she likes."

For a moment they looked at each other in puzzlement. Eli had recently been trying to make a computer think, and they both knew that that would be easier than trying to make Leslie Harcourt stay home and putter in the garage.

"This is a question for the Love Expert," Chelsea said, making Eli nod. "Love Expert" was what they called Eli's mom because she read romantic novels by the thousands. After each one she gave Eli a brief synopsis of the plot, then he fed it into his computer data banks and made charted graphs. He could quote all sorts of statistics, such as that 18 percent of all romances are medieval, then he could break that number down into fifty-year sections. He could also quote about plots, how many had fires and shipwrecks, how many had heroes who'd been hurt by one woman (who always turned out to be a bad person) and so hated all other women. According to Eli the sheer repetition of the books fascinated him, but his mother said that love was wonderful no matter how many times she read about it.

So Eli and Chelsea consulted Randy, telling her that Chelsea's older sister's husband was having an affair with a girl who wanted to marry him. he didn't want to marry her, but neither could he seem to break up with her.

"Ah," Randy said, "I just read a book like that."

Here Eli gave Chelsea an I-knew-she'd-know look.

"The mistress tried to make the husband divorce his wife, so she told him she was going to bear his child. But the ploy backfired and the man went back to his wife, who by that time had been rescued by a tall, dark, and gorgeous man, so the husband was left without either woman." For a moment Randy looked dreamily into the distance. "Anyway, that's what happened in the book, but I'm afraid real life isn't like a romance novel. More's the pity. I'm sorry, Chelsea, that I can't be of more help, but I don't seem to know exactly what to do with men in real life."

Chelsea and Eli didn't say any more, but after a few days of research, they sent a note to Eli's father on the letterhead of a prominent physician, stating that Miss Heather Allbright was pregnant with his child and his office had been directed to send the bills to him, Leslie Harcourt. Sending the bills had been Chelsea's idea, because she believed that all bills on earth should be directed to fathers.

But things did not work out as Chelsea and Eli had planned. When Leslie Harcourt confronted his mistress with the lie that she was expecting his child, the young woman didn't so much as blink an eye, but broke down and told him it was true. From what Eli and Chelsea could find out—and Eli's mother did everything she could to keep Eli from knowing anything—Heather threatened to sue Leslie for everything he had if he didn't divorce Randy and marry her.

Randy, understanding as always, said they should all think of the unborn baby and that she and Eli would be fine, so of course she'd give Leslie the speediest divorce possible. Leslie said it would especially speed up matters if he had to pay only half the court costs and only minimal child support until Eli was eighteen. Generously, he said he'd let Randy have the house if he could have anything inside it that could possibly be of value, and of course she would assume the mortgage payments.

When the dust had settled, Chelsea and Eli were in shock at what they had caused, too afraid to tell anyone the truth—but then if Heather *was* going to have a baby, then they *had* told the truth. One week after Eli's father married Heather, she miscarried and there was no baby.

Eli had been afraid his mother would fall apart at this news, but instead she had laughed. "Imagine that," she'd said. "But Miss Clever Heather *did* get her baby, whether she knows it yet or not."

Eli never could get his mother to explain that remark, but he was so glad she wasn't hurt by the divorce that he didn't mention the "miscarriage" again.

So now Eli had just seen the taillight of his father's car pull away, and he knew without a doubt that his father had been there trying to weasel out of child-support payments. Leslie Harcourt made about seventy-five thousand a year as a car salesman—he could sell anything to anyone—while his mother barely pulled down twenty thousand as a practical nurse. An old candy striper is how Randy described her job. "A glorified bed pan emptier" is what she said she was. "I hold hands and make people feel good. Unfortunately the don't pay people much for that. Eli, sweetheart, my only realistic dream for the future is to become a private nurse for some very rich, very sweet old man who wants little more than to eat popcorn and watch videos all day."

Eli had pointed out to her that all the heroines in her romance novels were running corporations while still in their twenties, or else they were waitressing and going to law school at night. That had made Randy laugh. "If all women were like that, who'd be buying the romance novels?"

Eli thought that was a very good consideration. His mother had the unusual ability to see right to the heart of a matter.

"What did he want?" Eli asked the moment he opened the door to the house he shared with his mother.

For a moment Randy grimaced, annoyed that her son had caught his father there. Escaping Eli's ever-watchful eye was like trying to escape a pack of watch-dogs. "Nothing much," she said evasively.

At those words a chill ran down Eli's back. "How much did you give him?"

Randy rolled her eyes skyward.

"You know I'll find out as soon as I reconcile the bank statement. How much did you give him?"

"Young man, you are getting above yourself. The money I earn—"

Eli did some quick calculations in his head. He always knew to the penny how much money his mother had in her checking account—there was no savings account—and how much was in her purse, even to the change. "Two hundred dollars," he said. "You gave him a check for two hundred dollars." That was the maximum she could afford and still pay the mortgage and groceries.

When Randy remained tight-lipped in silence, he

knew he'd hit the amount exactly on the head. He would tell Chelsea later and allow her to congratulate him on his insight.

Eli uttered a curse word under his breath.

"Eli!" Randy said sternly. "I will not allow you to call your father such names." Her face softened. "Sweetheart, you're too young to be so cynical. You must believe in people. I worry that you've been traumatized by your father leaving you without male guidance. And I know you're hiding your true feelings: I know you miss him very much."

Eli, looking very much like an old man, said, "You must be watching TV talk shows again. I do not miss him; I never saw him when you were married to him. My father is a self-centered, selfish bastard."

Randy's mouth tightened into a line that was a mirror of her son's. "Whether that is true or not is irrelevant. He *is* your father."

Eli's expression didn't change. "I'm sure it is too much to hope that you were unfaithful to him and that my real father is actually the king of a small but rich European country."

As always, Randy's face lost it stern look and she laughed. She was as unable to remain angry with Eli as she was to resist the whining and pleading of her ex-husband. She knew Eli would hate for her to say this, but he was very much like his father. Both of them always went after whatever they wanted and allowed nothing to stop them.

No, Eli wouldn't appreciate such an observation in the least.

Eli was so annoyed with his mother for once again allowing Leslie Harcourt to con her out of paying the child support that he couldn't say another word, but turned away and went to his own room. At this moment his father owed six months in back child support. Instead of paying it, he'd come to Randy and shed a few tears, telling her how broke he was, knowing he could get Randy to give him money. Eli knew that his father liked to test his ability to sell at every opportunity. Seeing if he could con Randy was an exercise in salesmanship.

The truth—a truth Randy didn't know—was that Leslie had recently purchased a sixty-thousand-dollar Mercedes, and the payments on that car were indeed stretching him financially. (Eli and Chelsea had been able to tap into a few credit-report data banks and find out all sorts of "confidential" information about people.)

Eli spent thirty minutes in his room, stewing over the perfidy of his father, but when he saw that his mother was outside tending her roses, he went back to the living room and called the man who was his father.

Eli didn't waste time with greetings. "If you don't pay three months' support within twenty-four hours and another three months' within thirty days, I'll put sugar in the gas tank of your new car." He then hung up the phone.

Twenty-two hours later, Leslie appeared at the door of Randy's house with the money. As Eli stood behind his mother, he had to listen to his father give a long, syrupy speech about the goodness of people, about how some people were willing to believe in others, while others had no loyalty in their souls.

Eli stood it for a few minutes, then he looked around his mother and glared at his father until the man quickly left, after loudly telling Randy that he'd have the other three months' support within thirty days. Eli restrained himself from calling out that within thirty days he'd owe not three months' support but four.

When Leslie was gone, Randy turned to her son and smiled. "See, Eli, honey, you must believe in people. I told you your father would come through, and he did. Now, where shall we go for dinner?"

Ten minutes later, Eli was on the phone to Chelsea. "I can*not* go to Princeton," he said softly. "I cannot leave my mother unprotected."

Chelsea didn't hesitate. "Get here fast! We'll meet in Sherwood Forest."

Three

"WHAT ARE WE going to do?" Chelsea whispered. They were sitting side by side on a swing glider in the garden on her parents' twenty-acre estate. It was prime real estate, close to the heart of Denver. Her father had bought four houses and torn down three of them to give himself the acreage. Not that he was ever there to enjoy the land, but he got a lot of joy out of telling people he had twenty acres in the city of Denver.

"I don't know," Eli said. "I can't leave her. I know that. She'd give everything she owned to my father if I weren't there to protect her."

Chelsea had no doubt of this after the story Eli had just told her. And this wasn't the first time Leslie Harcourt had pulled a scam on his sweet ex-wife. "I wish . . ." She trailed off for a moment, then stood up and looked down at Eli, his head bent low as he contemplated what he was giving up by not taking this offer from Princeton. She knew he hated the idea of high school almost as much as he loved the idea of getting on with his computer research.

"I wish we could find a husband for her."

Eli gave a snort. "We've tried, remember? She only likes men like my father, the ones she says 'need' her. They need her money and for her to forgive them."

"I know, but wouldn't it be nice if we could make one of her books she loves so much come true. She would meet a tall, dark billionaire, and he'd—"

"A *billionaire?*"

"Yes," Chelsea said sagely. "My father says that, what with inflation as it is, a millionaire—even a multi-millionaire—isn't worth very much."

Sometimes Eli was vividly reminded of how he and Chelsea differed on money. To him and his mother two hundred dollars was a great deal, but the woman who cut Chelsea's hair charged three hundred dollars a visit.

Chelsea smiled. "You don't happen to know any single billionaires, do you?"

She was teasing, but Eli didn't smile. "Actually, I do. He . . . he's my best friend. Male friend, that is."

At that Chelsea's eyes opened wide. One of the things she loved best about Eli was that he always had the ability to surprise her. No matter how much she thought she knew about him, it wasn't all there was to know. "Where did you meet a billionaire and how did he get to be your friend?"

But Eli just looked at her and said nothing, and when he had that expression on his face, she knew she was not going to get another word out of him.

But it was two days later that Eli called a meeting for the two of them in Sherwood Forest, their name for her father's garden, and Chelsea had never seen such a light in his eyes before. It was almost as though he had a fever.

"What's wrong?" she whispered, knowing it had to be something awful.

When he handed her a newspaper clipping his hand was shaking. Having no idea what to expect, she read it, then knew less than she did before she'd started. It was a small clipping from a magazine about a man named Franklin Taggert, one of the major heads of Montgomery-Taggert Enterprises. He'd been involved in a small accident and his right arm had been broken in two places. Because he had chosen to seclude himself in a cabin hidden in the Rocky Mountains until his arm healed, several meetings and contract finalizations had been postponed.

When Chelsea finished reading, she looked up at Eli in puzzlement. "So?"

"He's my friend," Eli said, in a voice filled with such awe that Chelsea felt a wave of jealousy shoot through her.

"Your *billionaire?*" she asked disdainfully.

But Eli didn't seem to notice her odd reaction as he began to pace in front of her. "It was your idea," he said. "Sometimes, Chelsea, I forget that you are as much a female as my mother."

Chelsea was not at all sure that she liked this statement.

"You said I should find her a husband, that I should find her a rich man to take care of her. But how can I trust the care of my mother to just any man? He must be a man of insight as well as money."

Chelsea's eyebrows had risen to high up in her hairline. This was a whole new Eli she was seeing.

"The logical problem has been how to introduce my mother to a wealthy man. She is a nurse, and twenty-one percent of all romance novels at one point or another have a wounded hero and a heroine who nurses him back to health, with true love always following. So it follows that her being a nurse would give her an introduction to rich, wounded men; but since she works at a public hospital and rich men tend to hire private nurses, she has not met them."

"I see. So now you plan to get your mother the job of nursing this man. But Eli," she said gently, "how do you get this man to hire your mother? How do you know they will fall in love if they do meet? I think falling in love has to do with physical vibrations." She'd read this last somewhere, and it seemed to explain what her dopey sisters were always talking about.

Eli raised one eyebrow. "How could any man *not* fall in love with my mother? My problem has been keeping men away from her, not the other way around."

Chelsea knew better than to comment on that. Making Eli see his mother as a normal human being was impossible. He seemed to think she had a golden glow around her. "Then how . . ." she hesitated, then smiled. "Robin and Marian Les Jeunes."

"Yes. I think Mr. Taggert is at the cabin alone. We find out where it is, write my mother a letter hiring her, give her directions, and sent her up there. They will fall in love and he'll take care of her. He is a proper man."

Chelsea blinked at him for a moment. "A . . . proper man?" She could see that Eli wasn't going to tell her another word, but she knew how to handle him. "If you don't tell me how you know this man, I won't help you. I won't do a thing."

Eli knew that she was bluffing. Chelsea had too much curiosity not to go along with any of his projects, but he wanted to tell her how he'd met Frank Taggert. "You remember two years ago when my class went on a field trip to see Montgomery-Taggert Enterprises?"

She didn't remember, but she nodded anyway.

"I wasn't going to go, but at the last moment I decided it might be interesting, so I went." Eli then began to tell Chelsea an extraordinary story.

Eli went on the field trip with his class solely for the purpose of stealing letterhead stationery. He didn't have any from the Montgomery-Taggert industries, and he wanted to be prepared in case they needed it.

As he was standing there, bored out of his mind, with a condescending secretary asking the children if they would like to play with the paper clips, Eli looked across the room to see a man sitting on the edge of a desk talking on the telephone. The man had on a denim shirt, jeans, and cowboy boots; he was dressed like the janitor, but to Eli the man radiated power, like a fire generating heat waves.

Quietly moving about the room, Eli got behind him so the man couldn't see him, then listened to his telephone conversation. It took Eli a moment to realize that the man was making a multimillion-dollar deal. When he talked of "five and twenty," he was actually talking of five *million* and twenty *million*. Dollars.

When the man hung up, Eli started to move away.

"Hear what you wanted to, kid?"

Eli froze in his tracks, his breath held. He couldn't believe the man knew he was there. Most people pay no attention to kids. How did this man know he was there? Or see him?

"Are you too cowardly to face me?"

Eli stood straighter, then walked to stand in front of the man.

"Tell me what you heard."

Since adults seemed to like to think that children could hear only what the adults want them to hear, Eli usually found it expedient to lie. But he didn't lie to this man. He told him everything: numbers, names, places. Whatever he could remember of the phone conversation he'd just heard.

The man's face had no discernible expression as he looked at Eli. "I saw you skulking about the office. What were you looking for?"

Eli took a deep breath. He and Chelsea had never told an adult about their collection of letterheads, much less what they did with it. But he told this man the truth.

The man's eyes bore into Eli's. "You know that what you're doing is illegal, don't you?"

Eli looked hard back at him. "Yes sir, I do. But we only write letters to people who are hurting others or ignoring their responsibilities. We've written a number of letters to fathers who don't pay the child support they owe."

The man lifted one eyebrow, studied Eli for a moment, then turned to a passing secretary. "Get this young man's name and send him a complete packet of all stationery from all Montgomery-Taggert enterprises. "Get them from Maine and Colorado and Washington State." He looked back at Eli. "And call the foreign offices too. London, Cairo, all of them."

"Yes sir, Mr. Taggert," the secretary said, looking in wonder at Eli. All the employees were terrified of Frank Taggert, yet this child had done something to merit his special consideration.

When Eli got over his momentary shock, he managed to say, "Thank you."

Frank put out his hand to the boy. "My name is Franklin Taggert. Come see me when you graduate from a university and I'll give you a job."

Shaking his hand, Eli managed to say hoarsely, "What should I study?"

"With your mind, you're going to study everything," Frank said as he got off the desk and turned away, then disappeared through a doorway.

For a moment, Eli just stared, but in that moment, with those few words, he felt that his future had been decided. He knew where he was going and how he was going to get there. And for the first time in his life, Eli had a hero.

Four

"AND THEN WHAT?" Chelsea asked.

"He sent the copies of letterhead—you've seen them—I wrote to thank him and he wrote back. And we became friends."

Part of Chelsea wanted to scream that he had betrayed her by not telling her of this. *Two years!* He had kept this from her for two years. But she'd learned that it was no good berating Eli. He kept secrets if he wanted to and seemed to think nothing of it.

"So you want your mother to marry this man. Why did you just come up with this idea now?" She meant her words to be rather spiteful, to get him back for hiding something so interesting from her, but she knew the answer as soon as she asked. Until now Eli had wanted his beloved mother to himself. Her eyes widened. If Eli was willing to turn his mother over to the care of this man he must . . .

"Do you really and truly like him?"

"He is like a father to me," Eli said softly.

"Have you told him about me?"

The way Eli said "Of course" mollified her temper somewhat. "Okay, so how do we get them together? Where is this cabin of his?" She didn't have to ask how they would get his mother up there. All they had to do was write her a letter on Montgomery-Taggert stationery and offer her a nursing job.

"I don't know," Eli answered, "but I'm sure we can find out."

Three weeks later, Chelsea was ready to give up. "Eli," she said in exasperation, "you have to give up. We can't find him."

Eli just set his mouth tighter, but his head was propped in his hands in despair. Three weeks they had spent sending faxes and writing letters to people, hinting that they needed to know where Frank Taggert was. Either people didn't know or they weren't telling.

"I don't know what else we can do," Chelsea said.

"It's getting closer to Christmas by the day and it's getting colder in the mountains. He'll leave soon, and she won't get to meet him."

The first week she'd asked him why he didn't just introduce his mother to Mr. Taggert, and Eli had looked at her as though she were crazy. "They will be polite to each other because of me, but what can they have in common unless they meet on equal ground? Have you learned nothing from my mother's books?"

But now they tried everything and still couldn't get his mother together with Mr. Taggert. "There is one thing we haven't tried yet," Chelsea said.

Eli didn't take his head out of his hands. "There is nothing. I've thought of everything."

"We haven't tried the truth."

Eli turned his head and looked at her. "What truth?"

"My parents were nearly dying for my sister to get married. My mother said my sister was losing her chances because she was getting old. She was nearly thirty. So if this Mr. Taggert is forty, maybe his family is dying to get him married too."

Eli gave her a completely puzzled look.

"Let's make an appointment with one of his brothers and tell him we have a wife for Mr. Taggert and see if he will help us."

When Eli didn't respond, Chelsea frowned. "It's worth a try, isn't it? Come on, stop moping and tell me the name of one of his brothers here in Denver."

"Michael," Eli said. "Michael Taggert."

"Okay, let's make an appointment with him and talk to him."

After a moment's hesitation, Eli turned to his keyboard. "Yes, let's try."

five

MICHAEL TAGGERT LOOKED up from his desk to see his secretary, Kathy, at the door wearing a mischievous grin.

"Remember the letter you received from Mr. Elijah J. Harcourt requesting a meeting today?"

Frowning, Mike gave a curt nod. He was to meet his wife for lunch in thirty minutes, and from the look on Kathy's face there might be some complications that would hold him up. "Yes?"

"He brought his secretary with him," Kathy said, breaking into a wide smile.

Mike couldn't see why a man and his secretary would cause such merriment, but then Kathy stepped aside and Mike saw two kids, both about twelve years old, enter the room behind her. The boy was tall, thin, with huge glasses and eyes so intense he reminded Mike of a hawk. The girl had the easy confidence of what promised to be beauty and, unless he missed his guess, money.

I don't have time for his, Mike thought, and he wondered who'd put these kids up to this visit. Silently, he motioned them to take a seat.

"You're busy and so are we, so I'll get right to the point," Eli said.

Mike had to repress a smile. The boy's manner was surprisingly adult, and he reminded him of someone but Mike couldn't think who.

"I want my mother to marry your brother."

"Ah, I see," Mike said, leaning back in his chair. "And which one of my brothers would that be?"

"The oldest one, Frank."

Mike nearly fell out of his chair. "Frank?" he gasped. His eldest brother was a terror, as precise as a measuring device, and about as warm as Maine in February. "Frank? You want your *mother* to marry Frank?" He leaned forward. "Tell me, kid, you got it in for your mother or what?"

At that Eli came out of his seat, his face red. "Mr. Taggert is a *very* nice man, and you can't say anything against him *or* my mother!"

The girl put her hand on Eli's arm and he instantly sat down, but he turned his head away and wouldn't look at Mike.

"Perhaps I might explain," the girl said, and she introduced herself.

Mike was impressed with the girl as she succinctly told their story, of Eli's offer to go to Princeton but his refusal to leave his mother alone. As she spoke, Mike kept looking at Eli, trying to piece everything together. So the kid wanted a billionaire to take care of his mother. Ambitious brat, wasn't he?

But Mike began to have a change of heart when Eli said, "Don't tell him that. He doesn't *like* his brother."

"Tell me what?" Mike encouraged. "And I love my brother. It's just that he's sometimes hard to take. Are you sure you have the right Frank Taggert?"

At that Eli whipped an envelope from the inside of his suit jacket. Right away Mike recognized it as Frank's private stationery, something he reserved for the family only. It was a way the family had of distinguishing private from business mail. His family frequently joked that Frank never used family stationery for anyone who did not bear the same last name as he did. There was even a rumor that on the rare times he'd sent a note to whichever female was waiting for him at the moment, he'd used business letterhead.

Yet Frank had written this boy a letter on his private stationery.

"May I see it?" Mike asked softly, extending his hand.

Eli started to return the letter to his pocket.

"Go on," Chelsea urged. "This is important." Eli reluctantly handed the letter to Mike.

Slowly, Mike took the single sheet of paper from the envelope and read it. It was handwritten, not typed. To Mike's knowledge, Frank had not handwritten anything since he'd left his university.

My dear Eli,

I was so glad to receive your last letter. Your new theories on artificial intelligence sound magnificent. Yes, I'll have someone check what's already been done.

One of my brother's wives had a baby, a little girl, with cheeks as red as roses. I set up a trust fund for her but told no one.

I'm glad you liked your birthday present, and I'll wear the cuff links you sent me next time I see the president.

How are Chelsea and your mother? Let me

know if your dad ever again refuses to pay child
support. I know a few legal people and I also
know a few thugs. Any man who isn't grateful
to have a son like you deserves to be taught a
lesson.

My love and friendship to you,
Frank

Mike had to read the letter three times, and even
though he was sure it was from Frank, he couldn't
believe it. Frank's only comment when one of his siblings produced yet another child was. "Don't any of
you ever stop?" Yet here he was saying his brother's
new baby had cheeks like roses—which she did.

Mike carefully refolded the letter and inserted it
back into the envelope. Eli nearly snatched it from his
hands.

"Eli wants his mother to meet Mr. Frank Taggert in
a place where they will be equal," Chelsea said. "She is
a nurse, and we thought she could go to this cabin in
the mountains where Mr. Taggert is staying, but we
can't find it."

Mike was having difficulty figuring out what she
was talking about. He looked at his watch. "I'm to meet
my wife for lunch in ten minutes—would you two like
to join me?"

Forty-five minutes later, with the help of his wife,
Samantha, Mike finally understood the whole story.
And more important, he'd figured out who Eli
reminded him of. Eli was like Frank: cool exterior,
intense eyes, brilliant brain, obsessive personality.

As Mike listened, he was somewhat hurt and

annoyed that his elder brother had chosen a stranger's child to love, but at least Frank's love for Eli proved he *could* love.

"I think it's wonderfully romantic," Samantha said.

"I think the poor woman's going to meet Frank and be horrified," Mike muttered, but he shut up when Samantha kicked him under the table.

"So how do we arrange this?" Samantha asked. "And what size dress does your mother wear?"

"Twelve petite," Chelsea said. "She's short and f—" She didn't have to turn to feel Eli's glare. He wasn't saying much, as he was extremely hostile toward Mike. "She's, ah, round," Chelsea finished.

"I understand," Samantha said, getting a little notebook from her handbag.

"What difference does her dress size make?" Mike asked.

Chelsea and Samantha looked at him as though he were stupid. "She can't very well arrive at the cabin wearing jeans and a sweatshirt, now can she? Chelsea, shall we go buy some cashmere?"

"Cashmere?!" Eli and Mike said in unison, and it made a bond between them: men versus women.

Samantha ignored her husband's outburst. "Mike, you write a letter to Mrs. Harcourt saying—"

"Stowe," Eli said. "My father's new wife wanted my mother to resume her maiden name, so she did."

At that Samantha gave Mike a hard look, and he knew that all sense of proportion was lost. From now on, anything Eli and Chelsea wanted, they'd get.

Six

RANDY GOT OFF the horse gratefully and went into the cabin. Things had happened so quickly in the last few days that she'd had no time to think about them. Yesterday afternoon a man had come to the hospital and asked if she'd please accept a private, live-in nursing job for his client, starting the next morning and lasting for two weeks. At first she started to say no, that she couldn't ask the hospital to let her off, but it seemed that her absence had already been cleared with the chief of staff—a man Randy had never seen, much less met.

She then told the man she couldn't go because she had a son to take care of and she couldn't leave him. As though the whole thing were timed, Randy was called to the phone to be asked—begged, actually—by Eli to be allowed to go with Chelsea's family on an extremely educational yacht trip. Maybe she should have protested that he'd miss too much school, but she knew that Eli could make up any work within a blink of an eye, and he so wanted to go that she couldn't say no.

When she put down the phone, the man was still standing there, waiting for her answer about accepting the job.

"Two weeks only," she said, "then I have to be back."

Only after she agreed was she told that her new patient was staying in a remote cabin high in the Rockies and the only way to get there was by helicopter or horse. Since the idea of being lowered on a rope from a helicopter didn't appeal to her, she said she'd take the horse.

Early the next morning, she hugged and kissed Eli as though she were going to be away from him for a year or more, then got into a car that drove her thirty miles into the mountains, where an old man named Sandy was waiting to take her to the cabin. He had two saddled horses and three mules loaded with goods.

They rode all day and Randy knew she'd be sore from the horse, but the air was heavenly, thin and crisp as they went higher and higher. It was the end of autumn, and she could almost smell the snow that would soon blanket the mountains.

When they reached the cabin, a beautiful structure of logs and stone, she thought they must be in the most isolated place on earth. There were no wires to the cabin, no roads, no sign that it had touch with the outside world.

"Remote, isn't it?"

Sandy looked up from the mule he was unloading. "Frank made sure the place has all the comforts of home. Underground electricity and its own sewage system."

"What's he like?" she asked. Because of the narrow trail, they hadn't been able to talk much on the long ride up. All she knew of her patient was that he'd broken his right arm, was in a cast, and that it was difficult for him to perform everyday tasks.

Sandy took a while to answer. "Frank's not like anybody else. He's his own man. Set in his ways, sort of."

"I'm used to old and weird," she said with a smile. "Does he live here all the time?"

Sandy chuckled. "There's twelve feet of snow up here in the winter. Frank lives wherever he wants to. He just came here to . . . well, maybe to lick his wounds. Frank don't talk much. Why don't you go inside and sit down? I'll get this lot unloaded."

With a smile of gratitude, Randy did as he bid. Without so much as a glance at the interior of the cabin, she went inside, sat down, and fell asleep immediately. When she awoke with a start, about an hour later, she found that Sandy and the animals were gone. Only a huge pile of boxes and sacks on the floor showed that he had been there.

At first she was a bit disconcerted to find herself alone there, but she shrugged and began to look about her.

The cabin looked as though it had been designed by a computer, or at least a human who had no feelings. It was perfectly functional, an open-plan L-shape, one end with a huge stone fireplace, a couch, and two chairs. It could have been charming, but the three perfectly matched pieces were covered with heavy, serviceable, dark gray fabric that looked as though it had been chosen solely for durability. There were no rugs on the floor, no pictures on the wall, and only one table with a plain gray ceramic lamp on it. The kitchen was in the corner of the L, and it had also been designed for service: cabinets built for use alone, not decorative in any way. At the end of the kitchen were two beds, precisely covered in hard-wearing brown canvas. Through a door was a bathroom with shower, white ceramic toilet, and washbasin. Everything utterly basic. Everything clean and tidy. And no sign of human habitation.

Randy panicked for a moment when she thought that perhaps her patient had packed up and left, that maybe she was here alone with no way down the mountain except for a two-day walk. But then she noticed a set of doors beside one of the beds, one on each side, perfectly symmetrical. Behind one, arranged in military precision, were some pieces of men's clothing: heavy canvas trousers, boots without a bit of mud on them.

"My, my, we are neat, aren't we?" she murmured, smiling, then frowned at the twin bed so near his. No more than three feet separated the beds. She did hope this old man wasn't the type to make childish passes at her. She'd had enough of those in school. "Just give me a little kiss, honey," toothless men had said to her as their aged hands reached for her body.

Laughing at the silliness of her fantasy, Randy went to the kitchen and looked inside. Six pots and pans. Perfectly arranged, spotlessly clean. The drawers contained a matched set of stainless steel cooking utensils that looked as though they'd never been used. "Not much of a cook, are you, Mr. Taggert?" she mumbled as she kept exploring. Other cabinets and drawers were filled with full jars of spices and herbs, their seals unbroken.

"What in the world does this man eat?" she wondered aloud. When she came to the last cabinet, she found the answer. Hidden inside was a microwave, and behind the tall door in the corner was a freezer. It had about a dozen TV dinners in it, and after a moment's consternation, Randy laughed. It looked as though she'd been hired to cook for the missing Mr. Taggert as much as anything else.

"Poor man. He must be starving," she said, and she cheered up at the thought. The beds so close together had worried her, but the empty freezer was reassuring. "So, Miranda, my girl, you weren't brought here for a sex orgy but to cook for some lonely old man with a broken arm. Poor dear, I wonder where he is now."

She didn't waste much time speculating but set to work hauling in supplies. She had no idea what Sandy had brought on those two mules but she soon found out. Packed in dry ice, in insulated containers, were nearly a whole side of prime beef and a couple of dozen chickens. There were lots of fishing gear, bags of flour, packets of yeast, lots of canned goods, and a couple of cookbooks. With every item she unpacked, she felt more sure of what her true purpose here was, and thinking of someone else who needed her made her begin to forget how easily Eli had said he didn't need her for the next two weeks. He very much wanted to travel with Chelsea and her parents to the south of France, then on to Greece aboard some Italian prince's yacht.

With a sigh, Randy put a frozen chicken in the microwave to thaw. She would *not* let herself think how Eli was growing up and needed her less every day. "My baby has grown up," she said with a sigh as she removed the chicken and began to prepare a stuffing of bread cubes, sage, and onion.

"Don't start feeling sorry for yourself," she said. "You're not dead yet. You could meet a man, fall madly in love, and have three more kids." Even as she said it, she laughed. She wasn't a heroine in a romance novel. She wasn't drop-dead gorgeous with a figure that made men's hands itch with lust. The trouble was that she was an ordinary woman. She was pretty in a dimpled sort of way—an old-fashioned prettiness, not the gaunt-cheeked style that was all the rage now. And she was—well, face it, about thirty pounds overweight. Sometimes she consoled herself that if she'd lived in the seventeenth or eighteenth centuries men would have used her as a model for a painting of Venus, the goddess of love. But that didn't help today, when the most popular models weighed little more than ninety pounds.

As Randy settled down to prepare a meal for her absent patient, she tried to forget the loneliness of her life, to forget that her precious son would soon be leaving her to go to school and she would be left with no one.

Two hours later she had a lovely fire going in the big stone fireplace, a stuffed chicken roasting in the never-before-used oven, and some vegetables simmering. She'd filled a bowl full of wildflowers from the side of the cabin and put a dry pine cone on a windowsill. Her unpacked duffel bags were by the bed the man didn't appear to use; her sweater was draped across the back of the chair, and she'd put an interesting rock on one end of the stone mantel. The place was beginning to look like home.

When the cabin door was flung open and the man burst in, Randy almost dropped the tea kettle. He was *not* old. There was some gray at the temples of his black hair and lines running down the sides of his tight-lipped mouth, but the virility of him was intact. He was a *very* good-looking man.

"Who are you and what are you doing here?" he demanded.

She swallowed. Something about him was intimidating. She could see that he was a man who was used to giving orders and being obeyed. "I'm your nurse," she said brightly, nodding toward his arm, which was in a cast nearly to his shoulder. It must have been a bad break for such a cast, and he must have great difficulty doing even the smallest task.

Smiling, she walked around the counter, refusing to be intimidated by his face. "Miranda Stowe," she said, laughing nervously. "But you already know that, don't you? Sandy said you had the medical reports with you, so maybe if I saw them I'd know more about your condition." When he didn't say a word, she frowned a bit. "Come and sit down, supper's almost ready and—here, let me help you off with those boots."

He was still staring at her, speechless, so she gently tugged on his uninjured arm and got him to sit on a chair by the dining table. Kneeling before him, she started to unlace his boots while thinking that sharing a cabin was going to be a lonely experience if he never spoke.

When he started to laugh, she looked up at him, smiling, wanting to share whatever was amusing him.

"This is the best one yet," he said.

"What is?" she asked, thinking he was remembering a joke.

"*You* are." Still smiling, he cocked one eyebrow at her. "I must say you don't *look* the part of—what was it you called yourself? A nurse?"

Randy lost her smile. "I *am* a nurse."

"Sure you are, honey. And I'm a newborn babe."

Randy quit unlacing his boots and stood up, looking down at him. "Exactly what do you think I am?" she asked quietly.

"With those"—he nodded toward her ample bosom—"you could be only one thing."

Randy was a softhearted woman. Wounded butterflies made her weep, but this tall, good-looking man, nodding toward her breasts in that way, was more than she could take. She was strong from years of making beds and turning patients, so she slapped him hard on his shoulders and pushed. He went flying backward in the chair, reaching for the table to keep from falling, but his right arm, encased in plaster, was on the side of the table so he went sprawling to the floor.

Randy knew she should have waited to see if he was all right, but instead, she turned on her heel and started for the cabin door.

"Why you—" he said, then grabbed her ankle before she could take another step.

"Let go of me!" she said, kicking out at him, but he pulled and she pulled in the opposite way until she fell, landing hard on him and hitting his injured arm. She knew the impact must have hurt him, but he didn't so much as show his pain by a flicker of an eye.

With one roll, he pinned her body to the floor. "Who are you and how much do you want?"

Puzzled, she looked up at him. He was about forty years old, give or take a few years, and his body felt as though it was in perfect condition. "For this job I receive about four hundred dollars a week," she said, her eyes narrowed at him. "For *nursing*."

"Nursing," he said in a derogatory way. "Is *that* what you call it?"

She pushed against him angrily but couldn't budge him.

"So how did you find me? Simpson? No, he doesn't know anything. Who sent you? The Japanese?"

Randy stopped struggling. "The Japanese?" Was the man's injury *only* in his arm?

"Yeah, they weren't too happy when I won on that last deal. But microchips are a dead item. I'm going for—"

"Mr. Taggert!" she said, interrupting him, as he seemed to have forgotten he was lying full length on top of her. "I have *no* idea what you're talking about. Would you please let me up?"

He looked down at her, and the color of his dark eyes seemed to change. "You're not like the women I usually have, but I guess you'll do." He gave her a lascivious, one-sided smirk. "The softness of you might make for a nice change from bony models and starlets."

At that remark, made as though he were in a butcher's shop poking chickens for tenderness, she brought her knee up sharply between his legs, causing him to roll off of her in pain. "Now! Mr. Taggert," she said, standing up and bending over him. "Just what is this all about?"

He was holding himself with one hand, and as he rolled to one side his injured shoulder hit the table leg. Randy's heart *almost* went out to him.

"I'm a . . ."

"A what?" she demanded.

"A billionaire."

"You're a—" She didn't know whether to laugh or kick him in the ribs. "You're a . . ." She couldn't conceive of the amount of money he was talking about. "You're rich, so you think I came up here to . . . to get your money?"

He was beginning to recover as he pulled himself up to sit heavily on a chair. "Why else would you be here?"

"Because you asked for a nurse," she shot at him. "You *hired* me."

"I've heard *that* story before."

She stood looking down at him, glaring, more angry than she'd ever before been. "Mr. Taggert, you may have a great deal of money, but when it comes to being a human being you are penniless."

She didn't think about what she was doing, that she was in the Rocky Mountains and had no idea how to get back to civilization. She just grabbed her sweater from the back of the couch and walked out of the cabin.

She followed a bit of a trail, raging in her anger, but she didn't look where she was going.

Not even Leslie had ever made her as angry as this man just had. Leslie lied to her and manipulated her at every chance, but he'd never accused her of being indecent.

She went uphill and down, unaware of the setting sun. One minute it seemed to be sunny and warm, and the next moment it was pitch dark and freezing. Putting on her sweater didn't help at all.

"Are you ready to return?"

She nearly jumped out of her skin when the man spoke. Whirling about, she could barely see him standing hidden amid the trees.

"I don't think I will return to the cabin," she said. "I think I'll go back to Denver."

"Yes, of course. But Denver is that way." He pointed in the direction opposite to the way she was walking.

She wanted to keep some of her pride. "I wanted

to . . . to get my suitcase." She looked from one side to the other for a moment, then charged straight ahead.

"Ahem," he said, then pointed over his right shoulder.

"All right, Mr. Taggert," she said, "you've won. I haven't a clue where I am or where I'm going."

He took two steps around her and parted some bushes with his hand, and there, about a hundred yards in front of her, was the cabin. Light glowed softly and warmly from the windows. She could almost feel the warmth of the fire.

But she turned away, toward the path leading to Denver, and started walking.

"And where do you think you're going?"

"Home," she said, just as she stumbled over a tree root in the trail. But she caught herself and didn't fall. With her back straight, she kept walking.

He was beside her in moments. "You'll freeze to death out here. If a bear doesn't get you first, that is."

She kept walking.

"I am ordering you to—"

She stopped and glared up at him. "You have no right to order me to do anything. No right at all. Now, would you please leave me alone? I want to go *home.*" To her horror, her voice sounded full of tears. She'd never been able to sustain anger very long. No matter what Leslie did to her, she couldn't stay angry for more than a short time.

Straightening her shoulders, she again started walking.

"Could I hire you as my cook-housekeeper?" he said from behind her.

"You couldn't pay me enough to work for you," she answered.

"Really?" he asked, and he was right behind her. "If you're poor—"

"I am *not* poor. I just have very little money. You, Mr. Taggert, are *very* poor. You think everyone has a price tag."

"They do, and so do you. So do I, for that matter."

"You must be very lonely if you think that."

"I've never had enough time alone to consider what loneliness is. Now, what can I offer you to make you cook for me?"

"Is *that* what you want? My pot roast?" At this thought there came a little spring to her step. Maybe she *did* have something to offer. And maybe she wouldn't have to spend the night running down a mountain chased by a bear.

"Five hundred dollars a week," he said.

"Ha!"

"A thousand?"

"Ha. Ha. Ha," she said with great sarcasm.

"What then? What do you want most in the world?"

"The finest education the world has to offer for my son."

"Cambridge," he said automatically.

"Anywhere, just so it's the best."

"You want me to give your son four years at Cambridge University for one week's cooking? You're talking thousands."

"Not four years. Freshman to Ph.D."

At that Frank laughed. "You, lady, are crazy," he said, turning away from her.

She stopped walking and turned to look at his back.

"I saw wild strawberries up here. I make French crepes so light you can read through them. And I brought fresh cream to be whipped and drenched in strawberries, then rolled in a crepe. I make a rabbit stew that takes all day long to cook. It's flavored with wild sage. I saw some ducks on a pond near here, and you would not believe what I can do with a duck and tea leaves."

Frank had stopped walking.

"But then you're not interested, are you, Mr. Billionaire? You could toast your money on a stick over the fire and it would no doubt taste just dandy."

He turned back to her. "Potatoes?"

"Tiny ones buried under the fire coals all day so they're soft and mushy, then drizzled with butter and parsley."

He took a step toward her. When he spoke, his voice was low. "I saw bags of flour."

"I make biscuits flavored with honey for breakfast and bread touched with dill weed for dinner."

He took another step toward her. "Ph.D?"

"Yes," she said firmly, thinking of Eli in that venerable school and how much he'd love it. "Ph.D."

"All right," he said, as though it were the most difficult thing he'd ever said.

"I want it in writing."

"Yes, of course. Now, shall we return to the cabin?"

"Certainly." With her head held high, she started to walk past him, but he pulled aside a curtain of bushes. "Might I suggest that this way would be quicker?"

Once again, not a hundred yards away, was the cabin.

As she walked past him, her nose in the air, he said,

"Thank heaven your cooking is better than your sense of direction."

"Thank heaven *you* have money enough to *buy* what you want."

She didn't see the way he frowned at her as she continued walking. If the truth were told, Frank Taggert wasn't used to being around women who didn't fawn over him. Between his good looks and his money, he found he was quite irresistible to women.

But then he usually didn't have anything to do with women like this one. Most of the women he escorted were the long-legged perfect sort, the kind who wanted sparkling baubles and nothing else from him. He'd found that if he grew bored with one of them, if he gave her enough jewelry, she soon dried her tears.

But this one had had a chance at a great deal of money and she'd asked for something for someone other than herself.

As he watched her walk back to the cabin, he wondered about her husband. What was he like to allow his wife to go alone into the mountains to take care of another man?

Once he was inside the cabin, he sat down hungrily at the table and waited while she reheated the meal she'd cooked, then served it to him. Then she made herself a plate and took it into the living area, put it on the heavy pine coffee table, sat on the floor, and began to eat as she watched the fire.

Annoyed, and with great difficulty because he was one-handed, he picked up his plate and flatware and moved it to the coffee table. He'd no more than sat down when she lifted her plate and took it to the table.

"Why did you do that?" he asked, greatly annoyed.

"The hired help doesn't eat with Mr. Billionaire."

"Would you stop calling me that? My name is Frank."

"I know that, Mr. Taggert. And what is *my* name?"

For the life of him, he couldn't remember. He knew she'd told him, but, considering the circumstances under which she'd told him, it was understandable that he didn't remember. "I do not remember," he said.

"Mrs. Stowe," she answered, "and I was hired as your *nurse*."

She was behind him, seated at the dining table, and when he twisted around, causing pain to shoot through his shoulder, he saw that she had placed herself with her back to him. Frowning in annoyance, he again moved his place setting so he could face the back of her.

"Would you mind telling me who hired you?" he asked. The chicken was indeed delicious, and he thought a week away from canned food was going to be worth sending some kid to school—well, almost, anyway. Maybe he could write off the expense as charity. This could be advantageous taxwise if he—

"Your brother."

Frank nearly choked. "My *brother* hired you? Which one?"

She still refused to look at him, but he could see her shoulders stiffen. They weren't fashionably square shoulders, but rather round and soft.

"It seems to me, Mr. Taggert," she said, "that a rather unpleasant joke has been played on you. I would hate to think that you had more than one brother who would have such animosity toward you as to perpetuate such a joke."

Frank well knew that each of his brothers would delight in playing any possible trick on him, but he didn't tell her that.

After her remark about his brothers he didn't speak again but tried to give his attention to the food. She wasn't going to put his French chef out of business, but there was a comforting, homey flavor to the food, and the proportions were man-sized. In his house in Denver, his apartment in New York, and his flat in London, each of his chefs served calorie-controlled meals to ensure Frank's trim physique.

She finished eating, then silently cleared her place, then his, while Frank, feeling deliciously full of food, leaned back against the coffee table and watched the fire. He'd never been a man who smoked, but when she served him a tiny cup of excellent coffee, he almost wished he had a cigar. "And a plump woman to share my bed," as his father used to say.

Relaxed, drowsy, he watched the woman as she moved about the room, straightening things, and then—

"What are you doing?" he demanded as she drove a nail into the wall between the two beds.

"Making separate rooms," she answered. "Or as close as I can come to it."

"I assure you, Mrs. Stowe, that that is not necessary. I have no intention of imposing myself on you."

"You have made yourself clear as to your thoughts of my . . . of my feminine appeal, shall we say?" She drove another nail, then tied a heavy cotton rope from one nail to another.

Aghast, Frank watched her drape spare blankets

over the rope, effectively creating a solid boundary between the two beds. With effort, he raised himself from the floor. "You don't have to do this."

"I'm not doing it for you. I'm doing it for me. You see, Mr. Billionaire, I don't like you. I don't like you at all, and I'm not sure anyone else in the world does either. Now, if you'll excuse me, I'm going to take a bath."

Seven

RANDY STEPPED INTO a tub of water so hot it made her toes hurt, but she needed the warmth, needed the heat to thaw her heart. Being near Frank Taggert was like standing near an iceberg. She wondered if he had ever had any human warmth in him, whether he'd ever loved anyone. She'd like to think he was like one of her romantic heroes: wounded by some callous woman, and now his cold exterior protected a soft, loving heart.

She almost laughed aloud at the idea. All evening he'd been watching her speculatively; she could feel his eyes even through her back. He seemed to be thinking about where she belonged in the world. Rather like an accountant would try to figure out where an expense should be placed.

"At least Leslie had passion," she whispered, lying back in the tub. "He lied with passion, committed adultery with passion, made money with passion." But when she looked into this Frank Taggert's eyes she saw no passion for anything. *He* would never lie to a woman about where he'd spent the night because he'd never care enough whether or not she was hurt by his infidelity.

All in all, she thought, it was better not to think at all about Mr. Billionaire. With longing, she thought of Eli and Chelsea, and wondered what they were doing tonight. Would Eli eat properly if she weren't there? Would he ever turn off his computer and go to bed if she weren't there to make him? Would—

She had to stop thinking about her son or she'd cry from missing him. It suddenly dawned on her that whoever had played a joke on Frank Taggert had also inadvertently played a joke on her. Obviously, someone thought that sending a plain, ordinary woman such as she to spend a week with a handsome, sophisticated, rich man like Mr. Taggert was the most hilarious of jokes.

Getting out of the tub, she dried off, then opened her night case to get her flannel gown and old bathrobe. At the sight of the garments within, she felt a momentary panic. These were not her clothes. When she saw the Christian Dior label on the beautiful pink nightgown she almost swooned. Pulling it out, she saw that it was a peignoir set, made of the finest Egyptian cotton, the bodice covered with tiny pink silk roses. The matching robe was diaphanous and nearly transparent. It didn't take a brain like Eli's to see that this was not something a woman who was merely a housekeeper should wear.

Wrapping a towel about herself to cover the beautiful gown and robe, she rushed out of the room, past the bed on which Frank Taggert sat, scurried behind the blanket partition, and began to rummage in her unpacked suitcase for her own clothes.

"Is there a problem?" he asked from behind his side of the blanket.

"No, of course not. What could be the problem?" She went through her bags frantically, but nothing was familiar. If a 1930s-era movie star were going to spend a week in the Rockies, these were the clothes she would have worn. But Randy had never worn clothes made of cashmere and silk and wool so soft you could use it as a powder puff.

Randy knew herself normally to be a soft-tempered person. She had to be to put up with Leslie's shenanigans. But this was enough.

Throwing aside the blanket room divider, three cashmere sweaters in her hand, she pushed them toward Frank Taggert. "I want to know exactly what is going on. Why am I here? Whose clothes are these?"

Sitting on the side of the bed, Frank was unlacing his boots. "Tell me, Mrs. Stowe, are you married?"

"Divorced."

"Yes, then I understand. I come from a large family that is constantly reproducing itself. I believe they have decided I should do the same."

"You—" In shock, Randy sat down on the edge of her bed. "They have . . . You mean, they want us to . . ."

"Yes. At least that's my guess."

"Your . . . guess?" She swallowed. "At this point, I'd decided your family had sent me here because the idea of a woman like me with a man like you would be very entertaining to them."

He didn't pretend to misunderstand her. While she'd been speaking, he'd been working at untying his boot laces with one hand. So far he'd not managed to even loosen the knot.

Not even thinking about what she was doing and certainly not what she was wearing, Randy knelt before him and untied his laces, then removed his boots. "I don't mean to pry," she said, pulling off his socks and giving each foot in turn a quick massage, just as she did for Eli and used to do for Leslie, "but why would they choose someone like *me?* With your looks and money, you could have anyone."

"They would like you. You look like a poster illustration for fertility."

She had her hands on his shirt collar as she began to unbutton it. "A what?"

"A symbol of fertility. A paean to motherhood. I'm willing to bet that this son of yours is your whole life."

"Is there something wrong with that?" she asked defensively.

"Nothing whatever if that's what you choose to do."

She was pulling his shirt off. "What better life is there for a woman than to dedicate herself to her children?"

"You have more than one child?"

"No," she said sadly, then saw his eyes as he seemed to say, I knew it. "So your brother sent me up here in the hope that I would . . . would what, Mr. Taggert?"

"From the look of your gown, I'd say Mike did this, since his wife, Samantha, is the personification of a romantic heroine."

"A romantic heroine?"

"Yes. All she wants out of life is to take care of Mike and their ever-growing brood of children."

"*You* have not been reading what I have. Today, the heroines of romance novels want a career and control of their own lives and—"

"A husband and babies."

"Perhaps. Stand up," she ordered and began unfastening his trousers. She'd undressed many patients, and she was doing so now without thinking too much about the action.

"How many heroes have you read about who said 'I want to go to bed with you but I don't want to get married and I never want children'?" he asked her.

"I see. I guess normality *is* a requirement in a hero."

"And to not want marriage and children is abnormal?"

She smiled coldly at him. "I've never met anyone like you, but I assume you are not married, never want to be, never will be, have no children, and if you did, you would only visit them by court order."

She had him stripped to his undershorts and T-shirt and he was certainly in fine physical form, but she felt nothing for him, any more than she'd have felt for a statue.

"What makes you think I have no wife? I could have married many times." He sounded more curious than anything else.

"I'm sure you could have, but the only way a woman would marry you is for your money."

"I beg your pardon."

Maybe it was rotten of Randy, but she felt a little thrill at having upset his calm. "You are *not* what a woman dreams of."

"And what does a woman dream of, Mrs. Stowe?"

Smiling dreamily, she pulled back the blankets on his bed. "She dreams of a man who is all hers, a man whose whole world revolves around her. He might go out and solve world problems and be seen by everyone as magnificently strong, but when he's at home, he puts his head on her lap and tells her he couldn't have accomplished anything without her. And, most important, she knows he's telling the truth. He needs her."

"I see. A strong man who is weak."

She sighed. "You don't see at all. Tell me, do you analyze everything? Take everything apart? Do you put everything into an account book?" She gave him a hard look. "What are you making your billions *for?"*

As she held back the covers, he stepped into bed. "I have many nieces and nephews, and I can assure you that my will is in order. If I should die tomorrow—"

"If you should die tomorrow, who will miss you?" she asked. "Who will cry at your funeral?"

Suddenly she was very tired, so she turned away from him, pushed the blanket partition aside, and went to her own bed. She had never felt so lonely in her life. Perhaps it was Eli's talk of going away to college, or maybe it was this man's talk of her looking as though she should have many children. When Eli left home she would be alone, and she didn't think some man was going to come riding up to her front door on a black stallion and—

She didn't think anymore but fell asleep.

She didn't know how long she'd been asleep before a man's voice woke her.

"Mrs. Stowe."

Startled, she looked up at Frank Taggert, wearing just his underwear, his arm in a heavy cast, standing there looking at her, his dark eyes serious. Only the fading firelight lit the room.

I'll bet this is how he looks when he makes one of

his million-dollar deals, she thought, and she wondered what he could possibly want of her.

"Yes?"

"I have a proposition to put to you. A merger of sorts."

Pushing herself upright, she leaned against the back of the bed, unaware that the gown showed every curve of her upper body. But Frank didn't seem to notice, as his eyes were intense.

"Ordinarily," he began, "the things you said to me would have no effect on me. My relatives have said everything you have said and more. However, it seems that when a man reaches forty and—"

"A billion," she interrupted.

"Yes, well, there does come a time when a man begins to consider his own mortality."

"Midas," she said, referring to the story of the man who turned everything, including his beloved child, into gold.

"Just so." He hesitated, glancing down at her bosom for the briefest second. "Contrary to what people think, I *am* human."

At that Randy pulled the covers up to her neck. She was *not* the one-night-stand type of person. In fact, she wouldn't even read romances in which the heroine had a multitude of lovers. "Mr. Taggert—" she began.

But he put up his hand to stop her. "You do not have to concern yourself about me. I am not a rapist."

She let the covers go. She could not see herself as a woman who drove men to uncontrollable acts of lust. "What is it you are trying to say to me?"

"I am trying to ask if you'd consider marrying me."

Eight

"MARRIAGE?" SHE ASKED, HER EYES WIDE. "TO ME?"

"Yes," he said seriously. "I can see that you're shocked. Most men of my wealth marry tall, statuesque blondes who train horses and wear couture. They do not marry short, unmanicured, plump—"

"I understand. So why aren't *you* married to one of these horsey women who spends her life trying on clothes?"

Her cattiness was acknowledged with a tiny bit of a smile. "I expect to be the man in my own household, and besides, it's as you say—they care only for my money."

"Mr. Taggert," she said, looking at him hard, "I'm not interested in your money *or* you."

He gave an ugly little smile. "Surely there are things you want that money can buy. I would imagine you live in a house with a mortgage and I doubt that your car is less than three years old. Does your ex-husband pay you any support? You're the type who would never take a person to court for nonpayment of debt. How long has it been since you've had any new clothes? There must be many things you want for your son."

That he'd described her life perfectly made her very angry. "Being poor is not a social disease. And since slavery was outlawed some years ago, I do not have to sell myself to get a new car."

"How about a white Mercedes with red leather interior?"

She almost smiled at that. "Really, Mr. Taggert, this is ridiculous. What's the *real* reason you're asking me to marry you? If you still are, that is."

"Yes. Once I make up my mind I never change it."

"I can believe that about you."

Again he gave her a bit of a smile, making her wonder if any of the tall blondes in his life had ever contradicted him. "My life is too perfect," he said. "It is beginning to bore me. It is perfectly in order. My servants are the best money can buy. There is never so much as a hairbrush out of place in any of my houses. For some time now I've thought it might be pleasant to have a wife, someone familiar to me. I like familiarity. The contents of each of my houses are exactly the same."

Blinking, she thought about this for a moment. "Same towels, same—"

"Same clothes in exactly the same arrangement, so that no matter where I am I know what is where."

"Oh my. This *is* boring."

"But efficient. Very efficient."

"Where would *I* fit into this efficiency?"

"As I said before, I have considered a wife, but the ordinary sort for a man of my wealth would be as perfect as my life already is."

"Why not marry several of them?" she asked helpfully. "One for each house. For variety you could change hair color, since I'm sure it wouldn't be natural anyway."

This time he did smile at her. Not an all-out teeth-showing smile but a smile nonetheless. "If wives were not so much trouble I would have done so years ago."

She couldn't suppress her own smile. "I think I am beginning to understand. You want me because I'll add chaos to your life."

"And children."

"Children?" she asked, blinking.

"Yes. My family is prolific. Twins, actually. I find I want children." He looked away. "Since I was a child I have been very aware of my responsibilities. As the oldest of many siblings, I knew I would be the one to run the family business."

"The crown prince, so to speak."

"Yes, exactly. Fulfilling my obligations has always been uppermost in my mind. But about two years ago I met a boy."

When he said nothing more, Randy encouraged him. "A boy?"

"Yes, he was at my brother's offices, skulking around from desk to desk, pretending to play but actually listening and looking at everything. I spoke to him, and it was like looking into my own eyes."

"And he made you want to have children of your own, did he? Sort of a wish to clone yourself, is that right?"

"More or less. But the boy changed my life. He made me see things in my own life. We have corresponded since that time. We have become . . ." He smiled. "We have become friends."

She was glad that he had at least one friend in the world, but he couldn't marry a woman and hope she would give him a son just like the boy he'd met. "Mr. Taggert, there is no way *I* could produce the kind of son you want. *My* son is a sweet, loving boy. He is the personification of kindness and generosity. He would die if he knew I told anyone this, but I still tuck him in every night and read aloud to him before he goes to sleep." She was *not* going to mention that she usually read advanced physics textbooks to him because that would have ruined the story.

Turning his head to one side, Frank said, "I would rather like my children to be a bit softer than I am."

It was beginning to dawn on Randy that this man was serious. He was coldly, and with great detachment, asking her to marry him. And produce children. For a moment, looking at him, she couldn't quite picture him in the throes of passion. Would he perhaps delegate the task to his vice president in charge of production? "Charles, my wife needs servicing."

"You are amused," he said.

"It was just something I was thinking about." She looked at him with compassion. "Mr. Taggert, I understand your dilemma and I would like to help. If it were only me I might consider marrying you, but others would be involved. Not others. Children. My son would be exposed to you, and if you and I did have—well, if we did have children, I'd want them to have a real father, and I can't imagine you reading fairy stories to a two-year-old."

For a moment he didn't move; he just sat on the edge of the bed. "Then you are saying *no* to me?"

"Yes. I mean *no.* I mean, yes, I'm saying *no.* I can't marry you."

For a few seconds he stared at her, then he stood up and silently went to his own bed.

As Randy sat there, she wondered if she'd dreamed the whole thing. She'd just turned down marriage to a very wealthy man. Was she terminally stupid? Had she lost all sense? Eli could have the best the world had to offer. And she could—

She sighed. She would be *married* to a man who wanted her so she could add chaos to his life. How amusing. Plump little Miranda walking about in circles in her attempt to leave the cabin. Daffy Miranda being stupid enough to fall for an elaborate joke played on a cold, heartless billionaire.

It was a long while before she fell asleep.

The next morning Randy was silently making strawberry waffles while Frank sat before the fire staring at the pages of a book on tax reform. He hadn't turned a page in fifteen minutes, so she knew he was thinking rather than reading.

No doubt I'm the first company he's tried to buy and failed, she thought. What will he do to win me over? Send candy to Eli? A man like Frank Taggert would never take the time to find out that Eli would like to have a new CD-ROM for his computer more than all the candy in the world.

As she watched him, she felt sorry for him. The feeling of isolation he projected surrounded him like an impenetrable glass bubble.

It was while she was making a sugar syrup for the strawberries and thinking how she'd like to see a little fat around the middle of Mr. Trim Taggert, that she heard the helicopter. Frank was on his feet before she was, and to her consternation, he flung open a door hidden in the log wall and withdrew a rifle. "Stay here," he ordered.

"Okay," she whispered, feeling a bit like a heroine in a Western movie.

Seconds later he was back; he put the rifle away, then went to the table. "Is breakfast ready?"

She heard him only by reading his lips, because the sound of the 'copter overhead was deafening. Maybe his curiosity wasn't piqued, but hers was. Quickly, she flung waffles and strawberries onto a plate, sloshed coffee into a cup by his hand, then was out the door.

The helicopter was directly overhead. A couple of duffel bags had already been lowered, and now a tall blond man wearing a dark suit, his briefcase in hand, was descending, his foot hooked into a loop of rope. Randy couldn't help smiling at this version of Wall Street calmly coming down through the tall trees, the mountains in the distance. As he got closer she started laughing, because she could see that while holding onto the briefcase and the rope, he was also trying to eat an apple.

He landed in front of her. He was quite good-looking: very blond, very white skin, blue eyes so bright they dazzled. Holding the apple in his mouth, he motioned the helicopter to go away, and Randy saw that the briefcase was handcuffed to his wrist.

"Hungry?" she asked, as he stood there smiling.

"Starved." He was looking at her in a way that made her feel quite good about herself, and she smiled back warmly.

"You here with Frank?" he asked.

"Not *with* him. I was hired as his nurse, but that turned out to be a joke. I'm just here until— Wait a minute. Maybe I could have returned on the helicopter." With her hand shielding her eyes, she watched the helicopter disappear over the horizon. She looked back at the man.

"Mike. Or was it Kane?"

"I beg your pardon?"

"If a joke was played on Frank, it would have to be either Mike or Kane." When she didn't respond, he smiled, then held out his hand. "I'm Julian Wales. Frank's assistant. Or actually, glorified go-fer. And you are?"

She let her hand slide into his large warm one. "Miranda Stowe. Randy. I'm the nurse, but mostly I'm the cook-housekeeper."

He gave her a look that made her blush. "Perhaps I'll find myself becoming ill and have need of your services."

Perhaps she should have told him she wasn't *that* kind of woman, but, truth was, his admiration made her feel good. Yesterday a marriage proposal and today a very nice flirtation.

She withdrew her hand from his—after two tugs. "Mr. Taggert is in there, and I have strawberry waffles for breakfast."

"Gorgeous, and you can cook too. You wouldn't like to marry me, would you?"

Feeling like an eighteen-year-old, she laughed. "Mr. Taggert's already asked." She was horrified that she'd said that. "I mean . . ." She had no idea what to say to cover herself, so she went back to the cabin while Julian, his eyes wide in disbelief, stared after her before following.

Frank didn't bother with greeting him, and Julian had learned not to expect any. Frank showed his gratitude for Julian's years of dedication with a large six-figure salary and many perks.

Without a word spoken between them, Julian

removed the briefcase from his wrist, unlocked it, and turned it over to Frank.

"Unfortunately," Julian said, "I arranged for the 'copter to pick me up two days from now. I planned to stay and do a little fishing. But I didn't know you had a guest. If it's not suitable for me to stay, I can walk out."

Buried in the papers, Frank didn't look up. "Take the couch."

"Yes sir," Julian said, then winked at Randy as she started to put a plate of hot waffles in front of him.

"Have you had breakfast, Randy?" Julian asked. When she shook her head no, he said, "How'd you like to join me outside? A morning like this is too beautiful to waste inside."

Smiling, plate in hand, she followed him out the door, and when she turned back, she saw Frank staring after them. "I'll just close this so we won't disturb you," she said, rather pleased that he was frowning.

Julian had put his plate on a stump and was removing his suit jacket and tie. "Hallelujah!" he said, unbuttoning the top of his shirt. "Two days of freedom." Sitting on the stump, the plate on his lap, he looked up at her. "There's room for two."

Maybe she shouldn't have, but she sat beside him, parts of her body warm against his.

"Did Frank actually ask you to marry him?"

She nearly choked. "I shouldn't have told you that. I have a complete inability to keep my mouth shut. It wasn't a *real* marriage proposal, just sort of a business arrangement."

Julian cocked one blond eyebrow. "I see what he gets, but I can't see what you get. Except the money, of course."

"Children. He seems to think he and I could, well, produce children."

At that Julian laughed. "Ol' Frank said that? Do you know him very well?"

"Not at all. Except he makes me cold even being near him."

"Ah yes. Many people feel that way, but don't underestimate him: He's as hot as anybody."

"For making money, maybe, but he doesn't exactly get my vote for lover of the year."

"You've been to bed with him then?"

"No!" she said with her mouth full. "Certainly not! I like there to be hearts and flowers and—Good heavens! I don't know what I'm talking about. Mr. Wales, I am not some romantic heroine to be fought over by two gorgeous men. I am rapidly approaching middle age, I'm overweight, I'm a single mother, and I'm sure that suit you have on cost more than I earned last year. If any other woman on earth were here I'm sure neither of you men would notice me."

He was smiling at her. "Randy, you know what you are? You're *real*. I knew it the moment I saw you. Usually the women near Frank are so perfectly beautiful they look as though they were manufactured. And you know that if he lost his money they'd never look at him again."

"Really, Mr. Wales, I—"

"Julian."

"Julian. I am a perfectly ordinary woman."

"Oh?" He took a big bite of waffle. "Ever been married?" When she nodded, he said, "When you divorced your husband, did you take him to the cleaners?" He didn't wait for her answer. "No, of course not. Looking at you, I'd say you 'understood' his need to run off with some empty-headed Barbie doll."

She looked down at her waffle, now growing cold. "You seem to be rather good at figuring out people."

"That's what Frank pays me for: to look into people's eyes and keep the deadbeats and con artists away from him."

At that moment, the cabin door opened and Frank appeared holding a fishing rod. "Actually, Julian, I've been meaning to do some fishing myself. Shall we go?"

Randy stood up. "I think Julian should change his clothes, and I'll need to pack you both a lunch. You can't leave without something to eat."

"You will come with me and cook our fish. Julian, sort out what is needed and follow us," Frank said, then he started walking down the trail away from them.

Randy wasn't about to obey what sounded like an order so she turned back to the cabin, but before she was through the door she knew she wasn't going to cut off her nose to spite her face and miss what sounded like a lovely day fishing. Julian stood where he was, staring open-mouthed after his boss. He'd worked with Frank Taggert for over ten years, and although during that time Frank had never once told Julian—or anyone else for that matter—about himself, Julian had been able to piece together a great deal. He knew his boss very, very well.

"He's in love with her," Julian whispered. "By all that's holy, he's madly in love with her. Only deep love could make Frank leave corporate merger papers and go fishing." For a moment Julian stared at his boss's back as it disappeared down the trail. Of course Frank knew so little about women that he'd mess this up—as he'd destroyed every relationship he'd ever had with a woman. Julian had to admit that Frank had never thought any woman was worth missing a meeting for or even postponing a call. And it was Julian who had the task of telling the women to get out. He'd had dishes thrown at him and heard curse words in four languages as he removed women from wherever Frank was at the moment.

It was this part of his job that was beginning to make him discontented, beginning to make him wonder if there was more to life than just doing whatever Frank Taggert wanted done.

Julian turned to look into the cabin, where he could see Randy putting food and utensils into a backpack. But now Frank had asked a woman to *marry* him. And knowing Frank, he'd presented the proposal as he would present something to a corporate board. No passion, no fireworks, no declarations of undying love. Just "I have a proposition to make you: Will you marry me?"

Julian grabbed his bags from the ground and changed into jeans and a sweater where he was, thinking all the while. No one knew Frank as he did. Too many people, like Randy, thought he had no heart, but Julian knew he did. Frank just kept rigid control over himself, but his loyalty was unbreakable. When Julian had smashed a Ferrari, it was Frank who'd flown in doctors from London and New York. When Mrs. Silen's husband had nearly taken her children away from her, it was Frank who'd silently and secretly stepped in and reversed the decision of the court. Frank often helped people; he just hated people knowing he did it. He liked his image of ruthless negotiator.

In his dealings with his employees and his relatives, he was always fair. Perhaps never warm, but fair. It was just with women that Frank seemed to be incapable of human feelings.

But two years ago something had changed Frank, and Julian didn't know what it was. And now this broken arm seemed to have changed him even more. He'd been playing handball as fiercely as he worked at business and he'd slammed against the wall, pinning his right arm under him. It was a nasty break, and Frank had been two hours in the operating room. Julian had been there, along with most of the Taggerts, the next day. They were a loud, happy family, exactly the opposite of Frank with his cool reticence. They teased him mercilessly about his being human just like other people.

As far as Julian knew Frank never so much as flinched from pain, but something seemed to have happened inside him because days later Frank cancelled some very important meetings and announced that he was retreating to his cabin high in the Rockies and he was not to be disturbed. Julian didn't dare ask Frank why, but his brother did, and Frank had said he'd wanted to heal and to think.

Nine

RANDY KNEW SHE'D never had such a wonderful day in her life as she did fishing with Julian. Everything he did or said seemed to be funny. He flirted with her, teased her, put his arms around her to show her how to bait a hook. He made her giggle and squeal like a girl again.

But throughout the day, Randy stole glances at Frank, who was standing alone, quietly and unobtrusively reeling in one fish after another. With his arm in a sling he must have been in pain as well as experiencing enormous difficulty, but he never showed any emotion.

"Interested in him?" Julian asked after she'd glanced at him for the thousandth time. Frank stood apart from them, almost as though he were unaware of them.

"Certainly not. I'm not a woman who wants a man for his money."

"Ah, I see. And what *do* you want from a man?" he asked with a false leer.

"Great love. Deep love. I want to be *sure* of him. I want undying loyalty." She smiled. "And a big house set among acres of fruit trees."

"Don't be fooled by Frank. He's the most loyal person I know. Once he takes you under his wing, he protects you."

She looked at Frank again. He was tall and broadshouldered, and those dark eyes of his were intriguing, but . . . But he was so very odd, one day asking her to marry him, then the next not so much as looking at her.

"A penny," Julian said.

"I was just thinking that he doesn't know I'm alive."

At that Julian laughed. "Frank *hates* fishing. The only reason he's here is to see that I don't touch you."

She blinked at him in disbelief. "But he's catching fish. He must like it."

"Frank is good at everything in life except women."

Randy stared at the rapidly moving mountain stream for a moment, then picked up the thermos of hot coffee and went to offer Frank some. "Having fun?" she asked as he drank.

"Marvelous. And you?"

She could see a muscle working in his temple. "The best. Julian is a truly wonderful man. Funny, happy, laughing. A woman could easily fall in love with him." Randy was watching him so hard she didn't blink. In spite of his coolness, she found herself drawn to him, as what woman isn't drawn to a man who asks her to marry him? Say something, she thought. Maybe even kiss me.

But Frank said nothing as he handed the empty cup back to her and looked at the water. "Julian is a fine man. Very good worker."

"He must have a thousand women friends with his looks and talents and charm." Randy knew she was pushing him, but she wanted some reaction out of him—if he felt anything at all for her.

"I have no idea of his private life." Turning, he looked away from her.

Randy moved closer to him. "And what about you? Lots of women in your life? Do you give out lots of marriage proposals?"

"Only one," he said softly.

Randy could have kicked herself. She was being rude and careless of another person's feelings. She put her hand on his arm. "Mr. Taggert, I—"

She broke off because he turned glittering eyes on her. "You what? Wanted to laugh at me?"

"Why no, I didn't."

"Then what? What is it you want from me?"

"I . . . I don't know."

Abruptly, he turned away from her. "Let me know when you figure it out."

Confused, embarrassed, Randy turned from him and headed down the trail toward the cabin. When Julian tried to stop her she told him she wanted to be alone, so he went back to stand beside Frank, who was pretending to be fishing, but he hadn't remembered to bait his hook.

Julian knew his boss—knew when he was angry, as he was now—so he didn't say anything as he set about building a fire. Maybe some of Randy's food, sizzling hot, would warm Frank up.

It was an hour later that the two of them were sitting around a campfire. In all the years Julian had worked for Frank their relationship had been based on business, but now Julian could feel things changing. Things were changing inside himself and inside Frank.

He took a breath. "Have you told Randy you're in love with her?"

Frank didn't say anything.

"You might be able to fool the rest of the world but you can't fool me. When did you know you were in love with her?"

Frank took a while to answer. "When I saw that she didn't like me."

"Frank, a *lot* of people don't like you."

He gave a one-sided smile. "But they don't like what I stand for or they don't like that I have money and they don't. It's not *me* they dislike."

Julian tossed a pine cone into the fire. "Don't kid yourself, Frank, it's you people don't like. Freezers are warm compared to you."

Frank smiled. "Women don't think so."

"True. Women do make fools of themselves over you when they first meet you. I've always wondered why."

"Money and power equal sex, and I have an excellent technique in bed."

"Go to school to learn it, did you?"

"Of course. How else does one . . ." He stopped, not wanting to say more.

"Randy is different, isn't she?" Julian waited for Frank to answer. Would he answer such a personal question?

"She is everything that I am not. She is warm where I am cold. She loves easily while I find it difficult to love. If Miranda were to love a man she'd love him unconditionally, with or without money. She'd love him always. I need that . . . that security. Women change toward a man. They love him today, but if he forgets her birthday she withdraws her love."

"Randy wouldn't like a man to forget her birthday."

"If I forgot it on the true date I'd take her to Paris a week later and she'd forgive me."

"Yes, she would. But Frank, how would someone like Randy fit in with your life? If I remember correctly, your last love interest had a doctorate in Chinese poetry and spoke four languages."

"She was a bore," Frank said with contempt. "Julian, something's happened to me in the last two years. I've had a change of heart. I know, lots of people think I don't have a heart but I do, or maybe I've just discovered that I have one. Many people have asked me what I'm earning money for, but I've never had an answer. I think it's been the challenge and the goal. You above all people know I haven't wanted to buy anything. I've never wanted a yacht that costs a hundred grand a day to run. I've just wanted to—"

"To win," Julian cut in, bitterness in his voice. Maybe it was jealousy, but sometimes he was sick of seeing Frank win.

"Yes, maybe so. Maybe that was it."

"What happened two years ago?"

"I met a kid. A boy named Eli, and it was like looking into my own eyes. He was so ambitious, so hungry for achievement." Frank chuckled. "He steals office letterhead and writes letters to people on it."

"Illegal."

"Yes, but he does it to help people. I looked at him and thought, I wish I'd had a son just like him. It was the first time in my life I ever wanted a child of my own."

"The Taggert bug," Julian said. "Bitten at last."

Frank smiled. "Ah yes, my prolific family. They seem to be born with the urge to reproduce themselves."

"But not you. At least not until now. Not until you met Randy."

"Yes. Randy. A real woman. I don't want the mother of my children to be anything but a mother to them."

"And a wife to you, I take it."

"Yes. I . . ." He took a deep breath. "When this happened"—he nodded toward his arm— "I had some time to think and to remember. If I'd broken my neck not one of those billion dollars I own would have missed me. Not one of them would have cried in misery at my death. And worst, when I got out of the hospital, there wasn't a woman, a soft, sweet woman whose lap I could put my head on and cry."

At that Julian raised one eyebrow in disbelief.

"I *could* have cried that day. Do you want to know what the Chinese poetry lady wanted to know? She asked me, Was breaking my arm and being in that much pain exciting? Was my pain sexually exciting?"

"Tell her," Julian said fiercely. "You *must* tell Randy what you feel."

"Tell her what? That I have been looking for a woman like her, someone so soft and sweet and loving that she'd get on a horse and ride into the middle of nowhere to nurse a man who's hurt? As far as I can tell she asked no questions. She was told she was needed, so she went. For a ridiculously low sum of money."

"Then tell her you need her."

"She'd never believe that. What do I need her for? I have a cook. Sex is easy to come by, so what else do I need?"

"Frank, no wonder women come to hate you."

"Women hate me when I refuse to marry them and make them part of my community property."

"You *don't* have a heart." They were silent a moment, then Julian spoke again: "If you don't tell her, you'll lose her."

"Julian, you know how I make money? I make money because I don't care. I don't care whether I win or lose. If there is a deal I really truly want, then I step out of it. You can't be ruthless if you care."

"Then you're saying that you want Randy too much to make an attempt to win her?"

Frank looked at Julian, and for just a moment he

saw past the coolness that was always there, and what he saw made him draw in his breath. "If I tried and lost, I couldn't go on living."

"You love her that much?" Julian whispered.

The mask returned. "I don't know why I . . . care for her, but I do."

"Therefore you will do nothing to try to win her."

"That's right," Frank said, staring into the fire.

Julian was quiet for a moment. "In spite of what you say, some women have genuinely cared for you. You, not your money. But without exception you have dropped them. Maybe when you started to care for them you got out. I don't know the reason, but I do know that I've always been the one to have to listen to them, calm them down and endure their rages after you've dropped them. Randy isn't one of the women on the circuit, some woman who's had affairs with a hundred men. She's just an ordinary, middle-class woman, and she likes you. She may say she doesn't, but I see it in her eyes. Today I did my best to get her attention onto me, but she was only interested in you. A nudge from you and she could love you."

He turned to look at Frank. "I don't want to have to try to explain you to Randy. I don't want to try to dry her tears with a box full of emeralds." He paused. "In fact, I don't want to do any of it anymore."

Julian gave Frank plenty of time to reply, but when he was silent, Julian stood up after a moment. "Frank, I've worked with you for ten years. I've admired and respected you and at times envied you. But at this moment I feel nothing but pity for you." As he turned away, he halted. "You know, I'm tired of not caring. I'm tired of buying and selling and never having a life of my own. This weekend I had a date with a wonderful woman, then you called and told me to bring you the papers. You didn't ask; you just told. So I left a message on her machine and came here. I doubt now that she'll ever speak to me again."

"I pay you well enough to do what I want."

"Yes, you do. You pay me so well that I don't need to work anymore. I could retire on what I've never had time to spend." Julian smiled. "And I think I'm going to do that. You will have my resignation on Monday."

For a moment Julian hesitated, waiting for Frank to call him back, but Frank said nothing, so Julian kept walking.

Ten

RANDY WAS STANDING by the sink, furiously grating carrots, when Julian returned. One look at his face and she knew not to say anything. To her surprise, he went to a blank log wall to the right of the fireplace, pushed a knot, and a door opened. Anger in every step, he disappeared inside the room.

Curious, carrot in hand, she went to peer inside the room. In contrast to the rugged, almost primitive cabin, the room was ultra modern, its walls painted a hard gloss white. Along three walls were tables, each covered with machines: computer, fax, television with the stock market playing on it, telephone, as well as machines she couldn't even identify.

Julian grabbed a microphone and in minutes he'd radioed for a helicopter to pick him up. "Wait a minute," he said, then turned to Randy. "Do you want to return with me?"

There was a slight emphasis on the word "me." For a moment Randy's heart seemed to stop beating. Even with anger in Julian's eyes, there was also interest. He hadn't just been flirting with her. This gorgeous man was actually interested in *her*.

But something held her back. "No, I'll stay," she heard herself whisper and couldn't understand what she was doing.

"Sure?" he asked, and she nodded.

Minutes later Julian was jamming clothes into his duffel bag. "He's not worth it. You know that, don't you? I should tell you what he said. He said—"

"No!" she said sharply. "I don't want to know what went on between you two. That's your business. He's injured and he needs me."

"No he doesn't. He doesn't need anyone. I thought he did, but—" He stopped. "It's not him, it's me. *I* need someone. Actually, what I need is a life of my own." At the cabin door, he paused. "Don't let him break your heart. A lot of women have tried to melt him but they couldn't. He . . ." Julian paused. "Look, this isn't about you. It's between Frank and me. He's in love with you."

"What? I know he—"

"He loves you. Which is why he'll never try to win you. Don't expect anything personal from him. Money, yes, but nothing else."

"But—" she began, a thousand questions swirling about in her head.

"I've said too much already. Take care," he said, then he was gone.

When she was alone in the cabin, Randy plopped down onto one of Frank's boring gray couches. "My goodness," she said aloud. "A lifetime of no adventure, and now everything is rolled into a couple of days."

An hour later Frank appeared at the door, and for a split second he looked startled to see her. "Why didn't you leave with Julian?"

Truthfully, she didn't know. "You owe me a Cambridge education," she said.

"Ah, yes, of course."

That wasn't the real reason she'd stayed, because who could charge thousands of dollars for a week's work; but then she didn't know the real reason she'd stayed. She stiffened her spine. "Do you want me to leave?"

"I want—" he began, then cut himself off. "I want you to do whatever suits you."

It was not what she'd hoped for. Had Julian been telling the truth when he said Frank Taggert loved her? Since she didn't love him, what did it matter? But there was something in his eyes. Something deep down in them that made her feel that he was lonely, maybe as lonely as she was when she thought of Eli going away to college and leaving her.

She wasn't sure what to say. "Have you eaten?" was all she could think of, and she was rewarded by the tiniest smile from him.

"You are going to make me fat."

It was the first personal remark he'd made—other than asking her to marry him, that is. "You could use a little fat on you. I have some I could lend you."

His eyes twinkled. "I'd like for you to keep all of yours. It's in the right places."

Blushing, she turned away to serve dinner, and when she turned back, he had his nose buried in the papers Julian had brought and he didn't say another word to her throughout the meal.

The light teasing between them seemed to have turned off something inside Frank, for he didn't speak again the rest of the evening. When he went outside to gather logs for the fire, Randy could see the nearly impossible task was hurting him, but when she offered to help he told her he needed no one.

Cursing herself for not having left with Julian, Randy took a bath, put on the seductive nightgown—the only one she had—and went to bed. "Wasted on him," she muttered, and she went to sleep immediately.

Thunder loud enough to split her eardrums woke her up. As she sat up, lightning lit the cabin, and she gave an involuntary scream. She was not used to such storms.

Frank was beside her instantly, just sitting there, not touching her, but at the next flash of lightning she flung herself into his arms.

She had forgotten how good a man could feel. His big, hard, strong body enveloped her, and before she could breathe he pulled her head back and kissed her.

It was not a kiss from a cold man, and in that moment she believed what Julian had told her: that Frank did love her.

He was kissing her neck. The cabin was lit with lightning and the roar of the thunder seemed to echo within her.

"Yes," she whispered as his hand went to her breast. "Yes, please make love to me."

Gently, he took her face in his hands, his eyes searching hers. "I have no protection with me."

For a moment she held her breath. She felt sure he didn't have a communicable disease. "I would like the consequences," she said, meaning how very much she'd like to have another child, to feel life growing within her, as she had with Eli.

"Yes," was all he said, then he was on her.

He was as hot in bed as he was cold out of it. She'd never seen him leering at her as men did, but he seemed to have noticed all of her body and to want her very much. Her gown was off her body in seconds and his hands were everywhere, caressing her, touching her, as though he wanted to memorize her.

Never had Randy enjoyed sex as much as she did with him. He seemed to know what she liked, seemed to find places she didn't know she wanted to be touched.

Somewhere during the night she thought she heard him say "I love you," but she wasn't sure. For herself, she was too taken away with touching Frank to think any words. Leslie had always been a man who rushed sex, always in a hurry to get onto the next task. Or the next woman, Randy had often thought.

But Frank seemed to have all the time in the world. When he entered her, she was nearly screaming with desire. She held him inside her for a moment, loving how he filled her. When he began the velvet strokes in and out, she thought she might die with the pleasure.

Watching her, he seemed to know when she was

ready to peak, then he thrust into her until she thought she might faint. "Baby," she whispered, not sure if it was a word she was calling him or a wish she wanted fulfilled.

Later, shaking in the aftermath, she snuggled in his arms and went to sleep, feeling safe and secure and at home.

But when she awoke the next day, she could tell by the light that it was afternoon and Frank was gone. She thought that perhaps he was outside, but he wasn't. There was no note, nothing. Only his unmade bed showed he'd been there at all.

An hour after she woke, Sandy appeared with the horses and said he'd been instructed to take her home.

Eleven

THE OUTSIDE OFFICES were decorated for Christmas, and in the distance was the sound of laughter and glasses clinking at the annual party at the Montgomery-Taggert offices. But inside Frank Taggert's office there were no decorations, no lights, just Frank sitting alone, staring unseeing at the papers on his desk.

In the last two months he had lost weight and there were dark circles under his eyes. And in the last months he seemed to have lost his edge in the business world; he seemed to have lost his hunger.

"Hello," said a tentative voice from his doorway, and he looked up to see Eli. He hadn't seen him in two years, not since that first meeting; they had conducted their friendship entirely by letters, Frank sending all his letters to Eli care of a P.O. box in Denver.

"Eli," was all that Frank could say, and the first hint of a smile in a long time appeared on his face. "Come here," he said, holding out his hands.

Closing the door behind him, shutting out the sounds of the other people, Eli walked around the desk to stand in front of his friend.

"You look as bad as I feel," Frank said. "I guess you're too big to hold on a man's lap, aren't you?"

Eli would have died before he admitted it, but part of his anger at his father was defiance, telling himself that he didn't need a father. "No, I'm not too big," Eli said, and he found himself swooped into Frank's arms and pulled onto his lap like a child. Eli was quite tall but Frank was taller, and Eli found how much he had missed the solid male touch of a father.

Much to his horror, Eli found himself crying. Frank didn't say a word, just held him until Eli stopped, then offered him a clean white handkerchief.

"You want to tell me about it?"

"My mother is going to have a baby."

"I didn't know she got married."

"She didn't."

"Oh. That's a bit of a problem. You need money?"

"Always. But she needs a man to take care of her. I'll never be able to go away if she doesn't have someone to take care of her."

"Any money you need—"

"No!" Eli said sharply. "I don't want you to give me money."

"Okay." Frank pushed Eli's head back down to his shoulder. "What can I do?"

For a while Eli didn't speak. "Why haven't you written me for two months?"

"I don't think you'd understand."

"That's what adults always say. They think children are too stupid to understand anything. My mother thinks I won't understand about the baby and why she's not married to the baby's father."

"You're right. We adults do tend to put children into situations then mistakenly think they can't understand them. Maybe we're trying to protect you."

Frank took a deep breath. "I did a very stupid thing: I fell in love. No, don't look at me like that. I guess it was all right to fall in love, but I was afraid and I ran away."

"Why did you run away? Why were you afraid? I love my mother, but I'd never run away from her."

"It's not the same as loving your mother. With this woman I had a choice." He pulled Eli closer. "I don't know how to explain it. In all my life I've never needed anyone. Maybe it was because I had so many people around me. I grew up in a huge family and I had a lot of responsibility from the first. Maybe I just wanted to be different and separate. Maybe I didn't want to be like them. Can you understand that?"

"Yes. I am different from other kids."

"You and I are misfits, aren't we?"

"What about the woman?" Eli urged. "Why did you leave her?"

"I loved her. I don't know how to explain it, since it makes no sense. I just looked at her and loved her from the first. I thought she was something other than what she was, and that made me angry at first, but then I saw that she was a sweet, gentle woman." He smiled. "Well, not too gentle."

He paused. "You know what I liked best about her? She judged me on my own merits, not on my money or even on my looks. She just told me she didn't like me and didn't want to be near me. She even ran out the door of the cabin and tried to go back to Denver."

"She has no sense of direction."

Frank looked surprised. "That's true, but how did you know that?"

"My mother has none and Chelsea has none," Eli said, covering himself.

"Better not let any woman hear you make such a generalization. Anyway, I wanted her to stay and cook for me, so I offered her money, a great deal of money. But do you know what she asked for?"

"Something for someone else," Eli said.

"Exactly. That's just what she did. How did you guess?"

Ignoring the question, Eli said, "What did she ask for?"

"An education for her son at the finest school in the world, from freshman to Ph.D."

"Yes," Eli said softly. "She would." He spoke louder. "But what happened?"

"We, ah, we . . . Later we . . ."

"I've learned a lot about babies in the last two months," Eli said in a very grown-up voice. "What happened later?"

"I left her. Radioed for a 'copter to pick me up and for someone to come on horseback and get her."

Eli could feel his body stiffening. "You just went off and left her there. Did she . . . love you?"

"I don't know. She's the kind that if she goes to bed with a man, she—I mean, she takes things seriously and falls in love with any man she . . . spends time with."

"But you *loved* her?"

"Yes. I loved her a lot after that night, and it frightened me so much I left. I got on a plane and I haven't been off since. I think I wanted to run away. Or maybe I just wanted time to think."

"What did you think about?"

"Her. How I wanted to be with her. She has a way of seeing the truth of any situation. She told me she wasn't poor, she just didn't have any money."

"My mom says the same thing."

"Smart mother. Very smart if she had you."

"What are you going to do now? About this woman you love, I mean."

"Nothing. There's nothing I can do. I'm sure she's forgotten me by now."

Eli lifted his head to stare earnestly at Frank. "I don't think she has. What if she cries every night for you the way my mom does for the man whose baby she's going to have?"

Frank raised one eyebrow. "I don't think so. A woman scorned, that sort of thing. I found out a long time ago that if you leave women, they never forgive you. They might say they have, but they get you back in other ways."

"But what if she's not like that? What if she loves you too and she would understand if you explained to her that you were frightened and a coward?"

"You make me feel worse. Okay, so maybe I was a coward. I've been thinking that I should try to find her. If I checked the hospitals they'd know where she was. I asked my brother Mike, but he's not speaking to me." Frank swallowed. "And after what his wife said to me, I wish she weren't speaking to me either."

"What are you going to *do?*" Eli demanded. "What are you going to do when you find her?"

Frank grimaced. "I'd like to think that I'd fall on my knees and declare my undying love for her, but I can't actually imagine myself doing that. Anyway, I've already asked her to marry me, but she turned me down."

"She what! You asked her to *marry* you?"

"Yes." Frank leaned back to look at Eli. "Why are you so interested in this?"

"It's my mother and that man she is going to have a baby with. I wish he'd marry her."

"If he's a good man."

"He is. I know he is."

"It's not your father, is it?"

"No!" Eli almost shouted, then calmed himself. "No, of course not. It's just . . ." He trailed off, not knowing what else to say.

"All right," Frank said. "let's change the subject. What do you want for Christmas? Computer equipment?"

"No," Eli answered. "I haven't done much work lately. I may have to get a job after school to help with the baby."

"Like hell you will!" Frank said. "I'll give you a check that will cover all expenses for a couple of years. And I will not take more of your pride!"

Eli knew he should have said no, but he couldn't. "Will you do me a favor?"

"Anything. Want a trip somewhere for you and your mom?"

"I want something for my mom, yes." Eli took a deep breath. "Can you ride a horse?"

"Rather well, actually."

"Do you own a black one? A big black stallion?"

Frank smiled. "I think I can find such an animal. I didn't know you liked horses."

"It's not for me. My mother was paying the bills last week, and she said that we had to face the facts: no handsome man was going to ride up to the front door on a big black stallion and rescue us, so we'd have to make ends meet another way."

"And you want *me* to ride up on a black horse and present a check to your mother?"

"Cash would be better. She'd never cash a check; she has a very strong conscience."

Frank laughed. "A black stallion, eh? And I guess you want me to do it tomorrow on Christmas Day, no doubt."

"Are you busy with your family on that day?"

"Somehow I doubt they'll miss me." For a moment he sat still, holding Eli and thinking. "All right, I'll do it. Shall I wear a black silk shirt, black trousers, that sort of thing?"

"Yes, I think my mother would like that."

"Okay, tomorrow at ten A.M. Now that that's settled, what do you want for your birthday?"

"The password to tap into the Montgomery-Taggert data banks."

At that Frank laughed harder than he had in

months. "Come on, let's get something to eat. And I'd have to adopt you before I let you tap into that, and somehow I don't think your mother would like to share you."

As Frank was escorting Eli out of the office, he said, "Would you like me to hire private detectives to find the man who did this to your mother? I could have his taxes audited."

"Maybe," Eli said. "I'll let you know the day after Christmas."

Twelve

"ELI," RANDY SAID, exasperated, "why are you so nervous?" Since early that morning, while Randy was up to her elbows in cranberry sauce and pumpkin pie, Eli had been going back and forth to look out the window every few minutes. "If you're searching for Santa Claus, I don't think he remembers where this house is."

She'd meant to make a joke, but it fell flat. She couldn't afford much in the way of gifts this year, and she was constantly worried about how she was going to support the two of them in the coming months. And then there would be three of them, and she didn't know—

She stopped herself from thinking of the bad things, such as about money and where and how. She also wouldn't allow herself to think of Frank Taggert, the rotten—

Calm down, she reminded herself. Anger was not good for the baby, nor for Eli either, for that matter.

"Is Chelsea coming over?" she asked.

"Not now. Later—" Eli broke off as his face suddenly lit up in a grin. In fact, his whole body seemed to light up. Then he gained control of himself, and, doing his best to appear calm, he went to sit on the sofa and picked up a magazine. Since the magazine was *Good Housekeeping,* Randy knew something was up.

"Eli, would you mind telling me what is going on? All morning you've been looking out that window and—" She stopped and listened. "Are those hoofbeats? Eli, what are you up to? What have you and Chelsea done now?"

Eli gave her his best innocent look and kept staring at the magazine.

"Eli!" Randy said. "I think that horse is coming onto the *porch!*"

When her son just sat where he was, his head down but looking as though he were about to burst into giggles, Randy smiled too, knowing that she was going to open the door to find pretty little Chelsea on her pony, hair streaming down her back, a Christmas basket in her hand. Randy decided to play along with the game.

Wiping her hands and putting on her best stern face, she went to the door, planning to look surprised and delighted.

She didn't have to fake the look of surprise. Shock would be more like it. She didn't see Chelsea's pony but an enormous black horse trying to fit itself onto her front porch. A man, dressed all in black, was on its back, trying to get the animal under control without tearing his head off on the low porch roof.

"You have any female horses around here?" the rider shouted above the clamor of the horse's iron-shod hooves on the wooden porch.

"Next door," she shouted back, thinking that she knew that voice. "Could I help you find your way?" she asked, stepping back from the prancing hooves.

After a few powerful tugs on the reins and some healthy curses muttered under his breath, the man got the horse under control, then leaned over to withdraw a fat envelope from his saddlebag.

"Mrs. Harcourt," he said, "I present to you—"

He didn't say any more as he looked at her. "Miranda," he whispered.

Randy could say nothing. One minute she was watching a man dressed in black trying to control a black stallion on her front porch, and the next she was inside the house, bolting the door.

Frank was off the horse in seconds, not bothering to tie the animal but leaving it where it was and going to the closed door. "Miranda! Please listen to me. I need to talk to you."

Randy stood with her back to the door and squinted at her son, who was bent over the magazine on the coffee table as though it were the most interesting thing he had ever seen. "Eli! I know you are somehow involved in this and I demand to know what's going on."

Outside, Frank wasn't sure what to do. He was confused as much as anything. He'd expected to meet Eli's mother, but instead here was Miranda, the woman he loved, the woman who had haunted him for the last two months.

Leaning back against the wall for a moment, he suddenly put everything together. Eli had coordinated with his brother Mike to get Miranda up to the cabin, then he and Miranda had taken it from there. For a moment Frank felt like a fool for having been so thoroughly duped, but the next moment he was smiling. How much better did he want life than this? The child he loved was the son of the woman he loved, and Eli had said that his mother was going to have a baby—*his* baby.

"Miranda," he said through the glass-paned door, "I must talk to you."

"Over my dead body," she shouted back. "And get your horse off my porch!"

Randy looked at her son. "When I get through with you, young man, you are going to be very sorry." She too had just put together the cabin and this man with Eli and Chelsea's eternal snooping.

Eli tried to seem more closely bent over the magazine, but he was actually fascinated by what was going on around him, and strained to hear every word that was being said.

Maybe it was the clothes, maybe it was because Frank was sick of doing things the proper way, but he picked up a flower pot from the porch and threw it through the glass of the door, then reached inside and opened the lock.

"How dare you!" Randy said when he was inside. "I'll call the police."

He caught her before she reached the telephone. He was sure there were words he should say, but he couldn't think of them. He just remembered making love to her that night, the most satisfying lovemaking he'd ever experienced. Without thinking, he grabbed her in his arms and kissed her. When he stopped and she started to speak, he kissed her again.

When he stopped kissing her, Randy was leaning back in his arms, her full weight borne by him. "Now listen to me, Miranda, I may not know how to be a hero out of a book, but I know that I love you."

"But you left me," she whispered.

"Yes, I did. My feelings for you were too strong for me to handle. I'd heard about this falling-in-love but I didn't know it was so horrible or so strong. I thought that being in love was something nice."

"No," she whispered, and he kissed her again.

"Now," he said, "I want you to listen to me: I love you and I love Eli. I have for a long time. I even told you about him at the cabin."

"Eli?"

"Yes, Eli. And I love our child you're carrying, and I mean to be the best possible father to it. I may not be any good at being a father or a husband, but I'll do my best and that's all I can promise. And I—"

Suddenly all the bravado left him, and he clutched her to him. "Marry me, Miranda. Please, please marry me. I'm sorry I left you that day. Everything happened to me too suddenly. I thought I could forget you, that maybe it was the moonlight and the trees and your strawberry waffles."

"What was it?"

"I don't know. Just you. I just love you. Please marry me."

Before Randy could say a word, Eli jumped up and yelled, "Yes! Yes, she'll marry you. Yes, yes, yes."

"I can't—" she began, but Eli, behind her back, started kissing the back of his hand, and Frank was so fascinated with this that he almost didn't understand what the boy was trying to tell him to do.

Frank took Eli's suggestion and didn't let Randy say another word but kissed her again. "Think of the children," he said.

"But I'm not sure—"

He kissed her again. "I love you. Don't you love me some?"

Randy smiled. "Yes, I do. You don't deserve it, but I do." She leaned back away from him. "What about Julian? You weren't very nice to him."

"My first taste of jealousy. He was bored to death after six weeks without me, so I hired him back at half again his salary. Miranda, marry me, please."

At that moment a siren went off in the next block and scared the horse, which ran inside the house for safety. Ran into Frank, Randy, and Eli, who all tumbled into a startled heap on the floor.

"Stupid animal," Frank muttered as the horse nudged his pockets, looking for apples.

"Whose idea was the horse?" Randy asked.

"Mine," the two males said in unison.

And it was that unison that made Randy know what to do. From the beginning Frank had reminded her of someone, and now she knew who it was: Eli.

"Yes," she said, her arms going around his neck. "Yes, I'll marry you."

Eli put his arms around both of them. "I got what I wanted for Christmas and my birthday," he said. "And I'd rather go to Cambridge than Princeton." But his mother and Frank didn't hear him because they were kissing again.

Smiling, Eli untangled himself from the two adults and the horse and ran to his room to call Chelsea and tell her the news.

Robin and Marian Les Jeunes had struck again.

Judith McNaught

~

Double Exposure

One

OBLIVIOUS TO THE spectacular view beyond the glass wall OF the Houston high-rise that housed the offices of *Foster's Beautiful Living* magazine, Diana Foster paced in front of her desk with a telephone cradled between her shoulder and ear.

"Still no answer at the house?" asked Kristin Nordstrom, a production assistant at the magazine.

Diana shook her head and hung the phone up, already reaching into the credenza behind her desk for her handbag. "Everyone is probably out in the garden, reinventing mulch or something," she joked. "Did you ever notice," she continued with a rueful smile as she shrugged into a lime green linen jacket trimmed in white, "that when you have really exciting news, the people you want to share it with are never where you can reach them?"

"Well, how about if you tell me the news in the meantime," Kristin suggested teasingly.

Diana paused in the act of smoothing wrinkles from her white skirt and flashed the other woman a smile, but she had to look up to do it. At thirty-two, Kristin was two years older than Diana and a full six feet tall, with the fair skin and blue eyes of her Nordic ancestors. She was also conscientious, energetic, and detail-oriented, three traits that made her an ideal member of the production department.

"Okay, you've got it. I've just decided to shoot

some of the photos for the 'Perfect Weddings' issue on location in Newport, Rhode Island. The opportunity dropped into my lap this morning, and it's going to put us under tremendous deadline pressure, but it's too good to pass up. In fact, if you're available I'd like to send you to Newport a week before the wedding to help our crew. Mike MacNeil and Corey will arrive a few days later. You can work with them while they shoot the actual photos. They're going to need an extra pair of hands, and it will give you an opportunity to find out what it's like to work on location, under pressure, in difficult conditions. How does that strike you?"

"Like a bolt of lightning," she said, her face illuminated by a broad smile. "I've always wanted to go on location with Corey's crew. Newport should provide a gorgeous setting for the layout," she said as Diana started for the door. "Diana, before you go, I want to thank you for everything you've done. You're a joy to work with—"

Diana waved off her gratitude with a smile. "Just keep trying to find Corey. Oh, and keep calling the house. If anyone answers, tell them to stay put until I get there. Tell them I have great news, but I want Corey there to hear it."

"I will. And when you see Corey, please tell her I'm excited about the chance to work with her." She paused, a funny, uncertain smile on her face. "Diana, does Corey realize how much she looks like Meg Ryan?"

"Take my advice and don't mention it to her," Diana warned with a laugh. "She gets accosted all the time by strangers who refuse to believe her when she tells them she *isn't* Meg Ryan, and some of them become downright unpleasant because they think she's trying to trick them."

The telephone rang, interrupting them, and Kristin reached across the desk to answer it. "It's Corey," she said, holding the receiver toward Diana. "She's on the car phone."

"Thank heaven!" Diana said as she hurried forward and took the phone. "Corey, I've been trying to reach you all morning. Where have you been?"

Corey registered the excitement in her sister's voice, but at the moment her attention was concentrated on the driver of an orange pickup truck who was determined to merge into a space on the expressway that was already occupied by Corey's car. "I was at the printer's all morning," she said, deciding it was wiser to change lanes and let him win the bluff than to have an orange "pin stripe" embossed on the door of her burgundy car. "I wasn't happy with some of the shots I got for the barbecue layout for the next issue, and I brought him some different ones."

"Don't worry about that issue, it'll be fine. I have something more important to tell you— it's great news. Can you meet me at the house in twenty minutes? I'd like to tell everyone at once."

"Did I just hear you say *not* to worry about an issue?" Corey teased, amused and surprised by this unusual attitude of optimism from her eternally cautious sister. Glancing in the rearview mirror, she changed lanes so that she could take the exit for River Oaks, rather than continuing to the office as she'd originally intended. "I'm heading for the house, but I insist on some sort of hint now."

"Okay, here goes: What would you say if I told you

an unbelievable opportunity for the 'Perfect Weddings'
issue just fell into my lap! The mother of the bride,
who is clearly anxious to further bolster her social sta-
tus, wants us to feature her daughter's wedding in
Beautiful Living. If we are willing to do that, she is
willing to guarantee us that it will be done in authentic
'Foster Style,' under our supervision, *and* she is willing
to pay whatever that costs, as well as all travel expenses
for our staff."

For months, Corey and Diana had been discussing
possible locations and themes for the "ideal" wedding
they wanted to stage and feature in that issue, but so far
they'd discarded all of them either because Diana
thought they were too expensive or because Corey
thought they were artistically unacceptable. Diana bore
the full burden for all Foster Enterprises' financial matters, but the responsibility for the beautiful photographic layouts that appeared in Foster's publications
was Corey's. "It sounds good from a budget standpoint,
but what about the location? What sort of setting would
we have?"

"Brace yourself," Diana said.

In the car, Corey smiled with helpless anticipation.
"I'm braced. Tell me."

"The wedding is to take place on the lawn of the
bride's uncle's home . . . a lovely little forty-five room
'cottage,' built in 1895, complete with frescoed ceil-
ings, fabulous plasterwork . . . and undoubtedly hundreds of other little architectural goodies you could
include in our next coffee-table book—you know," she
said, "those big, fancy, beautiful books that you turn
out in your spare time?"

"Don't keep me in suspense." Corey laughed, her enthusiasm soaring. "Where's the house?"

"Are you ready for this?"

"I think so."

"Newport, Rhode Island."

"Oh, my God, how perfect!" Corey breathed, her photographer's mind already envisioning scenic shots with fabulous yachts floating on sparkling blue water in the background.

"The bride's mother sent me pictures of her brother's house and grounds and then called me this morning after the package arrived. Based on something she let slip, I got the funny feeling he may be paying for the entire wedding. Oh, I forgot, she promised to provide us with six local people who'll work under our supervision. That should enable us to put some special touches in a few of the main rooms, so you'll have even more to photograph. All materials and freelance labor are at their expense, of course, and our people will have private rooms at the house. The hotels are already booked for the season, and you'll all need to work late anyway, so that's a practical solution. Also, they have servants and they'll have houseguests, so staying there to make certain no one tampers with our handiwork becomes a necessity."

"No problem. For an opportunity like this, I would work and sleep in Bluebeard's house."

Diana's voice lost a little of its happy confidence. "Yes, but can you do that in Spencer Addison's house?"

Corey's reply was instinctive and instantaneous. "I'd prefer Bluebeard."

"I know."

"Let's find another wedding to feature."

"Let's talk about it when you get home."

Two

BY THE TIME COREY turned off Inwood Drive and onto the long, treelined driveway that led to the house, she already knew she was going to go to Newport. Diana undoubtedly knew it too. Whatever either of them needed to do for the good of the other, or the good of the family, or the good of Foster Enterprises, they would do. Somehow, that had always been understood between them.

Corey's mother and grandmother would also have to go to Newport, because they were the creators of what was now popularly called the "Foster Style." It was a concept that Corey and Diana had managed to showcase and market on a national scale, via the magazine and a variety of books, but it was still a joint family venture. Her mother and grandmother would undoubtedly regard the chance to see Spencer again as a delightful side benefit rather than a repugnant drawback, but then he hadn't hurt them the way he'd hurt Corey.

Diana's car was already parked in front of the house, a sprawling Georgian-style mansion that served as the family's home as well as a sort of "testing ground" for many of the menus and home improvement projects that appeared regularly in *Foster's Beautiful Living*.

Corey turned off the ignition and looked up at the

house that she and Diana had helped to protect and preserve. So many momentous events in her life were linked to this place, she thought as she leaned her head against the headrest, deliberately postponing going inside, where she would have to listen to a discussion of the Newport wedding. She had been thirteen and standing in the foyer when she had met Diana for the first time, and she'd met Spencer Addison a year later on the back lawn, when she attended her first grown-up party.

And here, in this house, she had learned to love and respect Robert Foster, a broad-shouldered giant of a man with a gentle heart and brilliant mind who later adopted her. He had met Corey's mother in Long Valley, when he bought the manufacturing company where she worked as a secretary, and the rest had seemed like a fairy tale. Entranced by Mary Britton's lovely face and warm smile, the Houston millionaire had taken her to dinner his first night in town and decided that same evening that Mary was the woman for him.

The following night, he appeared at Corey's grandparents' house, where she and her mother lived, and began a whirlwind courtship that included the entire close-knit little family. Like a benevolent wizard, he materialized each evening with an armload of flowers and little gifts for everyone, and he stayed until the early hours of the morning, talking to the entire family until they went to bed and then sitting out on the swing in the backyard with his arm around Mary's shoulders.

Within two weeks, he'd befriended Corey, soothed all of her grandparents' possible objections to the marriage, and overridden Mary's own marital misgivings, then he whisked his new bride and her daughter from their little frame house on the outskirts of Long Valley into his private plane. A few hours later, he laughingly carried first Mary and then Corey over the threshold of his Houston home, and they had lived there ever since.

Diana had been vacationing in Europe with some school friends and their parents when the wedding took place, and Corey had dreaded meeting her new sister when she finally came home at the end of the summer. Diana was a year older, and supposed to be very smart. Corey was morbidly certain that besides all that Diana would be beautiful and sophisticated and the world's biggest snob.

On the day Diana returned from Europe, Corey hid on the balcony eavesdropping while her stepfather greeted his daughter in the living room and informed her that while Diana had been "lazin' around in Europe all summer," he had gotten her a new mother *and* a new sister.

He introduced Diana to Corey's mother, but Corey couldn't quite hear what they said to each other because their voices were too soft. At least Diana hadn't had a temper tantrum, as Corey had feared, and Corey tried to take some solace in that when her stepfather brought Diana into the foyer and called Corey to come downstairs.

Her knees knocking together, Corey had thrust out her chin and affected an "I don't care what you think of me" attitude as she walked stiffly down the staircase.

At first glance, Diana Foster was the personification of Corey's worst fears: Not only was she pretty and petite, with green eyes and shiny brown hair that tumbled in mahogany waves halfway down her back, she was also wearing an outfit that looked like it came right out of a teen magazine—a very short tan skirt with cream-colored tights and a plaid vest in shades of tan and blue, topped off by a tan blazer with an emblem on the pocket. She had breasts, too, Corey noticed glumly.

In comparison, Corey, who was two inches taller and wearing jeans, felt like a washed-out, overgrown lump of ugly clay with her ordinary blue eyes and streaky blond hair pulled up in a ponytail. In honor of the occasion, Corey was wearing her favorite sweatshirt—the one with a running quarter horse emblazoned in white across her flat chest. She tried to take some comfort from that as Diana stared at Corey in silence and Corey stared right back.

"Say something, girls!" Robert Foster commanded in his cheerful but authoritative voice. "You're sisters, now!"

"Hi," Diana mumbled.

"Hi," Corey replied.

Diana seemed to be staring directly at Corey's sweatshirt, and Corey's chin lifted defensively. Her grandmother in Long Valley had lovingly painted the horse on that sweatshirt, and if Diana Foster said one nasty word about it, Corey was fully prepared to shove her right off her dainty feet.

Finally, Diana broke the uneasy silence. "Do you— do you like horses?"

Wary, Corey shrugged and then nodded.

"After dinner, we could go over to Barb Hayward's house. The Haywards have a great stable with racehorses. Barb's brother, Doug, has a polo pony, too."

"I've only ridden a few horses and they've been pretty gentle. I'm not good enough for racehorses."

"I'd rather pet them than ride them anytime. I got thrown last spring," Diana admitted, putting a hesitant foot on the first step and starting up toward her bedroom.

"You have to get right back on if you get thrown," Corey sagely advised, feeling remarkably buoyed by Diana's easy admission of her own shortcomings. She'd always wanted a sister, and maybe—just maybe—this dainty, beautiful brunette girl would do after all. Diana didn't *seem* like a snob.

They walked upstairs together and hesitated in the hallway in front of their separate doorways. From the living room below, they heard their parents' merry laughter and the sound was so youthful and carefree that both girls smiled at each other as if they'd caught their grown-up parents acting like children. Feeling that she owed Diana some sort of comment or explanation, Corey said with frank honesty, "Your dad is real nice. My dad ran out on us when I was still a baby. They got divorced."

"My mom died when I was five." Diana tipped her head to the side, listening to the happy voices coming from the living room, "Your mom makes my dad laugh. She seems nice."

"She is."

"Is she strict?"

"Sometimes. A little bit. But then she feels guilty and she'll bake up a batch of brownies or a fresh strawberry pie for me—I mean us—before I—I mean we—go to bed."

"Wow, brownies," Diana muttered. "And fresh strawberry pie."

"My mom believes in everything being fresh whenever possible, and my grandma's the same way. No canned stuff. No boxed stuff. No frozen stuff."

"Wow," Diana muttered again. With a shudder she confided, "Conchita—our cook—puts jalapeño peppers in everything."

Corey giggled. "I know, but my mom's already kind of taken over the kitchen."

Suddenly she felt as if she—and her mother—had something nice to offer to Diana and her father, after all. "Now that my mom's your mom, too, you won't have to eat any more of Conchita's jalapeños." Teasingly she added, "Just think, no more chocolate cake with jalapeño frosting!"

Diana fell into the game at once. "No more jalapeño waffles with jalapeño syrup!"

They broke off, giggling, then their eyes met and they stopped, each feeling awkward and desperate, as if their future might somehow teeter on saying just the right thing during these first minutes together Corey gathered the courage to speak first. "Your dad gave me a great camera for my birthday. I'll show you how it works and you can use it whenever you want."

"I guess he's 'our dad' from now on."

It was an offer to share him, and Corey bit down on her lip to keep it from trembling with emotion. "I—I always wanted a sister."

"Me, too."

"I like your outfit. It's neat."

Diana shrugged, her gaze on the flashy horse that

seemed to be racing across Corey's shirt. "I like your sweatshirt!"

"You do? Really?"

"Really," she said with an emphatic nod.

"I'll call Grandma and tell her you like it. She'll make one just like it for you, only in your favorite color. Her name is Rose Britton, but she'll want you to call her Grandma, like I do."

A glow appeared in Diana's eyes. "Grandma? You come with a grandma, too?"

"Yep. Grandma's a terrific gardener, besides being an artist. And Grandpa loves to garden, too, but he grows vegetables instead of flowers. And he can build anything! He can put a deck on your house, or build you a playhouse, or design neat things for the kitchen, just like that." Corey tried to snap her fingers for emphasis, but she was still a little nervous and failed. "He'll build you anything you'd like. All you have to do is ask him."

"You mean I'm going to have a grandpa, too?"

Corey nodded, then she watched in delight as Diana lifted her gaze to the ceiling and happily proclaimed, "A sister, and a mom, and a grandma, and a grandpa! This could be *very* cool!"

It only got better.

As Corey had predicted, her grandparents fell in love with Diana on her first visit, and both girls began spending so much time in Long Valley with Rose and Henry Britton that their father irritably announced he was feeling left out. The following spring, when Mary gently mentioned that she wished her parents lived closer, Robert happily solved everyone's problems by instructing an architect to draw up plans to renovate and enlarge the estate's guest cottage, then he stood back in considerable awe as Henry insisted on doing most of the carpentry. After that, it was only a small concession to add a greenhouse for Rose and a huge vegetable garden for Henry.

Robert's magnanimous gesture was repaid a hundredfold with savory meals of fresh fruits and vegetables grown on his own land and artfully presented amid centerpieces of flowers or whimsical baskets, or in "canoes" made from hollowed-out loaves of French bread. Even the location of meals changed according to the whim and mood of what Robert routinely referred to as "his ladies."

Sometimes they ate in the vast kitchen with its brick walls and copper pots hanging from an arched wall above the row of ovens and gas burners; sometimes they ate in the garden on place mats made from green and white striped cloth to match the umbrella above the table; sometimes they dined beside the pool on the low recliner chairs that Corey's grandfather had fashioned and built from strips of wood; sometimes they ate on a blanket on the lawn, but with crystal goblets and fine china for what Mary called "a special touch."

This flair for dining and entertaining earned Mary a great deal of praise a year after her wedding, when she gave her first big party as Robert Foster's wife. At the outset, she was alarmed and intimidated at the thought of entertaining Robert's friends, people who she feared would think they were her social superiors and who she was certain would look upon her as an interloper, but Corey and Diana weren't worried at all. They knew whatever she did, she did with love and with flair. Robert Foster felt the same way. Wrapping his arm around her shoulders, he said, "You'll dazzle 'em, dar-lin'—You just be your sweet self, and do things your own special way."

After a week of consultations with the entire family, Mary finally decided to have a Hawaiian luau at pool-side beneath the palms on the lawn. And as Robert had cheerfully predicted, the guests were indeed dazzled— not only by the sumptuous food, gorgeously decorated tables, and authentic music, but by the hostess herself. On the arm of her husband, Mary moved among her guests, her slim figure wrapped in a lovely sarong, her free arm draped from wrist to elbow with spectacular leis made of homegrown orchids from their own green-house, and as she encountered each female guest, she presented her with a lei that matched the lady's apparel.

When several men complimented her on the amaz-ingly tasty food and then expressed amused shock at the discovery that Robert Foster had plowed up part of his lawn for a vegetable garden, Mary signaled her father, who proudly offered tours of the garden by moonlight. As Henry Britton showed the tuxedo-clad gentlemen along the neat rows of organically grown vegetables, his enthusiasm was so contagious that before the night was over, several of the men had announced their desire to have vegetable gardens of their own.

When the ladies asked for the name of her caterer, Mary stunned them by naming her own family. Marge Crumbaker, the society gossip columnist for the *Houston Post* who was covering the party, also asked her what caterer as well as what florist she had used, and Mary grew tense, knowing she might seem like a fool, but she admitted the truth: despite the popular notion that all domestic duties were sheer drudgery, and that any intelligent woman would want to find other, more appropriate uses for her time, Mary loved to cook, garden, and sew. She was in the midst of confessing that she also enjoyed canning fruits and vegetables when she noticed an elderly, white-haired woman who was sitting slightly off to one side, rubbing her arms as if she were chilled. "Excuse me," Mary explained with an apologetic smile, "but I think Mrs. Bradley is cold, and I need to find her a wrap."

She sent Corey and Diana into the house to find a shawl, and when they returned, they found Mary talking to their grandmother about the interview with Marge Crumbaker. "I just know I made us all sound like *The Beverly Hillbillies!*" she confided miserably. "I don't even want to know what she says about us in that column." She took the shawl from the girls and asked her mother to bring it to Mrs. Bradley, then she melted into the crowd to look after her guests.

Corey and Diana were stricken at the possibility of being held up to public ridicule. "Do you think she'll make fun of us?" Diana asked.

With a reassuring smile, Rose put her arms around their shoulders. "Not a chance," she whispered encouragingly, then she headed off to give Mrs. Bradley the shawl, hoping she was right.

Mrs. Bradley was glad for the lacy, handmade shawl. "I used to love to crochet," she said, holding it up to admire, her long, aristocratic fingers gnarled with arthritis. "Now I can't hold a hook in my hands, not even those big ones they sell in the stores."

"You need a hook with a large handle that's specially made to fit your hand," Rose said. She looked about for

Henry, saw him standing nearby, talking to a middle-aged man about growing edible flowers, and signaled him to come over. When Henry heard the problem, he nodded at once. "What you need, ma'am, is a hook with a big, fat, wooden handle that's shaped to the grip of your hand, with small indentations low on the handle, so it won't slip out of your fingers."

"I don't think they make any like that," Mrs. Bradley said, looking hopeful and despondent at the same time.

"No, but I can make you one. You come by the day after tomorrow and plan to stay for a couple of hours so I can fit it to your grip." He touched her twisted fingers and added sympathetically, "Arthritis is a curse, but there's ways to work around it. Got a touch of it, myself."

As he walked away, Mrs. Bradley watched him as if he were some sort of mythical knight in shining armor. Slowly she transferred her gaze to Rose and politely excused her to return to the other guests. "My grandson, Spencer, is attending another party nearby. I asked him to come for me at eleven o'clock, to take me home. You needn't stay here on my account."

Rose passed a sweeping glance over the banquet tables and, satisfied that she wasn't needed elsewhere, she sat down beside Mrs. Bradley. "I'd rather talk with you. You'll need to use thick yarn with Henry's hook. I intended to teach Diana how to crochet and I showed her a picture of a place mat, hoping to spark her interest. She turned up her nose at the notion of crocheting rectangles. She suggested we make them in the shape of apples, lemons, strawberries, and things like that. She drew up some sketches. They were simple and bold. You'd enjoy making them."

"Diana?" Mrs. Bradley interrupted doubtfully. "You don't mean little Diana Foster?"

Grandma nodded proudly. "I do, indeed. That girl has an artistic streak a mile wide—they both do. She paints and does charcoal sketches that are excellent. And Corey's fascinated with photography, and quite good at it. Robert bought her developing equipment for her fourteenth birthday."

Mrs. Bradley leaned forward and followed Rose's gaze, smiling a little when she spotted the girls. "I don't envy your life when the boys discover those two," she chuckled.

Unaware that they were being scrutinized and discussed, Diana and Corey observed the festivities from the sidelines near the dessert tables. It was not the sort of gathering to which teenagers were invited, and so they were pretty much on their own. At their father's request, Corey had been acting as "roving photographer," moving from group to group, trying to capture the mood of the party and the faces of the guests without being too obvious or in the way.

"Are you ready to go inside?" Diana asked. "We could watch a movie."

Corey nodded. "As soon as I use up the rest of this roll of film." She looked about for a face she hadn't photographed yet, realized she hadn't taken many pictures of her own family, and scanned the crowd to see where they were.

"There's Grandma, over there," she said, starting forward. "Let's get a pict—" She stopped short, and her breath seemed to catch in her throat as a tall young man in a white dinner jacket suddenly strolled out of the crowd. "Oh, *wow!*" Corey breathed, unknowingly

clutching Diana's wrist in a vice and stopping her
short. *"Oh, wow . . ."* she whispered. "Who is that?
He's over there, being introduced to Grandma," she
clarified.

Diana followed the direction of her stare. "That's
Spencer Addison. He's Mrs. Bradley's grandson, and
when he isn't away at SMU, he lives with her. He
always has." Racking her brain for any other tidbits of
information she'd heard over the years, she added, "He
has a mother somewhere and a half-sister who's a lot
older, but he doesn't have much to do with them . . .
Wait! I remember why he lives with his grandmother.
His mother kept changing husbands, and so Mrs.
Bradley decided Spencer should live with her a long
time ago. He's nineteen or twenty, I don't know
which."

Corey had never had a crush on a boy in her life,
and until that moment she'd harbored considerable
derision for all the girls she'd known who had. Boys
were just boys and no big deal. Until that moment.

Choking back a surprised giggle at Corey's mesmerized expression, Diana said, "Do you want to meet
him?"

"I'd rather marry him."

"First you have to meet him," Diana said with typical practicality and attention to protocol. "Then you
can propose. Come on, before he leaves—"

In her haste, she grabbed Corey's hand, but Corey
yanked it back in panic. "I can't, not now! I mean, I
don't want to just barge up to him and shake his hand. I
can't. He'll think I'm a jerk. He'll think I'm a kid."

"In the dark, you can pass for sixteen."

"Are you sure?" Corey asked, ready to rely completely on Diana's judgment. Although there was only a year's difference in their ages, to Corey, Diana was the epitome of youthful sophistication—poised, reserved, and outwardly confident. Earlier, Corey had felt she herself looked especially nice that night in her "nautical" outfit of wide-legged, navy blue pants and a short navy jacket trimmed in gold braid at the wrists with gold anchors appliquéd at the shoulders and gold stars on the lapels. Diana had helped her choose the clothes, then she'd styled Corey's heavy blond hair into a fashionable knot atop her head, which they'd both agreed gave Corey a more mature look. Now Corey waited in an agony of uncertainty while Diana gave her a close once-over.

"Yes. I'm sure."

"What if he thinks I'm a troll?"

"He won't think that."

"I won't know what to say to him!" Diana started forward, but Corey pulled her back again. "What'll I say? What'll I do?"

"I have an idea. No, bring the camera with you," Diana said when Corey started to put the camera down on a vacant lawn chair. "Don't worry."

Corey wasn't worried, she was petrified, but in the space of a moment, fate had thrust her out of childhood and onto a new path, and she was too brave and too excited to try to retreat to the safety of the old path.

"Hi, Spencer," Diana said when they reached their destination.

"Diana?" he said in the flattering tone of one who can scarcely believe his eyes. "You're all grown up."

"Oh, I hope not," she joked with a regal ease that Corey mentally vowed to copy. "I wanted to end up

taller than this by the time I grew up!" Turning to
Corey, she said, "This is my sister, Caroline."

The moment Corey yearned for and simultaneously
dreaded had arrived. Grateful to Diana for using her
real name, which sounded older and more sophisticated, Corey forced her gaze up the front of his white
pleated shirt, past his tanned jaw, until it finally col-
lided with his amber eyes, and she felt a jolt that made
her knees knock.

He held out his hand, and as if from far away, she
heard his deep voice—a velvet voice, intimate and
caressing as he repeated her name. "Caroline," he said.

"Yes," she breathed, gazing into his eyes and putting
her trembling hand in his. His palm was warm and
broad, and his fingers closed around hers. Her fingers
tightened involuntarily on his, inadvertently preventing
him from breaking the handclasp.

Beside her, Diana was rushing to her rescue, trying
to distract Mrs. Bradley and their grandmother from
Corey's enraptured pose. "Corey still has some film in
her camera, Mrs. Bradley. We thought you might like to
have a picture taken of you and Spencer, together."

"What a lovely idea!" Mrs. Bradley said, leaning
around Diana and breaking the spell by addressing
Corey directly. "Your grandmother tells me you're
quite the young photographer!"

Corey looked over her shoulder at Mrs. Bradley and
nodded, still gripping Spencer Addison's hand.

"How would you like Spencer and his grandmother
to pose, Corey?" Diana hinted.

"Oh, pose. Yes." Corey loosened her grasp on his
hand and slowly pulled her gaze from his. In a sudden
flurry of motion, she stepped back and raised her cam-

era, looked through the viewfinder, and aimed the camera straight at Spencer, nearly blinding him with the unexpected glare of her flash. He laughed, and she shot another picture.

"That was a little too quick," Corey said in breathless apology, hastily focusing again. This time he looked straight at her and smiled—a lazy grin that swept across his tanned features and touched his tawny eyes. Corey's heart did a somersault that she feared made her camera hand shake as she took that picture and the next one. Thrilled with the opportunity to have lots of pictures of him to look at in the morning, she forgot all about poor Mrs. Bradley and took two more shots of him in rapid succession.

"And now," Diana said, sounding as if she was about to choke on something, "how about a few shots of *Mrs. Bradley* with Spencer. If the pictures turn out," she added in a deeply meaningful voice aimed directly at Corey, "we could bring them over to *their house* in a couple days."

The realization that she'd completely forgotten about taking Mrs. Bradley's picture made Corey flush to the roots of her hair, and she immediately vowed to produce a photograph of the two of them that would do credit to a professional portrait photographer. With that goal in mind, the technicalities of photography temporarily replaced her preoccupation with her handsome subject. "The torchlight makes it tricky," she said. With the camera to her eye, she addressed Spencer. "If you could move over behind your grandmother's chair . . . Yes, just like that. Now, Mrs. Bradley, look at me . . . and you, too . . . Spencer . . ."

Saying his beautiful name sent shivers down her

spine, and she paused to swallow. "Yes, that's good."
Corey took the shot, but when the pair started to part,
she wasn't at all satisfied with the stiffness of the pose
she'd arranged. "Let's take just one more," she pleaded.
She waited while Spencer stepped back into the frame.
"This time, put your hand on your grandmother's left
shoulder."

"Aye-aye, Admiral," he said, teasing her about her
jaunty naval outfit, but following her order.

Corey held on to her composure at the endearing
little joke, but she tucked his words away in her
heart, to be savored later. "Mrs. Bradley, I'd like you
to look at me. That's good," she said, scrutinizing the
light playing on Spencer's features and its effect on
the ultimate outcome. She liked the way his large
hand looked as it rested almost protectively on his
grandmother's shoulder. "Now, before I take the picture, I'd like you each to take a second and think of a
really special time that you spent together, just the
two of you when Spencer was a little boy. A trip to
the zoo, maybe . . . or the day he got his first
bicycle . . . or an ice cream cone he dropped and still
wanted to eat . . ."

Through the viewfinder, she saw a fond grin drift
over Spencer's face, and he glanced down at his
grandmother's white head. At the same moment Mrs.
Bradley's face softened with a smile of remembrance
that made her eyes twinkle, and she looked up at him,
spontaneously lifting her right hand and laying it over
his. Corey snapped the shot and another immediately
after, her heart pounding with delight at the unexpectedly intimate moment she was almost sure she'd captured on film.

She let the camera slide down and smiled at both of them, her eyes shining with hope. "I'll have these developed at a camera shop. I don't want to try to do it myself, they're too important."

"Thank you very much, Corey," Mrs. Bradley said with gruff pleasure, but her eyes were still shining with whatever memory Corey had evoked.

"I'd like a picture taken with you, too, Spence, and then we have to go or we'll be late!" a plaintive female voice said, and for the very first time, Corey realized that there was a girl with Spencer. A beautiful girl, with a small waist and big breasts and long, slender legs. Corey's heart sank, but she obediently stepped back to take the picture, then she waited until the flickering torchlight threw a shadow over her rival's face.

The following week, Corey's pictures were ready to be picked up and Marge Crumbaker's column appeared in the *Post*. The entire family gathered around the dining room table and held their breaths while Robert opened it to the society section. An entire page was covered with pictures of the guests and decorations, the food and flowers, and even the greenhouse and garden.

But it was Marge Crumbaker's column that made the family beam as Robert Foster proudly read her words aloud:

" 'As she presided over this lovely party and looked after her guests, Mrs. Robert Foster III (the former Mary Britton of Long Valley) displayed a graciousness, a hospitality, and an attention to her guests that will surely make her one of Houston's leading hostesses. Also present at the festivities were Mrs. Foster's parents, Mr. and Mrs. Henry Britton, who were kind enough to escort many fascinated guests and would-be gardeners and handymen (if we only had the time!) through the new garden, greenhouse, and workshop that Bob Foster has erected on the grounds of his River Oaks mansion. . . .'"

Three

THE PARTY HAD been a great success and so were the pictures Corey took of Spencer Addison and his grandmother. Corey was so excited that she ordered two enlargements of the best picture—one for Mrs. Bradley and one for herself.

The day they arrived, she placed her framed copy on her nightstand, then she stretched out on the bed on her back to make certain she could see his picture with her head on the pillow. Lifting her head, she peered at Diana, who was sitting at her feet. "Isn't he gorgeous?" she sighed. "He's Matt Dillon and Richard Gere rolled into one—only better looking. He's Tom Cruise and that guy Harrison whatshisname—"

"Ford," Diana provided with typical attention to details.

"Ford," Corey agreed, picking up the picture and holding it above her face. "I'm going to marry him someday. I just *know* I am."

Although Diana was a little older, and definitely wiser and more practical, she wasn't immune to Corey's contagious enthusiasm or the energy with which Corey always tackled life's obstacles. "In that case," Diana said, getting up and reaching for Corey's phone, "we'd better make sure your future husband is home before we take the other copy over to Mrs. Bradley. We can walk over there, it's only two miles."

Mrs. Bradley didn't merely like the photograph, she loved it. "What a talent you have!" she exclaimed, her arthritic hand trembling a little as she touched Spencer's face in the picture. "I shall place this on my dresser. No," she said, getting up, "I shall place it here in the living room where everyone can see it. Spencer," she called out as he bounded down the staircase, heading for the front door. In answer to her summons, he strolled into the living room, wearing tennis whites and carrying a tennis racket—looking to Corey even more gorgeous than he had in a tuxedo.

Oblivious to Corey's hectic color, Mrs. Bradley gestured toward the girls. "You know Diana, and I'm sure you remember Corey from the party Saturday night?"

If he had said no, Corey would have died of humiliation and disappointment right there—expired on Mrs. Bradley's Persian carpet and had to be carried out and buried.

Instead, he looked at Corey with a smile and then nodded. "Hi, ladies," he said, making Corey feel at least twenty.

"The girls have just brought me a very special gift." She handed him the picture in its frame. "Remember when Corey asked us to think of a special moment while she took the picture?—look how it turned out!"

He took the picture, and to Corey's almost painful joy she saw his expression go from polite interest to one of surprised pleasure. "It's a wonderful picture, Corey," he said, turning the full force of his deep voice and magnetic gaze on her. "You're very talented." He returned the photograph to his grandmother, bent down, and brushed a quick kiss on her brow. "I have a tennis date at the club in thirty minutes," he told her. To the girls, he said, "Can I give you a ride home? It's on my way."

Riding beside Spencer Addison in his blue sports car with the convertible top down soared straight to the top of Corey's "Major Events of a Lifetime" list, and during the next several years, she managed to create a great many more events of a similar nature. In fact, she developed a positive genius for inventing reasons to visit his grandmother, whenever Spencer was home from college for an occasional weekend. His grandmother inadvertently collaborated in Corey's grand design by sending Spencer over to the Fosters' to deliver things she'd baked or to pick up some recipes or patterns she wanted to try with Grandpa's specially made crochet hook.

As the weeks passed, Corey used her interest in photography as an additional excuse to see Spencer and capture more treasured shots of him. Under the ploy of wanting to perfect her ability with "action photography," she went to Spencer's polo matches, his tennis matches, and anywhere else she could possibly go where he was likely to be. As her collection of his pictures grew, she started a special scrapbook and kept it under her bed, and when that was filled, she started another, and then another. Her favorite shots of him, however, were always displayed around her bedroom, where she could see them.

When her grandmother asked why most of the pictures in her room were of Spencer Addison, Corey dissembled with a long, involved, and mostly trumped-up explanation about Spencer's unique photogenic qualities and how concentrating on a single "subject" in a variety of settings helped her to gauge her improvement as a photographer. For good measure, she threw in a lot of jargon about stop-action photography and the effect of aperture settings and shutter speeds on the final result. Her grandmother walked out of Corey's bedroom looking a little dazed and thoroughly confused, and did not broach the subject again.

The rest of the family undoubtedly suspected Corey's true feelings, but they were all kind enough not to tease her about them. The object of her unflagging devotion seemed perfectly at ease around her, as if he had no idea that she lived for his visits, and he visited often, although mostly on errands for his grandmother. The reasons he came to the house didn't matter to Corey; what mattered was that he was rarely in a hurry to *leave*.

If she had advance notice of his arrival, she spent hours in her room frantically restyling her hair, changing her clothes, and trying to decide on a good topic for conversation when she had a chance to talk to him. But regardless of how she looked, or what topics she chose, Spencer unfailingly treated her with a gentle courtesy that evolved into a kind of brotherly affection by the time she was fifteen. He took to calling her "Duchess" and teasing her about being beautiful. He admired her latest photos and joked with her and talked to her about college. Sometimes he even stayed for dinner.

Corey's mother said she thought he came over to the house and stayed for a while because he'd never had a real family, and so he enjoyed being with theirs.

Corey's father thought Spencer enjoyed talking with him about the oil business. Corey's grandfather was equally certain that it was his garden and greenhouse that interested Spencer. Corey's grandmother was adamantly of the opinion that he knew the value of healthy cooking and eating, which was her forte.

Corey clung to the hope that he enjoyed seeing and talking to *her,* and Diana was young enough and loyal enough to completely agree with Corey.

Four

SOMEHOW, COREY MANAGED to maintain the facade of wanting only a platonic friendship with him until she was sixteen. Until then she'd kept a tight rein on herself, partly because she was terrified of overwhelming him with her ardor and losing him completely, and partly because she hadn't found a risk-free opportunity to show him that she was old enough and more than ready for a romantic relationship with him.

Fate handed her that opportunity the week before Christmas. Spence had come over to the house to deliver an armload of Christmas gifts from his grandmother to each of the Fosters, but for Corey there was a special gift from him to her. He stayed for dinner and then for two games of chess with her grandfather. Corey waited until afterward, when the family had gone upstairs, then she insisted he wait while she opened his gift to her. Her hands shook uncontrollably as she spread the tissue in the big box aside and lifted out a large beautifully bound book of photographs by five of the world's leading photographers. "It's beautiful, Spence!" she breathed. "Thank you so much! I'll treasure it always."

She knew he was on his way to a Christmas party being given by some friends of his, but as she ushered him across the foyer in her new high heels, long plaid skirt, white silk blouse, and wine-colored velvet blazer, she had never felt more confident and mature. Because she'd known he was coming that night, she'd put her hair up into a chignon, with tendrils at her ears, because the style made her look older, and because Diana and she agreed it made her blue eyes look bigger.

"Merry Christmas, Corey," he said in the foyer as he turned to leave. Corey acted on sheer impulse because if she'd thought about it, she'd never have had the nerve. The house was decorated for the Christmas season in pine boughs and holly—and hanging from the crystal chandelier above the foyer was a giant bunch of mistletoe tied with red and gold ribbon. "Spence," she burst out, "don't you know it's bad luck not to honor the Christmas traditions of your friends when you're in their home?"

He turned, his hand already on the front door handle. "It is?"

Corey nodded slowly, her fingers clasped behind her back in a pose of nervous expectation.

"What tradition am I violating?"

In answer, she tipped her head back and looked meaningfully at the mistletoe overhead. "That one," she said, struggling to keep her voice steady. He looked up at the mistletoe, then down at her, and his expression was so dubious and hesitant that Corey abruptly lost much of her nerve.

"Of course," she fabricated hastily, "the tradition doesn't require you to kiss me. You can kiss anyone who lives in the house." Trying to turn it into a joke, she continued. "You can kiss a maid. Or Conchita. Or our cat. My dog . . ."

He laughed then and took his hand off the doorknob, but instead of leaning forward and kissing her cheek, which was about all she'd let herself hope he'd do, he hesitated, looking at her. "Are you sure you're old enough for me to do this?"

Corey got lost in those tawny eyes, mesmerized by something she saw flickering in their depths. *Yes,* she told him silently, beckoning him to kiss her. *I know I'm old enough. I've been waiting forever.* She knew the answers were in her eyes, and she knew he saw them, and so she smiled a little, and with her hands still clasped behind her back, Corey softly and deliberately said, "No." It was an instinctive piece of highly effective flirtation, and just as instinctively he recognized it . . . and succumbed.

With a husky, startled laugh, he took her chin between his thumb and forefinger, tipped her head back, and brushed his lips slowly back and forth across hers . . . just once. It took only a moment for the kiss, but it was another, longer, moment before he took his hand from her chin and an even longer one before Corey opened her eyes. "Merry Christmas, Duchess," he said softly.

Corey felt the blast of icy air as he opened the door. When it closed behind him, she reached out automatically and switched off the foyer lights; then she stood there in the dark, reeling from the tenderness she'd heard in his voice after the kiss. For two years, she had fantasized about Spencer Addison, but not even in her fantasies had she ever imagined that his voice could be as stirring and as tender as a kiss.

Five

THE ONLY BLIGHT on her happiness was that Spencer had said he planned to stay at college over spring break, studying for final exams, and that he didn't intend to be back in Houston until after he graduated in June.

Corey, who hadn't had much interest in dating, decided to use the months between January and June to broaden her knowledge of the workings of the male mind by going out regularly with a variety of boys. Spence was almost six years older than she, and a hundred times more worldly, and she was beginning to worry that her lack of dating experience would eventually embarrass him or somehow stop him from getting any more deeply involved with her.

She was popular at school and there were a gratifying number of boys who were eager to take her out, but it was Doug Hayward who quickly became her favorite and most constant escort, as well as her confidant.

Doug was a senior at her high school, the captain of the debate team, and the quarterback of their football team, but his greatest attraction from Corey's standpoint was that he, too, was hopelessly in love with someone else who lived far away. As a result, she could talk to him about Spence and get some male insight from an older boy who, like Spence, was smart and athletic and who also regarded her more as a sister than a real girlfriend.

It was Doug who tutored her on what "older men" liked in their girlfriends and who helped her come up with ideas to capture Spencer's attention and then his heart. Some of Doug's ideas were useful, some impractical, and some downright hilarious.

In May, just after Corey's seventeenth birthday, they had a long discussion about kissing techniques—a subject in which Corey felt woefully inexperienced—but when Doug earnestly attempted to demonstrate some of the techniques they'd discussed they ended up convulsed with laughter. When he told her to slide her hand around his nape, Corey made a comic, threatening face and slid her hand around his throat instead. When he attempted to lightly kiss her ear, she got the giggles and laughed so hard she bumped his nose.

They were still laughing as he walked her to her front door that night. "Do me a favor," Doug joked, "if you ever tell Addison what we did tonight, don't mention my name. I don't want my right arm broken by some jealous running back before I ever get to play college football."

They'd already discussed the possibility of making Spence jealous as a way of forcing him to notice Corey, but the methods Doug came up with had seemed trite and transparent to Corey, and the outcome far too uncertain. "I can't see Spence getting jealous over anything connected with me," she said with a sigh, "let alone having him get physical about it."

"Don't bet *my* life on it. There's nothing like knowing your girl has been kissing someone else to make a sensible guy lose his mind. Believe me," he added as he left, "I know from experience."

Corey watched him walk down the sidewalk to his car in the driveway, her imagination running away with itself as his words revolved in her mind and an idea took shape.

She was still standing on the porch long after his taillights disappeared. By the time she finally went inside, she'd made a decision and was working out the fine details of the plan.

As soon as Spence came home in June, she had Diana suggest to their mother that Spence be invited to the house for dinner later in the week. Mrs. Foster readily complied. "Spence seemed delighted," she announced to the family when she hung up the phone in the kitchen.

"That young man appreciates the benefits of healthy home cooking," Rose said.

"He likes those father-son chats he and I have about business and making money," Mr. Foster asserted. "I've missed them, too."

"I'd better finish that project in the workshop," Henry mused aloud. "Spencer has an eye for fine woodwork. He should have gotten his degree in architecture instead of finance. He's fascinated with anything that has to do with building things."

Corey and Diana looked at each other with a conspiratorial smile. They didn't care why Spence came, so long as he came and stayed after dinner so that Corey could get him outside and execute her plan. Diana's contribution was to get everyone else to go to the movies once they'd had dinner and a little time to visit with him. Diana had chosen a movie that Corey had already seen so that no one would think it odd when Corey decided to stay home.

By the time Spence finally rang the doorbell, Corey was a mass of quivering nerves, but she managed to look serenely composed as she smiled into his eyes and gave him a quick, welcoming hug. She sat across from him at dinner, surreptitiously studying the changes that a half year had made in his beloved face, while he talked about attending graduate school in the fall. His tawny hair seemed a little darker to Corey, and the masculine planes of his face harder, but that lazy, heart-stopping smile of his hadn't changed a bit. Every time he grinned at some quip of hers, Corey's heart melted, but when she smiled back at him, her expression was teasing, not worshipful. By her own count, she'd been out on forty-six dates with boys since he left her in the foyer at Christmas, and although the majority of them had been with Doug, her six-month crash course on dating, flirtation, and men in general had served her very well.

She was counting heavily on it as Diana herded the entire family into the car and Spence picked up his sport jacket, obviously intending to leave also. "Could you stay for a little while longer?" Corey asked, giving him what she hoped was a vaguely troubled look. "I— I need some advice."

He nodded, his forehead furrowing with concern. "What sort of advice, Duchess?"

"I don't want to talk abut it here. Let's go outside. It's a beautiful evening, and I won't have to worry about our housekeeper overhearing us."

He walked beside her, his sport jacket slung over his shoulder and hooked on his thumb, and Corey wished she could feel one tenth as relaxed as he looked. The night was balmy, devoid for once of the awful humidity that made Houston summers into a steam bath. "Where do you want to sit?" he asked as she walked by two umbrellaed tables and headed toward the swimming pool further back on the lawn.

"Over here." Corey gestured to a lounge chair next to the swimming pool, waited until he sat down on it, then she boldly sat down beside him. Tipping her head back, she gazed up through a canopy of blooming crape myrtles to the stars twinkling in the moonless sky while she fought desperately to recover her fleeing courage. She made herself think only of his Christmas kiss and of the tenderness in his eyes and voice afterward. He had felt something special for her that night. She was still positive he had. Now she needed to make him remember it and feel it again. Somehow.

"Corey, what did you bring me out here to ask me?"

"It's a little difficult to explain," she said with a nervous laugh that caught in her throat. "I can't ask my mother because she'll get all upset," she added, deliberately eliminating what she knew would be his only escape routes from the discussion. "And I don't want to talk about it with Diana. She's all excited about starting college in the fall."

She stole a glance at him and saw him watching her with narrowed eyes. Drawing a fortifying breath, she plunged in. "Spence, do you remember when you kissed me at Christmas?"

His answer seemed a long time in coming. "Yes."

"At the time, you may have known I didn't have much experience . . . Did you know—notice—that?" The last question hadn't been in her rehearsed speech, and so she waited, wanting him to deny that he'd noticed. "Yes," he said flatly.

Irrationally, Corey was crushed. "Well, I've gotten a lot more experience since then! A *whole lot* more!" she informed him haughtily.

"Congratulations," he said shortly. "Now get to the point."

His tone was so sharp and impatient that Corey's head snapped around. Not once in all the times that she'd been with him had he *ever* spoken to her like that. "Never mind," she said, nervously rubbing her palms on her knees. "I'll find someone else to ask," she added, abruptly abandoning the whole scheme and starting to stand.

"Corey," he snapped, "are you pregnant?"

Corey gave a shriek of horrified laughter and dropped back to her seat, gaping at him. "From *kissing?*" she laughed, rolling her eyes. "What did you do, skip health and hygiene class in the sixth grade?"

For the second time in moments, she saw Spencer Addison exhibit another unprecedented emotion—chagrin. "I guess you aren't pregnant," he said wryly, shooting her a rueful smile.

Utterly delighted to have him off balance for a change, Corey continued to tease him, trying without success to control her wobbly grin. "Don't football players take biology at SMU? Listen, if *that's* why you have to go to graduate school, save the tuition and talk to Teddy Morris in Long Valley, Texas. His dad's a doctor, and when Teddy was only eight years old, he told us everything there is to know on the playground by the swings." Spencer's shoulders were shaking with laughter as Corey finished. "Of course, he used a pair of turtles for teaching tools. They *may* have mated by now."

With traces of a grin still tugging at the corners of his mouth, he shifted position so that his shoulders were against the raised back of the chaise lounge and his left leg was bent at the knee, resting beside Corey's hip. His right leg, which had been injured twice in games last year, was stretched out beside the chair, his heel resting on the flagstones. "Okay," he said mildly, folding his arms over his chest and lifting his brows, "let's hear it."

"Is your right knee bothering you?"

"Your *problem* is bothering me."

"You don't know what it is yet."

"That's the part that's bothering me."

The banter was so endearingly familiar, and he looked so relaxed and powerful—as if he could carry the entire world's problems on his wide shoulders— that Corey had a crazy impulse to simply curl up beside him and forget kissing. On the other hand, if she executed her plan successfully, she might end up stretched out beside him *and* being kissed. An infinitely preferable alternative, she decided as she paused for a quick mental check of her appearance to make certain she looked as desirable as possible. Something slinky and low-cut would have been preferable to the white shorts and sleeveless knit top she was wearing, but at least they showed off her tan well.

"Corey," he said in a no-nonsense tone, "the problem?"

Corey drew a long, fortifying breath. "It's about kissing . . ." she began haltingly.

"I already got that part. What do you want to know?"

"How can you tell when it's time to stop?"

" 'How can you—?' " he repeated in disbelief; then he recovered and said flatly and piously, "When you're enjoying it too much, it's time to stop."

"Is that when *you* stop?" Corey countered.

He had the decency to look ashamed of his answer; then he looked annoyed. "This discussion is not about me."

"Okay," Corey said agreeably, rather enjoying his discomfiture, "then it's about someone else. Let's call him . . . Doug Johnson!"

"Let's drop the pretense," Spence said a little testily. "The fact is that you're seeing someone named Johnson and he's pushing for more than you want to give. If you want advice, I'll give it to you: Tell him to pound sand!"

Since she hadn't been certain what tactics Spence would use to evade her trap, Corey was ready with several variations of the same scheme, all of which were designed to maneuver him back onto the path. She tried out the first variation. "That won't help. I'm seeing lots of *different* people, actually, but things seem to go too fast after the kissing gets started."

"What are you asking me?" he said warily.

"I'd like to know how to tell when things are getting out of hand, and I'd like some specific guidelines."

"Well, you aren't going to get them from me."

"Fine," Corey said, defeated, but bluffing to save her pride. "But if I end up in a home for unwed mothers because you wouldn't tell me what I needed to know, then it's going to be as much your fault as mine!"

She made a move to stand, but he caught her wrist and jerked her back down onto the seat. "Oh, no you don't! You aren't going to end this discussion with a remark like that."

A moment ago, Corey thought she was defeated, but now she realized that victory was actually in her grasp. He was floundering. Uncertain. Retreating from his original position. Corey prepared to advance, but *very* cautiously.

"What—exactly—do you need to know?" he asked, looking sublimely uncomfortable.

"I'd like you to tell me how to know when a kiss is going to get out of hand. There has to be some sort of clue."

Defeated by his own uncertainty, Spence leaned his head back and closed his eyes. "There are several clues," he muttered, "and I think you already know damned well what they are."

Corey widened her eyes and innocently said, "If I knew what they are, why would I be asking you about them?"

"Corey, it is impossible for me to sit here and give you a play-by-play description of the stages of a kiss."

Corey opened the trapdoor and got ready to shove him in. "Could you demonstrate?"

"Absolutely not! But I can give you a good piece of advice: You're dating the wrong bunch of people if they're all pushing you for more than you want to give."

"Oh, I guess I didn't make myself clear. What I'm

trying to say is that I think *I* might be the one who is giving the guys the wrong idea." Mentally, she stood beside the open door and made a sweeping gesture to him. "I think the problem may be how *I* kiss *them*."

Spence walked straight into her trap. "How the hell do you kiss?" he demanded, then he looked furious at his blunder. "Never mind," he said, leaning forward suddenly.

Corey put her hands on his shoulders and gently forced him back. "Now, don't get hysterical," she said in a soothing voice. "Just relax."

Beneath her palms his shoulders were still tensed, as if he wanted to bolt, and she had a fleeting image of him on the football field, only tonight he'd caught a pass he hadn't expected and didn't want, and now he couldn't find anyone else to hand it off to.

The thought made her smile into his narrowed eyes; it made her feel as if she, not he, were calling the plays for a change. It gave her confidence. It made her absurdly happy. "Spence," she said. "Just run the ball down the field. It's very simple. Honest."

Her ability to find humor in his predicament only made him more irritable. "I cannot believe you seriously want me to do this!"

From beneath her lashes, Corey gave him a look of limpid appeal. "Who else can I possibly ask? I suppose I could ask Doug to show me what I do that—"

"Let's get on with it," he interrupted shortly.

His knee was still beside her hip, preventing her from moving closer to him. "Could you move your knee?"

Wordlessly, he shifted his left leg out of the way

without altering the position of his upper body. Corey scooted closer, turning so that she could look at him.

"Now what?" he demanded, his arms crossed obstinately over his chest.

Corey had a rehearsed answer in mind for exactly this moment. "Now you pretend you're Doug—and I'll be me."

"I don't want to be Johnson," he said, sounding bitter about everything.

"Be anyone you like, but be a good sport, okay?"

"Fine," he clipped. "Now I'm being a good sport."

Corey waited for him to move, to reach for her, to do *something*. "You can start whenever you're ready," she said when he didn't budge.

He looked resentful. "Why do *I* have to start?"

Corey looked at his balky expression and felt an almost uncontrollable impulse to burst out laughing. She had started out tonight hoping to fulfill the most cherished dream of her lifetime—to be kissed by him— *really* kissed—by him. As badly as she'd wanted that, the prospect of it had made her feel nervous and inadequate. Now it was a foregone conclusion that she was going to be kissed, but it was Spencer who was uneasy and off balance, and it was she who was amused and very relaxed. "You have to start," she informed him, "because that's the way things . . . start." When he still didn't seem able to move, she peered at him with sham concern. "Do you *know* how to start?"

"I think so," he drawled.

"Because if you aren't certain, I can give you a hint Most guys—"

Corey broke off as the absurdity of her suggestion

registered on him, banishing his annoyance over his assigned task and making his eyes gleam with amusement.

"Most guys do what?" he asked with a grin as he reached out and moved her closer to his chest. "Is this how Johnson starts?" He bent his head and Corey braced herself for some sort of wild kiss that would make her faint. What she got was a swift clumsy kiss that was slightly off center and made her shake her head in the negative.

"No?" he joked. He pulled her forward into a bear hug and nipped her ear. "How was that?"

He was being playful, Corey realized, and she suddenly feared that this sort of kissing was all there was going to be. She resolved not to let all her carefully made plans lead only to this, but she couldn't help laughing as he quickened his demonstration of how he pictured poor imaginary Doug Johnson treating her. "I'll bet this technique is a real favorite of his," he said, starting to kiss her and deliberately bumping her nose instead. "Did I miss?" He switched to the other side and bumped her nose again. "Did I miss again?"

Laughing, Corey leaned her forehead against the solid wall of his chest and nodded.

He caught her chin, turned her face aside, and rubbed his nose against the side of her neck like a playful puppy. "Let me know when I'm driving you out of your mind with passion," he invited, and Corey laughed harder. "Am I great?" he asked, nuzzling the other side of her neck. "Or am I great?"

Her eyes swimming with mirth, Corey raised her gaze to his and nodded vigorously. "You're completely great—" she said, "but you just aren't—Doug."

He grinned back at her, sharing the joke, and in that prolonged moment of silent companionship, with his hands linked loosely behind her back and his eyes smiling into hers, Corey felt utterly content. Alive. At peace. So did he—she knew it with every beat of her heart. She knew it as surely as she knew he was about to kiss her again and that the joking was over.

His gaze holding hers, he tipped her chin up and slowly lowered his head. "It's time," he said softly, as his mouth descended, "for a more scientific approach to the problem."

At the first touch of his lips on hers, Corey's entire body stiffened with the shock of the contact. He obviously noticed her reaction, because he took his mouth away and touched it to her cheek, kissing her there as he continued in a throaty murmur, "In order for us to obtain reliable data . . ." His mouth slid slowly to her jaw. ". . . both parties have to . . ." His lips traced a warm path to her ear. ". . . collaborate in the . . ." He lifted his mouth slightly, his hand curving around her nape, tilting her face into better position. ". . . experiment."

His mouth captured hers in a slow, insistent kiss that steadily increased in pressure, forcing Corey's lips to part beneath his and setting off tremors of passion inside her that began to collide and combine with stunning force. With an inner moan of pleasure and need, Corey slid her hands up his chest and gave herself over to the kiss, letting him part her lips, yielding to the probing of his tongue, then welcoming it with mindless desperation.

His fingers shoved into the hair at her nape, loosening the pins that held her hair, and suddenly the mass of golden strands were pouring over them like a veil, and everything was out of control. She was kissing him back, falling forward into his arms while his tongue plunged into her mouth, breathlessly insistent, stroking and caressing.

His hands slid over her breasts, cupping them possessively, and Corey crushed her mouth to his, her nails digging into his arms, her body pressing intimately against his surging erection while his arm clamped around her hips, pressing her tighter to him, holding her as he rolled her onto her side.

Years of love and longing more than compensated for lack of experience, and Corey returned each endless, scorching kiss, her hands sliding over the bunched muscles of his back and shoulders, her parted lips surrendering to and then boldly conquering the man whose long fingers were caressing her breasts, tormenting her, tantalizing her with the same promise of pleasure her mouth was giving him. Time ceased to exist for her, obliterated by the turbulence of raging desire and a sensual mouth that was hungrily devouring hers with increasing urgency . . . and a knee that was nudging her legs apart while his hands . . . stopped.

He tore his mouth from hers and lifted off her so abruptly that Corey felt completely disoriented, and when she saw the awful expression on his face, she was afraid to breathe.

His brows were drawn together into a dark frown of utter disbelief as he stared down at their bodies, then he seemed to notice that his hand was still on her breast and he jerked it away, glaring at his own palm as if it had somehow offended him. His accusing gaze snapped from his hand to her face, and his expression slowly transformed from angry to utterly thunder-struck.

Understanding dawned, and Corey expelled her breath on a rush of joyous relief. He had lost control and he didn't like it. He hadn't imagined she would ever be able to do that to him, but she had done it. *She* had done that to him. Filled with pride and satisfaction and a world of love, Corey smiled slumberously at him, her hand still resting on his chest. "How'd I do?"

"That depends on what you were *trying* to do," he said curtly.

She leaned up on her elbow, so happy that she had been able to make him want her that nothing he could have said would have spoiled her joy. "Now that you've had a demonstration," she teased, "would you care to tell me at what point things got out of hand?"

"No," he said, and sat up.

Corey sat up beside him, thoroughly enjoying the situation, her smile disarmingly innocent. "But you were supposed to notice and tell me if things got out of hand because of something *I* did. Do you need another demonstration?"

"No more demonstrations." He stood as he said it. "Your father would get out his shotgun if he knew what happened out here tonight, and he'd be justified."

"Nothing happened."

"If this is your idea of 'nothing,' then that's why the boys in your life are trying to take things too far."

She walked beside him trying to look deeply concerned when she felt like laughing with delight. "Would you say, then, that things went too far between us?"

"They didn't go too far. They *could* have gone too far."

Six

HE LEFT, AND COREY didn't see him again until the following Thanksgiving. When he finally came over to the house, Corey had the feeling that she couldn't have gotten him off to a solitary spot if her life depended upon it, and she told herself that if the kiss hadn't affected him, he wouldn't be so wary.

Diana was inclined to agree, and Corey again enlisted her aid in helping to accomplish her dream, a dream she'd cherished for years. She wanted it to come true so fiercely, so completely, that she couldn't believe fate would ever prevent it. In order to accomplish her goal, she was careful toward the end of Spence's visit to seem a little distracted and just a touch sad. Once she'd made certain he couldn't help but notice, Corey left him alone in the living room with Diana, then she hid around the corner to see how things went. "Poor Corey," Diana said—as they'd rehearsed.

"What's wrong?" Spence asked quickly, and Diana's heart soared at how concerned he sounded.

"She's been looking forward to the Christmas dance at school all semester. She's on the decorations committee and everything. She's had the dress she's going to wear for months."

"What's the problem?"

"The problem is that Doug Johnson was going to take her—he's on Baylor's football team—but he phoned this morning to tell her that his family has decided to go to Bermuda for Christmas, and they won't even consider letting him stay behind. I feel terrible for Corey."

"She's better off not going out with jocks, anyway. You know what they're like and what they think they're entitled to from any girl they honor with a few hours of their time."

"You were a jock," Diana said with a laugh.

"And that's how I know what I know."

"The point is, she's not going to be able to go. The dance is a big thing, especially for graduating seniors."

"Why doesn't she ask someone else to take her?" he suggested, sounding puzzled that Diana was bringing the problem to him.

"Corey has lots of friends, but they already have their own dates."

To Corey it seemed like hours before he said, "Are you suggesting I take her?"

"That's entirely up to you." Diana got up then and headed out of the room, and as she passed Corey in the dining room, they exchanged a silent "high five." Corey was halfway into the living room before she remembered to wipe the grin off her face and replace it with a more woebegone expression, but Spencer didn't notice; he was putting on his jacket to leave.

"My mother is coming home for Christmas," he said.

"That will be nice."

"I'm looking forward to seeing her," he admitted, looking a little embarrassed by his sentimentality. "The point is," he continued abruptly, "I haven't seen her in three years. Diana explained that you don't have a date for the Christmas dance. I'll be in Houston, so if you don't mind having an old man take you to your dance, and you can't find anyone else, then I will."

Corey felt faint with joy and relief, but she was wise enough to refrain from a display of too much exultation and risk suffocating him. "It's very nice of you to offer."

"I'm on my way back to Dallas. You can tell me when I come home Christmas week if you want me to take you."

"Oh, I do," Corey said quickly. "I can tell you right now. The dance is the twenty-first. Could you pick me up at seven?"

"Sure. No problem. And if you get a better offer, just let me know." He turned on the front step as he zipped up his jacket, and Corey said in a daring, grown-up way, "You're a complete sweetheart, Spence."

In answer, he chucked her under the chin as if she were a six-year-old and left.

Seven

ON DECEMBER 21 at seven, when Corey came down-stairs in her gown of royal blue silk and matching blue high heels, she didn't look or feel like a child. She was a woman, her eyes shining with love and anticipation; she was Cinderella on the way to her ball, watching for her Prince Charming at the living room window.

Prince Charming was late.

When he hadn't arrived by seven forty-five, Corey called his house. She knew his grandmother wasn't planning to return from Scottsdale until the next day and that she'd given the servants some time off before Christmas, so when no one answered the phone at the Bradleys', Corey was certain it was because Spence was on his way.

When he still wasn't there at eight fifteen, her father gently suggested that he go over to the house and see what was keeping Spence or if something was wrong over there. In an agony of suspense and foreboding, Corey waited for her father to return, certain that only death or injury would keep Spence from honoring his commitment.

Twenty minutes later, Mr. Foster came back. Corey took one look at his angry eyes and hesitant expression, and she knew the news was bad. It was worse than bad; it was devastating: Her father had spoken with the family chauffeur, who lived in an apartment above the garage, and the chauffeur had told him that Spence had decided not to come home for the holidays, after all. According to the chauffeur, Spencer's mother, who'd been expected for Christmas, had decided to go to Paris instead, and as a result, Spencer's grandmother had decided to extend her stay in Scottsdale until the New Year.

Corey listened to that shattering recitation in anguished disbelief, fighting back tears. Unable to bear either sympathy or righteous indignation from her family, she went upstairs to her room and took off the beautiful gown she'd chosen with such care to dazzle and impress him. For the next week, she jumped every time the phone rang, convinced he would call to explain and apologize.

On New Year's Day, when he had not done either one, Corey calmly removed the blue gown from her closet and carefully packed it in a box, then she removed every single picture of him from all the walls, mirrors, and bulletin boards in her room.

Afterward, she went downstairs and asked her family never to mention to Spencer that she had waited for him or had been disappointed in any way that he failed to show up. Still furious at the hurt Corey had suffered, Mr. Foster argued vehemently that Spencer was getting off much too lightly and deserved to be horsewhipped, at least verbally if not physically! Corey calmly replied that she didn't want to give Spencer the satisfaction of knowing she'd waited and watched and worried. "Let him think I went to the dance with someone else," she said firmly.

When Mr. Foster still argued that, as Corey's father, he was entitled to the satisfaction of "having a few words with that young man," Corey's mother had put her hand on his arm and said, "Corey's pride is more important, and that's what she's saving with her plan."

Diana, who was as angry with Spencer as her father was, nevertheless sided with Corey. "I'd love to give him a good swift kick, too, Daddy, but Corey's right. We shouldn't say anything to make him think he was ever that important to her."

The next day, Corey donated the beautiful blue gown to a charity resale shop.

She burned the unmounted photographs.

The photo albums she'd kept under her bed were too big and too handsome to burn, so she packed them into a large box along with the framed photographs she'd taken of him. She lugged them up to the attic, intending the remove the pictures some day and use the albums and frames for photographs of more worthy subjects than Spencer Addison.

When she went to bed that night, Corey did not cry, nor did she let herself ever again fantasize about Spencer Addison. She had packed away more than his pictures that day; she had put away the last traces of adolescence with all its lovely, impossible dreams.

After that, fate presented her with only two opportunities to see Spencer, had she wanted an excuse to talk to him—his grandmother's funeral that spring and his wedding to a New York debutante that summer. Corey attended the funeral with her family, but when they went to talk to Spencer, she deliberately let herself be obscured by the crowd of mourners. With her gaze on the flower-strewn coffin, Corey paid her last respects to the elderly woman in silence, with a prayer, while tears of sorrow slid unnoticed down her cheeks. And then she left.

She did not attend Spencer's wedding with her family either, even though it took place in Houston, where the bride's maternal grandparents lived, nor did she attend the reception. She spent his wedding night doing exactly what she knew he would be doing that night: she went to bed with Doug Hayward.

Unfortunately the young man to whom she had chosen to surrender her virginity was a much better friend and confidant than he was a lover, and she ended up weeping her heart out in his awkward embrace.

In time, she forgot about Spencer entirely. There were other, better, things to concentrate on, to anticipate and celebrate.

For one thing, the Foster family was becoming quite famous. The family's joint interest in gardening, cooking, and handiwork that had seemed like a lark to many had become something of a trend, popularized by Marge Crumbaker, who continued to give it glowing mentions in her column.

During Corey's freshman year at college, an editor at *Better Homes and Gardens* saw one of the columns, and after coming out of the house and attending a Fourth of July party, the editor decided to do a huge feature on what she dubbed "Entertaining—Foster Style."

When the magazine came out, there were pictures featuring tables set with Grandma's hand-painted china and handmade place mats, with beautiful flower arrangements that Corey's mother created from flowers taken from their own garden and their little greenhouse. Also included were pictures of some of the family's favorite meals, beautifully photographed and described in detail, with recipes and directions for growing the fresh herbs, fruits, and vegetables that were used for the family meals. But the most memorable part of the article came at the end, where Corey's mother had tried to oescribe her feelings about what she and her family did and why they did it: "I think the real pleasure of having a party or preparing a meal, or planning a garden, or creating a furnished room, comes from doing it with people you love. That way there's satisfaction in the effort, no matter how that effort turns out."

The magazine dubbed that last sentence, "The Foster Ideal," and the phrase stuck. After that, other magazines contacted the Fosters asking for articles and pictures, for which they were willing to pay. Corey's mother and grandparents were only able to produce the raw material, so Diana wrote the articles and Corey took the photographs.

In the beginning, it had all been a family hobby.

Robert Foster died of a stroke five months after the stock market made its downward plunge in 1987. When his attorney and accountant gave the family the details of his dire financial situation, they understood why he'd been so tense and preoccupied during the last year, and why he had wanted to shield them. After that the family hobby became a business that enabled them to survive. Marge Crumbaker's columns had already made Mary Foster into a celebrity hostess, but in the aftermath of Robert's death, that no longer had any meaning to anyone, particularly his grieving family.

In the end, it was Elyse Lanier, the wife of one of Houston's leading entrepreneurs, who hit upon a way to help them stay afloat. A few weeks after Robert's death, she phoned Mary and gently asked her if she'd be willing to accept the responsibility for the food and decorations for the Orchid Ball. When Mary said yes, Elyse used her considerable influence to make the rest of the ball's committee agree.

It was the first time in the ball's history that one person had ever been entrusted with so much. On Elyse's part, it had been an act of friendship and support, one that Mary never forgot. Several years later, when Elyse's husband was elected Houston's mayor, Mary finally found a way to express her gratitude. She did it in the form of a large picnic basket, the size of a compact car, which bore a huge red, white, and blue ribbon when it was delivered to the Laniers.

In it were hand-painted dishes, wineglasses, coffee cups, candlesticks, napkin rings, and salt and pepper shakers, along with handmade napkins and place mats. It was a full picnic service for twenty-four people. Each piece was lovingly crafted. Each item bore the Laniers' monogram in red, white, and blue.

Despite the Fosters' instant renown as Houston society's "caterers of choice" after the Orchid Ball, there would never have been enough money to maintain their house or their living style from catering alone, and the hard work quickly began taking a heavy toll on Corey's mother and grandparents.

In the end, it was Diana who decided the family should be capitalizing on the fame they'd acquired in various home and entertainment magazines, rather than trying to run a catering business for which they were actually ill-equipped. She was the daughter of an entrepreneur, and although Robert Foster had suffered the fate of many other wealthy Texans in the seventies and eighties, Diana had clearly inherited his proclivity for business.

She drew up a business plan, packed up the magazine articles and recipes that had been published over the years, and put together a large collection of Corey's photographs taken of family projects.

"If we're going to do this," she announced to Corey as she left to see a banker friend of her father's, "we have to do it big and with plenty of financial backing. Otherwise we'll fail, not from lack of ability, but from lack of funds to keep us going for the first two years."

Somehow, she got the funds they needed.

The first issue of *Foster's Beautiful Living* magazine came out the following year, and although there were some difficult, and even terrifying, setbacks along the way, the magazine caught on with the public. Foster Enterprises began putting out recipe books and then coffee-table books, where Corey's photography won acclaim and generated even more income for the family.

All of that had led up to Newport, Corey thought wryly. After more than a decade of years and dozens of cameras, she had come full circle: she was about to take a camera with her and go see Spencer Addison again . . .

Corey pulled out of her reverie, glanced at her watch, and hastily opened the car door. As she walked up the front steps of the house, she suddenly realized that the prospect of seeing Spencer again no longer upset her. For more than a half hour, she'd been sitting in the car, dredging up old and awful memories that she'd buried in the attic with all his pictures and photo albums. Now that she'd taken out the memories and examined them as an adult, they no longer hurt.

She had been a dreamy adolescent with an enduring crush on "an older man." He had been the unwilling, and in the end, unkind, recipient of her adoration. It was as simple as that.

She was no longer an adolescent, she was nearly twenty-nine, with a large group of friends, a long list of accomplishments behind her, and an exciting life ahead of her.

He was . . . a stranger. A stranger whose marriage had ended five years after it began and who had stayed on the East Coast, where he'd developed some sort of pleasant relationship with his only remaining relatives—his half-sister and his niece, who was about to be married.

Now that she'd thought the whole thing through, she could hardly believe she'd reacted so badly to the thought of seeing him. The prospect of photographing that wedding and featuring it in *Beautiful Living* was challenging and exciting to her professionally and she *was* a professional. In fact, her feelings for him were so totally impersonal, and her infatuation with him so silly in retrospect, that she decided she really ought to ship the box in the attic to Newport, along with the other supplies that would be sent ahead. She had no use for those photographs, but they were a chronicle of his youth, and he might like to have them.

Her family was seated at the kitchen table with lists spread everywhere. "Hi, guys," Corey said with a grin as she slid into a chair. "Who's going to Newport with me?"

Her answer was relieved smiles from her mother, her grandmother, her grandfather, and Diana.

"Everyone is going but me," Henry Britton said, glancing at the walker he used now to get around. "You girls always get to have all the fun!"

Eight

COREY'S PLANE WAS two hours late, and it was nearly six o'clock by the time the taxi turned down a quiet street lined with palatial homes built at the turn of the century when the Vanderbilts and Goulds spent summers in Newport. Spence's house was at the end of the road, and one of the most imposing of them all.

Shaped like a wide U that faced the street, it was a three-story masterpiece of architecture and craftsmanship with soaring white columns that marched across the front and joined both wings. No matter how Corey felt about Spencer Addison, she adored his house on sight. A high wrought-iron fence surrounded the lush lawns, and the driveway was secured by a pair of ornate gates that swung open electronically after the cab driver gave her name on the intercom.

A butler answered the front door, and she followed him across an octagonal foyer that was easily sixty feet across with pale green marble pillars supporting a gallery above. It was a rotunda meant to welcome bejeweled women in fabulous ball gowns and furs, Corey thought wryly, not modern businesswomen in dark suits and definitely not a female photographer in a turquoise silk shirt and white gabardine pants with a matching jacket over her arm. If jewels were the ticket of admission, she'd never have gotten in the front door of this place, not even with the wide gold bracelet at her wrist or the turquoise and gold earrings at her ears. These were authentic pieces and very fine, but this place called out for emeralds and rubies. "Could you tell me where I'll find the group from *Beautiful Living* magazine?" she asked the butler as they approached the main staircase.

"I believe they are out on the back lawn, Miss Foster. If you wish, I can show you to them now and have your suitcases taken upstairs to your room." Corey was more anxious to see how things were progressing outside than she was to unpack, so she accepted the butler's offer and followed in his wake.

In contrast to the foyer, which had been quiet and serene, nearly all the other rooms she passed were hotbeds of activity, with furniture being rearranged and wedding decorations being put up.

Her mother's handiwork was clearly evident in the dining room, where a forty-foot table had been set with exquisite china and crystal on handmade lace cloths, but the unmistakable "Foster Signature" would be the individual centerpieces that would be placed on the table the morning of the wedding for each pair of diners. All of the centerpieces would contain the same kinds of flowers, but each arrangement would be unique, and all of them were meant to be taken home by the ladies whose places at the table they had adorned during dinner, a token—Mrs. Foster said in her monthly column in *Beautiful Living* magazine—of the hostess's affection for her guests.

The author of that column was standing on the back lawn, oblivious to the glorious expanse of blue water on the pink and gold sunset taking place on the horizon as she directed four of the six freelance helpers that Spencer's sister had provided. Corey's grandmother was standing beside her, irritably shooing away her two assistants with the obvious intention of rearranging the wires that were being wound in and around the framework of the flowered arches the bride would walk under on her wedding day.

Corey came up behind them and gave them both a hug. "How's it going?"

"About like you'd expect," Corey's mother said, kissing her cheek.

"Chaos!" her grandmother said flatly. Age had not made many changes in her except that she had acquired a disconcerting bluntness that her doctor said was common to many of the elderly. If something was true, she came right out and said it, though never with any malice. "Angela—the bride's mother—is interfering with everything and getting underfoot."

"How's the bride holding up?" Corey asked, avoiding asking about Spencer.

"Oh, she's a sweet enough girl," Gram said. "Pretty, too. Her name is Joy. She's dumber than a box of rocks," she added as she walked off to correct one of her helpers.

Stifling a nervous laugh, Corey glanced over her shoulder, then exchanged knowing glances with her mother, who said a little worriedly, "I know how important it is to use real events like this for our magazine layouts, but they're very wearing on Gram these days. She doesn't like working under any sort of deadline pressure anymore."

"I know," Corey said, "but she always insists she wants to be part of it." She looked around at the bustle and activity taking place on the grounds, at the newly erected gazebo being covered in climbing roses, at the banquet tables beneath the big white tent near the water, and she smiled at the transformation taking place. "It's going to be splendid."

"Tell that to the bride's mother before she drives us all crazy. Poor Spence. If he doesn't strangle Angela before this is over, it will be a miracle. When she isn't worrying, she's complaining, and she's nipping at his heels like a hyperactive terrier all the time. She's the one who wanted Joy's wedding to take place here, and she's the one who wanted *us* here, and it's Spence who's paying the bill. Diana was right about that. Spence never complains and Angela never stops."

"I wonder why he's paying for the wedding when Angela's husband is supposedly a German aristocrat with relatives all over the social register."

Mrs. Foster paused to pick up a long strip of crepe paper skittering across the grass near her foot. "According to what Joy told me—and the child is quite a chatterbox—Mr. Reichardt has noble ancestors but little money to go with it. At least not the sort of money Spence has, and when you think about it, Angela and Joy are really his only family. I mean, his father remarried when Spence was still a baby and never wanted anything to do with him, and when his mother was alive, she was too busy enjoying herself to ever bother with him. To be fair Mr. Reichardt, Joy isn't his daughter. Joy's father was Angela's second husband. Or was it her third? Anyway, according to Joy, Spence is paying the bill because his sister thinks it's important that Joy be married in a style that befits the stepdaughter of a fancy German aristocrat."

Corey chuckled at the problems of the rich and multi-married. "What's the groom like?"

"Richard? I don't know really. I haven't seen him, and Joy doesn't talk about him. She spends most of her time with the caterer's son, whose name is Will. I gather they've known each other for several years, and they seem to enjoy each other's company. By the way, have you seen Spence yet?"

Corey shook her head as she reached up to shove her hair off her forehead. "I'm sure we'll bump into each other sooner or later."

Mrs. Foster nodded toward three people walking their way. "Here come Mr. and Mrs. Reichardt with

Joy. Dinner is in two hours, and I suggest you say hello to them and then excuse yourself to go unpack. The next two hours will be the last peace and quiet you get until you leave this madhouse in three days."

"Sounds like a good idea. I have some phone calls to make before dinner, anyway."

"By the way," she added, "Gram and I eat in the little room by the kitchen, not in the dining room with the family."

Corey heard that with a sharp twist of annoyance. "Are you telling me that Spencer is treating us like servants?"

"No, no, no," Mrs. Foster said with a laugh. "We prefer to eat in the kitchen. Believe me, it's much more pleasant than listening to Mr. and Mrs. Reichardt and the two other couples who are friends of theirs and staying here for the wedding. Joy usually eats in the kitchen with us. She likes it better there, too."

Mrs. Foster had likened Angela to a terrier, but Corey thought it a false analogy after meeting the trio. With close-cropped, white-blond hair and brown eyes, Angela was as exotically elegant—and as nervous—as a Russian wolfhound. Her husband, Peter, was a doberman pinscher—sleek, aristocratically aloof, and temperamental. Joy was . . . Joy was a cute cocker spaniel, with wavy, light brown hair, and soft, inquisitive brown eyes. As soon as the introductions were over, the wolfhound and the Doberman ganged up on Corey's poor mother and dragged her off to show her something they didn't like about the way the living room was being decorated, leaving Corey alone with Joy.

"I'll show you up to your room," the eighteen-year-old volunteered as Corey started toward the house.

"If you have something else to do, I can ask the butler where it is."

"Oh, I don't mind," Joy said, coming to heel on Corey's left and trotting off beside her toward the house. "I've been looking forward to meeting you. You have such a nice family."

"Thank you," Corey answered, a little startled by what she instantly sensed was a very genuine girl who was far more interested in getting to know Corey than she was in talking about herself or her wedding.

A flagstone terrace with French doors wrapped around the back and right side of the house, which both had spectacular water views. Corey started across the terrace toward the doors at the back, but Joy turned right. "Come this way, it's quicker," she told Corey. "We'll cut through Uncle Spence's study and avoid—"

Corey stopped short, intending to insist on *not* using that entrance, but she was too late. Spencer Addison was walking across the terrace, heading toward the steps that led down to the side lawn, and even if she hadn't seen his face, Corey would have recognized that long, brisk stride.

He saw her and stopped abruptly, a welcoming grin sweeping over his tanned face as he shoved his hands into his pockets and waited for her and Joy to reach him. Once that special smile of his had made her heart thunder, but now she felt only a swift, sharp jolt of recognition. At thirty-four, wearing casual gray pants and a white shirt with the sleeves rolled back on his forearms, he *still* managed to look every bit as handsome and sexy as he had when he was twenty-three years old.

He turned up the heat of his smile as she came close, and when he spoke, his baritone voice was richer, more intimate than she remembered. "Hello, Corey," he said as he slid his hands out of his pockets and made a move to hug her.

Corey responded with a smile that was appropriate for greeting a casual acquaintance whom one hasn't seen for many years—a friendly, serene smile, but not too personal. "Hello, Spence," she replied and deliberately held out only one hand so that he had to settle for a handshake. No hug.

He understood it and he settled for it, but his handclasp lasted longer than was necessary, and so she ended it.

"I see you've already met Joy," he said, shifting the conversation to include his niece. To her he added a mild reproof, "I thought you were going to tell me when Corey arrived."

"I just arrived a few minutes ago," Corey said. Once, the thought that he wanted to see her or was eager to see her, as his words implied, would have sent her spirits soaring. Now, she was older and wiser and doing a rather excellent job, she thought, of handling this first meeting and remembering that Spencer was and had always been all charm and sex appeal and no substance. She glanced at her watch and then apologetically at him. "If you'll excuse me, I have some phone calls to make before dinner." On the off chance that Spencer intended to volunteer, she directed her request specifically to Joy. "Would you mind showing me where my room is now?"

"Oh, sure," Joy said happily, falling into step beside her. "I know exactly where it is."

With a polite nod in Spence's direction, Corey left him standing on the terrace. He turned and watched her walk away; she knew he did because she could see his reflection in the glass panes of his study doors, but the knowledge scarcely affected her. She was completely in control and proud of it. She couldn't deny the jolt of nerves she'd felt at the first sight of him, or the increase in her pulse rate when he smiled into her eyes and took her hand in his, but she attributed all that to a natural phenomenon, a sort of irritating but understandable response to an old, forgotten stimulus. Long ago, he had affected her that way, and even though her emotions were no longer engaged, her body was reacting like one of Pavlov's dogs to the sound of a bell.

Joy led her through the foyer and up a sweeping staircase with beautiful wrought-iron scrollwork. The staircase ended in a wide gallery that wrapped around the foyer on three sides. Long hallways branched off the gallery at regular intervals, and Joy headed down the first of them, then continued walking until they came to a pair of double doors at the end. As she reached for the brass door handles, she confided with a smile, "My mother and stepfather wanted their friends to have this, but Uncle Spence said it was 'reserved' for you." She threw open the doors with a flourish and stepped aside to give Corey her first, unobstructed view, then she looked expectantly at her, waiting for a reaction.

Corey was speechless.

"It's called the Duchess Suite," Joy provided helpfully.

In dumbstruck silence, Corey walked slowly into a vast room that looked as if it belonged in Nicholas and

Alexandra's summer palace. The suite was decorated entirely in pale blue and gold. Above the bed an ornately carved golden crown secured panels of ice blue silk that draped the bed at its corners, ending in graceful swirls on the pale blue carpet. The thick, tufted coverlet was of blue satin and so was the headboard with its arched gilt frame.

"It's called that because the original owner of the house had a daughter who became the duchess of Claymore when she married. This was the room she used whenever she came home from England, and it was called the Duchess Suite from then on."

Corey found it hard to concentrate on Joy's narrative as she looked around. The draperies at the windows were of blue silk with elaborate swags fringed in gold, and in the corner was a French secretary with carved panels on the doors and a dainty chair pulled up in front of it that was also upholstered in blue.

"When my uncle bought the house a few years ago, he had the entire place renovated and all the furniture in all the guest rooms restored, so that they all look pretty much the way they did a hundred years ago, when the house was built."

Corey pulled out of her daze, and turned to Joy. "It's—breathtaking. I've only seen rooms like this in pictures of European palaces."

Joy nodded, and added with a grin, "Uncle Spence said he used to call you Duchess when you were my age. I guess that's why he wanted you to have this suite."

That announcement had a definite softening effect on Corey's attitude toward Spence. He'd been inexcusably thoughtless of her feelings as a young man, but he'd evidently mellowed a little with age. It hit her then

that she was giving him far too much credit for what
was a very small gesture that hadn't inconvenienced
him in the slightest.

"Dinner's at eight o'clock. I'll see you then," Joy
added as she left.

Nine

FROWNING WITH INDECISION, Corey hesitated in front
of the mirror in her room and studied her appearance.
The black jersey jumpsuit she'd decided to wear had
narrow black shoulder straps attached to the bodice
with a pair of golden loops, a scooped neckline, and a
low back. It clung to her figure like a soft glove, ending in a gentle flair at her ankles, but she wasn't certain if it was too dressy for dining next to the kitchen,
or perhaps too casual for this house. It would definitely make a good impression on Spence though . . .
Spence!

Angry at herself for even considering his reaction,
she stepped into a pair of flat-heeled sandals, clipped
on a pair of gold disks at her ears, and snapped the
wide gold cuff she'd worn earlier onto her wrist. She
took a step toward the door, then a step back toward the
mirror to check her face and hair. She was wearing her
hair down tonight, loose around her shoulders; she no
longer had to worry that Spencer Addison might think
she was too young for him. She needed a little more
lipstick, she decided, and quickly applied some. She
glanced at her watch and could not believe how late it

was. It was fifteen minutes after eight. She had just taken exactly twice as long to get ready as she had the night of the last Orchid Ball in Houston. Thoroughly disgusted, she turned her back on the mirror and marched to the door.

The little room by the kitchen was not the dark cubbyhole Corey had imagined, but rather a cozy alcove behind the kitchen that had a large, semicircular booth in it surrounded by tall windows that looked out on the darkened lawn. Corey heard her mother's voice as she rounded the corner, and she was already smiling at the sound when she walked into the room.

And saw Spence.

He was sitting at one end of the booth, his left arm stretched casually across the top of it, grinning down at Corey's mother, who was seated on his immediate left. Corey's grandmother was next to Corey's mother, facing the kitchen doorway, and Joy was seated next to her. The table had been set for five people. Four of them were already there. He was staying to eat with them.

Corey's smile froze, her step faltered, but she recovered just as her grandmother saw her and announced her arrival to the gathering. "Here's Corey, now. You're late, dear. My, you look nice tonight! Is that a new outfit?"

Corey felt like sinking through the floor. The implication was that she'd dressed especially for the occasion, which of course she had, and she was horribly certain that Spencer had noticed.

Spencer Addison had definitely noticed how she looked.

At the moment, what he noticed most was that her entire body had stiffened when she saw him sitting at the table. She hadn't expected him to be there, Spence realized. And she didn't want him there. The realization baffled and hurt him.

He watched her moving toward the booth with that same easy grace she'd had as a teenager, and he smiled at her. In return, she smiled *through* him, and he had a sudden insane impulse to get up out of the booth, block her path, and say, *Dammit, Corey look at me!* He still could hardly believe that this cool, composed young woman who seemed to scarcely remember him was the same Corey Foster he'd known.

One thing hadn't changed about her, Spence noted—she still lit up a room when she walked into it. Within moments after she slid in across from him and started talking with the others, the entire atmosphere at the table seemed to brighten. At least that much about tonight was the same as it had been so long ago. Except, in those days, Corey had been glad to see him.

An image of those days danced in his mind . . . recollections of an adorable kid with a camera around her neck who popped up at his tennis matches. *"I got a great shot of your first serve, Spence."* It had been a lousy serve, and he'd said as much. *"I know,"* she'd agreed with that infectious smile of hers, *"but my shot of it was just great."*

He remembered the times when he'd gone over to the house unexpectedly. She had been so glad to see him then, her smile dawning like sunshine. *"Hi, Spence! I didn't know you were coming over."*

And then, one day, when she was about fifteen, he looked around and saw her walking toward him across the back lawn, her honey-colored hair blowing around her shoulders, sun-streaked and glinting in the sun, her eyes the bright clear blue of a summer sky. A golden girl—all sparkle and zest, long legs and laughing face. She had been his golden girl from that day on—changeable, constant, glowing.

Even now, he could see her standing beneath the mistletoe, her hands clasped behind her back. She was sixteen and looking very grown up.

"Don't you know it's bad luck not to honor the Christmas traditions of you friends in their homes . . ."

He had hesitated. *"Are you certain you're old enough for this?"*

Of course, he'd known she had a fierce crush on him, and he'd known the time would come when she would grow up, grow out of it, and grow away from him. It was natural, inevitable that boys her own age would replace him in her heart. It was right that should happen.

He'd expected it, and even so, it had bothered him a little when it happened. More than a little. He hadn't even seen the change coming until the night she asked him to be a kissing partner in an experiment. God, he had felt like such a pervert for what he'd done to her that night, and even worse for what he had wanted to do to her—to a *seventeen-year-old* girl!

His golden girl.

He'd forgotten about her Christmas dance, and that was all it took to sever whatever feeble feelings she had left for him. She went with someone else, a last-minute substitute, which was what he had been. According to his grandmother, she went with someone closer to her own age "and a far more suitable companion for an innocent girl" than Spence was. Corey was so involved with her own life by then that she hadn't even bothered to say anything to him at his grandmother's funeral a few months later. Diana had excused her by saying Corey had an afternoon date. She hadn't bothered to attend his wedding either, even thought she could have brought her date . . .

The conversation swirled around him at the table as one course followed another, and he participated now and then, but with only half his attention. He preferred to watch Corey when she wasn't looking at him, and since she never glanced in his direction for more than a moment, he had plenty of opportunity. He was genuinely surprised when dessert was served; he'd eaten without tasting his food, and he certainly didn't want any dessert.

What he did want he could not have; just this one night, just for this one meal, he had wanted it to be the way it had been the last time he had had dinner with her family. That was the night Diana had asked him to volunteer to take Corey to her school dance. She had a new man in her life by then—Doug somebody—and several others, as well.

Spence had already been relegated to least-important man in her life, but at least she'd still been able to spare a smile for him. The fact that she now found him completely dispensable in his own damned house at his own damned table was worse than annoying; it was terribly disappointing. And he knew exactly why it was. He'd been looking forward more than he wanted to admit to seeing her again, to having her happy family around him again. When he'd seen her coming across the back lawn earlier today, with her sun-streaked hair blowing in the breeze, he'd thought . . . He'd thought a lot of stupid, impossible things.

"Uncle Spence?" Joy's puzzled voice cut through his thoughts, and Spence looked at her. "Is something wrong with your glass?"

"My what?"

"Your water glass. You've been staring at it and turning it around in your hand."

Spence straightened in his seat and prepared to pay attention to the present and forget the past. "I'm sorry. My mind was on something else. What have you all been talking about?"

"The wedding mostly, but we're all bored with that subject. Anyway, everything's all taken care of."

Corey sensed instinctively that Spence was about to join in the conversation, and since she was more comfortable, not having to talk to him, she tried to keep everyone focused on Joy. "We're not bored with the wedding at all," Corey said quickly. "And even though you think everything is taken care of, there are always last-minute details that people forget. Sometimes they're really important."

"Like what?" Joy asked.

Corey thought madly for something to discuss that hadn't already been covered. "Well, *um* . . . did you remember to apply for a marriage license?"

"No, but the judge is going to bring it with him."

"I don't think you can do that," Corey said, wondering if Angela, in her preoccupation with making the wedding into a social extravaganza, had failed to handle the more mundane, less showy details. "I've been a bridesmaid in several weddings, and you always have to apply for a license in advance, then there's a waiting period of a few days, oh—and blood tests."

Joy shivered at the mention of blood. "I get faint at the sight of needles, so I don't have to have one. The judge who's performing the wedding is a friend of Uncle Spence's, and he has the right to decide. He said I didn't need one."

"Yes, but what about the license and the waiting period?"

Spence spoke for the first time in fifteen minutes, and even though Corey was braced for the sound of his deep voice, it still did funny things to her heart. Nostalgia, she was learning, was not a feeble force. "It's all taken care of," he said. "There's no waiting period in Rhode Island."

"I see," Corey said, looking away from him the instant he finished speaking. Rather than try to think of another topic, she did what the others were doing and began to eat her dessert. Unfortunately, Joy wasn't interested in her own slice of cheesecake; she was interested in Corey and Spence. "It's funny," she said, looking from Spence to Corey and back to Spence, "but I thought you two used to be good friends."

Spence was so annoyed with Corey for treating him like an insignificant nonentity that he abruptly decided to make his presence, and his feelings, known. "So did I," he said curtly. He had slammed the conversational ball directly into Corey's court, and with amused satisfaction, he noticed that the "gallery" of three all turned to her to see how she was going to return it.

Corey lifted her head and met his challenging look. Mentally she reached across the table and flipped his plate into his lap, but all she did was smile and shrug. "We were."

"But you don't seem to have anything to say to each other," Joy said, looking baffled and a little disappointed. The gallery looked to the right at Spence, then to their left, at Corey, but Corey had cleverly eaten a bit of cheesecake, effectively forcing Spence to deal with that issue. "It was a long time ago," he said flatly.

"Yes, but Uncle Spence, *only two days ago* you were upset because Corey delayed her flight for a day. I started thinking maybe there'd been a—like, relationship—between you two when you were younger."

Now, when he didn't want Corey's attention, he got it. In fact, he got everybody's attention. Corey lifted her brows and gave him a serenely amused look that managed to convey that he deserved whatever embarrassment he suffered in a conversational confrontation that he had provoked. The other three spectators waited expectantly. "I was not upset because she delayed her flight," Spence said. "I was upset because I thought she had canceled her trip." They continued to look at him until he was prodded into a half lie. "Corey, is an excellent photographer, and she was part of the 'deal' your mother made with the magazine to cover your wedding. It was a legal, binding contract. Naturally, I expected Corey to honor her commitments."

Corey's mouth dropped open at that enormous piece of hypocrisy, and her mother, who sensed Corey's impulse to throw her cheesecake into Spence's face, rushed to the rescue. "Corey always honors her commitments," she told Joy with gentle firmness. "She has very *strong* feelings about that."

"Actually," Corey added, heading off what she felt certain would be another probing question from Joy, "Spence was a friend of the whole family's not of mine in particular."

Corey was pleased with that explanation, and Joy looked satisfied, but unfortunately Corey's grandmother was neither. "I don't think that's entirely true, Corey."

"Yes, Gram," Corey said in a warning voice, "it is."

"Well, maybe it is, dear, but you were the only one in the house who wallpapered your bedroom with his pictures."

Corey wanted to kill her, but at the moment all she could do was argue on a technicality. "I did not *wallpaper* my room with his pictures."

"That room was a shrine to Spencer," the elderly lady argued. "If you'd lit candles in there, people would have prayed. Goodness, you even had photograph albums filled with his pictures under your bed."

"Then what happened?" Joy asked.

"*Nothing* happened," Corey said, aiming a quelling look at her grandmother.

"You mean, one day you just—just stopped caring about Uncle Spence and took down his pictures? Just like that?"

Corey gave her a bright smile and nodded. "Just like that."

"I didn't know it could happen that way," Joy said somberly. "A person can just stop caring—for no reason?" For the first time since her questions had begun, Corey had the feeling that Joy wasn't merely curious, she was troubled.

Corey's grandmother obviously noticed the same

thing and attributed Joy's anxiety to bridal nerves. Patting Joy's clenched hand, she offered reassurance: "Corey had a very good reason, dear. One you will never have, I'm sure."

"She did?"

"Yes. Spence broke her heart."

Mentally, Corey threw up her hands and yielded to the inevitable. Short of gagging her grandmother with a napkin and dragging her out of the booth by her ankles, Corey knew there was nothing to stop what was to come. Torn between misery and mirth, she waited for her dignity to be sacrificed on the altar of truth, for the sake of a nervous bride-to-be. Since she couldn't prevent it, and since she knew Spence was also going to suffer some unpleasant moments, she leaned back, folded her arms, and decided to enjoy his discomfort. He looked completely flabbergasted, Corey noted with some amusement, his coffee cup arrested halfway to his mouth.

"I did what?' he said irately, and actually looked to Corey as if he expected *her* to come to his rescue by denying it. In answer she lifted her brows and gave him an unsympathetic shrug.

"You broke her heart," Corey's grandmother asserted.

"And just exactly how did I do that?" he demanded.

She gave him a deeply censorious look for failing to own up to his wrongdoing and retaliated by addressing her answer to his niece, instead. "When Corey was a senior in high school, your uncle asked to take her to the Christmas formal. I've never seen Corey so excited. She and Diana—Corey's sister—shopped for weeks for just the right gown to dazzle him, and they finally found it. When the big day arrived, Corey spent most of it in her room primping. Then, just before Spence was due to arrive, she came downstairs. My, how she sparkled in that gown! She looked so beautiful and grown-up that her grandpa and I had tears in our eyes. We took pictures of course, but we saved some film so Corey would have pictures of Spence with her."

She paused for a sip of water, letting the suspense build, and Corey had the fleeting thought that her grandmother had a previously undiscovered flair for high drama. Poor Joy was on the edge of her seat, frowning at her uncle for whatever he'd done to spoil such a night. Spence was frowning at Corey's grandmother, and Corey's mother was frowning at her plate. Corey was beginning to enjoy herself.

"Then what happened?" Joy implored.

Corey's grandmother carefully put her glass where it had been, then she lifted her sorrowful gaze to Joy. "Your uncle stood her up."

Joy turned a look of such disbelief, such accusation on Spence that Corey almost pitied him. "Uncle Spence," she breathed, "you *didn't!*"

"He did," Corey's grandmother averred flatly. Spence opened his mouth to explain, but she wasn't through with him. "It broke my heart the way Corey kept watching for him at the window. She could not believe he wasn't coming."

"And so you missed the formal?" Joy asked Corey, displaying the sort of appalled sympathy that only females are capable of feeling for each other under those particular circumstances.

"No, she did not," Spence said.

"Oh, yes she did."

"I think you're mistaken about that and some other things," Spence said, his jaw tight with annoyance at being made to look like an even bigger villain than he'd actually been. "I did stand Corey up that night," he said, addressing his defense mostly to his wide-eyed niece. "I forgot I was supposed to take Corey to the dance, and I went to Aspen for the holidays instead of going home to Houston. It's obvious now that I shouldn't have let my grandmother handle my apology, but she was very upset and very insistent. I'm guilty of those two things, but the rest of the story you just heard—he hesitated, searching for a respectful way to say Corey's grandmother was completely wrong— "isn't the way I remember it. Corey already had a date for the dance, and she already had her gown, but her date had to cancel at the last minute. The other boys she knew who would have taken her already had dates of their own, so Diana suggested I offer to take Corey, which I did. I was not a volunteer, I was a recruit, and the only reason Corey wanted to go with me was there wasn't anyone else available—except for her very last choice, which was whoever she called in as a last-minute substitute for me. I," he finished bluntly, "was her next-to-last choice."

Having had his say, he gave Corey's grandmother a conciliatory smile and said, "My memory isn't the greatest either, but I have a very clear recollection of all that because I felt very badly when I realized I'd forgotten about the dance. I was very relieved when I was told that Corey went with someone else."

"You would have had a clearer recollection," Gram informed him smugly, "if you had been there, as I was, when she went upstairs in that beautiful blue gown— the gown she bought had to be royal blue because that was your favorite color—and took it off. I don't know what gave you the idea you weren't her first choice, but I do know that if you had heard her crying herself to sleep, as I did that night, you would never forget the sound of it either. She was beyond heartbroken. It was pitiful!"

Although some of what he'd heard didn't make sense, as Spence stared at the elderly woman, he knew instinctively she was telling the truth. His niece knew it, too. Filled with shame, he looked at their accusing faces while his mind tormented him with images of his golden girl coming down the stairs in her royal blue gown and waiting for him at the windows. He thought of Corey crying herself to sleep in a bedroom filled with his pictures, and he felt physically ill. He didn't know why she'd invented a story about needing a substitute date for the dance, but when he looked at Mrs. Foster, who was avoiding his gaze, one thing was obvious: everybody had known how Corey felt about him back then, but him.

He looked at Corey, but she had leaned her elbows on the table and covered her face with her hands, and he couldn't see her face. His jaw tight with self-disgust, he glared at his water glass, thinking of the barb he'd thrown earlier about honoring commitments. No wonder she couldn't stand the sight of him!

Across the table, Corey looked between her fingers at the stricken expression on Spence's face and then the satisfied smile on her grandmother's, and the whole scenario was so beyond her worst imaginings that she had an uncontrollable impulse to . . . giggle.

"Corey," Spence said, lifting his eyes to her covered face, prepared to take whatever verbal flogging she wanted to give him. "I didn't know. I didn't realize—" he began awkwardly, and to his horror, her shoulders started to shake. She was crying!

"Corey, please don't—!" he said desperately, afraid to reach for her and make things worse.

Her shoulders shook harder.

"I'm sorry," he said in an aching voice. "I don't know what else to say—"

Her hands fell away, and Spence stared in disbelief at a pair of laughing blue eyes that were regarding him with amused sympathy, not animosity. "If I were you," she advised in a laughter-choked voice, "I'd leave it right there and say good night. If Gram isn't convinced you feel guilty enough, this could actually get worse." Her transformation from cool stranger to his enchanting ally was so sudden, so undeserved, and so poignantly familiar that Spence felt a surge of pure tenderness pour through him.

He slid out of the booth, gave Corey's grandmother a wink, and held his hand out to Corey. "In that case, I'd rather do my groveling outside, and deprive her of the opportunity to witness it."

"I really ought to let you do it," Corey said with that infectious smile he'd always loved, "but you're already too late. I'd already forgiven and forgotten the whole thing. In fact, I shipped those old photograph albums here with some of my equipment and supplies.

I intended to give them to you. So, as you can see, there's no need to go outside *or* grovel."

Spence put his hand firmly beneath her elbow. "I insist," he said with quiet implacability.

Joy slid out of the booth behind Corey. "I guess I'd better spend some time with Mom and Peter and their guests."

Mrs. Foster waited until the three were well out of earshot. "Mother," she said with a sigh, "I cannot believe you did that."

"I only said what was true, dear."

"Sometimes the truth hurts people."

"Truth is truth," the elderly lady said smugly as she eased her way out of the booth. "And the truth is that Spencer deserved a thrashing for what he did that night, and Corey deserved an apology. I accomplished both tonight, and they're both better off for it."

"If you're hoping that they'll fall in love now that you've cleared the way, you're very wrong. Corey is the living example of 'once burned, twice shy.' You've said that a hundred times about her."

"Well, that's the truth, too."

"Do you think," Mrs. Foster said, her mind shifting away from Corey and Spence and back to the basic problem, "you could just *think* about the truth, and not say it quite so often?"

"I don't think so."

Mrs. Foster stepped aside so that her mother could precede her down the hall. "Why not?"

"I'm seventy-one years old. I don't think I should waste any more of my time on words that don't mean anything. Besides, at my age, I'm allowed to be eccentric."

Ten

LAUGHTER AND RAISED voices echoed from the dining room, where Angela's dinner party was in full swing, but outside the night was soft and hushed as they strolled across the side lawn toward the water. Corey was amazed at how utterly relaxed and at peace she felt, walking at Spence's side. She could not remember ever being near him when she'd felt anything but an excited, nerve-racking tension, and she vastly preferred this new feeling.

She no longer had anything to hide or regret—her grandmother's dissertation at dinner had exposed her girlhood infatuation, laid it bare for all to see, and in the process she'd revealed it to Corey for exactly what it was—a very sweet, adolescent infatuation with an unknowing victim, not the painfully embarrassing, neurotic obsession with a selfish monster she'd feared it was. Spence's tanned face had actually paled while he listened to her grandmother's eloquent description of what Corey had "suffered" at his hands.

Before she had left for Newport, Corey had forced herself to view the whole awful debacle with philosophical indifference, but she was still hurt by it. Tonight, she had ended up laughing at herself in her grandmother's dramatic tale, and then laughing at the "villain" and trying to rescue him from any more guilt than he was already being made to feel. Confession, she decided, was definitely good for the soul, even if

that confession was forced out of you by your grandmother. She had finally put an end to any and all
attachment she ever had to Spence; all that was left was
nostalgia, and her freedom gave her a sensation of sub-
lime serenity.

He stopped beneath a big tree near the water's edge,
and Corey leaned her shoulders against it, looking out
at the crescent of twinkling lights from houses in the
distance, waiting for him to say whatever he'd brought
her out here to say. When he didn't seem to know how
to begin, she found his uncharacteristic uncertainty a
little touching and extremely amusing.

Spence gazed at her pretty profile, trying to gauge
her mood. "What are you thinking about?" he asked
finally.

"I'm thinking that I've never known you to be at a
loss for words before."

"I don't quite know where to begin."

She crossed her arms over her chest, lifted her
brows, and tipped her head toward the water in a silent,
joking suggestion. "Want some help?"

"I don't think so," he said warily. She laughed,
and the sound of it made him laugh, and suddenly
everything was the way it had always been with
them, only better, richer for him because he was
beginning to understand its value. He was shamefully
pleased that she'd had his pictures all over her room
and belatedly delighted that she'd evidently wanted
him to take her to her Christmas dance from the very
beginning.

Rather than start with the dance, he started with the
pictures. "Did you really have my pictures all over your

room?" he teased, gentling his tone so she wouldn't think he was gloating.

"Everywhere," she admitted, smiling at the memory; then she looked up at him and said, "You surely had to have known I had a terrible crush on you when I was tagging after you taking pictures of you."

"I did. Only I thought it ended when you were seventeen."

"Really? Why?"

"Why?" he uttered, a little dumbfounded that she didn't know. "I suppose I regarded it as a clue when you asked me to help you practice kissing techniques so that you could use them on some guy named . . ." He searched his memory for a name. "Doug!"

Corey nodded. "Doug Johnson."

"Right. Johnson. In fact, Diana told me Johnson had planned to take you to the Christmas dance and then had to cancel at the last minute, which was why I volunteered. I naturally assumed you had a crush on him after that, not me. How could I have possibly thought you cared about me after all that?" He waited for her to see the logic in his thinking, and when she only regarded him in amused silence, he said, "Well?"

"There was no Doug Johnson."

"What do you mean 'there was no Doug Johnson'?"

"I wanted you to kiss me, so I invented Doug Johnson and used him as an excuse. I wanted you to take me to the Christmas formal, so I used Doug's named again. The only reason I dated boys was so that I'd know how to act on a date with *you*, when you asked me." She gave him a sideways smile, and Spence had an insane impulse to lean down and kiss it off her lips—an impulse that approached a compulsion when she shook her head at the memory of her infatuation and added softly, "It was you. It was always you. From the night I met you at the luau until a week after the dance, when you didn't call to apologize or explain, it was only you."

"Corey, there was another reason I forgot about the dance and went to Aspen. I'd expected my mother to come to Houston for Christmas, and I was looking forward to it more than I let anyone know. I'd been making excuses for her absence and lack of interest my whole life, and although it sounds absurd now, I actually thought that if she got to know me as an adult, then maybe we could have some sort of relationship. When she phoned at the last minute to say she'd decided to go to Paris instead, I ran out of excuses for her. I got drunk with some friends, none of whom had 'normal families,' and we all decided to go to Aspen, where one of them had a house, and forget Christmas."

"I understand," Corey said. "You'd told me you were looking forward to her visit, but I'd already guessed she was more important to you than you wanted anyone to know. You were a hobby of mine, remember. There wasn't much about you I didn't know or try to find out."

Flattered and touched, Spence braced his palm high on the tree trunk, longing to lean down and kiss her, but there was one more thing he needed to say. "I should have called you to explain, or at least apologize, but I let my grandmother convince me that I'd already done enough damage and that I should stay completely out of your life. She told me that you went to the dance with someone else—which she believed—and that I was not a fit companion for an innocent young girl—which she also believed. I already felt like a complete pervert for what I did to you that night by the pool, so her tirade hit me in a very vulnerable place."

Corey saw his gaze drop to her lips and a little of her newfound serenity deserted her even before he said in a husky voice, "Now that we've finished the explanations, there's only one thing left to do."

"What's that?" Corey asked warily.

"We have to kiss and make up. It's traditional."

Corey pressed further back against the tree trunk. "Why don't we just shake hands, instead."

He smiled solemnly and shook his head. "Don't you know it's bad luck not to honor the traditions of your host?"

The forgotten sweetness of the memory was nothing compared to what she felt as he laid his palm against her cheek and whispered, "A golden girl told me that one Christmas, a long time ago." He bent his head and brushed a kiss slowly over her lips, and Corey managed to savor the moment without participating, but Spence wasn't finished. "If you don't kiss me back," he coaxed, sliding his mouth over her cheek, "the tradition isn't fulfilled. And that means *very* bad luck." His tongue lazily traced the curve of her ear, sending shivers down her spine to her toes, and Corey smiled helplessly, tipping her head back a little as he traced a warm path down her neck. "*Extremely* bad luck," he warned, retracing his path, and then the teasing was over. He cradled her face in his palms, his thumbs slowly caressing her cheeks, and Corey was mesmerized by the intensity in his eyes. "Have you any idea," he said gruffly, "how much I hated Doug Johnson after that night?"

Corey tried to smile and felt the sudden, inexplicable sting of tears instead.

"Have you any idea," he whispered as his mouth descended purposefully toward hers, "how long I've wanted to do this . . ."

Corey felt her defenses crumbling and tried to forestall him with humor. "I'm not completely sure I'm old enough."

A sensual smile curved his lips, and she watched them form a single word: "Tough," he said, and curved her into his arms, capturing her lips in a kiss that was as rough and tender as his answer had been.

Corey told herself there was no danger in a kiss, no defeat in cooperating just a little, as she slid her hands up his hard chest and yielded to the coaxing insistence of his tongue. She was wrong. The instant she did, his arms tightened and his mouth opened over hers in a fierce, demanding kiss that assaulted her newfound serenity and made her clutch his broad shoulders for balance in a world that was beginning to spin. His tongue drove into her mouth, and with a silent cry of despair, Corey wrapped her arms around his neck and kissed him back.

She leaned into him and forced him to gentle the kiss by softly stroking his tongue with hers and felt the gasp of his breath as he drew her tighter to him, his arms angling over her hips to hold her pressed to his rigid thighs. She kissed him slowly, sliding her fingers over his jaw and around his nape, and he let her set the pace, his hand drifting in a slow caress over her spine and bottom, his mouth moving endlessly on hers, following her lead. And just when Corey was beginning to feel in complete control, he took it away. His fingers shoved into the hair at her nape, and he ground his lips into hers, pressing her back against the tree with his body, freeing his hands to rush over her breasts, then slowly covering and caressing them until Corey thought she would die of the sweet torment and the longing for more.

Time ceased to exist, measured only in a series of endless, shattering kisses and arousing caresses that began slowly and built toward a crescendo; then they pulled apart. So they could begin all over again.

Corey heard herself moan when he tore his mouth from hers for the very last time. He buried his face in her neck, then he drew a long, labored breath and tightened his arms around her, holding her face against his heart.

She stayed there, her eyes closed tightly against the moment when her mind would take over and rage against the stupidity, the insanity of what she'd just done to herself, but it was already too late. Reality was setting in. She was clearly mentally ill! She had some sort of sick obsession with Spencer Addison. She had tossed away her adolescence on him, and now, all he had to do was say something sweet—and she fell into his arms like a lovesick idiot. She had never in her life felt as she had tonight except once . . . long ago on a summer night by the swimming pool. A tear dropped from her eye and raced down her cheek. She did not mean anything to him, and she never had . . .

"Corey," he said in a roughened voice as he touched his lips to her hair. "Would you care to explain to me why I seem to lose my mind the moment I touch you?"

Her heart did a somersault, her mind went into silent shock. For the second time tonight, she had an absurd impulse to laugh and cry at the same time. "We are both clearly insane," she said, but overall, she felt much better than she had the moment before. She moved away from him, and he put his arm around her shoulders, walking with her back to the house.

Lost in her own thoughts, Corey scarcely noticed that he was walking her to her room until they'd turned down the hall and she saw the double doors of the Duchess Suite in front of her. She turned in front of them and looked up at him. This last half hour was the closest thing to a date they'd ever had, and she had an irreverent impulse to smile at him and say, "Thank you for a lovely evening." Instead she said, "Since we've already kissed good night, I guess there's nothing else to do or say."

He grinned at her and braced his hand against the doorframe, relaxed and confident. A little too confident, she thought. "We could always do it again," he suggested.

"I don't think that would be a good idea," she lied.

"In that case, you could invite me in for a nightcap."

"I think that's an even worse idea," she primly informed him.

"Liar," he said with a grin, then he bent and gave her a hard swift kiss and opened the door. Corey walked serenely into her room, closed the door, and collapsed against it, dazed by the last half hour she'd spent in his arms. Her gaze landed on the clock on the little secretary. It was almost midnight. They'd been outside for well over an hour.

Eleven

STANDING ON THE back lawn, Corey watched Mike MacNeil and Kristin Nordstrom setting up some of the camera equipment for exterior shots of the work underway, but there was little the pair could do until tomorrow, when the flowers were in place on the bridal arches and the banquet tables beneath the white tent were decked out in "Foster Style." At the moment, there was a small army of gardeners, carpenters, and florists bumping into the caterers, who were scheduled to serve a rehearsal dinner on the terrace tonight after the rehearsal itself was over.

To Corey's trained eye, everything looked as if it was going very well. She saw Joy talking earnestly to one of the caterer's staff, and whatever she was saying to the young man made him smile at her and the rest of his companions guffaw. The caterers were a family operation, Corey knew, and besides being very good, they obviously enjoyed working together. She saw Corey and waved, and Corey waved back, then she headed over to Mike and Kristin, who'd arrived that morning in a van. "How's it going, Mike?"

"Everything's under control. No problems." He was five feet four inches tall, fifty pounds overweight, and he looked as if he were about to collapse on top of the heavy trunk he was dragging across the grass. Corey knew better than to offer to help. "How do you like your new location assistant?"

He looked over his shoulder at Kristin, who was effortlessly carrying an identical trunk. "Couldn't you have found someone a little taller and a little more robust?" he asked wryly.

Since Corey had more than enough work to occupy her, she watched for a few minutes and then headed back to the house.

Back to Spence.

She'd fallen asleep with her arms around her pillow, thinking of him, and today, she could think of little else. He wasn't helping, either. This morning, he'd strolled into the little breakfast room where they'd dined last night, and in full view of Corey's mother and grandmother and his astonished niece, he'd rumpled Corey's hair and pressed a kiss on her cheek.

At noon, she saw him coming down a crowded hallway near his study with a sheaf of papers in his hand that he appeared to be engrossed in reading. Without looking up, he nodded to a houseguest and moved around three servants. As he passed Corey, seemingly without seeing her, he made a sharp turn and walked straight into her, backing her through an open doorway and straight into a closet, closing its door behind them. While she was still sputtering, he dropped the papers, pulled her into his arms, and kissed her senseless. "I've missed you," he said just before he let her go. "And don't make plans for dinner. We're dining alone tonight on your balcony. My balcony overlooks the back lawn, which means we'd have as much privacy as we have in the halls."

Corey knew she should object, but she didn't want to. She was leaving on Sunday, which gave her only tonight and tomorrow night to see him. "Only if you promise to behave," she said instead.

"Oh, I will—" he agreed solemnly, then he pulled her back into his arms and kissed her until she was clinging to him, "—just like this." He let her go with a familiar smack on her rump. "Now get out of here before I decide to keep you here and we end up suffocating. There's no air in this damned closet."

The entire time they'd kissed there'd been a parade of footsteps down the hall and Corey shook her head. "No, you go first and make certain the coast is clear."

"Corey," he said, "I can't leave this closet right now. I'm in no state to greet houseguests, believe me."

Embarrassed and pleased, she put her ear to the door, then stealthily reached for the handle when the coast seemed clear. "I ought to lock you in here," she tossed over her shoulder.

"Try it and I'll pound on the door and tell everyone you've stolen the silver."

Corey was smiling at that memory when she saw Joy walking slowly and dejectedly toward a stand of trees on the perimeter of the lawn. She looked so miserable that Corey hesitated and then went after her. "Joy—is something wrong?" she said, coming up behind her.

"I'd rather not talk about it," she said, hastily brushing her fingertips over her cheeks before she turned and gave Corey a watery smile.

"If you don't want to tell me why you're crying, then will you talk to your mother or someone else? You shouldn't be upset like this on the day before your wedding. Richard will be here tonight. He won't want to see you unhappy."

"Richard's very sensible, and he'll say I'm being foolish. So will everyone." She shrugged and started slowly to the house. "Let's talk about something else.

Tell me more about you and Uncle Spence." She hesitated, and then said in a voice tinged with desperation, "Do you think you really loved him when you were my age?"

If the question had been asked in idle curiosity, Corey would have sidestepped it, but she had the feeling that Joy was turning to her for help and that anything other than the truth might somehow do a great disservice to her. "I want to answer you honestly, but it's hard for me to look back at my feelings for him without also realizing how hopeless and one-sided they were, and then to discredit them because of it."

"Would you have eloped with him?"

The question was so unexpected that Corey laughed and nodded. "Only if he'd asked me."

"What if he hadn't been from a wealthy family?"

"I only wanted him, nothing else would have mattered."

"So you did love him?"

"I—" Corey hesitated, looking back. "I believed in him. I admired and respected him. And I did it for all the *right* reasons, even then. I didn't care that he was a football hero at college, or what kind of car he had. I wanted to make him happy, and he always seemed to enjoy being with me, so I truly believed I could." With a rueful smile, she admitted, "I used to lie in bed at night, imagining that I was going to have his baby, and that he was asleep beside me with his arms around me, and that he was happy about the baby. It was one of my favorite fantasies, out of about ten thousand fantasies. If all those things add up to love, then yes, I did love him. And I'll tell you a secret," Corey finished wryly, "I have never felt that way about anyone else since."

"Is that why you've never gotten married?"

"In a way, it is. On the one hand, I don't want to risk feeling that way about anyone again—I was completely obsessed. On the other hand, I'd never settle for anything less if I were to marry someone." They'd arrived at the house, and to Corey's surprise, Joy gave her a hug. "Thank you," she said fiercely.

Corey watched her walk back across the lawn toward the caterers, then she started slowly toward the dining room, where she was planning to spend the rest of the afternoon taking photographs, but she felt uneasy. She decided to talk to Spence about Joy. Something was wrong.

Twelve

TRYING NOT TO make a sound, Corey repositioned an antique candelabra on the dining room table. From the head of the table, out of range of the shot she was setting up, Spence said, "Don't worry about making noise. Do what you need to do."

He had brought his paperwork there so they could be together while she worked. Corey was afraid to admit to herself how much she loved his company and how wonderful it felt to have him pursuing her after all these years. "I don't want to distract you."

A lazy, intimate smile swept across his handsome face. "In that case, you'll have to pack up and leave Newport."

Corey knew exactly what he meant, but the sweetness of flirting with him, and even getting the upper hand, was too tempting to pass up. "Be patient. We'll be out of here Sunday morning, and you'll have this ramshackle old house all to yourself again."

"That isn't what I mean, and you know it," he said calmly, refusing to participate in her game.

That surprised her. Sometimes, she was positive they were indulging in a long-overdue flirtation, but just when she'd adjusted to that and tried to play by the rules, he ended the game and turned serious on her.

"Can you stay a few days longer?"

Corey hesitated, struggling to resist the temptation. "No, I can't. I have assignments already booked for the next six months."

She waited, half in hope, half in fear, that he'd urge her to stay longer and she would agree. He didn't. Evidently he wasn't *that* serious. Refusing to acknowledge that it hurt her, Corey turned her attention to safer matters and glanced at the papers spread out in front of him. "What are you working on?"

"I'm considering the pros and cons of a business deal; weighing all the alternatives, balancing the element of risk with the possibilities of gain; going over the research. The usual process of decision making."

"It isn't usual for me," Corey admitted, crouching down and eyeing the effect of the flower arrangement with the candles and heirloom china. "If I went through all of that, I'd never be able to make any decision at all." Satisfied, she walked over to the tripod and took the picture, then she adjusted for a slightly different angle that would catch the rays of the sun dancing off the crystal and snapped off two more shots.

Spence watched her, admiring her deft skill for a moment, then turning his attention to her other more alluring attributes. He studied the curve of her cheek, the generous softness of her mouth, and watched the sunlight dancing on her hair. She'd pulled the wavy mass up into a ponytail with tendrils at her ears, and it made her look about eighteen years old again. She was wearing white shorts and a T-shirt, and he indulged himself with a leisurely visual caress of her long slim legs and her full breasts while he imagined how she was going to feel in his arms in bed tonight.

She could set him on fire with a kiss, and tonight he intended to fan that fire and let it blaze out of control until it consumed them both. And then he was going to build it up again. He was going to make love to her until she pleaded with him to stop, and then he was going to make her plead for him to start again.

They were meant for each other; he knew that now just as surely as he knew Corey didn't want to trust him with her heart again. He could persuade her to give him her body tonight, but he needed time to persuade her to give him her heart, and she was trying not to give him that time. He already knew now amazingly steadfast she was once she made up her mind; she had been steadfast in her devotion to him years ago, and now she was just as dedicated to keeping her emotional distance from him. For the first time in his adult life, Spence felt powerless and fearful, because short of tying Corey up, he couldn't think of a way to make her give him the time to prove himself.

"Stop staring at me," she said with a smothered laugh, without glancing in his direction.

"How do you know I am?"

"I can feel your eyes on me."

He heard the tiny tremble in her voice, and he smiled, then he returned to the discussion they'd been having about decision making. "What method do you prefer for making your decisions?"

Corey looked over her shoulder. "Seriously?"

"I'm very serious," he said, his voice deep with meaning.

Corey ignored that. "For the most part, I act on instinct and impulse. I seem to know in here"—she touched her heart—"what decisions are best. I've learned that from experience."

"That's a risky way to handle important things."

"That's the only way I can handle them at all. The truth is, if I spend too much time weighing alternatives, balancing the risk against the gain, I become paralyzed with uncertainty, and I end up making no decision at all. My judgment is best when I rely on impulse and instinct."

"That's probably a part of your artistic nature."

Corey smiled. "Maybe, but it's just as likely that it's genetic. My mother is the same way. If you give either of us too much time to think, or offer us too many possibilities, we don't act at all. She told me once that if my stepfather hadn't rushed her into marriage before she could sort out all the drawbacks from the benefits, if she hadn't been forced to act on instinct instead of logic, that she wouldn't have married him at all."

Mentally, Spence filed that revealing information about Corey away for future use.

"Is that why you've never married—too many possibilities for failure and too much time to think about all of them?"

"Could be," Corey evaded, and quickly turned the discussion back to him. "What happened to your marriage?"

"Nothing happened to it," he said dryly, then he realized that he wanted her to understand. "Sheila's parents had died the year before my grandmother died, and neither of us had anyone else. When we realized we had only that in common and very little else, we decided to get a divorce while we were still able to be civil to each other."

Corey opened her camera case and carefully slid the camera into its compartment, then she turned around and leaned against the dining room table, her forehead furrowed into a frown. "Spence . . . speaking of marriage, I wanted to talk to you about Joy. I don't know that she's certain she's doing the right thing. Does she have anyone she confides in? I mean, where are her friends, her bridesmaids, her *fiancé?*"

She half expected him to wave the matter off; instead he leaned his head back and ran his hand around behind his neck as if the subject somehow made his muscles tense. "Her mother has picked her friends, her bridesmaids, *and* her fiancé," he said bitterly. "Joy isn't stupid, she'd simply never been allowed to think for herself. Angela had made every decision for her and then inflicted them on her."

"What's her fiancé like?"

"In my opinion, he's a twenty-five-year-old egomaniac who is marrying Joy because she's pliable and will reinforce his own inflated opinion of himself. I also think he likes having a connection through marriage to German nobility. On the other hand, the last time I saw the two of them together, Joy seemed to like him very much."

"Will you talk to her?" Corey asked as she turned back and finished packing up her equipment.

"Yes," he said, his voice so near that his breath stirred the hair on her nape, then his lips grazed her skin and Corey felt an alarming jolt from even that simple contact. "Will you mind having a late dinner? Although I don't give a damn about any of these people, I do have a duty as host to fulfill at the rehearsal dinner."

He'd asked her to join him downstairs during the rehearsal festivities, but she'd declined. Corey knew it was insanity to have dinner with him in her room, but she told herself she'd keep things under control, and that they weren't even eating on the bed, they were eating on the *balcony*—"A late dinner is fine. It will give me a chance to take a nap."

"That's a *very* good idea," he said, and with such emphasis that Corey turned around and tried to see his face. He looked completely innocent.

Thirteen

ALTHOUGH COREY'S BALCONY faced the side lawn, another set of her windows offered a perfect view of the party taking place on the terrace below and an ideal chance to observe Spence without fear of having him know it. It occurred to her that she'd been with him for only two days and she was right back where she'd begun—watching for a glimpse of him. Sighing, she leaned her shoulder against the window frame, but she continued to watch.

He was a man of great contrasts, she thought tenderly—a tall, powerfully built man who exuded a tough, hard-bitten strength that was at complete variance to the sensuality of his mouth and the glamour of his sudden smile. He looked as if he could still carry a football and plow his way through a defensive line, and yet he exuded the relaxed elegance of a man who was born to preside over a mansion like this one.

Tonight, he was playing his role of host with ease, appearing to listen intently to what a group of men were telling him, but Corey saw him look at his watch for the third time in ten minutes. He'd had dinner sent up five minutes ago, and the table on the balcony was already set with china and silver and covered platters. She glanced at the clock and watched the minute hand make its last small lurch. It was ten o'clock. She looked out the window and smothered a laugh as Spence abruptly put his drink down, nodded briefly to the men who were talking to him, and left them there, his long, swift strides taking him straight toward the doors that led into the house. He'd fulfilled his social obligations; now he was in a hurry.

Because he wanted to have dinner with her.

And after dinner, he intended to have Corey for dessert.

Wryly, Corey glanced at the table on the balcony, where a hurricane lamp was already casting its mellow glow. It was a perfect seduction scene—a private balcony, candlelight, champagne chilling in a bucket, music in the distance, and a very large, luxurious bed with satin sheets within immediate reach. She was immensely flattered by his attention to detail, but she was not going to let him make love to her. If she did, the desolation she would feel when he kissed her good-bye and sent her on her way would make the episode eleven years ago pale in comparison.

Corey was very clear on all that. What she was not clear about was why he suddenly seemed to find her so irresistible. Last night, as she had lain awake, trying to find a reason for his display of passion, she'd decided it was a case of guilt over the picture her grandmother had painted for him of Corey waiting at the window for him to take her to the dance.

That theory was invalidated by the way he'd behave today—he was in serious amorous pursuit, and he was using an entire arsenal of sensual weapons on her, from his voice to his hands. He'd even asked her to extend her trip, though he'd backed off without pressing her. It didn't make sense. Outside, on the lawn, here were stunning women who put Corey completely in the shade, and she'd watched several of them trying to flirt with him. Spence was gorgeous, sexy, and rich. He had an unlimited supply of women who were just like him from which to choose. *That* was the real reason he'd never been interested in Corey, not even when she was almost eighteen and the age difference between them wouldn't have mattered so much.

Now he was suddenly pursuing her with single-minded determination, and she knew there had to be an explanation. It was possible he simply enjoyed the novelty of trying to seduce a childhood friend. She shoved that thought aside; it was completely unjust. Spence wasn't cynical or jaded; she wouldn't be so helplessly in love with him now if he was.

Corey moved away from the window so that he wouldn't see her there and guess she'd been watching him on the terrace.

When there was no answer to his knock, Spence tried the knob and let himself in. He was halfway across the suite when he saw Corey outside on the balcony, standing at the balustrade in a long, bright green silk shift that covered her from her neck to her ankles with the exception of a slash at the neck. She was waiting for him, he thought with an inner grin. After all these years, his golden girl was waiting for him again. Fate had given him a second chance he didn't deserve, and he intended to seize it any way he could.

Dinner with Corey was one of the most enjoyable meals he'd had in years. She regaled him with funny stories about events in life that he'd almost forgotten. Afterward, they sipped brandy and Corey got out one of the photo albums she'd brought to give him. The light from the hurricane lamp wasn't very good, but Corey argued that bad lighting was a help, not hindrance, for viewing her earliest photographic attempts. Spence let her have her way because the champagne and brandy were having a mellowing effect on her, and he wanted her to be relaxed tonight.

With his elbow on the table and his chin on his fist, he divided his attention between her animated face and the pictures she was showing him. "Why did you keep that shot?" he asked, pointing to a picture of a girl in riding breeches who was sprawled on the ground in a sitting position, her hair half-covering her face.

Corey gave him a winsome smile, but he had the feeling she was a little embarrassed. "Actually, that was one of my favorites for a while. I gather you don't recognize her?"

"Not with her hair in her face."

"That happens to be Lisa Murphy. You took her out during your junior year of college when you were home during the summer."

Understanding dawned and Spence swallowed a laugh. "I take it you didn't like her very much?"

"Not after she took me aside and told me I was a pest and that I should stay away from you. We were all at a charity horse show that day. Actually, I didn't even know you were going to be there."

The last page contained one of the snapshots of Spence with his grandmother that Corey had taken at the luau. They looked at it in silence for a moment. "She was very special," Corey said softly, touching her fingertip to the elderly lady's cheek.

"So were you," he said quietly, as he closed the album. "Even then."

Corey knew instinctively that the part of the evening she longed for and dreaded was about to begin. She took the coward's way and tried to forestall the inevitable with humor and a change of location. "I'm sure you didn't think I was 'special' when I was hanging out of trees taking pictures of you," she joked, walking over to the balustrade.

He walked up behind her and put his hands on her shoulders. "I always thought you were special, Corey."

When she didn't reply, he said, "Would you be surprised if I told you I have a picture of you?"

"Was it one of the ones I used to stick in your wallet when you weren't looking?"

An instant ago he was about to kiss her, and he ended up burying his laughing face in her hair instead. "Did you really do that?"

"No, but I considered it."

"The picture I have of you is from the front of *Beautiful Living*."

"I hope you found enough room for it somewhere," she joked. "It's only an inch tall."

He brushed his lips over her temple, his voice a tender murmur. "I want a larger photograph that shows the way you glow in the moonlight when you're in my arms."

Corey tried not to let what he was saying or doing affect her, but warmth was already spreading through her entire body, and when he slid his arm around her waist and drew her against his full length, she felt an ache of longing begin to build. "I'm insane about you," he whispered.

"Spence," she pleaded softly, "don't do this to me." But it was too late, he was already turning her in his arms, and when his mouth opened over hers, insistent and hungry, Corey gave herself up to the torrid kiss, surrendered to the turbulence that followed in the wake of male hands that caressed her breasts and slid down her spine, forcing her into vibrant contact with his arousal. When he finally lifted his mouth from hers, Corey felt seared by the kiss and branded with his body.

"Stay for a few days," he whispered, rubbing his jaw against her hair.

A few days . . . She deserved a few sweet days to remember and cherish. And then regret. "I—I have to work for a living—a schedule—"

He shoved his hands through the sides of her hair and turned her face up to his. "Put me on your schedule. I have work for you."

She thought he was joking about it being work, and she leaned her forehead against his chest. She was going to stay with him. God help her, she was going to do it. "What you're suggesting is not work," she said, her voice trembling with fear and love.

Spence sensed that she was wavering, and he pressed the advantage he'd gained before she could change her mind. "I'm serious," he said using the only method he'd been able to think of all day that might make her agree to stay. "I've been putting together notes for a book on this house and several others built at the same time. I need photographs to accompany the text, and you could—"

She shoved him away so abruptly that he almost lost his balance. "So that's what this whole seduction routine has been about!" She wrapped her arms around her middle and backed away, her voice shaking with tears and fury. "You wanted something!" He reached for her, but she jerked free and backed away. "Get out of here."

"Listen to me!" Spence caught her just inside the open doors. "I love you!"

"If you want me to take pictures of this place, then call the William Morris Agency in New York and talk to my agent, but first you'd better send him a blank check!"

"Corey, shut up and listen to me. I invented all that about the book. I'm in love with you."

"You lying, conniving—Get out of here!"

She was trying so damned hard not to cry, and he knew she'd hate him more if she broke down in front of him. He dropped his arms to his sides, but he wasn't giving up. "We'll talk about this in the morning."

By the time Spence reached his own room, the enormity of his mistake had hit him. No matter what he tried to tell her in the morning, she wasn't going to believe him. After this, there was no way he could prove to her that he had no ulterior motives and that all he wanted was her.

Furious with his blunder, he yanked off his jacket and unbuttoned his shirt while he let himself consider the one ugly possibility that had been there all along: Corey wasn't in love with him. He knew damned well she felt *something* for him; it ignited the moment he touched her, but he could be mistaking that "something" for love. He was on his way to the liquor cabinet when he passed his bed and saw the note propped on his pillows.

It was a hastily written letter from Joy, telling him that she was eloping with Will Marcillo, the caterer's son, and asking Spence to tell her mother in the morning. The rest of the letter was a desperate effort on his niece's part to make Spence understand why a conversation she'd had with Corey earlier that day had convinced her she had to marry the man she loved. According to Joy's disjointed explanation, Corey had admitted to her that she had never loved anyone but Spence and she wanted to have his babies, but she was afraid to risk her feelings again. That, according to Joy, was exactly how she herself had felt about Will, only Joy was no longer afraid to take the risk.

Spence read the letter again, then he put it down on a table and stared at his bed, his mind whirling with

Joy's revelations, fitting them together with the things
he'd discovered about Corey and then coming to a full
stop at the impossible predicament he'd put himself in
tonight by lying to her about his motives for wanting
her to stay.

According to Joy's note, Corey loved him. She
wanted to have his babies. She was afraid to take a risk.

According to Corey, she either acted on impulse and
instinct, or else she lost her courage and didn't act at all.

Spence had inadvertently fixed it so that nothing he
said would make Corey believe he wanted only her.
Tomorrow a wedding was scheduled to take place, but
there was no bride and no groom. He couldn't say anything to make her believe him, but there was a possibility he might still be able to *do* something. He hesitated
for a moment, and then he made his decision and
picked up the telephone.

Judge Lattimore had just gotten home from the
rehearsal dinner. He was very surprised to hear from
Spence. He was more surprised when he understood
why.

Fourteen

COREY WAS ALREADY setting up equipment for the
wedding shots on the lawn at seven o'clock in the
morning when she was handed a note from Spence
telling her to come to his study immediately. Convinced he had some new form of lie to tell her, she cir-
cumvented him by taking Mike and Kristin with her.

Anger made her steps long and fast as she walked across the lawn. She still could hardly believe he'd done what he had, merely to get free professional photographs for his damned book. On the other hand, Corey's freelance fees were very high, and she'd lived among the wealthy long enough to know how incredibly cheap some of them were when it came to spending money on anything other than themselves. Cheap was bad enough, but deceitful and manipulative were unforgivable, and to use her as he had—to touch her and kiss her—and then to tell her he *loved* her. That was obscene.

As soon as she stepped into his study, Corey realized she needn't have worried that he had any sort of cozy tryst in mind. Angela was seated in a chair wearing a dressing robe and clutching a handkerchief; her husband was standing rigidly beside her chair in his robe, looking poised to attack. Spence looked immune to whatever drama had taken place in there. With his hip perched on the edge of his desk and his weight braced on the opposite foot, he was looking out the window, idly turning a paperweight on his desk.

He looked up at Corey as she walked in with her assistants, but instead of the animosity or the cajolery she expected to see, he looked perfectly composed, as if last night hadn't happened. He nodded toward the chairs at his desk in an invitation for Corey, Mike, and Kristin to have a seat. Unable to bear the suspense, Corey looked from him to Angela. "What's wrong?"

"She's gone, that's what's wrong!" Angela cried. "That nitwit has eloped with that—that busboy! I shouldn't have named her Joy, I should have called her Disaster!"

Corey sank down into the chair, her shock giving

way to happiness for Joy and then to the awful realization that Joy's last-minute elopement was a calamity for Corey and the magazine. It was too late to substitute another wedding for the next issue, much too late. They were already at deadline now.

"I notified the groom's family an hour ago," Spence told her. "They'll speak to as many of their guests as they can reach. Those guests who can't be reached will be met here by one of their relatives, who will explain the situation."

"This is a nightmare!" Angela gritted.

"It's also created an enormous problem for Corey's magazine. They've invested a great deal of time and money in all this." He paused to let that sink in before he continued. "I've had longer than anyone else to consider alternatives, and I think I've come up with a plausible solution. I suggest we let Corey go ahead and photograph the wedding."

"There isn't going to *be* a wedding!" Angela burst out bitterly.

"What I'm suggesting is that Corey be allowed to photograph everything—"

"Except the bride and groom who *won't be here!*" Angela exploded.

"Corey can use stand-ins," Spencer explained.

Corey understood exactly what he was suggesting, and she rushed in to help him explain, her mind already racing ahead to the angles she'd used to get appealing photographs without revealing the faces of the bride and groom. "Mrs. Reichardt, we can take long shots of another couple dressed as a bride and groom. What I need is a crowd in the background . . . It doesn't have to be a large one, but—"

"Absolutely not!" said his sister.

"I won't have it!" Mr. Reichardt stormed.

Spence's voice had a razor edge to it that Corey had never heard before. *"You* haven't paid for it, I have." He shifted his attention back to his sister and continued. "Angela, I understand how you feel, but we have a moral and ethical obligation to do what we can to make certain Corey's magazine doesn't suffer because of Joy's . . . impulsiveness."

Corey listened to him in stunned silence, trying to understand how his mind worked. Last night, she'd decided that he was so cheap that he'd been romancing her in the hope of getting free photography for his book. This morning, he was lecturing about ethics and morality and passing up an opportunity to cancel everything associated with the wedding, forfeit what deposits he had to forfeit, and still save himself a small fortune.

"But what will we tell *our* guests?" Angela demanded. "Some of the guests are friends of yours, too, don't forget that."

"We will tell them we're delighted with the bride's decision, and sorry that she can't be here . . . but that we'd like them all to celebrate at the reception as if the newlyweds were present." Finished, he looked to Corey for approval, and she gave it to him in the form of a relieved smile, but in fairness to Angela she added, "It is very unusual."

"So are many of the wedding guests," Spence said dryly. "They'll probably enjoy the novelty of a reception for a canceled wedding. That's something they won't have already done. A new experience, you might say, for a bunch of jaded cynics."

Angela looked ready to hit him. She surged to her

feet and stormed out of the room with Reichardt at her side.

Spence waited until they were gone, then he said briskly, "Okay, let's handle the details. We need a bride and a groom and a judge."

Corey knew he was waiting for her to speak, but as she looked at the forceful, dynamic man who was willing to help shoulder her burdens, her heart was reclassifying him from enemy, to alley and friend, and there was nothing she could do to stop it. He saw the change reflected in her eyes and his tone softened to a caress. "I'll find a stand-in for the judge."

"In that case, all we need are stands-ins for the bride and groom." Corey looked at Kristin and Mike. "How about you two?"

"Get serious," Mike said. "I'm fifty pounds overweight and Kristin is six inches taller than me. The caption beneath our picture would have to read 'Pillsbury Doughboy Weds the Green Giant.' "

"Stop thinking about food," Kristin chided, "and start thinking of solutions."

Silence ensued for a long moment before Spence finally said in a tone of exasperated amusement, "What am I, chopped liver?"

Corey shook her head. "I can't use you for the groom."

A look of surprised hurt flashed across his eyes. "As I recall you used to find me rather photogenic. Now that I'm older, are you afraid I'll break your lens?"

"You'd be more likely to melt it," she said wryly, imagining his tall, muscular physique in a raven black tuxedo with a snowy shirt contrasting against his tanned skin.

"Then what's the problem?"

"You'll be busy with the guests, making explanations and trying to keep them smiling." She paused to make her point. "Spence, it's imperative that I have lots of happy faces in these shots. Their success depends much more on the mood of the crowd than on my technique."

"I can accomplish that and still be the 'groom.' I'll tell the staff to open up all six of the bars on the lawn and keep passing drinks until the last guest leaves or we run out of liquor. If necessary, we'll have taxis lined up in front in case they're needed."

"In that case," Corey said with a relieved sigh, "the job is yours. Kristin, you get to be the bride. Spence is several inches taller than you."

Spence opened his mouth to object, but Kristin beat him to it. "I'd have to lose twenty pounds to get into Joy's wedding gown, and it would still only hit me at the knees."

"Corey, there's only one solution and it's obvious," Spence said flatly. "You'll have to be the bride."

"I can't be the bride; I'm the photographer, remember? We'll have to ask someone else."

"Even I cannot trample on good taste to the extent of asking a wedding guest to put on Joy's gown and play bride for us. You have several tripods here. You can set up the shot, rush into the picture, and have Mike or Kristin press the button. That's all there is to it."

Corey bit her lip, considering his suggestion. She didn't need more than a couple shots of the bride and groom—one in the garden beneath the gazebo, the other somewhere at the reception off to the side, so using tripods wasn't a problem. "Okay."

"Would anyone like a glass of champagne?" Spence offered, looking completely satisfied with the situation. "It's customary to toast Corey and me."

"Don't make jokes like that," Corey warned, and the tension in her voice surprised everyone, including her.

"Bridal nerves," Spence surmised, and Mike guffawed.

They got up to leave, but Spence laid a detaining hand on Corey's arm. "I want to ask you for a favor," he said when the others were gone. "I understand how you felt last night, but for the rest of the day, I'd like you to pretend it never happened."

When Corey eyed him in dubious silence, he grinned and said, "No favor, no wedding. I'll cancel it and the deal's off."

He was completely unpredictable, inscrutable, and utterly irresistible with that teasing glint in his eyes. "You are completely unscrupulous," she informed him, but without any force.

"Lady, I am the best friend you've ever had," he countered, and when she gaped at the arrogance of that claim, he explained, "I have, in my possession, Joy's elopement letter. In it, she says very clearly that it was her conversation with *you* yesterday that convinced her she'd regret it for the rest of her life if she didn't marry the man she loved. Contrary to what my sister thinks, you brought all this on yourself. Now, do I get my favor or do I cancel the wedding?"

"You win," Corey agreed, laughing. She wasn't certain whether she was relieved or disappointed that he didn't want to talk about last night.

"No dark thoughts about me for the rest of the day—agreed?" When she nodded, Spence said, "Good.

Now, is there anything else I can do to make things easier for you before the wedding?"

Corey shook her head. "You've already accomplished a great deal. I'm very grateful," she said earnestly. "And very impressed," she reluctantly admitted, tossing him a grin over her shoulder as she left.

Spence studied the easy grace of her movements while he considered her last remark. If Corey was "very impressed" by what she knew he'd accomplished, she'd be dazzled by the rest of it. Upstairs, Joy's wedding gown was already being altered to the size of one of Corey's dresses. In Houston, Spence's attorney was drawing up a letter notifying the tenants in his grandmother's house that their lease was being terminated, and preparing a large check from Spence to compensate them. In Newport, Judge Lawrence Lattimore was on the phone with a sleepy clerk from City Hall who was being talked into issuing a marriage license on a Saturday.

All things considered, Spence decided, it had not been a bad morning's work.

Even so, he had the disquieting feeling that he was forgetting something important—something other than informing Corey that she was about to become a bride. He hoped to God that she'd been sincere about her love of spontaneity and acting on instinct; he hoped she'd been sincere when she told Joy she'd always loved him and wanted to have his babies.

That last part didn't bother him as much as the first. Corey loved him, he knew she did, but he wasn't thrilled about the sort of wedding she was about to have.

Of course, based on their early history, she was bound to feel an enormous amount of satisfaction at having forced him to go to such bizarre lengths in order to get her to the altar.

He smiled to himself, imagining the tales she would tell their children about this day, but his smile faded as he walked out of his study and stood on the terrace, watching the sailboats gliding across the water. If he was mistaken, she was going to be furious, and if he wasn't mistaken, then he shouldn't be feeling quite this uneasy. On the other hand, he could merely be suffering from an ordinary case of wedding nerves.

Spence turned his back on the view and walked over to his desk to make some more phone calls. At the very worst, Corey could get an annulment and no one would ever need to know they'd been married.

Fifteen

STANDING NEAR A rose-covered gazebo where he was about to be married by a thoroughly inebriated judge to a totally unsuspecting photographer, Spence chatted amiably with two women who didn't know they were about to become his in-laws.

Corey had wanted happy faces for her pictures, and he'd provided two hundred of them for her, with the aid of an amazing quantity of French champagne, a fortune in Russian caviar, and a brief, amusing speech he'd given that had gained their full cooperation. In fact, all the guests seemed to be having a thoroughly enjoyable time.

The bridegroom certainly was.

Lifting his champagne glass to his mouth, Spence watched his bride-to-be study the angle of the sun as she readied the last of the tripods for the shots of the actual wedding. The long train of her ten-thousand-dollar wedding gown had gotten in her way, so she'd tied it up into a makeshift bustle, and her long lace veil was currently slung over her shoulders like a crumpled stole. He decided she was the most exquisite creature alive. Utterly fetching. Completely unself-conscious. And she was about to become his. He watched her hurrying toward him, her eyes glowing with pleasure at the shot she'd lined up. "I think we're all set," she told him.

"It's a good thing," Spence chuckled. "Lattimore is roasting alive in that gazebo in those robes you've made him wear for the last hour, and he's been quenching a very big thirst."

Corey's grandmother summed it up differently as she reached up to rearrange Corey's veil. "That judge is drunk!" she declared.

"It's okay, Gram," Corey said, twisting around to watch her mother unwind her train and stretch it out carefully behind her. "He isn't really a judge. Spencer says he's a plumber."

"He's a lush, that's what he is."

"How's my hair?" Corey asked when they were finished.

Spence particularly loved her hair today, even though it wasn't loose around her shoulders the way he wanted to see it tonight, in bed. They'd pinned it up into curls at the crown to keep it from looking untidy in the pictures. "It looks fine," Mrs. Foster declared, reaching up to straighten the headpiece.

Spence offered Corey his arm and grinned. He was so damned happy, he couldn't stop smiling. "Ready?" he asked.

"Wait," Corey said as she straightened his black tie. Spence envisioned a lifetime of Corey straightening his ties.

Corey felt a sharp ache in her chest as she looked up at the elegant man in a tailor-made tuxedo who was smiling down at her with all the tenderness of a real bridegroom. She'd dreamed this dream a thousand times in years gone by, and now it was only make-believe. To her horror, she felt the sting of tears and hid them quickly behind an overbright smile.

"Will I do?" Spence asked, his deep voice strangely husky.

Corey nodded, swallowed, and smiled gaily. "We look like Ken and Barbie. Let's go."

Before they could take the first step onto the white carpet that stretched between the rows of chairs and into the gazebo, someone in the front of the row turned around and good-naturedly called, "Hey, Spence, can we get this thing going? It's hot as hell out here."

It hit Spence at that moment what he'd forgotten. He looked around for something to use and saw a piece of gold wired ribbon lying in the grass.

"Ready?" Lattimore said, running his finger around the collar of his robe.

"Ready," Spence said.

"Okay if we make it sh . . . short?"

"That's fine," Corey said, but she was leaning back, trying to see where Kristin was with the spare camera they'd decided to use for extra shots.

"Miss . . . uh . . . Foster?"

"Yes?"

"It's customary to look at the groom."

"Oh, sorry," Corey said. He'd been very nice and very cooperative, and if he wanted to play his part to the fullest, she didn't mind in the least.

"Place your hand in Spence's hand." On the right, Corey saw Kristin move into position and lift her camera.

"Do you, Spencer Addison, take Cor . . . er . . . Caroline Foster to be your lawfully wedded wife so long as you both shall live?" the judge said so quickly the words ran together.

Spence smiled into her eyes. "I do."

Corey's smile wavered.

"Do you, Caroline Foster, take Spence Addison to be your lawfully wedded wife . . . husband . . . so long as you both shall live?"

Alarm bells began ringing in Corey's brain, but they sprang from a source she couldn't understand.

"For God's sake, Corey," Spence teased gently, "don't jilt me at the altar."

"It would serve you right," she said on a breathless laugh, trying to concentrate on the whereabouts of Mike.

"Come on. Say yes."

She didn't want to. It seemed wrong to perpetrate this sham. "This isn't a movie, these are still shots," she said.

Spence reached out and took her chin between his thumb and forefinger, tipping her face up to his. "Say yes."

"Why?"

"Say yes."

He bent his head and as his lips moved closer to

hers, she could almost hear Kristin rushing forward for this unexpected shot.

"You can't kiss her until she says yes," Lattimore warned in a slur.

"Say yes, Corey," Spence whispered, his mouth so close to hers that his breath touched her face. "So the nice judge will let me kiss you."

Corey felt a helpless giggle well up inside her at his cajolery and his insistence on being kissed. "Yes," she whispered, laughing, "but it better be a very good k—"

His mouth swooped down, smothering her voice, and his arms closed around her with stunning force, gathering her to him, stifling her laughter while the judge happily proclaimed, "I now announce you man and wife, give her the ring." The crowd erupted into laughing applause.

Caught completely off guard by the deep, demanding kiss, Corey clutched his shoulders for balance as her senses reeled; then she flattened her hands, forcing him away. "Stop," she whispered, tearing her mouth from his. "That's enough. Really."

He let her go, but he laced his fingers tightly through hers and kept them there while something round and scratchy slid against her knuckle.

"I need to change out of this gown," Corey said as soon as they stepped out of the gazebo.

"Before you go—we have to—" the judge began, but Spence intervened. "You can congratulate me in a few minutes, Larry," he said smoothly. "I'll meet you in the library, where it's quiet, as soon as I take Corey upstairs. There's a cab out front to take you home after we talk."

In the space of time it took to leave the gazebo and

start down the hall to her suite, Corey's emotions had plummeted from an enthusiastic high over the outstanding photographs she was certain they'd gotten to an inexplicable depression, which she tried to rationalize as a normal letdown after a day of extraordinary tension and hard work. She knew Spence wasn't to blame. He'd played his role as surrogate bridegroom with a combination of unshakable calm and boyish enthusiasm that had been utterly charming.

She was still trying to sort out her tangled emotions when he opened the door to her suite and stepped aside, but when she started to walk past him, he stopped her. "What's wrong, beautiful?"

"Oh, please," she said on a choking laugh, "don't say anything sweet, or I'll burst into tears."

"You were a gorgeous bride."

"I'm warning you," she said chokily.

He drew her into his arms, cupping the back of her head and pressing her face to his heart in a gesture that was so tender and so unexpected that it moved her another step closer to tears. "It was such an awful farce," she whispered.

"Most weddings are an awful farce," he said in quiet amusement. "It's what comes afterward that matters."

"I suppose so," she said absently.

"Think about the weddings you've seen," he continued, ignoring the startled looks of several wedding guests who saw them through the open door as the guests walked down the hall. "Half the time the groom is hungover or the bride has morning sickness. It's pitiful," he teased.

Her shoulders shook with a teary laugh, and Spence smiled because the sound of her laughter had always delighted him, and making her laugh had always made him feel as if he were better, stronger, nicer than he really was. "All things considered, this is about as close to a perfect wedding as you could hope for."

"Not to me it isn't. I want a Christmas wedding."

"Is that the only thing you dislike about this wedding—the season of the year, I mean? If there's anything I can do to make you happier about all this, tell me and I'll do it."

You could love me, Corey thought before she could stop herself, then she pushed the thought aside. "There is absolutely nothing more you can do beyond what you've done. I'm being ridiculous and overemotional. Weddings do that to me," she lied with a smile as she stepped back.

He accepted that. "I'll deal with Lattimore, and then I want to change clothes. In the meantime, I'll have some champagne sent up here, and then I'll come up and share it with you—how does that sound?"

"Fine," she said.

Sixteen

A SHOWER HAD partially revived Corey's spirits, and she surveyed the selection of clothes hanging in her closet, wondering what the appropriate attire was for a stand-in bride who was about to have champagne with a surrogate groom after their pretend wedding. "This will work," she said with relief as she reached for the billowy cream silk pants and long tunic she'd brought along because they were flexible enough to wear to almost any social event in a Newport mansion.

She was standing in front of the bathroom mirror, brushing her hair, when she heard Spence knock on the door and then let himself in. "I'll be right there," she called, pausing long enough to put on pearl earrings. She straightened and stepped back from the mirror. She looked much happier and more contented than she felt, she decided with relief. Because what she felt was . . . haunted. She had worn a bridal gown and veil and stood beside Spence in a rose-covered gazebo while he held her hand in his, smiling tenderly into her eyes. He had even slipped a ring on her finger afterward . . . The memories of their "wedding" seemed to be permanently imprinted on her mind. No, she told herself, not permanently, only temporarily. Memories would soon give way to the reality. The wedding had been a hoax, the "ring" of a piece of gold ribbon with a wire in it. The reality made her ache.

Spence had taken off his tuxedo jacket, loosened his tie, and opened the top buttons of his formal shirt. He looked every bit as sexy and elegant that way as he had during the wedding; he did not, however, look nearly as relaxed. His jaw was rigid, and his movements were abrupt as he ignored the champagne chilling in a gold bucket and jerked the stopper out of one of the liquor decanters on the cabinet. He poured some into a crystal tumbler and lifted the glass to his mouth. "What are you doing?" Corey asked, watching him take two deep swallows of straight bourbon.

He lowered the glass and looked at her over his shoulder. "I'm having a very stiff drink. And now I'll fix one for you."

"No thanks," Corey said with a shudder. "I'd rather have the champagne."

"Take my advice," he said almost bitterly, "have a regular drink."

"Why?"

"Because you're going to need it." He fixed her a drink that at least had ice cubes and some club soda to dilute it and handed it to her. Corey sipped it, waiting for him to explain, but instead of talking, he stared at the glass in his hand.

"Spence, whatever is wrong, it can't be worse than you're making it seem to me right now."

"I hope you still feel that way in a few minutes," he said grimly.

"What *is* it?" Corey said desperately. "Is someone ill?"

"No." He put down his drink, then he walked over to the fireplace and braced his hands on the mantel, staring into the empty grate. It was a pose of such abject defeat that Corey felt a fierce surge of protective tenderness. She walked up behind him and laid her hand on his broad shoulder. It was the first time since coming to Newport that she had voluntarily touched him except when he was kissing her, and she felt his muscles tense beneath her hand. "Please don't make me wonder like this, you're scaring me!"

"An hour ago, my idiotic niece called to tell me she was now married to her beloved restaurateur."

"So far, that sounds good."

"That was the only good part of the phone call."

Visions of car crashes and ambulances flashed through Corey's mind. "What was the bad part, Spence?"

He hesitated, then he turned and looked directly at her. "The bad part is that, during our conversation, we also discussed the elopement letter she left for me last night. It appears that in her haste to explain how you'd influenced her decision to elope, Joy was a little remiss about the verbs she used. Specifically, she failed to clearly differentiate between past and present tense."

"What do you mean she explained *how* I influenced her?" Corey asked warily.

"Read the letter," he said, taking two folded piece of paper out of his pants pocket and handing Corey the one on top.

Corey saw at a glance what he was talking about.

> Corey told me she loved you and wanted to have your baby, she said you're the only man she's ever felt that way about, and that's why she's never married anyone else. Uncle Spence, I love Will. I want to have his babies someday. That's why I can't marry anyone else. . . .

Despite the mortification she felt, Corey managed to affect a calm, dismissive smile as she handed the letter back to him. "In the first place, I was describing how I felt about you when I was a teenager, not an adult. Secondly, the conclusion she drew about why I haven't married was hers, not mine."

"As you can see, that's not quite the way it read."

"Is—is that all that's bothering you?" Corey said, relieved that he wasn't going to challenge her explanation.

Instead of answering, he shoved his hands into his pockets and studied her in impassive silence for so long that Corey took a nervous sip of her drink. "What's bothering me," he said bluntly, "is that I don't know how you feel about me now."

Since she didn't have the slightest idea how he felt about her and he wasn't volunteering any information about it, Corey didn't think he had any right to ask the question or expect an answer. "I think you're one of the handsomest men I've ever married!" she joked.

He was not amused. "This is no time to be evasive, believe me."

"What do you mean?"

"I mean that I know damned well you feel something for me now, even if it's just common garden-variety lust."

She gaped at him. "Does your ego need a boost?"

"Answer the question," he ordered.

Struggling desperately to put a light tone on the matter and end it, she said, "Let me put it this way: If we ever do an article on 'Great Kissing,' you'll be featured in the Top Ten, and I'll give you my vote. Well?" she teased. "What do you think?"

"I think you'd be accused of bias for voting for your own husband."

"Don't call yourself my husband," Corey said. "It isn't funny."

"It isn't a joke."

"That's what I just said," Corey pointed out impatiently.

"We're married, Corey."

"Don't be ridiculous."

"It may sound ridiculous, but it is also true."

Corey searched his impassive features, shaking her head in denial of what she saw in his eyes. "The wedding ceremony was a sham. The judge was a plumber."

"No, his father and his uncle are plumbers. He's a judge."

"I don't believe you."

Instead of replying, he handed the second folded piece of paper to her.

Corey opened it and stared. It was a copy of a marriage license with Corey's name on it and Spence's name on it. It was dated that day and signed by Judge Lawrence E. Lattimore.

"We're married, Corey."

Her hand closed into an involuntary fist, crumpling the paper; her chest constricted into a knot of confused anguish. "Were you playing some sort of sick joke on me?" she whispered. "Why would you want to humiliate me this way?"

"Try to understand. I told you what Joy said, and I thought this was what you wanted—"

"You arrogant bastard!" she whispered brokenly. "Are you trying to tell me that you actually married me out of pity and guilt, and you thought I'd *like* it? Am I so pathetic to you that you thought I'd be happy to settle for getting married at someone else's wedding, in someone else's gown, with a piece of wire ribbon for a wedding ring?"

Spence saw the tears in her eyes, and he caught her by the shoulders. "Listen to me! Corey, I married you because I love you."

"You love me," she scoffed, her shoulders shaking with laughter, her face wet with tears. "You love me. . . ."

"Yes, dammit, I do."

She laughed harder and the tears came faster. "You

don't even know what love is," she sobbed. "You 'loved me' so much that you didn't even bother to propose. You didn't see anything more with turning my wedding into one great big joke."

From her perspective it was all true, Spence knew that, and the knowledge was as painful to him as the tears racing down her pale cheeks and the anguish in her eyes. "I understand how you feel about me right now."

"Oh, no you don't!" She twisted out of his grasp and angrily brushed tears off her pale cheeks. "But I'll try to make it clear once and for all: I don't want you! I didn't want you before, I don't want you now, and I will never want you!" Her palm crashed against his cheek with enough force to snap his head sideways. "Is *that* clear enough for you?" Whirling on her heel, Corey started for the closet where her suitcases were. "I'm not spending the night in the same house with you! When I get to Houston, I'm going to start annulment proceedings, and if you dare try to oppose me, I'll have you and that drunken judge arrested in less time than it took you to arrange this marriage! Is *that* clear?"

"I have no intention of opposing an annulment," he said in a glacial voice. "In fact," he added as he tossed something onto the bed and walked to the door, "I suggest you use that to cover the cost of your attorney." The door slammed shut behind him.

Corey collapsed against the wall and buried her face in her hands, her body shaking with silent sobs.

At last, a numbness finally swept over her, and she shoved away from the wall and went over to the telephone. She asked the servant who answered to locate her mother and grandmother and tell them to come up to her room immediately, then she instructed him to find Mike MacNeil and have him call her.

When Mike called, Corey told him something had come up, and she had to fly home tonight. The phone rang as soon as she hung it up. "Miss Foster," the butler coolly informed her, "Mr. Addison's car is on its way to the front and will be waiting for you there as soon as you are ready to leave."

Despite the fact that she was desperate to get out of that house, Corey was irrationally infuriated at being summarily ejected from the premises that way. She finished packing in record time and closed her suitcase. As she put the last one on the floor, she remembered the object her "husband" had tossed onto the bed. Expecting to see a money clip with bills in it, she glanced toward the head of the bed, where she thought it had landed.

Lying atop a pile of ice blue satin pillows, glittering in the pale light from the setting sun, was a spectacular diamond ring that looked as if it should have belonged to a duchess.

Her mother and grandmother knocked on her door, and Corey called to them to come in while she picked up her purse and reached for her suitcases. Mrs. Foster took one look at Corey's pale face, saw the suitcases, and came to a full stop. "Dear God, what's wrong?"

Corey told them in a few brief sentences and nodded toward the ring on the bed as she left. "Please see that he gets that back. Then tell him if he ever comes near me again, I'll swear out a warrant!"

After Corey left, Mrs. Foster looked at her mother in stunned silence, then she finally said, "What a stupid thing for Spence to have done!"

"He deserves to be horsewhipped," Gram decreed without animosity.

"Corey will never forgive him for this. Never. And Spence is impossibly proud. He won't ask her again," said Mrs. Foster with a sigh.

Her mother walked over to the bed and picked up the ring, turning it in her fingers with a smile. "Spence will have to send a bodyguard with Corey when she wears this."

Seventeen

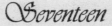

"WHAT DO YOU mean he won't sign the release so that we can use the pictures we took in Newport?" Corey exploded.

"I didn't say he had flatly refused to sign them," Diana said carefully. In the week since Corey had been back from Newport, she'd thrown herself into a dozen projects to keep from thinking about either her marriage or the annulment proceedings she'd started, and she looked exhausted. "He said he would sign them, but only if you brought them to him personally tomorrow night."

"I am not going back to Newport," she warned.

"You won't have to. Spence will be in Houston taking care of some business."

"I don't want to see him in Houston or anywhere else."

"I think he knows that," Diana said wryly. "You not only started annulment proceedings, you asked for a legal injunction to prevent him from coming near you."

"What do you think he'd do if we put the magazine out without the releases?"

"He said to tell you that if we do, his attorneys will dine on our corporate carcass."

"I hate that man," she said wearily.

Diana wisely refrained from arguing that point and stuck to the matter at hand. "There's a relatively pain-less way around this. He said he's staying at the River Oaks house, so tomorrow night—"

Furious at the control he was exerting over the mag-azine and over her, Corey said, "Tomorrow night is the Orchid Ball. He'll have to sign the releases during the day, instead."

"I explained to Spence we're one of the sponsors and have to be there. Spence said he would expect you at the house before the ball, at seven o'clock."

"I am not going there alone."

"Okay," Diana said, sounding as relieved as she felt. "Mother and I will wait in the car for you while you're with Spence, then we'll leave from there."

Eighteen

COREY HADN'T BEEN back to Spence's house since his grandmother lived there, and it seemed strange to be returning after so many years.

She knew he'd leased the house to tenants who'd kept most of the servants on, and the place was as beau-tifully maintained as it had always been. Since Spence was staying there now, Corey assumed either he had decided to sell it and it was vacant, or else the people who'd lived there for years had moved out.

All the carriage lights were lit on the front porch, just as they'd always been whenever guests were expected, but tonight, a strange colorful glow was visible through the closed draperies in what Corey knew was the living room.

"I won't be long," Corey told Diana and her mother as she got out of the car and walked up the front steps.

Clutching the release form in her hand, she rang the bell, her heart drumming harder as footsteps sounded in the foyer, and harder still when the door swung open and Mrs. Bradley's former housekeeper said with a warm smile, "Good evening, Miss Foster. Mr. Addison is waiting for you in the living room."

Corey nodded, then she walked through the dimly lit foyer. Bracing herself for the impact of seeing Spence for the first time since that hideous scene in Newport, Corey rounded the corner and walked into the living room.

Then she braced herself again, trying to assimilate what she was seeing.

Spence was near the middle of the candlelit room, leaning casually against the grand piano with his arms crossed over his chest.

He was wearing a tuxedo.

The room was decked out for Christmas.

"Merry Christmas, Corey," he said quietly.

Corey's disoriented gaze drifted over the thick garlands draping the mantel, to the beribboned mistletoe on the chandelier overhead, to the huge Christmas tree in the corner with its red ornaments and twinkling lights, then it came to a stop at a small mountain of presents beneath the tree. All of them were wrapped in gold foil, and all of them had huge white tags on them.

And all the tags said "Corey."

"I cheated you out of a Christmas dance and a Christmas wedding," he said solemnly. "I'd like to give them to you anyway. I still can, if you'll let me."

Spence had envisioned a dozen possible reactions from her, from laughter to fury, but he had never considered the possibility that Corey would turn her back on him and bend her head and start to cry. When she did, his heart sank with defeat. He reached for her and dropped his hands, and then he heard her choking whisper: "All I've ever wanted was you." Relief made him rough as he spun her around and yanked her into his arms, wrapping them tightly around her.

His wife laid her hand against his jaw and tenderly spread her fingers over his cheek. "All I've ever wanted was you."

In the car outside, Mrs. Foster looked at the embracing couple silhouetted against the draperies. Her son-in-law was kissing her daughter as if he never intended to stop or let her go. "I don't think there's any need for us to wait," she told Diana with a happy sigh. "Corey won't be going anywhere tonight."

"Yes she will," Diana said with absolute certainty as she put her car into gear. "Spence cheated her out of one Christmas dance, and he intends to make up for it tonight."

"You don't mean he intends to take her to the ball," Mrs. Foster said worriedly. "The tickets have been sold out for months."

"Spence managed to reserve somehow, and we're sitting together at it." With a fond smile, she added, "We shouldn't have any trouble finding the table. It has an unusual centerpiece. Instead of white orchids, it has a big red sleigh filled with holly."

Epilogue

WRAPPED IN A RED velvet robe, Corey stood at the windows of the chalet, looking out across the snowy, moonswept hills of Vermont, where they had decided to spend their first real Christmas. Her husband insisted this was also their second honeymoon—the one they would have had if Corey had gotten her Christmas wedding—and he was playing the role of ardent bridegroom with passion and élan.

She turned and walked over to the bed where Spence was asleep, then she leaned down and pressed a kiss to his forehead. It was almost dawn, and he'd made love to her until they were both exhausted, but it was Christmas morning, and she was absurdly anxious to see him open his presents. He gave her presents all the time, and she'd shopped for months for just the right gifts for him.

A smile touched his lips. "Why are you awake?" he asked without opening his eyes.

"It's Christmas morning. I want to give you a present. Do you mind?"

"Not at all," he said with a husky laugh, and pulled her down on top of him.